# For the Sake of Revenge

## An Alaskan Vampire Novel

By

DL Atha

ISBN: 978-0-9793356-5-5

This book is dedicated to my husband, Erich, who has allowed my laptop to spend many nights in our bed with very few complaints—again. And to our three darling children who inspire me with their antics every day.

With Special thanks to Debbie Hewett, who has been with this project when it was only a tossed around idea and a few hastily typed pages. Your support is priceless.

And to Dr. Jennifer Burks who has been one of my closest friends and greatest allies. Thanks for believing in me and for helping me to have fun.

Also a special thanks to the beta readers who helped with proofing and idea bouncing:
Dr. Jarrett Lea
Dr. Patric Anderson
Dr. Robert Sanders
Christy M. Copeland
Michelle Westbrook
Tammie Young
Margaret Clymer
Danielle Ritch
Kristy Brewer
Sherra Bean
Jeff Burks
Ron Martin
Phyllis Atha

Other books by DL Atha

*Blood Reaction: A Vampire Novel*

Here lies the girl
who fell for death
He stole her heart
and took her breath
He kissed her as he took her life
She should have watched out for that scythe

– Submitted by: Hali, Londonderry, to Haunted Bay

# For the Sake of Revenge

## An Alaskan Vampire Novel

# Chapter 1

"*Uppyr*." I breathed the word out between sips of steaming hot tea as I squinted down at the aged label clinging to the ancient bottle I held in my other hand.

*Have I read that right?* I questioned myself. It had been a few years since I'd read any Russian writings, but as I studied the word again, I was certain of its meaning.

"Vampire," I spoke aloud this time, translating from Russian to English, hoping it sounded less insane.

I gave it a few seconds to let the syllables sink in, saying it over a few times in my head.

No, it still sounded insane.

A second word was elegantly scrawled onto the label, but in the dim lighting, I couldn't make it out. Casting a sideways look at the cold fire burning in the hearth, I scooted as far forward on the couch as I could without leaving the coziness of the blanket I'd wrapped up in and focused all my efforts on reading the label; my face screwed up with the effort.

"*Krov*," I sounded it out, searching my mind for the meaning.

Blood. Grandmother had used the word from time to time, usually in some ancient reference to a curse—or when hunting. Occasionally, these two strangely different subjects had collided in her world.

"*Uppyr krov*. Vampire blood," I spoke aloud to the empty house. Then I laughed, but only a little. I am of Russian descent after all, and we don't limit ourselves to the normal thoughts of traditional Americans; hence always keeping a broom visible in the corner of the living room and the horseshoe over the doorway. The horseshoe isn't an Alaskan custom. Mom had just borrowed the idea from her southern friend Gloria, but in her world, you could never be too careful.

With the exception of a date on the label—January 26, 1808—there were no other markings on the bottle. No serial numbers or expiration dates stamped into the glass to suggest it was modern; the vial was slightly misshapen with an old and withered cork stuffed deep into the neck of the glass.

Despite the date written on the bottle, the contents flowed freely. No dried remnants clung to the sides of the vial; no clots stuck to the bottom.

*It looks very fresh for two-hundred-year-old blood*, I thought skeptically to myself as I traded the bottle for my teacup, setting the relic down beside the lamp.

Earlier in the day, I'd found the bottle in an unpretentious wooden chest hidden in a secret compartment of my mom's old steamer trunk. I'd been working most of the afternoon on sorting decades' worth of heavily worn coats and mothy long-sleeved underwear from out of the steamer when I lost my balance leaning over the tall sides of the trunk. My fingers had inadvertently pushed through what turned out to be a false bottom as I caught myself.

At first, I'd jerked my hand back as if my fingers had landed in a clutch of spiders, but unable to resist my curiosity, I'd tentatively stretched my hand back in and palpated until I stroked the free edge of what felt like a wooden box.

I clawed at it until the false bottom of the steamer trunk could no longer take it, giving up its treasure with a sudden split. Antique dust exploded up into the space around me as I landed hard on my butt, a small wooden trunk held aloft in one hand as my other stretched out behind to keep me upright. Musty air tickled my nose, and I sneezed hard before regaining my balance.

I carried my treasure with me as I retrieved some tissue and sat down on the couch to study my find. Getting comfortable, I turned the small wooden box over slowly in my hands as my imagination ran away with the possibilities of what it could contain. Surely something good or whoever had hidden it wouldn't have bothered, right?

About the size of a shoebox, the trunk certainly appeared to be an antique. The wood was a dark, rich chocolate and into the top, an Orthodox cross was deeply carved. Besides the etching, there were no other markings. Instead, the wood had been so meticulously polished, or had simply been handled enough, that I could see the outline of my face in the grain of the wood. Nothing seemed to hold it together. I couldn't find a nail or a bolt. The wooden pieces were so precisely cut that it fit together like a puzzle.

*Kinda like Mom*, I mused. *She'd needed nothing to hold her together either.*

I wiped away a layer of fine dust from the side of the trunk and my features stared back, reflected in the polished wood. Halfheartedly, I smiled at the woman in the reflection, conceding for the first time in my life that I did in fact look like my mother.

God, how I missed her.

She'd been a lady of few possessions and even fewer secrets, so it seemed odd she'd have kept this box hidden from me. More likely, it had been placed there years before by someone in our family tree. I remembered my grandmother saying the steamer had been handed down from her great-grandfather. Potentially, the trunk could have sat hidden in the false bottom of the steamer for well over a century—maybe two. Mom had probably never laid eyes on it or the mysterious contents.

Nor did it seem to want to share its secrets with me. The lid was tightly adhered, and I couldn't get enough leverage with my fingernails to push the lid open. I'm not known for my patience, and soon I was prying at the lid with an old kitchen knife—tenderly of course. I was tense with anxiety when the lid finally erupted off with a twist of the knife, the contents exploding around me.

Old yellowed papers floated through the air, small fragments breaking off and waltzing on the breeze of the fireplace. Hastily, I waved the musty fragments away, anxious to get to the good stuff but I was sorely disappointed as I pulled out only more stacks of ancient vellum that seemed to age further in front of my eyes.

I'd expected something far more important than papers to have been so carefully concealed and something of monetary value would have been helpful considering the financial straits I was in.

Digging deeper, I found two books that I laid aside before my fingers curled around the cold, curved bottle, whose label I was now deciphering.

At first, I thought it was worthless in the shallow light of the living room—some old glass bottle of God only knew what. An ancient wine or maybe perfume I'd guessed as the liquid had swirled in the confines of the bottle.

But here in the brighter light of the lamp with the words "vampire blood" inscribed on the side, the bottle had become far more interesting. Valuable even. Collectors paid through the nose for stuff like this.

I shuffled through the trunk again, looking for anything that pertained to the bottle of blood. Studying the tattered papers first, I was dissatisfied with their contents. Most were letters to family, sent back and forth from Alaska to Russia, and were pretty mundane. Somebody was betrothed, a great aunt had died, a new grandbaby was born. They were all handwritten in Russian, the writing fading in and out in an elegant old-world script that made the words all the harder to translate, but none of them mentioned anything about vampire blood.

Only the books remained, and I set the trunk at my feet as I flipped through these. The first book creaked as I opened it, the binding worn and heavily creased but stiff from lack of use. It appeared to be some sort of medical text, and I flipped through the pages, grimacing a little at the torturous appearing illustrations of old medical procedures. There were various drawings of bleedings and even one detailed sketch of how to drill a hole in a man's head. The dude in the drawing was way too calm.

The smaller of the two volumes was short but thick, the mahogany cover worn to the point that in some places the color of the leather had faded to only an off white. Barely legible was the name 'Klim Semenov, Surgeon' engraved into the leather of the bottom right corner. The gold that had once been present in the lettering had chipped away and now only flecks could be seen glittering in the lamplight. A tattered bookmark lay about halfway through the book.

Inside the cover at the bottom right in Russian was scrawled 'Personal journal of Klim Semenov, Surgeon New Archangel Outpost, Alaska, Russian American Trading Company.'

I glanced back at the bottle and realized it was the same handwriting on the label. Like the blood, the journal was now more interesting, and I planned to search it cover to cover for anything that pertained to the bottle.

It would be slow going; the book was old and the script elaborate, yet faded. But I had all afternoon and little else to do, so I threw a couple of green logs on the fire, ignoring the tufts of smoke from the burning moss, wormed deeper into my blanket and began to translate.

The surgeon's writing was anything if not meticulous, and the first few pages were fairly mundane. He was the only doctor for the fort at New Archangel, so he cared not only for the hunters, fur traders, soldiers, and clergy but also for any of the natives who cared to visit him.

New Archangel was the first name given to the city of Sitka, Alaska, where I had grown up and currently lived. Originally a fort, the town had been established as the capital for the Russian American Trading Company, which had a charter from the Tsar of Russia, giving the company sole rights to the fur trade. Over the years, the town became known by the Tlingit Indian name, Shee-Atika, which in turn became Sitka. Alexander Baranov, the manager of the company, had defeated the Tlingit

Indian tribe here for the final time in 1804. You can't grow up in Sitka and not know these simple facts; the history is everywhere.

Most of the entries discussed the weather in New Archangel and the doctor's assumptions of how it affected the health of the fort. He described some illnesses, a few cases that sounded suspiciously like food poisoning, and another couple cases of the flu. At least three entries were dedicated to the coming and going of the ships that frequented New Archangel's harbor, most of which brought new rounds of sickness.

My eyes were nearly crossed two hours and thirty pages later when the surgeon's neat, elegant script became harried, the words smudged either by tears or sweat.

The top of the page dated the entry as January 26, 1808, the same date inscribed on the bottle of blood. In contrast to the surgeon's usual concise, methodical entries, this one was several pages long. The writing was crooked and messy, as though it were written with emotion this time and not just science. I read through it once, and even though I was fluent in Russian, I had to force myself to start over and read it aloud, translating as I went.

*"Tonight, a creature, which I considered to be myth only, was laid upon my examining table. I was raised on such tales, but being trained in the art and science of medicine, I considered such stories the fodder of children and the nightmares of the poor and uneducated. If I had not seen the evidence myself, examined the beast with my own hands, I would have laughed at such a story.*

*"A fortnight ago, January 12, 1808, a young serf died in opposition of the Church. In truth, he committed suicide. The man, his Christian name was Adrik, was accused of raping a wealthy young woman of high social stature—Irena Ivonvosky. Irena was to be, upon the death of her father, the Duchess of the Ivonvosky estate. As such, she was betrothed to a nephew of the Tsar.*

*"The accusation of rape was an odd charge given the degree of Adrik's conviction, as he was long known to be a religious. Despite a reliable witness, Adrik denied the charges and refused to repent and acknowledge his crimes. Thus, he was excommunicated from the Church. Apparently driven to madness by the loss of his religion, Adrik committed suicide. The morning following Adrik's suicide, his closest and only friend, Ivan, removed the body and buried it on unhallowed ground and without the typical precautions afforded those who die outside the Church. He was not staked or decapitated. Neither was he bound.*

*"By the judgment of the Baranov, being himself a man of science, Adrik's body was left undisturbed and no precautions were taken against the chance of him rising a vampire. Except for his burial on unhallowed ground, the body remained unmarred and intact.*

*"The men and women of the fort were naturally excited and frightened by the unusual condition of Adrik's death. Ivan was beseeched by the citizens of the fort to return to Adrik's burial site and stake him, as he was the only man who knew where the body lay. He refused, and the Baranov upheld his decision.*

*"Fourteen nights had passed since Adrik was placed in the ground by Ivan with no untoward events. The anxiety surrounding the fort was just beginning to fade when the young woman, Irena, who had accused Adrik of the heinous crime of rape, was found dead in the home she shared with her father. Her body now lies on a cot in the very room in which I write this journal entry.*

*"The condition of her body leaves no question as to what manner of beast attacked her. Of the state of her body, I can only say that I will be haunted forever by those memories. No human encounter could have left her thus. Her father, convinced that she had suffered the same fate as Adrik, staked her himself when he found her covered in the marks of vampirism and clinging to life. It was disturbing, for the woman was still yet living when her father ran her through with the stake.*

*"After such a display, a search party was raised, led by Ivan,*

*and the vampire was hunted and staked near the location of his previous burial. It was Ivan who performed the first blow. The corpse was then brought to me so that I could perform the rituals to keep him safely interred.*

*"I was aghast when the body was laid out upon my examination table. Unlike Irena's remains, the vampire's body was nearly pristine except for the multiple stakes that penetrated his chest. Only three had hit the heart, but it was enough to immobilize him.*

*"But leaving nothing to chance, the archimandrite stood at the corpse's feet, our Holy Cross held up in defense, lest the vampire be able to withstand the power of the stakes.*

*"As a human, Adrik had been a fine specimen of manhood. Tall and with fair complexion, he had been quite vigorous and had the strength of two men. He had been hardworking and loyal, of normal intellect despite his peasant birth but something of an introvert. His face had been kind with emotions easily read from his expressions. In my estimation, the man was completely lacking in guile.*

*"Tonight, I looked down into that same face I had been familiar with for over two years and could see no vestiges of human emotions. As I walked around the corpse, I could feel its eyes upon me, even though they did not move within their sockets. His presence leaves a palpable fear in the room. Even in his weakened state, his body trembled with rage at my handling of him.*

*"Legend says that the vampire cannot die, that he can merely be contained. And since he cannot die, his body cannot undergo the natural process of returning to the dust from whence it came. Unless Adrik can be re-communicated, he will remain as he is for an eternity, and so while his body can be controlled, it can never be fully destroyed.*

*"Knowing what I had to do to protect the fort did not make the deed any easier, and I admit I was forced to take several slugs of vodka to steady my trembling hands. I have taken several more since.*

*"First, I removed his clothes, marveling at his body as I did so. My hands shivered at the coolness of his skin. Despite his paleness, his lips were blood red, and I shuddered knowing how they had obtained their unnatural color. The dehydration that should have overtaken his body in the grave has not occurred; instead, his skin has a fullness and a softness that not even the tender skin of a child can compare. The ligature marks that had once surrounded his neck are now absent; his skin is whole and unmarred except the penetration of the stakes. I know this as it was I who examined him upon his human death. I helped Ivan cut the noose from his neck, after all, on the morning after his hanging.*

*"I daresay the vampire is quite striking, even more so than when he lived as a man. The hair of his head is thicker, blacker. His eyes are the bluest I have ever seen, and his lips so full that even I can feel my heart stir. His limbs remain heavily corded with muscle and have lost none of their robustness. But I labor over his appearance too much to avoid describing the desperate tasks that had to be completed.*

*"I began first at his head. Into his mouth, I packed unpeeled garlic as deeply into his throat as I could. His form jerked for the first time, and I nearly cut my hand on the razor quality of his fangs. I took a deep steadying breath and pressed on until not another bulb would fit and his cheeks bulged with the herb.*

*"Moving to his chest, I inspected the blood that issued from around the stake. It was garishly bright red against his white skin, and it did not clot but instead remained fresh and living in appearance. What a shock to see blood so healthy oozing from a man I pronounced as dead a fortnight ago.*

*"I could not resist the chance to study such a medical anomaly, and glancing at the archimandrite, our highest ranking Church official, I gratefully found him occupied studying the stitching of his clothing. I took advantage of his preoccupation and sliced a scalpel deeply into the vampire's elbow. Blood flowed freely, and I collected that which flowed out into a basin. I will examine it later when I have more time as it does not seem to clot, and even now as I write this, a few*

*hours after I collected it, the substance remains unclotted. The basin filled, I then crossed his arms over his body, securing his wrists with twine.*

*"Next, I rubbed his body down with garlic oil and his skin split and bled. He shuddered underneath my hands and even managed to hiss once through the garlic bulbs in his mouth as I placed ropes of garlic between his legs and bulbs between his buttocks and under his scrotum. The pain must have been excruciating, for his body shook like a man dying of tetanus, and at one point, large blood-filled tears ran down his cheeks.*

*"I checked once more that the stakes were secure and that they passed completely through the breadth of his body. And with nothing left to do, I looked deeply into the eyes of the gentle man that I had once known him to be. Despite the animal that he has become, I will always remember him for the quiet and kind manner in which he conducted himself. I daresay that had I been born a serf, it is doubtful I would have bowed so graciously to the yoke.*

*"I, for one, do not believe the charges that were brought against him. It bruised my heart to cause him such pain tonight, and it is only with the knowledge that his suffering will keep the fort safe that I was able to perform these acts against him.*

*"I begged the archimandrite to reverse his excommunication, to let his body decompose and his spirit find rest. The priest only smiled at me, saying that he could not re-communicate a reprobate, unwilling to confess. I say that the priest is an unnaturally cold man who knows little of mercy.*

*"The vampire now bound and his body delivered back to the grave, I have poured the blood that I collected into several small bottles for further study. I shall examine the contraband fluids when the memory of tonight is less vivid. I pray that I find a dreamless sleep this evening, if I am able to find sleep at all. I have no desire to meet this aberration again whether in the harshness of reality or the terror of nightmares.*

*"I performed the same rituals on the Duchess Irena. I am asked by the Baranov, now an unwilling believer in the legends*

*himself, if she could rise a vampire, but as I am a surgeon of the living and not the dead, I honestly cannot say with any certainty.*

*"Irena appeared dead, her blood clotted thickly around the stake that pierced her heart and lungs, so I suspect that she is indeed dead. I remind myself that it was her father, the duke, by whose hand she died. The vampire, Adrik, had marked her, but she was staked while she yet lived. So perhaps she will be spared the curse. However, given our experiences tonight, I recommended that we take no chances and performed the rituals on her as well.*

*"Her father, who has certainly gone mad, was carried away to the warship that even tomorrow was scheduled to transport both he and his daughter home. Pity fills me for the man; he seems as stunned at the act that he committed against his own child as the rest of us. He will undoubtedly remain a broken man, and I suspect he will not reach Russia alive, so deep is his melancholy.*

*"As for myself, I shall never disclose these events to any living person. Without a doubt in the circle of men in which I acquaint myself, I would be called a fool or a heretic at my securing of his blood, if my peers believed my tales at all.*

*"At the very least, my sanity would be questioned. I shall only talk of this in the confines of my journal, now my only confidant in this matter. The men whom I experienced this with will, no doubt, seek the most expedient transport away from New Archangel, or possibly from Alaska itself.*

*"I cannot blame these men. I would leave if I were not the father of three half-breed children whom I am now unwilling to live without."*

# Chapter 2

I laid the journal aside, carefully replacing the ribbon in between the pages I'd finished and leaned my head back against the couch behind me as I tried to wrap my head around what I'd just read. My grandmother gazed down at me from her portrait hanging above the mantle. Homesick for the days of my childhood, I wished both she and Mom were here to help make sense of such a story.

I suppose normal people would have never given this tale any credibility at all. But then again, I am Russian. And Tlingit Indian. When you combine the two cultures, a new plane of superstition is reached. Which was why I didn't just toss the book in the trash immediately.

I'd grown up in a house where superstition was the norm. In our home, we celebrated our birthday the weekend after; that way you didn't count your chicks before they hatched. As a teen, I couldn't sit at the corner of a table because that meant I wouldn't get married for seven years. We absolutely did not put our keys on the kitchen counter. I can't even begin to explain that superstition, and whistling in the house would have brought on a spit over the shoulder by my grandmother.

A vampire wouldn't have been that out of the norm in my mother's world, and certainly not in my grandmother's. In a town where oddity was widely accepted, my family still managed to stand out. Grandmother's chants were legendary, and Mom never went anywhere without salt. I didn't have many friends because we only spoke Russian in our house. Try explaining that to your second grade class.

But looking back, I realized just how wonderful and peaceful my childhood had been. If only I could have appreciated the simplicity of it before it was too late. But like a typical teen, I'd been embarrassed by our meager life and our ties to a past so hopelessly outdated.

Mom had been what most people call a 'tree hugger' or a 'hippie.' We spent much of our free time in the forest harvesting herbs and plants. She tried to teach them to me, but I ignored her lessons, rolling my eyes as I stuffed the earphones of my Walkman deeper in my ears.

I didn't appreciate our cramped but paid-for home or the hand-me-down clothes from distant relatives. I complained about my no-name pants and how we didn't have enough potato chips and cookies. I never missed an opportunity to point out how poor we were but failed to notice the true gift of the two women with whom I shared a roof. Two generations of wisdom and experience, and I missed it completely.

Somehow I'd overlooked the fact that these two women were steadily in touch with the world, both what could be seen and what couldn't, and I had discounted Mom's specific gift to see through people.

The cost of my disdain was her life.

Ten years had passed, but the thought of what I'd put Mom through made my skin crawl, made my breath catch in my chest. Sweat broke out on my forehead, and suddenly the hot tea I'd been drinking all afternoon wasn't that appetizing.

I was a child the last time I saw my mother. Eighteen years old and an adult by society's standards but a child still. Naïve, innocent and completely unaware that I was all of these things.

I'd just graduated from high school. The ink wasn't even dry on my diploma, and I was itching to blaze a trail out of Sitka. I was sullen as I helped my mom load our folding table into the back of the truck. I was even more sullen as Mom and I sold homemade native jewelry to cruise-boat tourists on a street corner across from the school park.

It was July. The skies were partly clear, and the mountains surrounding Sitka reached up their snowcapped peaks to bask in the sunlight. Along every fence line and unused space, the uncultured but flourishing salmonberries were ripening. I'd just popped a few into my mouth, bursting them with my tongue and reveling in the sweet tartness spreading out across my taste buds when a handsome man in a heavily starched uniform stopped in front of me.

I was busy folding tissue paper around a necklace that a dangerously thin woman in high heels had purchased, so I didn't see him at first. My head was bowed as I put too much work into intricately folding the thin peach-colored paper that disguised what I was certain was inadequate craftsmanship.

Lifting my head to thank the lady, my gaze caught his, and with that simple act, the world reversed on its axis. Or at least that's how it felt. Unintentionally, I caught my breath and held it as if I was falling and bracing for the impact. The sky above my head whirled into a mixture of blue and white. I felt faint as I realized my knees were locked the same as if I'd been standing in front of the entire church congregation.

Mom bumped me with her hip to bring me back to reality, causing me to unlock my knees and take a deep breath. The blood returned to my head, and I was a tad bit clearer. I looked questioningly at Mom, and she nodded her head at the man. He must have said something I realized, but I'd heard nothing after my eyes met his, not even the noise of the cars rolling by or the clanking of the boats in the harbor.

In one hand, he held one of my bracelets. His other hand rested lightly on one lean hip. His dress uniform was crisp, his shoes polished to a high shine.

Swallowing the salmonberry juice, I managed to mumble the price, looking down at my feet while I answered. He laughed, thoroughly amused by my reaction to him, but he bought the bracelet—didn't even try to talk my price down. As he counted the money from his wallet, he asked my name.

"Tamara," I managed to say. It was just above a whisper

when the sounds at last made it across my tensed vocal cords.

"Joel," he said, answering the unspoken question on my face as he turned to walk away.

I watched him and his fellow soldier walk down the sidewalk towards downtown, past a little girl's lemonade stand where he stopped and bought a cup of the sour liquid. I think he was pretending, but I heard him tell her it was delicious. Tossing the drink back, he winked at me over his shoulder and disappeared around the corner.

If I sold more jewelry the rest of that day, I don't remember it. What I do remember was the perfection of his green eyes and how they stood out from his dark skin. The moss that carpeted the forest floor would have been jealous of the color. A deep green with highlighting flecks that matched the wispy lichens hanging from the trees; I'd blush whenever he roamed that cool gaze across my body. It was like being dipped into a cold mountain spring; my skin would tingle with the thought.

Joel returned the next day and then the next, and despite the warnings of my mother, I lost myself completely in him. I lived for his furloughs and those stolen hours when he was AWOL from the military base in Kodiak. Just a few short months later, he asked me to marry him, and I didn't hesitate even a split second in saying yes. Mom tried every way short of force to change my mind, but I was headstrong and impulsive, so nothing she said made any difference.

My decision made, I turned my back to her and climbed aboard a ferry that would take me away from Alaska, my mother, and everything familiar. Her tear-stained face watched me through the glass windows of the boat while the crew readied the ferry, and I turned from that too.

It was cruel the way I ignored her as Joel and I waited for the boat to pull away from the harbor. She didn't leave me; I could feel her back there, willing me to see reason. But it wasn't until the ferry pulled sluggishly away from the bay and we began to melt into the rain that I looked back at her one more time. I could barely make out her lone figure, shoulders drawn forward and hunched against the rain.

It was the last time I saw her alive.

I gave up a lot that day for Joel. My mom and grandmom, my best friend and sometimes boyfriend Peter, my way of life and even my future. I'd had a scholarship at a small college in Juneau for a nursing degree, and I kissed that goodbye too. A little niggle of doubt had fluttered at the base of my belly. Maybe it was the way Joel held me too tightly at times or the way I caught him looking at me out of the corner of my eye when I laughed too loudly or took too long to order at the drive-in. But I wanted him so badly that I ignored that tiny voice at the back of my mind that whispered to be careful.

Whatever misgivings I had were erased as the ferry pulled into Seattle Harbor. I'd never been anywhere except the villages that dot southeast Alaska, so the view of Seattle with its sparkling cascade of lights shimmering on the waters of the harbor seemed to vindicate my decision to leave Sitka. Mom was wrong about Joel.

*She's just jealous because she never escaped that island,* I told myself.

In less than a week, Joel and I moved into a cramped apartment in a bad part of town. There was only one bedroom, a tiny living room, and a battered kitchen. The paint that clung determinedly on the walls consisted more of smoke than anything else. The walls were thin and the neighbors talked too much. I didn't care. I was happy.

Joel got a job, and I was a good housewife. A fresh coat of paint and some thrift store furniture, and we had a great little place. Every morning, I woke him up early for work, laid out his clothes while he was in the shower, and packed his lunch.

The world was perfect, and Mom's concerns had been swept firmly into a corner of my mind until one morning, I woke up late and got a little behind in my morning routine. Joel's work buddy was lying heavily on the horn as I struggled to get his lunch packed. Kissing him quickly on the cheek, I pushed the lunchbox into his arms as he grabbed his coat.

"Sorry," I whispered as he walked out the door. His mouth

was set in a tight thin line. It was the first time I'd ever seen him angry.

*He's irritated that his friend is blaring that horn so early in the morning*, I convinced myself.

About an hour later, I noticed his sandwich sitting on the counter. I wasn't worried about it; he had plenty else to eat in his lunch. But that afternoon when he walked in the door, he busted my lower lip as I leaned in to give him his usual welcome-back peck.

It was hell after that day. There were stretches of time when things were okay, but they always ended in more punches, followed by a few meaningless apologies and a few I love you's.

The police didn't come the first night he hit me, or the next. It took over a month before the neighbors realized anything was wrong. They didn't say anything, and I didn't blame them. Those beautiful eyes of Joel's could slant a threatening jade at anyone who even appeared to intervene. Eventually, the neighbors would just look away. Sometimes they called the cops when I couldn't hold in the screams; sometimes they turned up their radios.

We moved a lot, as abusive and abused people normally do. The system is so easily manipulated despite all of the electronics. In reality, there's little communication between the different districts and counties.

Once the police became familiar with us, Joel would announce that we were leaving. The first couple of times we moved, I forwarded my new address to Mom and Peter in a short letter, where I bragged that everything was perfect. The two of them could be counted on to produce a flurry of letters or emails on my trusty AOL account, but I didn't answer.

Pride was a barrier I just couldn't cross, and over time, not writing or calling became the easier option. After the first few moves, I didn't bother with the change of address, and Mom and Peter had no idea where I was. Ten years with no contact. How could I have been so selfish? Now all of that lost time was my greatest regret.

So much pride. It had held me from my home, from

admitting my errors, and from contacting the people who had always truly loved me. Mom. Grandmom.

And Peter.

I'd sit sometimes for hours, while Joel was at work, thinking of Peter's face, the lift of his golden hair, the feel of his hands. If only pride had let me reach out to him. He would have moved mountains to save me.

Peter had warned me about the man I was marrying, but I'd thought he was a boy, and a jealous one at that. I'd told him as much the last time I saw him. Smiling at him with pity like a child who's losing his favorite toy when he told me how much he loved me, I'd brushed him aside for Joel too. I couldn't call him and admit just how right he'd been and how very wrong I was. I could be as stubborn as I was impulsive.

Nearly a year had passed before the realization hit that the Joel who drank too much and beat up on women was who he actually was, that the man I'd fallen in love with had been a fabrication from the start. It took another two years to realize that I couldn't change him, and then it took another five years before I found the strength to walk away.

Joel and I had been married for nine years when I caught sight of a thin, disheveled girl in a store window. I was waiting at the bus stop, having been to the county health units for some birth control pills—one of the few secrets I was willing to keep from Joel—when I noticed this woman out of the corner of my eye.

Her back was slightly bowed, her hands picked nervously at her clothes, but it was the lack of luster in her eyes and skin that really made me stop and take a second look. Unhappiness radiated from her; it was palpable and even in the crowded bus stop, no one stood within five feet of her.

It was the first time I'd seen myself so clearly. Perhaps it was denial that kept me from recognizing in the mirror at home just how far I'd fallen from my former self. Or maybe it was getting a look at what everyone in the bus stop was so eager to avoid.

The thick black hair that had at one time fallen down my

back in long waves to my waist was gone, replaced by a thin, limp mop of hair cut off at the shoulder. My once rounded curves were too sharp. My face was angular, and my eyes had gone dull with apathy. Chronic fear and anxiety were taking their toll. How embarrassed I was to be that girl who stood alone in the crowd while everyone else was talking on their cell phones or making small talk with the other passengers.

I left the bus stop that day a different person, still abused but no longer ignorant of the truth. My insides were in turmoil; my blood boiled as it traced hot paths down my hands and legs. I hated Joel with a rage that was frightening with its intensity as I walked home. I vowed to rip him apart with my bare hands; I wanted to feel his blood running down my arms and between my fingers, but by the time I got home, I knew I couldn't hurt him because I was partially to blame. I should have left years before.

The rage rushed out of me like hot air from a balloon, and once more, Joel had the upper hand. That's how abusers and criminals operate. That's why they usually win even when they're outgunned and outmanned; they're never concerned about who's at fault, and so they never fail to strike first.

That night, I made his dinner. I smiled and pretended nothing had changed. But after he fell asleep, I slipped a dollar bill out of his wallet. My hands trembled as if I was a shoplifter at my first crime, but I did the same thing every night, no matter how difficult the evening had been. And each time, it got easier.

Part of Joel's control was that I didn't have any money, and he'd never let me work. I looked for cash nearly any way I could. I picked aluminum cans out of the neighbor's trash. I scoured the bus stop for lost change. I hocked one of the tools that Joel didn't use very often. I went to the food pantries so I could squirrel back some of the grocery money he counted out to me each week.

I ached to call Mom. I knew she'd help me, but I wanted to fix this myself. Besides, I'd done enough to hurt her. Joel was unpredictable and dangerous, and I didn't want to nor did I have any right to drag her into our drama.

Time passed so slowly it seemed, slower than all the years that I'd just accepted my fate, but finally my stash of cash was big enough that I felt I could succeed. I began to plan.

I picked out an older retail district on the other side of Seattle, a place I'd never heard Joel speak about. Using the Internet at a nearby library, I found a shelter that promised to help locate a job within walking distance of its campus. It was first-come-first-served the shelter manager had told me since I didn't have kids. I'd have to be there right at six in the evenings if I wanted a bed for the night, and at seven in the morning if I wanted breakfast.

I packed nothing except a pair of pants, a shirt, a set of underclothes, and my raincoat in a plastic grocery bag, which I hid in a maxi pad box in the bottom of a bathroom cabinet. The money was buried beneath an ivy plant that had managed, against all odds, to thrive in the kitchen windowsill.

The best opportunity in weeks happened on a Tuesday night. Joel came home, angrier than usual. He turned to the booze early in the evening and was soused by dinnertime.

He was sitting on the couch when I set his dinner on a TV tray in front of him. My hands were shaking so hard, I knocked his beer off the tray. I didn't bother to duck as he backhanded me. Blood ran from my left nostril, but I wiped it on my jeans absentmindedly as I sopped the beer up with a towel.

Following our usual routine, I sat beside him while he watched TV and muttered about the price of gasoline. Every now and then, he'd squeeze my knee and say, "You've got to learn to be more careful, babe. I don't like to hit you like that."

Nodding my head at his inane remarks, I struggled not to be stiff, to act normal, but it felt like there was a neon sign blinking over my head advertising my escape.

If there was, he never noticed. Another hour, and a half a case of beer later, he finally slumped over onto the couch and fell asleep.

Too afraid to move, I set there trembling for a good thirty minutes until his breathing was steady enough that I found the courage to slide away from his heavy hands.

The money was the priority, so I sacrificed the ivy. Dumping it into the sink and pulling the plastic sack of cash out of the bottom, I made a beeline for my clothes before grabbing my purse. My birth certificate and social security card were hidden in the lining at the bottom.

Ever so slowly, I eased the door open. The movement seemed to suck the air out of the room with it, and I looked over my shoulder expecting to see Joel wake up to tear me a new one. But he never budged. The step out the door was not an easy one, but inch by inch, I made it across.

I ran down the street like a mad woman, and only an elderly couple smoking cigarettes on their front porch paid me any attention at all. The woman took a deep draw, the end of her smoke growing hot, as she looked away from me and down the empty street. She blew the smoke out as leisurely as she dismissed me from her thoughts. In my part of town, no one was terribly concerned to see a woman escaping into the night.

It was six blocks to the dollar store, but I never stopped. I'd planned to come here, it being one of the few strip centers that still had a pay phone. With the cab on its way, I slumped against a concrete wall to wait.

About an hour and ninety dollars later, the dim lights of the shelter came into view. The cheap bulbs, surrounded by little halos of mist, were a beautiful display—a beacon of hope. It might as well have been Vegas; I'd hit the jackpot.

The night air was chilly, and it misted rain against my raincoat, but the cold air was invigorating. Rain dancing on the concrete smelled like freedom, and I danced a little as well, my feet kicking up their own little showers with every step.

It was a long night waiting for the shelter to open. Seattle and a few of her suburbs can be dangerous places, and the shelter wasn't exactly prime real estate unless you were looking for a spot out of the way of the eyes of the police. Luckily, the rain picked up and even the drug dealers found other places to go. So for most of the night, I was alone and happy for it.

The shelter was a godsend. The staff was good on their

word; they helped with the job search, and soon I was checking groceries at a little mom and pop store not too far from where I slept. I never missed the deadline for a bed, and in a couple of months, I counted out the deposit money for my first place.

That's when I really started to feel free. Work was enjoyable; I loved talking to the customers as I checked their groceries. Most of them had shopped in this same store for half a century, and they continued to, not because of our great prices but for the atmosphere.

At night, I went to the library and played on the web. I checked out tons of books and read voraciously. I splurged on Chinese take-out once a week. I went to the free concerts advertised on the flyers posted around town. The tram carried me downtown on Saturdays and I went to the fish market.

Life was good.

Except the guilt over Mom.

I passed a payphone on my way to work every morning which served as a constant reminder that I should call her. The door on the booth stood open wide, never occupied by a single caller and beckoned me to enter.

*"It's a sign,"* my conscience whispered to me daily.

Sometimes I'd take a different route home just to avoid the phone, but it was always on my mind. Even when I didn't see it, I dreamed about it. Mom's voice rang in my ears at night. I could feel the buttons under my fingers as I dialed the number.

Exhausted and unable to take the dreams anymore, I finally gave in and stopped in front of the payphone on my way home from work. I paced in front of the booth, working on my breathing for twenty minutes, before I picked up the receiver and fed in the change that the mechanical operator required.

It rang twice before Mom answered, and my nails were white from my tight grip on the receiver before I finally got the nerve to respond.

"Mom," I whispered into the phone. My voice broke.

The other end was silent.

I cleared my voice. "Mom?" I questioned, wondering if she

was still there and knowing that I had no right to expect her to be.

My name was her only response for several minutes. We had volumes to say, but all that would come were tears.

The machine asked for a lot of money that day before we were done talking, but when we said our goodbyes, it was as if the last ten years hadn't happened.

I was still her daughter. How could I have ever doubted her?

I called her weekly after our initial phone reunion. She wanted me to come home, but I convinced her we'd both be safer if I was nowhere near her. Joel was still a danger. He wasn't the kind of man who took kindly to losing.

The weeks that followed will always be special to me. Mom and I became close again, even if it was over the phone. Money was too tight on either end for an impromptu trip, but we both started saving.

The summer, although months away, seemed a good time. I'd have a pretty good sum of money saved by then, and the cruise boats would be docking in Sitka several days a week. Mom could sell jewelry, and I could get a job with one of the seasonal tourist businesses for a couple of weeks. The owner of the grocery store where I worked promised I'd have a job when I returned. And return I would; I wouldn't stay and risk my Mom's life by giving Joel a stationary target.

I was so certain Joel would show up that I pleaded with Mom to move to Seattle with me. She refused; Sitka had been our family home for generations. "Joel is not going to run me away from my own home," she said.

I begged her then to keep the doors locked and have her mail kept at the post office. I wouldn't have put it past him to steal her phone records and try to track me. My heart told me she was in danger, but after a few months, life was still good. Nothing had happened and I dropped my guard. I filed for divorce. I had to. The end of the year was coming and taxes would be due. I, for one, planned on filing separately.

The phone book had more listings for attorneys than I could count and the sheer number of them made my vision blur as I ran my index finger down the list. Ever the resource, the manager of the shelter recommended a young attorney just a few streets over from the grocery who specialized in confidentiality.

I saw the lawyer on a Wednesday. It was a cool winter day. The skies over Seattle were heavy with wet leaking clouds, and I was glad to sit in her waiting room and dry off a bit before she called me back.

An hour later, she promised to treat my address as top secret, and I had no doubts she would. The divorce agreement would be simple. I wanted nothing except Joel's signature. The attorney promised to file that afternoon.

Outside her office, the clouds remained heavy. I called their bluff and walked home in the dry, and as I neared my apartment, I caught a look at myself in the glass of a dollar store window. This time, the woman who stared back at me was smiling. Her hair had a new shine, and it was growing. Where angles had been, curves now took their place. Her face was full; her complexion clear. I was optimistic about the future as I flashed a bright smile to my reflection.

Two weeks later on a Saturday night, everything came crashing down.

The clock to the right of my front door had struck ten when I turned out the lights that fateful evening and headed to bed. Nothing had been out of the ordinary about the evening. Mom and I had talked the day before. She'd mailed a cashier's check to help me buy a cell phone. I'd eaten a turkey sandwich for dinner and some chips that had passed their expiration at the store but were still perfectly good.

The historical fiction novel I finished that evening set on the counter waiting to be returned to the library in the morning. No romance mind you, as I didn't need any nightmares. The neighbors were all quiet when I climbed in bed and bundled up in the covers. Sleep came so easy I don't remember closing my eyes or counting numbers like on a lot of nights. I must have begun to dream right away, and that's where the normalcy ended.

Drawn from the haziness of a dream, I opened my eyes to the sensation that I wasn't alone. I was facing the far wall of my bedroom; my eyes strained to find something in the darkness, and I stretched one hand across the covers, watching as the hair rose of its own accord from my wrist to my neck. Behind me, the air stirred and flipping over, and I found my mom sitting on the edge of my bed.

Black hair draped down her back like a thick heavy curtain. It fell on either side of her shoulders, shadowing her face, which was smooth and sculpted. Her normally dark eyes glowed with a blue light. She was more beautiful than was humanly possible; I would say she looked young, but that would be wrong. She was timeless.

*This is a dream*, I told myself, which did nothing to calm the building anxiety. Besides, it was a lie. She was an apparition, and I was frightened not because I thought she might hurt me but because of what it meant. She was either dead or very close to it.

She didn't say anything, only watched me while she stroked my face and hair. I lay quietly under her soothing touch, knowing it would be the last time I ever felt it.

"I've come to ask your forgiveness." Her voice was like the tinkle of fine wine glasses in the midst of a toast.

"No," I said, shaking my head. "It's me that needs to be forgiven. I betrayed everything you and Dad ever taught me. I let a man take it all from me." My voice hoarsened with disgust at myself.

"I need to know you forgive me for not finding you years ago. I should have done more to protect you from him," she whispered, her skin cool against my cheek as she leaned towards me. "Please, Tam."

"You have my forgiveness, Mom. But you don't need it," I answered, knowing that I had to say whatever it took to put her at peace. This was not the time to be selfish. I couldn't even bear to ask her if Joel was involved. I couldn't say his name and see her lose any of her peace.

"Thank you, Tamara. Be strong. Have faith in yourself and know I will always love you," she whispered as she kissed my forehead, her form beginning to dissolve.

The room was cool, the way I liked it, but still I was drenched. My damp hair was stuck to my face, and I had to pull strands from my eyes as I sat up to clutch at the empty spot on my bed. The scent of rosemary hung in the air, and I inhaled deeply of the fragrance. The evergreen had been Mom's favorite spice.

Searching the darkness for her, I called out in one last selfish, desperate call for her. "Mom! Don't leave me. I need you."

Her image flickered in the corner, and she reappeared one final time, a peaceful smile touching and lighting up her face in silvery shadows. Unable to stop the tears that leached from my eyes, I watched as her form flickered once more then dissolved completely into a thin vapor.

The last remnants of her spirit dissipated on the air, and a numb feeling crawled through my body. I shook with the chills even as sweat pooled in my armpits. My mind danced between logic and soul. Maybe it was simply a bad dream. I took a deep breath, reminding myself of everything I'd been through in the last ten years. Bad dreams were to be expected, right? It crossed my mind that Joel had found me and not her. Maybe this was a warning from my subconscious.

I tried to rationalize, but my heart knew the truth. It was Mom's spirit coming to me after a bad death. According to my family's beliefs, the dead didn't necessarily leave the earth for forty days after dying. If someone experienced an untimely death, their spirit would be restless. They spent this time seeking forgiveness or visiting their loved ones. My grandmother believed that during sleep you could visit the other world of death and return by waking up. It was an old Russian concept, but she never doubted it.

I crawled trembling out of bed and, grabbing only a jacket and some change off the counter, I ran to the nearest payphone, my bare feet slapping the wet pavement loudly.

Mom's number rang over and over, her answering machine picking up on the first ring after the first two calls. Panic settled around me like netting. Desperate, I begged the operator to connect me to the Sitka Police Department.

A woman answered the phone informally. She was clearly a transplant with her southern California accent. My voice was shaking as I explained my bad dream and why the police needed to check on my mom. Unconvinced, she snickered a little and said someone would get back to me. I waited five minutes and called again. It was the same response the next six calls.

The only other number that I remembered from Sitka, besides my mother's, belonged to the local church Mom had faithfully attended. I dialed it frantically, my fingers flying across the small buttons of the payphone as I cursed my lack of a cell phone once more.

The number rang twice before a calm but strong male voice answered on the other end. I hesitated at the familiar sound. Momentarily stunned, I lost my courage and my voice.

"Hello? Who's there?" he questioned.

"Peter?" I spoke hesitantly.

"This is Father Peter. Who's asking?" he questioned.

"It's Tamara. Umm..." I paused here, embarrassed that I so clearly remembered his voice when mine might have held no place in his memory at all. "Lena's daughter. It's been a really long time." I swallowed hard. "You might not even remember me."

He laughed softly, a pleasant sound that took the edge off of my jitters, if only for a minute.

"Of course I remember you, Tamara. We only spent most of our childhood together. But I'm a little confused at your call. It's nearly three a.m. Is something wrong?" he asked.

I took a deep breath, looking for some steadiness in my voice and not finding any, I plunged ahead. "This will sound kind of crazy, I know, but I've had a dream that Mom's spirit came to me, and now I can't get a hold of her." Tears threatened to steal my voice and I choked them back, at least for the moment. "I...

I… I don't know what Mom has told you over the years, but I ended up in a bad way. A bad relationship, and I'm afraid that something awful has happened to her because of me."

The last few words rushed out of my mouth before a muffled sob escaped my lungs.

"Have you called the police?" Peter asked, his voice rising a little with my anxiety.

"Yeah, they said someone would get back to me, but I've been waiting a while and haven't heard anything. I was wondering if someone from the church would drive out and check on her. I know it's really late but something isn't right." My inner voice already knew what my mind refused to accept. "This is ridiculous, I know, but my gut says something is wrong."

"I'll go myself right now, Tam. What number can I call you back on?" he asked, slipping back to my old nickname.

I gave him the payphone number and sat down on the curb to wait. An hour later, Peter called saying Mom wasn't home. Two days' worth of newspapers lay on the deck, and her steps hadn't been swept of snow or ice.

I sat on the curb still in my nightgown and jacket, undisturbed by the strange looks of passersby, until Peter called back. Her body had been found at the bottom of a mountain ravine not too far from her home.

A passing policeman eventually drove me to my apartment. I guess I'd sat there for hours until a concerned citizen had called 911. I used the cashier's check Mom had sent days before her death to pay for my ticket back to Sitka, and I was still numb when I stepped off the ferry.

I'd come home, but it was too late.

# Chapter 3

That had been the worst day of my life by far, and I couldn't relive those memories yet without getting emotionally bogged down. It was just too soon. Someday, Peter had told me on the phone, I'd be able to look back and remember them without feeling as though my heart were going to explode. I thought it was far more likely that my heart would turn to stone before it quit hurting.

Blotting at the tears that had built up and trickled down my cheeks with the arms of my fleece overshirt, I stood up to shake off the memories that threatened to overwhelm me. I reminded myself that I had to be strong. It had been her last request.

*And I will be strong,* I told myself as I put the journal and supposed vampire blood on the mantle. I'd find a way to make Joel pay.

I stowed the rest of the letters and the textbook back in the trunk and tucked it in between the couch and the end table. Not wanting to miss twilight as it crept across the bay, I hurried outside, determined to close the door to the past, at least until after the sun had set.

The daylight was drawing to a close, and still I had a lot to get done. Wood had to be carried in for the night, there were fish to clean that a neighbor had delivered this morning, and the mail needed to be checked. The steps had to be cleared of the day's snow and rain.

I finished cleaning the fish first. I hadn't done it in years, but I managed to produce a few decent filets and only a handful of razor thin fin cuts that stung in the briny water.

I carried in several stacks of wood from the porch to the fireplace, scowling at the wood chips that dropped onto the floor, and moved more in from the rick in the backyard to dry out on the porch. Although it made a bit of a mess on the living room floor, I didn't like to go out after dark to get more wood.

Dusk hadn't quite settled when I walked the tree-lined driveway to the mailbox. Still it was dark enough in the shadow of the trees that I had to study the ground carefully in front of me. Not much waited in the box: a flyer for the local five and dime, the electric bill and a condolence card for losing Mom. She'd had so many friends and the cards were a near constant reminder of exactly what I'd lost.

Stomping up the steps of the porch to remove the mud from my shoes, I swept the three steps smooth and clean as I ascended before I stowed the broom in the corner and turned towards the view of Thimbleberry Sound. Two large lawn chairs rested against the back wall of the porch, but I didn't sit down. Instead, I leaned against the front rail and let the mist hit my face, watching as the rain peppered the surface of the Pacific.

Thimbleberry Sound spread out in front of my family home, its waters blending into the rougher waters of the Pacific at the edge of my vision. Dusk had fully arrived, and the sound was in limbo between day and night. The water itself was placid, expect for the pockmarks of rain, and in the semi darkness, I could just make out the rippling of the ocean as it lapped at the rounded islands jutting from the ocean floor. In the distance, the ice-capped peaks of the granite mountains rose majestically into the clouds.

It had been an unusually clear day until this evening when the gathering clouds on the horizon had stormed the coastline, and now wispy mists trailed in with the rain. More clouds gathered in the west, promising a night of wind and probably a little snow.

I could feel the storm coming, feel it brewing in my soul, and

I liked it. Weather should have texture I'd always thought. It should pelt your skin and leave you breathless. I'd happily embraced the rain while Joel had batted at it nervously. Tonight, I lifted my face to the breeze of the sea.

The misting rain tasted of salt as I licked my lips, and I was unprepared for the barrage of emotion that the taste dredged up. Every good kiss I'd ever had tasted of the ocean.

A bashful brushing of lips by Peter while we fished as teens. A sultry kiss from Joel that left the taste of salt dancing across my tongue.

How badly I'd craved Joel's kisses. How I'd yearned to drink the salt from his skin with my lips. It was as if my reserves were depleted and Joel was the element it would take to complete me. But just as too much salt will kill anyone, too much of Joel was equally dangerous, and he'd nearly poisoned me instead.

Angrily, I scrubbed the salt from my mouth with the back of my hand, refusing to enjoy even one memory of him. I surveyed the sound again, but this time without the rose-colored glasses of unbidden memoires. Instead, I squinted hard, searching the waters for boats that studded the surface too late in the day. My ears strained in the coming darkness for footsteps; determined that Joel would not catch me unawares.

Even after five months apart, I knew that I wasn't free of him. Somewhere out there, I sensed him watching, waiting. I could feel it in my bones. I should, he'd broken them often enough. Joel was the shudder I felt at random times, the sensation that someone was watching me when no one was around. It was him that brought me grasping for the lamp from a dead sleep. It was his face I'd see in the mirror if I turned my head too fast. I saw him in every car that passed me or at the other end of the grocery store. My neck was sore from looking over my shoulder.

And yet, nothing was tangible. I had no proof, except that I knew him. I was a wanted woman. He'd come for me just like he'd come for Mom. And while I had no illusions about my future, I also had no plan.

I'd been to the police every day since I'd arrived home about my fears with little success. I had, as of yet, been unable to convince anyone in authority that Joel was a danger to me or that he'd proved fatal to my mother. All I'd accomplished by my daily visits to the police was to begin to sink in my own self-doubts and fears. How much more alone could I get?

One officer had offered to help with a restraining order, but I hadn't bothered. Everyone knows it's just paper, and who needs more litter? I couldn't afford security for the house, and I wouldn't leave. My one purpose was to see Joel punished. I hoped it would be through the legal means of the court, but I wasn't fool enough to have much faith in that. My gut told me death really was the only thing that would part us.

Night had fully overtaken the ocean, and I was just about to walk back into the house when I caught the twin beams of a car below my house on the highway. There are few roads on the island, and Mom's house is the last house on the highway before the residential area ends and the Tongass National Forest begins. And I wasn't expecting any visitors.

Unless you're familiar with it, the driveway is easy to miss. In fact, it's closer to impossible to find. My lungs clutched my breath deep in my chest as the car slowed and turned into the drive, the brakes whining as it slowed its pace. Wary of whom it might be, I first darted closer to the door and then changed my mind and ran quickly down the steps. 911 was not likely to be of much help if it was Joel. The shrubbery close to the house was thick, and I slipped in behind it. The only thing I had for protection was Dad's pocketknife, which I'd used to clean the fish earlier. I slid it from my jeans, opening it with one hand to my side. I didn't feel any braver; my hands were nearly fluttering from nerves.

The lights of the car cut through the blackness as it wound up my drive, glinting on the rain dotting the spruce trees. Accustomed to the graying light of the past half-hour, the lights hurt my eyes and I closed them, shrinking closer to the ground until I heard the car door close and the headlights faded away.

I waited, still hidden, until the porch steps creaked with

somebody's weight, and slowly I rose up far enough to peer around the edge of the house. Just as I saw the figure of a man, he rapped his knuckles loudly on the door, and I jerked backwards, my head making contact with the sharp wooden corner of the house.

"Dammit!" I cursed. My head swam a bit, and I stumbled forward a step.

The man on the porch swung around as startled as me, but to his credit, he didn't curse or shriek. Instead, he swung his arms up defensively as he scanned the darkness to the side of the house. He was very tall, his long legs eating up the width of the front porch as he crossed it at the sound of my voice. He was way too tall to be Joel, and I let my breath out in a rush.

Pissed off but no longer scared, I raised a hand to the aching spot on the back of my head. Warm blood grazed my fingers, and I jerked them away, another curse word escaping, but more quietly this time, into the darkness. I stepped out of my hiding space just as the man swung down directly in front of me.

"Tamara? Is that you?" the man asked, reaching for one of my elbows.

"Peter?" Ten years had nothing on Peter and I gawked for a moment at how even more handsome he had become during my absence before I found my wits. "What are you doing here? You nearly gave me a fricking heart attack. Geez!" I exhaled harshly. And then I remembered who I was talking to.

"Sorry. I... I forgot," I stammered as I pushed past him, embarrassed to be caught hiding in the bushes like some frightened tourist.

"Forgot what?" he asked.

I kept walking, not bothering to look back over my shoulder. "Forgot you're a priest now, and I've already said three curse words in thirty seconds." I stopped for a second and blew out my breath in a big sigh. "Come on in. I'll be just a minute. I cut my head on the siding."

In the bathroom, I slung through the cabinets looking for some antibiotic cream but gave up. A cold, wet washcloth would have to do, along with the two ibuprofen I tossed back. I pressed the washcloth to my head as I went back to the living room.

Peter was standing at the mantle twisting the bottle of blood I'd found earlier around in his hands. "What is this?" he asked, one lip curled up in disgust. "It looks like blood."

Taking it from his hands, I shoved it deep in my jacket pocket. "Grab a seat," I said, but he ignored me.

The fire had died down a little; the room was starting to get chilly, so I stoked the coals and added a couple of logs. The ache in my head turned to a hard pounding as I bent to get the wood. It was a relief to throw the last log on and lean up against the doorjamb. The room was too charged to slip onto the couch.

"I tried to call several times today but never got an answer," he said accusingly. Arms across his chest, Peter stood by the mantle, looking as uncomfortable as I felt. I could see the resentment that I hadn't called him since I'd gotten home. I was zero for two, left without saying good-bye ten years ago and returned without saying hi. This wasn't the way our reunion should have been. Mom would have kicked my butt. Disgusted at my complete lack of decorum, I could have kicked my own butt.

"I've been meaning to call you. It's just that I've been busy here getting all of Mom's stuff in order. I haven't even checked the answering machine today." I gestured towards the mess that was the living room.

He nodded his head stiffly, pretending to understand why I'd blown him off.

"I'm sorry about your mom. I know it hurt not making it for the funeral."

I half-smiled to be polite, but he didn't know what it was like and how much I blamed myself for what had happened to her. "Thanks, and thanks for driving out here that day to check on her. I have to say, I was really surprised when I heard your voice. I thought you never wanted to..."

"End up in the Church. Yeah, I know. I didn't. You know how much I fought against it," he finished the sentence for me and let out an uncomfortable laugh.

"Well, I for one always knew you'd join the family business," I murmured.

"The ministry is *not* a family business, Tamara." Irritation made him use my full name.

This wasn't going well at all. I tried to backtrack.

"That's not exactly what I meant. I only meant to say you can count back many generations of Orthodox ministers."

"It's not a business," he said testily. "It took me a little longer than my dad or brother, but I finally realized that this truly is my calling. I was meant to be in the Church."

"I didn't mean the business part literally," I said as I reached up to dab at my head again. The pain was starting to die down. The ibuprofen had worked its way into my system, and I felt a little calmer.

"I didn't mean to startle you. Is your head okay?" he asked, starting to take a step closer. "Um... why were you in the bushes anyways?"

I waved him off. "Don't worry about it. I'm just jumpy. Living this far out is lonely after living in Seattle," I lied, refusing to let him see the weak, victim side of me and hoping to convince myself at the same time.

"Have you talked to a realtor?" Peter asked, pointing around the room with his index finger. "This place is worth a mint these days. Things have changed since you left."

"I can't sell this house. It belonged to my grandmother and then to my mom," I answered, pretending shock that he'd mention such an idea. I didn't tell him it had crossed my mind too. "You know how much this place means to me," I added in irritation.

"No. I can't say I did. In fact, I thought you never cared much for this place, or for anyone in Sitka for that matter." He scowled down at me from his substantial height, his arms crossed stoically across his chest again. "I meant *anything* in Sitka. I didn't think you cared for anything here. As I remember, you left in quite a hurry."

The space between us crackled with tension as we eyed each

other warily and I snapped back, “So, is this your usual welcome to the neighborhood pastoral spiel or is this just something special you cooked up for me?”

Before the words had even cleared my teeth, I regretted what I’d said. He should have been angry at my words, but instead he was hurt. He deserved to be angry after all he’d done for Mom and I over the last few weeks, but it was sadness that clouded his expression.

Peter had been my closest friend. We were near to inseparable growing up, and it had been him that had held me when my dad had died, his chest I cried into when school got too tough, or when I thought I couldn’t take another minute in Sitka.

He’d also been my first love, and besides Mom, no one in the world had known me better. He’d always been supportive despite his own burdens. His father was the local minister just like his father before him and his before him. His family could trace their genealogy back for several generations. So much was expected of him.

Preacher’s kid and all, there was no room for mistakes. He’d spent most of his childhood feeling trapped by the history of his family and the inevitably of what lay ahead. Mom had always hoped Peter would take the restless out of me, and Peter had craved the open roads of my future.

Maybe Mom would have gotten what she wanted if I hadn’t wanted to escape this island so badly. But Peter was destined to follow in his family’s footprints, and I’d always known that, even if he didn’t. It was too constricted of a life for me. I could see my future ahead of me, laid out like a timeline that you see in a history book, like it had already happened.

At the time, Joel was like a breath of fresh air in a stale room. There had been nothing predictable about him, nothing that was laid out in stone. Such a contradiction to the predictability of Peter. I didn’t feel guilty about rejecting that life, but I wished I hadn’t rejected Peter. I should have told him ten years ago how I felt instead of treating him like he had the plague and running away with the first man who could get me off the island. My goodbye to him had been a hasty message scribbled onto a piece of paper that I'd slipped into his mailbox. For all I knew, his parents had read it before him.

The crackling of the fire and Peter's angered breathing were the only sounds in the room. I'd sucked my breath in after my smart-ass remark, and it was still hovering somewhere near my diaphragm. Finally, I let it out, giving in to the inevitable and took a deeper one for courage.

"Peter, I owe you a huge apology." Only a few feet stood between us, and I looked up at him, meeting his gaze. "Ten years ago, I abandoned everything that was important to me, including you. I was horribly selfish. Guess I still am, actually, because I should have found you as soon as I got home and told you just how wrong I was to leave without a goodbye and an explanation. But truth be known, I'm embarrassed at the absolute mess of things I've made with my life and with the way I left our relationship; I would've fully expected you to tell me to go to hell."

I waited, expecting to hear him say the words—hoping to actually. I think if he'd told me to go to hell, I'd have felt better.

"I'm a priest, Tam. 'Go to hell' is not really in my vernacular."

He smiled and I melted. The heaviness that had hung in the air evaporated, and we both laughed at his words.

"Forgiveness on the other hand is, Tam, and you've always had it. I came tonight because I wanted to see an old friend and tell her that I never forgot her. Or gave up on her."

Speech had abandoned me, and so I reached for his hand, giving it a tight squeeze until I could find something to say. I held onto his hand for dear life while I blinked back a few tears.

Holding his warm hand in mine was like wrapping up in your favorite blanket or slipping into your best jeans. I knew his every tendon, the scar he'd gathered as a child on his palm and the valleys between the bones of his hands. It took effort to let go.

"Thanks for coming, Peter. Maybe I can forgive myself one day."

Indecision sparked momentarily across his face before he spoke. "Your mom lit a candle for you every day at the church. She never gave up. Sometimes she prayed alone and sometimes I prayed with her, but she always prayed. She would want you to quit blaming yourself for what happened. More than anything, she believed in a bigger power than ourselves and a greater plan than what we are capable of seeing."

"I didn't deserve her," I murmured.

"You did deserve her. If you could just have seen the happiness on her face the day after you two reconnected, you would know that."

"Thanks," I started to say, but the word got stuck in my throat as my eyes welled with fresh tears. Instead, I lifted up on my toes and kissed his cheek.

His cheek flamed under my lips, and he looked at the ground hesitantly for a moment. "Call me sometime, Tam. Here's my card. It's got all my numbers. Maybe you could stop by the church; everyone would love to see you—me included," he said as he placed the card in my hand, his eyes holding mine only for a second before he dropped my gaze and turned towards the front door.

I curled my fingers around the sharp edges of the card, feeling them bite into my skin. I nodded a goodbye as he crossed the porch and walked to his car.

The sounds of his tires on the gravel had disappeared before I looked down at his card. 'Peter Solinov, Minister,' the card read, followed by the address of the church and a variety of different phone numbers.

Church. I hadn't been in years. It was tempting, but I knew the prodigal child could hardly return now even if Peter didn't, and I laid the card on top of an unread stack of newspapers, reminding myself that I shouldn't drag him into all of my drama.

I locked the door behind him, listening to the quiet of the highway in the wake of his leaving. The doorknob was already turning cool to the touch as I twisted the lock into place.

The back door, which opened out onto a small deck

overlooking the mountain vista, was already secured, but that didn't keep me from checking it again just for good measure.

My watch sounded the hour in annoying little beeps, yet another reminder that I was the last person on the planet to not have a cell phone. It was only six o'clock but all of the sunlight leached from the day.

Alaskan winter nights are long. In fact, I'd forgotten how they lingered. I'd been in Sitka little more than two weeks and already I was beginning to feel the short days wearing on me. It was easy to get bogged down in your thoughts when the daylight, often times muted by the cloud cover, lasted a mere seven hours. Tomorrow, I'd make a point to get out, do some hiking. It had been years since I'd walked the trail to Heart Lake. It was well traveled and frequented by the locals, and I'd feel pretty safe there.

I'd gotten into the habit of staying up very late, sometimes till four or five in the morning, and then sleeping till around ten. Perhaps it was a delusion, but I felt safer. Joel was never a night owl, and since I'd known him, he'd never managed to stay up past one in the morning. If he was going to sneak up on me, he was going to have to lose some sleep.

Normally, I'd peruse a couple of magazines from Mom's "to donate to the local hospital pile" or read a book from the library. Sometimes, I studied for the philosophy class I'd signed up for before I left Seattle. I wasn't going back there anytime soon, but the syllabus was still an interesting read and had helped me think outside my usual parameters.

My newest loan from the local library was lying on the kitchen table. I started to slip my jacket off as I walked by the coat tree, my hand grazing the bottle I'd hidden from Peter's sight in the jacket pocket. I could only imagine what reason he'd thought a person might have for keeping a bottle of blood on the mantle. Luckily, he'd forgotten it when our argument erupted.

The liquid swam in the confines of the bottle as I twirled it in my hands, eddies forming and bursting within the glass as the fluid turned in upon itself. The color glimmered in the light and mesmerized me with its intensity. I found it hard to look away, especially knowing the unusual story behind it.

Returning the bottle to the mantle, I lay back onto the couch and watched the blood shimmering in the firelight. I could almost hear Mom telling me to throw it out and couldn't help but smile knowing she'd slept with it at the foot of her bed most of her life. She would have been mortified because she would have believed it was real.

Me. I was a little more skeptical. Vampires are a mainstay of Russian folklore and old wives tales but still, I knew very little about the old legends. Glad that I had something to think about other than Joel and Mom, I decided I'd make a trip to the library and the bookstore tomorrow. If I remembered right, the bookstore had an entire section of Russian literature, and the library would be bound to have something related to the subject. I'd stop there on my way to the hiking trails.

With tomorrow planned out, I spent the rest of the evening sorting through more of Mom's belongings. Eventually, I drifted off to sleep with images of vampires and bottles of blood playing across my mind.

# Chapter 4

I woke at nearly nine o'clock and still it was barely light. Rain pelted the windows, and when I lifted myself off the couch to look out the picture window, I couldn't even make out the sea for the cloud cover. Fog had rolled in heavy from the ocean and billowed puffy layers across my porch.

I considered going back to sleep, and I'd nearly let the quilt fall back across my shoulders when I reminded myself that bad habits are easy to form and I'd made plans for today. If I didn't watch it, I'd be sleeping all the time, and that wasn't good for anyone. It's the risk of living in Alaska in winter.

I forcefully threw the quilt back, my back protesting a little as I pulled myself to a sitting position on the couch and determinedly made my way into the kitchen. Soon the coffee pot was percolating, and I was completely dressed when I sucked down my third cup. Thank God for coffee. And I meant that literally; no one can survive in Sitka without it.

I poured a thermos full of the black gold as I shrugged on my raincoat. My plan was simple. I'd avoid the police station today. I would avoid thoughts of stalking soon to be ex-husbands. Instead, I'd drink lots of hot coffee, eat chocolate, and read books that had nothing to do with murder.

I was going to solve a different kind of mystery this morning—a vampire mystery. Not wanting to drink alone, I called Mom's best friend Gloria. Like everyone, it'd been years since I'd seen her. She'd meet me at the bookstore at noon.

Town was as bustling as it gets in Sitka in the wintertime, so there was no waiting for coffee, and a few minutes later, I was tucked between a couple of bookshelves, my thermos resting between my knees and several books about vampires scattered around my feet. Who knew they were such a hot topic?

As I'd expected, I'd found a couple of books in the Russian lore section. Sitka is, after all, known for its Russian influence, and Russian books are very popular with the tourists. I perused one book of Russian fairytales until my knees and back got stiff, so I moved to a table carrying my stack of vampire books with me.

I was deep into the old fairytale of a bridegroom and a vampire. I'd heard the story many times as a child, but I can't say it made much more sense now than twenty years ago. I was intently looking for some deeper meaning when I felt a strong but warm hand on my shoulder. I nearly jumped out of my skin, the coffee sloshing around with my movement.

"Tam. It's me. I'm sorry, baby. I didn't mean to startle you." Gloria was smiling down at me apologetically. She and Mom had been best friends for as long as I could remember. Many a winter night had been whiled away at her house. She and Mom guzzled whiskey laced coffee, and Gloria's two kids and I cooked popcorn over the fireplace and drank sodas. Friends in the wintertime are a commodity that you can't live without in Alaska.

Gloria was a transplant, moving here years before from the Deep South. She said she'd come to escape the heat. Her Cherokee Indian heritage showed up in deep mahogany skin that stretched beautifully over high cheekbones. Her complexion was smooth and even. Her lips were still full and dark eyebrows arched gracefully over eyes as dark as coal. She was tall, nearly six feet, and her arms encircled me in a deep hug before I had time to set my coffee aside. Except for the silver in her hair, you'd never know she was pushing sixty.

"It's okay. I was deep into this story, I guess." I stood to hug her back. "Gloria, I'm so glad to see you," I said as I leaned into her tall frame.

"Tamara, I can't believe you're here. It's been ages," she said, squeezing me all the tighter.

"Better late than never," I answered, guilty all over again at the problems I'd caused. I knew it was Gloria that had consoled Mom when I left.

"You look great," she said, stepping back to take my shoulders in her hands. "Your Mom told me about everything you've been through, and I'm so glad you're home."

"Thanks. You look wonderful. Time's been kind to you." I wasn't lying. She looked really good. It's amazing what a cloudy environment will do for your skin.

She laughed, "Time is never kind, Tam. We run out of it too quickly and yet complain about how we look wearing the years we get." She paused as she studied my face. "You look more like your mom than I expected you would. She was my best friend and one lady I'm never going to quit missing."

I nodded my head, tearing up a little as I spoke. "I miss her more than I ever realized I would. She was my best friend too in the end. I only wish I'd been smart enough to have taken advantage of that earlier." Guilt hit me hard, then and I blurted out, "It's my fault she's dead. You know that, right?" I questioned.

"Tamara! Why would you ever say that? None of this is your fault." She took my hand from across the table, folding it over in her long brown fingers.

"I think Joel killed her. To get back at me for leaving him. I knew he would and I left him anyway," I said, a few tears tracing a path down my cheeks.

"Have you talked to the police?" she questioned.

I rolled my eyes. "Only every other day. They all but run when I walk through the doors of the station. They say it was accidental. That Mom was getting older and not getting around as good as she used to and just fell. But I know the truth, and it's my fault."

"Getting older my ass," Gloria drawled as only a southerner can. "Lena was in great shape, and she got around better than most anyone I know, including that little upstart of a detective," Gloria said, a little miffed that anyone would say her friend was old. "Tam, baby, listen to me. I've had a bad feeling about this whole thing myself. Now I'm not sure what happened exactly, but I know none of this is your fault. You are *not* to blame no matter if your soon-to-be ex did this or not. But I don't I think she just fell off that mountain."

"So you think it's possible. That I could be right and Mom's death wasn't an accident?" I questioned. She was the first person who'd conceded that my suspicions might be correct.

Gloria looked away for a minute, her eyes studying the wet street outside the window before she took a deep breath and met my gaze again. Her hand circled tighter around her coffee cup, one turquoise ring digging into the Styrofoam. "I know your mom was worried about something. I'm not sure about what; she wouldn't say, but she seemed jumpy. You know, just a little nervous, and that wasn't like her."

"Had anything happened I don't know about?" I questioned, watching her face intently.

Gloria took a quick sip of her coffee and crossed her arms across the table, leaning forward a tad. "Not anything specifically. She just acted a little strange. About a week before she died, we were out one night at a crab boil on the beach. There were lots of people there. Seemed like the whole town had come down, and it was really noisy. Everything was going fine. She was cracking crabs, laughing and talking like normal, and then her hands stopped in midair and her face froze. She looked like she'd seen a ghost. I asked her what was wrong, but she said nothing and went back to cracking. She just seemed a little spooked the rest of the night. I'm not sure what happened or what she saw."

"Or *who* she saw," I finished the thought for her.

"A couple of nights later, I went to see her at the house and her doors were locked. In all the years I'd known Lena, I had never known her to lock a door. Then to make matters even stranger, she had all her mail held at the post office. When I asked about it, she just shrugged, saying she didn't want anything falling into the wrong hands."

My insides knotted up and I felt sick. I hated myself for dragging Mom into this. "It was Joel. I know it was. It's killing me, Gloria, because I want him to pay. I want him to suffer. But the police won't give me the time of day. They say there's no evidence and everything's circumstantial. There are days I feel like I could kill him with my bare hands, and yet I'm scared to death of him. To make matters worse, I have no idea where he even is now. Is he here? Has he left the island? I have no idea."

"Tamara, you listen to me," she said sternly. "He may never pay on this earth, but he will pay. Even if he isn't responsible for Lena's death, he's certainly done enough damage to you. Someday when the good Lord gets ahold of him, he's gonna be *mighty* uncomfortable. Right now, you need to take care of yourself. Go somewhere and make a new life. That's what your mom would want. She would have happily died to protect you. You have to know that."

"Gloria, I can't keep running, and yet I'm about to lose my mind with all of the worry with where Joel might be and what he's going to do next. I want revenge for everything he's done to me and to Mom. We deserve it." I could hear the weariness in my voice.

"You're right. You do deserve justice. But remember that vengeance is the Lord's. Not ours. It's not ours to dole out."

She was right of course. But that didn't stop me from wanting it anyways. Gloria didn't understand how much I'd suffered at Joel's hands nor could she possibly understand just how guilty I felt for my part in Mom's death.

I smiled, hoping it would break the tension that had developed. "I guess you're wondering why I'm reading vampire novels with all of this mess going on," I laughed, gesturing at the books spread out haphazardly across the little table. I had so many that they were piled on one another.

"Well, it did cross my mind, and I thought it was good. You need something to take your mind off all this drama," she laughed, pleased that I'd put the crazy talk away.

"Okay. Here goes. Do you remember the old steamer trunk Mom kept at the foot of her bed?" I took a long sip of my coffee while she nodded.

"It was a bona fide mess the couple of times I saw her open it," Gloria added.

"Yeah. Well, I was cleaning it out. Going through the heaps of old coats and long out-of-date undergarments and stuff. You know how Mom was, she never threw anything away. I was straining to get one last jacket out, and I lost my balance leaning over the side. When I did, my hand busted through the bottom into some secret compartment. And I found an antique wooden box."

"So Lena didn't know about it?" Gloria smiled, enjoying the mystery.

"I don't think so; Mom never mentioned it, and I had to pry the thing out of its hiding place. From the looks of the steamer, it had been hidden for years. Anyways, inside the box was this old journal written by a surgeon around the time Sitka was first founded. If I remember right, the year was 1808, and I think Sitka was founded in 1804. But that's not the amazing part. I was able to translate the journal since Mom and Grandmom insisted I learn Russian and there was one entry that described the staking of a vampire. So I've been doing some research. It gives me something else to think about. In fact, I'd promised myself that today would be free from thoughts of Joel," I added, slightly embarrassed to be caught doing vampire research. I didn't mention the blood.

Gloria smiled, running a hand through her silvering hair. "Who doesn't love a good mystery?"

"I know. Right!" I said.

Taking another long draw of her coffee, Gloria leaned in excitedly. "Well, I have some clues to add to this. You see, Lena once told me that her great-grandfather wouldn't go into the forest alone and never at night, no matter how much company he had. He never went hunting with the other men. Did she ever tell you that?"

"No," I answered, shaking my head. "I don't remember her saying too much about him except that he was really old and really superstitious even by her standards."

"This was her great-grandfather on your grandmother's side. Supposedly, he firmly believed in vampires and claimed to know where one was buried. He said his grandfather had nightmares about burying one and talked about it in his sleep. But when pressed, he wouldn't name where the grave was so everyone just thought he was making it up."

"What'd Mom think?" I was pretty sure I already knew.

"She didn't think he was crazy. But she sure didn't want anything to do with him."

"So Mom's great-grandfather never told anyone where the grave was?" I asked.

"Not that your mom ever mentioned. He took the secret to his grave. Your grandmom was buried somewhere close to him," she said, pointing over her shoulder towards the cemetery. "I'm sure his stone is long gone by now. I only heard her tell the story once or twice because Lena didn't like ghost tales and the like. But you knew that. She was the queen of superstition and when a Southerner says that, it means something!"

"Yeah, she was a big chicken about that kind of stuff. But then she'd pick up a hitchhiker and drive them wherever they wanted to go. And never lock a door. Go figure."

"Your Mom was one of a kind. That's for sure." Gloria downed the rest of her coffee in one long draw. "Well Tam, I gotta go. My man's about to leave on a hunting trip, and I've got to see him off."

She caught my hand in hers before she stood to leave. "Honey, listen," she said, more remnants of her southern accent sneaking into her speech. "Revenge is its own kind of prison. Don't buy into it."

I promised to call her again soon and waved goodbye until she'd disappeared down a side street into the misting rain.

After she left, I finished my coffee and flipped through a few more of the books. It seemed nearly every culture of the world had vampire legends. The physical descriptions weren't the same, but the principles were fairly constant. The Russian culture had certainly contributed a lot to the lore.

I picked out the most informative book and paid for it at the counter. The sales lady had been eyeing me surreptitiously, and I didn't want to give her the wrong impression; that I was just one of those chronic bookstore stalkers. Which I was of course. I'd been known to read entire books just sitting in the bookstore. Luckily, this book was from a discount rack, so it wasn't very pricey.

It was raining hard as I walked to Mom's truck. The wind blew in sharp gusts from off the ocean until the rain came down slanted, and it stung like nails if I didn't keep my face tucked into the neck of my coat as I walked. I'd planned to hike the trail to Thimbleberry Lake, and I had to remind myself of an Alaskan truth. The weather is just the weather.

*Don't be a sissy,* I said to myself as I climbed into the cold, but at least dry, truck cab.

By the time I'd reached the trailhead, I'd had to warn myself against being a sissy time and time again, and I kept repeating the mantra until I'd hiked to Thimbleberry Lake, which was about a mile from where I'd parked. The rain had turned to snow, which I preferred, with the increase of elevation, and the view of the lake was crisp and brilliant.

I stood absorbing the view for a few minutes, allowing my breath to catch up with me before I walked on towards Heart Lake, which sat at a higher elevation. The spruce trees whistled around me, the wind occasionally knocking off small clumps of snow and ice, which landed in mock cannonballs that made birds start from the branches or caused me to take a step back. The temperature had cooled even further. I rubbed my hands together for warmth as I hiked with little success.

The trail was well traveled even in the winter. I met three hikers headed back down the mountain. One older lady hiked alone, a pole in each hand helping her to balance as she worked her way down the slope of the mountain. A few minutes later, I met a couple as they hiked hand in hand. I smiled, giving them a silent nod and wave as we passed. Ahead of me, I could see two women pushing through the snow headed up the mountain a little off the beaten path. They were certainly getting a workout. To the rear, I could hear the laughter of some teenagers skipping class out for a walk.

Reaching Heart Lake, I settled next to its shore on a snow-covered rotting log. I opened my thermos and took a long draw of my coffee. The java was like a shot of warmth to my bones, and I took another long drink before I tightened the lid back in place.

I was warmly dressed but still the wind had crept in amongst all my layers. I snuggled my hands deep in my pockets as I studied the alpine lake in front of me. On a summer day, it would be hard to tell where the lake ended and the mountains began, the water was that clear. But here in the winter, the reflection was more like frosted glass with mountains shimmering across its surface. Randomly situated, tufts of heavy mists trailed across its surface.

On three sides, mountains ensnared in thick blankets of snow loomed in the background and even I, having been raised here in their shadows, was awestruck by their beauty. That same awe was tempered by the inherent danger. Visitors died here every summer by forgetting that where great beauty is, danger is not usually far off. That was no truer than here in America's last frontier.

This year, Mom was listed as one of the casualties of the mountains, and I shuddered to think of her lying here in the elements, cold and alone, until she breathed her final breath. It seemed a cruel twist of fate that a woman who knew the terrain so well would come to her end at its hands. It was her who took the Girl Scouts out on their camping trips each year. She helped teach the nature classes to our native children every summer and she could name every plant and how it was used in the woods.

Before I was born, she'd spent her time with her new husband in the woods, camping and living off the land for the pure enjoyment of it. She and Dad had canoed for days at a time, traveling downstream, fishing as they went, hiking into the higher elevations to hunt sheep and searching the lower lands for black-tailed deer. Mom was no stranger to the forest.

There's something cleansing about the cold mountain air, and it took all of the fluff from my mind and let me see the real condition Mom was in during her last few days alive. So much for not thinking of Mom or Joel; I just couldn't keep my mind from going down that road.

I slid down on the ground, using the log to rest my back against and began to rehash Gloria's words. Something, someone had spooked her. She'd become careful, locking doors and holding her mail. No doubt she wanted to keep my address a secret. She'd died to protect my whereabouts.

No, these mountains did not kill my mom. Being up here where she and I had spent so much time together silenced the voice of doubt that had been lying to me since I'd arrived home. In the back of my mind, I could hear Peter and Gloria telling me to leave. They were probably right. I usually made the wrong decision, but I couldn't walk away from my home and my mom again. I needed a little peace, even if it came from bad choices.

Thinking of bad decisions made me think of the time. It had gotten late. The setting sun was only visible as a lighter crescent of blue clouds that hovered in the valley of two sheer-faced mountains. The snow under my feet had taken on that luminescence that can only be gained in those few moments of twilight before being swallowed by the fullness of night.

It would be dark this evening. Very dark, as the sky burdened with heavy clouds would let in none of the moon's brightness. I'd stayed too late and still it took too long to decide to push myself out of my warmed up spot against the log. The wind slapped me as I stood up, and I shivered at the sting, wishing that I was already back, warm and cozy, in my truck. There was a couple swallows of coffee left, and I downed them before clipping my thermos to the waistband of my jeans.

The hike back down the mountain was cold and brisk, and I berated myself nonstop down the trail as I realized how totally alone I was on the side of the mountain. The locals I'd seen out for exercise along the trail had long since made it back down while I hadn't. If I looked over my shoulder at the mountains behind me once, I looked a hundred times. I was getting more nervous with every passing moment. How foolish to present myself such an easy target for Joel.

My truck sat forlornly at the trailhead when I finally emerged from the tree-lined path. Despite the moderate snow that was falling, the windshield of my truck had been wiped clean and a piece of paper, stuck under a wiper blade, fluttered in the breeze. My palms got clammy just looking at it. Someone knew I was here. But who? Joel was my first thought naturally but then again Gloria knew I was hiking today. Peter could certainly find me. He knew this was one of my favorite spots. Nervously, I eyed the empty parking spaces as I searched the darkness for any threats, but nothing and no one bothered me as I walked across the parking lot.

I snatched the paper off of the windshield as quickly as I could and slipped into the cab, the hairs raised on the back of my neck the entire time. If I didn't know better, I'd swear someone was watching me. Jamming my finger onto the electric lock, I took a deep breath as I studied the trees lining the forest and the road to my left, but nothing stood out to explain my increased anxiety. Still, I felt like someone was out there. Watching, waiting.

With my heart racing, I unfolded the paper, expecting to see Joel's neat, even handwriting. Even his penmanship was perfectly controlled, but instead, the note was scrawled in a large friendly script that I immediately recognized even though it had been more than eight years since I'd seen it.

Eight years instead of ten because Peter had written often when I first moved to Seattle. His letters followed me until I finally began returning them to the post office. I didn't want to send them back, but I was scared for Peter's safety. If Joel had checked the mail before me, things would have gone poorly for the both of us, and so when we picked up our bags and moved the next time, I didn't bother filling out a change of address.

The note I held in my hand today smelled of Peter, just as those letters had eight years ago, and then, as now, the scent brought a warm feeling to my insides and a soothing reminder that Peter had loved me once. I hadn't deserved his love, of course, but he'd loved me nonetheless, and I'd come to the realization over those first two years apart that I'd loved him more than I'd realized. Immaturity kept me from discerning it from the lust and excitement I felt with Joel, but my love for Peter was the feeling that lasted long after the excitement of Joel had worn away.

The only thing I could give Peter back was his safety, and so I'd burned his letters in the kitchen sink, washed them down the drain and resolutely forced him from my mind all those years ago.

I inhaled deeply of the note I held in my hand once more before I read it. 'Dinner at my place? Seven? Or whenever, I'll be waiting for you. Hope you enjoyed your hike.'

My heart sunk into my belly at his words. I wanted to go. My soul ached to see him but how could I after what I had done to him? And knowing that Joel was here, somewhere waiting for me made Peter as much a target as myself. In fairness, I had to protect him from my drama. He was a minister now and didn't need my reputation for disaster and mayhem affecting him or his position in the church. People in Sitka have a long memory and no know had forgotten what I had put Mom or Peter through.

I started towards home, determined to put Peter's safety before my craving to be with him, but as my driveway approached, I couldn't force myself to turn in. Surely one dinner wasn't the end of the world and not going would be an insult, I convinced myself as I drove on into town towards Peter's house. On the way, I picked up a bottle of Pinot Grigio, a tip from the liquor store owner as I shopped for something suitable to take to his house.

Peter's driveway was partially obscured in a clump of azaleas, but I'd turned in so many times as a teenager when Mom would give me the truck for the day that I had no problems finding it. His family home was nestled a couple of miles off of the main road in the protective arms of a mountain that rose precipitously from his backyard. His people had lived at this address for years. Not necessarily in the same house, as houses come and go, but this location had been his family's home base for at least as many generations as my family. No matter where in the world the Solinovs ended up, they always came back here to be born, married, and buried.

The house hadn't changed much since I'd been gone except that it now blended even more into the landscape. The rock chimney, the focal point of the home both inside and out, was covered with a deep green moss that had once only dotted its surface. Ferns had overtaken the bases of the trees his mother had planted when we were teenagers, and those same trees had spread branches that now cocooned the sidewalk. The wood siding on the house had faded to a steel gray color that matched the slate mountains in the backdrop. In the far left backyard, I could see the remnants of the tree house Peter and I had played in as children.

It was fairly large and sprawling by Sitka standards, but you wouldn't know it from standing outside where the trees and shrubbery were arranged to conceal its size. But from the inside, hallways branched in nearly every direction leading to the several bedrooms that had housed his brother and four sisters.

Just seeing the house made me a bit nervous. The last time I'd walked through these doors, I'd told Peter I was leaving for Seattle. It was in front of the fireplace that he'd pleaded with me to listen to reason. I had promised I would then later I'd hastily shoved a note telling him good-bye into his mailbox. I felt guilty just standing in the yard. *I shouldn't be here*, I told myself, and I turned to go. I didn't make it more than a few feet before I heard the door open swiftly behind me.

"Hey, you can't leave. You just got here," Peter yelled across the expanse of the front yard. I jumped at the sound of his voice, nearly dropping the wine bottle I carried in my hand.

He was leaning around the door, and I could only see him from the neck up. "Wow. You really are jumpy. I thought you were just joking last night when you were hiding in the bushes," he teased. "How's your head by the way?"

Taking a steadying breath, I turned back towards him even as I was thinking of some good excuse to get out of the evening. "I just realized I've got to…" I started to lie, but I couldn't think of a good excuse quickly enough. "A bad case of nerves is all," I finally said as I walked back towards the front door. "And my head is still sore. Thanks for that," I snipped.

"Well, you're not letting a case of nerves ruin dinner. Come on in," he said, stepping back from the doorway so I could pass.

"Oh," I said as I walked through the front door and realized he was shirtless, his chest shining with sweat. "I can come back. Clearly, I'm early. It's just that you said 'any time,' and so I came straight over, but I can come back later. Or I can come another day. Or we could forget it all together if you want." I was getting more flustered with every passing moment, and my mouth just wouldn't stop moving.

"Tam, it's okay. Relax. It's my fault. I was working out in the garage and lost track of time. Let me just get a quick shower. There are some glasses set out in the kitchen and some snacks. The salmon could marinate awhile longer anyways so it's all good."

I nodded my head, avoiding looking in his direction at all. Instead, I was studying the entryway as if I'd never seen one before in my entire life.

"Do you want me to take that?" Peter asked as I stared fixedly at the chandelier hanging from the vaulted ceiling.

"Oh, I almost forgot. Yeah, it's a bottle of Pinot," I said as I handed it to him. The skin of his thumb brushed my hand, and I couldn't stop my eyes from moving to his. I'd forgotten how green they were against the honey color of his skin, but I'd never forgotten how I enjoyed looking at them.

"Make yourself at home, Tam. The fire's going in the living room, and I'll be back in a few."

With his back safely to me now, I watched him walk away, admiring the columns of muscles that framed his spine as he strode from the room.

Peter had always been handsome. Tall, at least three inches over six feet, he'd towered over every guy in our high school. In middle school, he'd filled out early, and by the time he was eighteen, every woman in town, no matter their age, had a hard time keeping their eyes off him. His body was hard-muscled from woodworking with his father and the continual climbing his family did in the mountains. His thick hair was a golden brown, and he always had a light five o'clock shadow, the good kind, which was just a shade darker than his actual hair color. Looking at him certainly did not make you think Christian thoughts.

But if his body was beautiful, his heart was divine. He was one of the few men who could pull off humility and kindness without looking weak and walked on. *Why had I ever broken up with him?* I questioned myself again.

Oh, yeah. Excitement. Escaping the familiar. The usual reasons women throw away good men.

After discarding my shoes and coat, I walked to the living room, anxious to warm my hands in front of the fire. It had always been my favorite room in Peter's house. In the corner, the native rock chimney dominated the wall. The stones had been carved out and placed meticulously by some past relative of Peter's, and it truly was a work of art. The walls were hand-hewn logs from the surrounding forests and stained a natural color that was both warm and inviting.

Comfortable leather furniture had replaced the country blue fabric his mom had preferred, and the bookcases were lined with rows of seminary books, woodworking manuals, a few classics and Peter's all-time favorites—westerns. The air smelled of cedar, leather, and men's cologne and whispered of days filled with hard work and quiet nights spent reading in front of the fire.

I thumbed through a couple of photo albums that were lying on the coffee table, smiling at the memories the faded pictures brought back. There were several of my family at church functions and a few of Peter and I at school events. Our senior prom pictures were displayed proudly followed by our graduation pictures. The second album was filled with pictures taken after I'd left and looking at them brought tears to my eyes. I wiped them away quickly when I heard Peter's bedroom door open. Carefully, I placed the albums back where I'd gotten them.

"How was the hike?" Peter asked from behind me. He held two glasses of wine, one of which he slipped into my hand as he lowered himself down onto the stone hearth to sit beside me.

"The cold air was good. Cleared my head a little and I feel better," I said as I took a drink of wine. I lied, forcing myself to sound happier than I actually felt, but I had no intentions of ruining Peter's evening with the details of Mom's case. He knew I suspected foul play, since I'd mentioned it to him the night I called and asked him to check on her, but we hadn't discussed it since.

"Pinot Grigio is my favorite," he said. "How'd you know?"

"Yeah, I got a little tip from the owner of the liquor store," I said sheepishly. "I didn't mean to tell anyone I was coming over here. He just kind of figured it out. It seems he remembered us. Or me. Probably me mainly."

"Everyone remembers you," Peter answered.

I let my breath out in a huff. "That's what I'm afraid of and I don't want to ruin your reputation, Father." I smiled sarcastically but I wasn't joking.

"It's okay. I don't care if anyone knows you're here. I'm not ashamed. Everyone knows one of the benefits of being Orthodox is not having to be celibate your entire life." Our eyes met and I felt my cheeks flame.

"So what were you working on when I drove up?" I asked in an attempt to change the subject away from celibacy.

"Let me show you," he said, standing up and offering his hand. I let him pull me to my feet against my better judgment. His hands were warm, strong and slightly calloused. He didn't let go of mine immediately but instead led me in the direction of his workshop for a few steps before our hands slipped apart.

His workshop was connected to the house through a series of hallways. His father used to work out there for hours, and he'd taught Peter everything he knew. The smell of fresh cedar drifted through the hallways as we got closer until I would have sworn I was standing on the side of a mountain.

As we walked into the workshop, I gasped in awe. Spread across braces was the partially finished hull of a boat carved from a giant red cedar tree trunk. At least ten feet in length and three feet wide, the canoe would carry five or six people easily when it was completed, which could take years. Hand carving a canoe is no easy feat.

"Peter, oh my gosh, it's beautiful! How long have you been working on this?" I questioned as I ran my finger carefully down the sides. It was still rough-hewn and splinters would be abundant.

"About a year. I spend some time on it whenever I get a chance, which sometimes is every day and then sometimes I can't touch it for a week or two."

"Well, it proves you're a dedicated man, and why you don't have the hands of a minister," I teased.

"I guess we'll know for sure when I get it done, and it's not necessary for ministers to have soft hands, by the way, so long as we have soft hearts."

"You've always had a soft heart. That's what made you such a good friend," I said.

"As I remember it," Peter answered, his eyes holding mine, "we were more than friends."

The room had suddenly gotten much smaller, and the air seemed to have lost some of its oxygen. I became very aware of Peter's proximity, the outline of his chest and the fullness of his lips.

"I need some water," I said, breaking our gaze as I turned

and walked back to the kitchen. Behind me, I heard him let out a sigh of frustration.

In the kitchen, I grabbed a bottle of water from off the counter and sat down at the bar while Peter put the salmon steaks on to cook.

"So how are your parents? I should have asked earlier," I said, hoping for a neutral topic as I reached for some bread arranged on a tray on the counter.

"Mom died a couple of years back, heart disease, and Dad retired to the lower forty-eight. He just couldn't face living here without her. You know, seeing their friends all the time. It was just too much. The land has been in the family for generations of course, so he just turned it over to me when I came back here."

"I'm sorry to hear about your mom."

He nodded a thanks as he flipped the salmon over, basting it with a traditional marinade. It smelled delicious, and I was beginning to get an appetite.

"So what's it like being back here? You miss the big city?" he questioned.

"It's different. But it's nice," I said. "I miss the Fish Market and the music that was a constant in Seattle. And I miss the crowds, which is strange, I know, but Sitka feels kind of lonely now after living there. But it's good to be back and see the mountains again, and there's just nothing like the Sitka air. I haven't smelled anything this clean in a really long time."

We made small talk awhile longer about the whereabouts of some old classmates and family friends while Peter plated the salmon and fresh grilled vegetables and placed our plates at the massive wooden table in the attached dining room. The table was situated in front of a large picture window. The rain had returned, and the water zigzagged randomly down the window in long streaks. I tried to guess which direction the stream would go, but I missed it every time, and the water would streak in the opposite direction to what I expected. Visibility was low with the mists sweeping in from the sound, and I couldn't see more than a few feet away from the windows, but rather than closing us in, the fog only added to the privacy that surrounded us tonight.

The evening was perfect. Dinner was delicious. The salmon was cooked to absolute perfection. Of course, it didn't hurt that he'd caught the fish himself just a few days back. The conversation was pleasant, sticking to easy subjects like Seattle and our old times together. I stopped at one glass of wine, since I had to drive home, but Peter was finishing his third glass by the time we were done eating.

I insisted on helping him clean up despite his protests and forced him to talk about himself for a while. I was anxious to know what he'd been up to for the last ten years.

As I wiped down the table and dried the dishes, Peter described how he'd traveled for a year or two overseas before going to seminary, and in between semesters, he'd done missionary work in the outskirt villages of far northern Alaska. He'd dated a little, had a couple of serious relationships, but in the end, he hadn't been able to commit, and then he'd returned home and stepped into the role the men in his family had filled for generations in Sitka.

When we were finished and the kitchen was spotless, I insisted I had to get home. It was getting quite late, and I was already dreading returning to my house at this hour. Peter walked me to the entryway, and while I put on my shoes and coat, he went outside and started my truck to take the chill off.

"Thanks for dinner and for starting my truck. Especially for starting my truck," I said when he came back in the front door. His honey skin was spattered with raindrops and a few had collected on his eyelashes framing the green of his eyes. I couldn't look anywhere but at his face. He seemed to be having the same problem and for several seconds the only sounds were the hum of the gentle rain and our quiet breathing.

Peter finally broke the silence. "I'm surprised you came, Tam," he said. "To be honest, I thought I might be sitting here waiting for you all night."

"Well, if we're being honest, Peter, I almost didn't come."

He sucked in his breath harshly and started to say something before I cut him off. "But you need to know why before you judge me, okay?"

Nodding his head, he took a deep breath as if he were steadying himself for my answer.

"The only reason I considered not coming was for your safety. It's not that I don't want to be with you. I do. But I don't deserve you. Parts of me are broken, Peter and those same parts want something that you wouldn't understand because you're too good. And I'm also dangerous because Joel is out there somewhere, Peter. I don't know where or when he's going to pop up, but he is out there. I spent a long time with him. Too long, I realize, but if I know one thing about him, it's that he will not give up. So you see, it was very selfish of me to come here tonight, but I so badly wanted to see you. I just hope I haven't made a terrible mistake."

"I can take care of myself, Tam," he responded quickly. "I'm not afraid of him."

"You should be," I said. "But you're too good to understand how evil someone like him can be. Please don't under estimate him."

Pulling my coat on, I reached up and kissed him goodnight on the cheek. "Talk to you soon," I promised.

I was halfway out the door when he caught my arm in his hand pulling me towards him.

"I can take care of you too, Tam."

His lips brushed mine in a soft whisper of a kiss before I escaped into the blur of the rain, grateful that he could not distinguish the tears that began to course down my cheeks.

# Chapter 5

I waved one last goodbye as I climbed into the truck, but I had to pull over as soon as I got out of his driveway to brush the tears from my vision. His words had simply affected me too much to focus on the road. *"I can take care of you too, Tam."* It kept replaying in my mind.

What would it be like to collapse into the safe embrace of Peter's arms? Could I turn all of my fears over to him and not worry about my safety or Mom's case or Joel's whereabouts? Could I let my desire to see Joel pay fade away while I fell in love with Peter again? It was such a tempting idea that I seriously considered it. So much that I put the truck in reverse. All I had to was go back. Peter would be waiting for me.

*"Are you prepared to watch Peter die?"* My subconscious asked me. *"Do you want to add another name to your death toll?"*

And knowing the answer to those questions, I put the truck in drive and drove towards home. I'd gotten myself into this mess, and I was going to have to get myself out. I forced myself to put away any leftover romantic thoughts and focused on the road ahead.

The highway was empty and quiet as I finished driving home and I studied the yard, as I'd made a habit of doing, while I pulled in and parked. The truck engine shut down with a loud wheeze as if it was as nervous as I was about coming home to a darkened yard, but nothing appeared out of the normal. Since my house set at a higher elevation than Peter's, the rain had turned to snow, and it had laid out a white blanket across the yard on which glinted the light from the kitchen window.

My right foot was striking the top step of the porch before I realized that something was out of place. I stopped, my leg frozen in midair, as I studied the space around me. Had I missed Joel out there somewhere? God knows there were plenty of places for him to hide in just my yard alone. Not to mention the acres of forest around the house.

To my left, everything was as it should be. Snow dusted the railing of the porch, and beyond the railing, the yard gleamed with the frozen precipitation that clung to the deep green grass that grows in Sitka even in winter.

But to my right, where only the empty space of the porch should have been, a rick of firewood stretched from just under the picture window all the way to the railing on the far side.

Chills showered across my back as I studied the meticulously stacked wood. Each log was so evenly cut that the pieces were the same length. Not at all the way most people cut wood with the logs ending up in several varying sizes. Each cut had been precise, methodical. Only an obsessive-compulsive person can stack wood like that. Only someone who really likes to be in control could have chopped this rick of wood. Beside the stack sat a five-gallon bucket filled to the brim with kindling and rolled up newspapers for fodder.

The porch had been swept, and the broom stood evenly to the left of the front door. My work boots had been moved to the corner, the toes precisely matched up and facing the house. The welcome mat had been squared up with the door so that it matched up perfectly, and on top of it lay a bundle of orange lilies—Mom's favorite.

How perfectly Joel! He was here; somewhere he was in Sitka waiting for me, and he was a first-class manipulator. Manipulating people was a science he understood all too well. He'd slipped into my life today in the most subtle of ways. What was I going to do? Call the cops and complain that he'd chopped a stack of wood for me and left a bouquet of flowers? I'd look like the complete nut the cops already thought I was.

And yet, he'd gained a little control of my life. Wormed his way in, even if only a little bit. My wood was stacked the way he liked it. My boots were where he wanted them.

Pissed off and nauseated at the same time, I kicked the welcome mat as hard as I could, sending it skittering off the deck and into the darkness of the unlit yard. The slap of the plastic against the snow echoed across the porch. I moved the boots, making sure they were twisted and not facing each other.

Wearily, I turned the key in the knob, and although I stopped and listened every few feet for breathing or any other noise that might let me know he was here, I knew he wasn't. Joel would much prefer to play with me for a while. How he would enjoy knowing that tonight I'd be unable to think of anything but him. How my fear would turn him out and keep him smiling, satisfied, all night long.

I made sure the front door was locked as I retraced my steps through the house, double-checking all the windows. I guess if for no other reason than it gave me something to keep in my control, but nothing was out of place—nothing was out of the ordinary.

Still, I was a nervous wreck. How could I not be? It crossed my mind again to call the police about Joel's intrusion into my life but decided against it. There was no way I wouldn't come out on the losing end of that conversation.

I could picture it. "Officer Kendrick, I'd like to report a crime. My soon to be ex-husband is stalking me."

"What did he do, Tamara?" he'd ask.

"He came to my house uninvited and chopped a full rick of wood. While he was here, he cleaned up the porch and left some flowers."

*Click* is all I'd hear from the other line.

No, that would never do. Instead, I tried to push Joel from my mind and focus on the mundane part of life that must go on no matter what's happening around you. I warmed up some soup and made a small batch of hot tea to drink now and put some coffee on for later in the evening when I'd need its power to keep my eyes open. I was not going to change my routine for Joel just in case he did plan to return tonight.

The fire would need to be rekindled, but I refused to use the wood Joel had stacked for me. Instead, I trudged through the snow to the remains of a leftover pile at the far side of the yard. The wood was a little damp, but it would have to do.

By the time I got back with a few logs, my hands were pained from the cold; my feet were wet, but I didn't stop to change shoes or warm my hands before I worked on the fire. Luckily, embers from this morning remained, and I fed them logs until they were blazing. Wearily, I leaned my head against the mantle.

It was a hard night to be alone in this house with reminders of Joel sitting right outside the front door and memories of Mom staring at me from every corner of the house. I flipped through the radio stations and thumbed through a two-month-old magazine, but nothing kept pictures of Mom and Joel out of my thoughts.

I finally slapped the magazine away and turned the radio off. I tried to eat, but the soup didn't settle well, and the tea was bitter in my mouth. I pushed them both away as a few tears began to trickle. Angry at my own self-pity, I wiped them harshly away.

Physically I was fine, but mentally I felt exhausted to the bone. Watching over my shoulder for Joel and searching for justice for Mom was leaving me threadbare. I was going to have to empty my mind of this for a while—one way or the other.

Mom had never been a heavy drinker, but she had enjoyed a little whiskey now and again. Her decanter was still sitting tucked in behind her picture of my dad on her bedroom bureau. I poured a good-sized dollop of the golden good stuff and stretched out onto the couch. But not before I pulled my dad's twenty gauge out from the closet and put the stock within reach.

The first shot of whiskey went down a little hot. I hadn't drunk in a while, and I sputtered a bit, but the second went down like silk before landing warmly in my belly. I chased it with a little coffee and settled back into the couch, pulling a pleasantly worn quilt onto my shoulders.

I decided to continue my little research project I'd started the previous night. The surgeon's journal was tucked in between the couch and the end table, and I started with it rather than the vampire book I'd purchased. I glanced quickly towards the mantle, the bottle of presumed blood sitting where I'd left it.

I began with the doctor's account of the vampire's staking so it was fresh in my mind, reading again of the poor man's tragic life, the accusation of rape before being excommunicated and dying outside the church.

The entries that followed seemed routine. What sounded like a few panic attacks and some unknown infections popped up over the next few weeks and were naturally blamed on the recent vampire attack. The doctor ignored them for the most part, feigning ignorance or any knowledge of such an occurrence. Just as he expected, what few witnesses remained quickly moved on, finding other stations in the Russian Trading Company or leaving on the warship that had set sail the following morning.

Finally, in an entry dated nearly six months after the staking, the surgeon's handwriting lost its refined swirls, becoming shaky and uneven once more. It took three tries to translate due to the length of the passage but also to make sense of his very erratic penmanship. Something had no doubt given him quite a scare. I read it aloud as I ran my fingers across the impressions made by his harried writing.

*"Tonight, I prepare for my journey to Russia. I had thought to make Alaska my permanent home, but the events that followed the staking of the vampire some months back have made that an impossibility.*

*"Even now, my three children sit weeping in the small home*

*they share with the native woman I have called 'wife' for several years. They do not understand why I leave them and their sense of abandonment is acute. I cannot blame them for is it not the greatest betrayal a child can suffer? Worse yet is that I cannot even tell them my reasons, and my children will forever believe that I left them for no other reason than a selfish desire to return to my homeland or out of shame at their dark skin and I cannot take them with me when it is forbidden by the Tsar.*

*"How can I tell them that I leave to save them when I am unable to make them understand how I am saving them? How can I tell them that their father has dabbled in the dark arts? Even now, I question not only my sanity but also my purity before God.*

*"Let me explain.*

*"On the night of the vampire's capture, it was I who treated the body and prepared it for reburial. It was only I and the archimandrite who were present with the body at close quarters. The Baranov had wanted to limit the number of men who came in contact with the aberration in hopes of controlling the aftermath. Thus, I was able to take much blood from the veins of the beast, and in doing so filled up several vials of the substance, which have remained hidden to all men, including the Baranov.*

*"In the glow of the lamp each evening for these many days, I have stared at the contents of the vials, wondering what could be done with this unholy bounty. As a scientist, I recognized that the substance within these bottles should be studied, examined. As a devout member of the Church, I knew I should cast it aside, as it is cursed. The scientist in me won out and the bottles rest safely in my cabinet.*

*"I am a heretic to be sure. The Church would most likely excommunicate me, as Adrik was, if they knew what power I possessed here in my small clinic. And it IS power, I am certain of that. For the substance inside these glass bottles has not decayed in any way. The liquid is as bright and free flowing as ever. No clots have as of yet began to form. It is as alive as the*

*day six months back when I pulled it from his veins.*

*"Because of this, I know the legends are true. That the accursed Adrik lies waiting beneath the ground. While we sleep, he strains against his shackles, and when we awake, his body goes lax as his mind burns with plans of retribution. Awake, conscious, but bound by the power of the Cross, and therefore, he thinks but cannot act. He burns with lust but cannot attain his desires. He hungers but cannot starve. Exhausted, he cannot sleep.*

*"I am certain of this because I have done the most unconscionable thing. I have consumed his blood! Not much, only a few drops, and yet what seemed an inconsequential amount now torments me in the greatest of ways!*

*"It was an experiment of science, and I have suffered no deleterious effects, save one. I can feel him. In my mind, Adrik's presence hovers, and he tugs at my soul. He calls to me in screams at night and in whispers when the sun has dominion in the sky.*

*"In my nightly dreams, I am with him in his casket. Inky blackness that not even his vampiric eyes can separate surrounds him while the stench of rotting wood clogs his lungs. His clothes decompose and add to the filth that bathes his skin. The water, at first only a trickle, has filled the coffin, and together we drown nightly. Insects slither across his bare skin. His every sensation is now mine. Our minds join in the abject horror of facing the eternity before us while we burn, literally afire with thirst.*

*"The thirst for human blood is present to be sure, but it is more. His soul begs for revenge. You see, Adrik was an innocent man. His soul is laid bare to my eyes, and there are no dark shadows in which he can tuck away secrets.*

*"Still, he is beyond my help. Beyond the help of any mortal, save the archimandrite, who could in a single act of mercy restore Adrik to the fold of the Church and wipe his slate clean. But it is this same man whose hands are surely stained as crimson as Adrik's are now.*

*"But I am only a physician. A writer at times when my hands*

*can find time to spare a few words. So tonight, before I seek to escape Adrik's dominion over my mind, I will write the truth. I will put to paper how Adrik came to be in this state so that, at least, there is a written record of the terrible things that went on here. I will stand witness to the truth that this man was defiled.*

*"To give his story justice, I must begin long before the curse of vampirism forever marked him. It seems Adrik was cursed from the moment his feet first touched the soil of New Archangel.*

*"No, it was with his very birth that he was cursed! He was, after all, born into the wretched condition of serfdom. Simply put, his life was never his own. Now it seems it shall never be. Being born an estate serf who worked the land, he was sent in lieu of monetary capital by his master as an investment in the Russian American Trading Company, of which I myself am a part. He was one of only a handful of serfs sent with the Russian American Trading Company, this not being a common practice.*

*"He arrived on board the Neva, the mighty warship sent from Russia to voyage around the world, under the command of Captain Lisianski. The voyage in and of itself was not an easy one. It was plagued with disease from time to time and lack of funding at others.*

*"With no direct intentions, it happened that the Neva was in the vicinity of New Archangel when Alexander Baranov made to retake the site upon which New Archangel now sits. Fate tried to intervene for poor Adrik in this instance and caused the winds to die down such that the sails of the Neva hung limp and useless. An odd thing off the coast of Alaska to be sure. But Baranov, being stronger than fate itself, had the Neva pulled into the sound by four hundred canoes manned by Aleutians Indians.*

*"The Battle for New Archangel was not a particularly bloody battle, but it was long. Unbearably long, actually. Baranov found the Tlingit to be a surprisingly guileful group of fighters. It was their most favored fishing grounds they were protecting after all.*

*"Knowing Baranov was coming, the tribe had built a fort*

*across the marsh and along Indian River, which wound through the forest to the sea. It was a heavily fortified encampment, quite suited for withstanding the heavy cannon fire of us, the Russians, and fire we did for days.*

*"Unable to blow them out, Baranov sought to starve the Tlingit instead. As I said, they were heavily fortified and provisioned, but as any city under siege, eventually hunger sets in. The Tlingit sent an envoy promising surrender and Baranov's forces waited patiently until one evening, a chanting began that lasted well into the night. It ended with hair-raising screams that could have pierced the slumber of the dead.*

*"The Russians, it was said, were a twisted lot of anxiety, and those present say the screams delved straight to the soul. It raised the hair on the soldiers' arms, made them reach for the crosses strung round their necks with trembling hands.*

*"Expecting the gates of the Tlingit encampment to open, our Russian troops waited until it became apparent that the gates would yet remain closed. Not a sound could be heard except the cries of scavenger birds circling above. The forest was quiet, as if the wind itself could not even find the energy to breathe through the trees.*

*"Finally, exhausted and unwilling to wait any longer, Baranov gave the order to take the encampment, bloodshed or not. What they found is difficult to describe. Captain Lisianski could scarcely detail the carnage. I have read his account, and, I daresay, it turns the stomach sour.*

*"The fort was empty of the living save two small children and one woman. The Tlingit had long since escaped into the forest, knowing the mountain trails as no white man can, leaving behind only the bodies of their children. Or perhaps it was the slave children. We shall never know, and does it really matter? We are hardly in a position to condemn them, having our own class of slaves that we treat as poorly.*

*"I tell none of this to judge the Tlingit, only to set the scene for what happened to Adrik. You see, that wretched man was one of the first sent through the gate. It was he that stumbled upon the first of the two living children, and by a wicked twist of*

*fate took the life of one young child. The boy died in Adrik's arms, his blood spilling onto the cursed dirt of the fort while Adrik desperately tried to staunch the wound with his hands. Needless to say, it did not work.*

*"From that moment, Adrik's demeanor changed. Melancholy became his constant companion. Nightmares became so frequent that he could never lay his head down without being brought from sleep by these visiting demons. Any other man would have recognized this terrible event for the accident it was, but Adrik became nearly inconsolable with grief.*

*"I treated him myself with a variety of potions and concoctions that helped none at all. The most comfort the man received came from the services of the priests who prayed with him daily. During his free time from his serf duties (which was scarce), he accompanied the priests in the instruction of the native children and in visiting the sick and afflicted. I suppose it was Adrik's way of paying penance, however unnecessary it may have been.*

*"Returning from an evening with the priest, Adrik had the bad luck to catch the eye of a wealthy young woman named Irena. Her father, Duke Ivonvosky, had brought her abroad with him, unusual for the nobility but not unheard of. She was betrothed to a nephew of the Tsar.*

*"Perhaps her father sought to keep her pure by keeping her close to him, but I fear he had lost that battle months ago. In his defense, I do not think he realized the deepness of his daughter's depravity, and so his sins against Adrik shall surely be forgiven him.*

*"Adrik was uncommonly handsome, especially for one born of such low station. A baser man would have used the beauty of his face to find favors, and there would have been many in high stations that would have enjoyed his attributes. Adrik's interests, however, were towards no woman but to the Church alone.*

*"Rebuffed despite her numerous advances, Irena's anger was kindled against Adrik. I must assume when she missed her*

*monthly cycle, she chose him to be the scapegoat to pay for her previous sins. Her father never doubted her claims of rape by the one man who was truly not capable of such a crime. Had it been anyone else, I would have believed the charge, for Irena was an uncommonly beautiful woman.*

*"Knowing Irena could no longer marry into the royal family, the duke was outraged and promptly strung Adrik up outside her cabin, delivering a near fatal beating with the knout, that terrible whip so beloved by Russian nobility.*

*"Unable to obtain a confession from Adrik on pain of mortal death alone, the duke turned towards the afterlife instead. The archimandrite, our highest priest, fared no better and so ignoring his divine calling of mercy, he promptly excommunicated poor Adrik. You see the duke wanted a full confession that would secure his daughter a pension from the Tsar.*

*"It seems the archimandrite preferred a god made of gold. 'Wide and easy is the path that leadeth to destruction,' saith the Bible. I only hope it will lead that false prophet straight to hell.*

*"Unable to confess a sin that he did not commit and unable to bear the future as a condemned man absent from God, Adrik developed a hunger for revenge that would last beyond his mortal life. Thus, he turned to vampirism by the act of suicide. What a potent combination, excommunication and suicide! He became the undead, the stricken! Not worthy of burial on hallowed ground; not worthy of the great ceremonies that properly put the dead to rest.*

*"The English have a saying that hell hath no fury like a woman scorned. I think they have forgotten the rest of that poem which is that Heaven has no rage like love to hatred turned.*

*"Never have I felt a rage so deep, so visceral as Adrik's; his love for mankind has died, and hatred has taken a firm root in the remains of his once quiet heart. His rage breeds a deep thirst.*

*"It is daylight as I write this, and so I am able to bear it; he becomes subdued by the rising of the sun. It seems the power of*

*his mind wanes during the light of day, but I must not fool myself. His thoughts are ever-present with me; he knows no rest. No peace.*

*"For fear of what I might do with his thirst burning in my own breast, I locked myself in the block house the night before last, the same cell in which the dejected Adrik took his own life and sealed his fate.*

*"During the night, I cried aloud with his hunger—my hunger. I strained my arms through the bars, begging for release by anyone. Thankfully, the wind blew, the rains pelted, and no one heard my cries until this morning.*

*"For I am certain, I would have given in to the hungers that filled me, his promises of immortality, and of a strength which I dare not think on too much. Especially now that age is robbing me of the virility that was once mine.*

*"On rising the next morning, I smiled at the soldier who found me, telling him I was getting old, absentminded even, and had accidently let the cell door shut behind me. 'Why had I come here?' he asked. I told him I must have dreamed I had a new patient in the cell house.*

*"For two nights hence, I have contained myself in the cell at dusk, asking my assistant, who is also my nephew, to free me once the sun is well positioned in the sky. He thinks it odd but does not say anything and does as he is told.*

*"As for the blood I have collected, I am unsure of what to do with it. In my heart of hearts, I know I should pour the cursed fluids out upon the earth, but with this same heart, I am afraid to do this very thing. For I cannot say with any certainty what unnatural thing will arise out of it. I know it will not decompose but instead will last for an eternity. And yet, I fear it will fall into the wrong hands as it would make a very powerful weapon indeed. I can scarcely imagine the men that could be controlled with such a substance. What armies could be empowered by this blood or of what men might be capable just to obtain it?*

*"Have I sold my soul for this knowledge? Will I rise a vampire upon my death? No, I think it more difficult than that. I think it*

*takes the vampire's mark upon your skin or commitment of the sin of heresy or suicide. Neither of which I have.*

*"And do not the old legends speak of consuming the vampire's heart to regain your strength or to cure the disease of vampirism? Have I done anything different? At least, this is how I console myself in the dark of night when his cries are so loud in my head that in sheer desperation I clasp my hands over my ears, burying my head in between my knees. It does no good; I hear him still. What pure hell is this? What have I done?*

*"Of a few things, I am certain. I have tasted his power, his promises of immortality on this earth, and I must leave. For I cannot bind myself each night, and I am certain that one evening when the sun has sunk below the horizon, I will rise like my nocturnal companion begs and go to him. I will dig him from the earth and remove the stakes from his diseased heart, if only to release myself from the hell I have created by my own curiosity. And then how many people will die? How much blood will it take to satiate his thirst for revenge?*

*"So while I still perform under my own power and my mind is more or less mine, I have booked passage away from here. I leave the fort clinic in the capable hands of my nephew, whom I have personally trained in the art of medicine. As for my children, I leave them only with the hope that by my very desertion of them, I will yet save them. May God forgive me all my sins."*

That was the last entry, and as I flipped through the rest of the journal, it produced only yellowed, empty pages.

It had taken nearly three hours to decipher and translate the fading text, and my eyes were strained as I leaned back into the couch to think about what I'd read. *Did I believe his account?* I wasn't sure I did, but I wasn't a complete doubter either. I was open to the possibility that there was a lot I didn't know about this world. Mom had been, and that gave her an understanding of the world that I'd never had when I was younger.

I was still wrapped up in thoughts of the surgeon's account

when the outdated wall phone rang in the kitchen. It was late, nearly one o'clock in the morning, and I started, nearly knocking my tea over, when it began whining on the wall.

Was it Peter calling to make sure I'd made it home? Maybe Gloria calling to check in and make sure I hadn't dropped off the deep end. I didn't know anyone else here well enough anymore that they'd call me this time of the night, I reasoned.

Suspiciously, I stared at the phone. Cold dread at the thought of answering it washed across me and a pit opened up in my stomach, but I knew I had no choice. I walked slowly across the living room and into the kitchen, hoping it would quit ringing, but it was still clamoring as I lifted the receiver to my ear.

"Hello?" I whispered into the earpiece.

"You warm tonight, babe?" a familiar voice questioned.

I didn't say anything. What was there to say? Any warmth I'd felt was rapidly evaporating from my entire body.

"Nothing to say to me, girl? I came by to try to help you out. Make sure my girl is all right and you can't even say 'thanks' or 'how are you?'"

I swallowed hard, knowing he could hear the tightness of my throat across the line.

"No? Nothing? I'm surprised. You and preacher boy talked half the night. I thought you two was never going to shut up."

"He's just a friend, Joel." The words were out of my mouth before I realized it. I hadn't planned on responding at all, but the fact that he mentioned Peter made me sick to my stomach.

"Well, he better be is all I got to say. You just remember who you belong to, girl."

"He's got nothing to do with any of this, Joel."

"I guess that depends on you, Tam."

"Why can't you just leave me alone?"

"Till death do us part, isn't that what you promised, Tam?"

"I'm going to call the police now."

"You should be careful up in the mountains. It can get lonely up there. The nights are awfully cold and it gets darks so early.

I've heard you can lose your footing in the blink of an eye. Real shame about what happened to your momma."

"I'm hanging up now," I said, but the line was dead before I got the words out. My hand was shaking as I lowered the receiver back onto the phone.

I started to call the police like I'd threatened I would and the number was part way dialed before I hung up and walked back into the living room and collapsed in sheer exhaustion onto the couch. I had years of experience with the police, and I knew nothing would come of just a phone call. Joel hadn't explicitly threatened me, only veiled innuendo that proved nothing. It wasn't the police's fault. Their hands were tied.

Across the room, the fire danced in the stone hearth, and I watched the flames, letting their comforting patterns mesmerize me. The bottle of blood sat where I'd left it on the mantle; the glass bottle shimmered in the light of the fire, the vial casting a long shadow backwards onto the wall. I could not look away, could think of nothing else except what the surgeon had said.

I was tantalized by his words. *A powerful weapon,* he'd said. Power and immortality. I could no easier forget the idea than the surgeon two hundred years earlier. Would this bottle of ancient blood help avenge my mother? Would it at least give me the edge I needed? Could I use it against Joel?

Gloria's words replayed a continuous circuit in my head. The police report resurfaced in my mind's eye, the words searing into my consciousness. The knowledge that Joel had been here today set me on edge and made my teeth rattle. Hearing his voice had only made it worse.

Desperation can force you into some strange situations, allow you to believe in things you normally wouldn't, and give you the ability to do things that on a routine day you'd never consider. And I was, above all else, a desperate woman.

I had only three options. I could leave the island, like Peter and Gloria had recommended. Give in to the fear but stay alive and run for as long as I could stay ahead of Joel, and I knew he'd find me. Eventually. He'd promised I could never escape him.

Or I could give in now, like I always had, and go back to Joel. Listen to his ridiculous logic that everything that had happened was my fault. How easy it would be to slip back into the role he'd taught me.

My final option was to make my own way. Create a path that was as illogical and as ill-advised as the path that had taken me away from my home ten years ago. I wasn't getting anywhere with the police, and I wasn't going to change their minds. It was a dead end. If I wanted justice, I'd have to get it myself.

Maybe it was the whiskey that still burned a path of liquid courage down my throat, or sheer desperation, or maybe it was a potent combination of both that caused me to take the first few steps to the fireplace.

The blood undulated within the bottle with my motions as I shimmied the shriveled cork from out the mouth of the bottle. It clung stubbornly to the glass but finally released its hold. The tip crumpled in my fingers, but the inner surface that touched the blood pulled out whole like cork from a fine bottle of wine, looking as if it had been placed yesterday.

I took a tentative sniff, expecting the accumulated smell of two centuries of rot to overwhelm my senses, but instead, only the scent of fresh blood wafted from the mouth of the bottle.

Still, it was enough to be nauseating, and I held my breath as I lifted the bottle to my lips. Hesitating for a few long seconds, I finally tipped the bottle up, deciding to chug it and worry about the taste later.

Three swallows was all I could manage, and I forced back nausea, placing a hand over my mouth to keep the fluid safely where it needed to be. I gagged harder, my eyes watering, and I could taste the blood all over again as it sloshed across my tongue and the flavor filled my sinuses. Clamping my hand over my mouth even tighter, I swallowed the blood back down against the stomach acid that had risen into my throat.

Then I sat and waited. For exactly what I wasn't sure. I guess I expected to hear the voice of the vampire whispering in my ear, see a vision, or something dramatic. Instead, nothing happened as I sat cross-legged in front of the fire.

The house had warmed with the fire, a nice comforting glow that complemented the whiskey. My muscles, tensed from finding evidence of Joel on my porch, had finally relaxed; the kind of limp-noodle feeling you get after an adrenaline rush. I leaned forward resting my head in my hands, giving into the warmth that coursed through my body and stared deeply into the undulating flames of the fire, letting my mind go where it wanted.

My head still ached slightly from whacking my head the night before, and I lay back against the couch, setting the bottle of blood to my side. I sighed with the warmth of the fire on my skin after the chill of the day, and I felt my eyes began to drift closed. I didn't object, letting the world go dark around me.

# Chapter 6

For once, sleep came easily, and I dreamed of average, forgotten things that made no sense; the small dog Joel and I had kept for a few years, doing laundry at the dilapidated coin-operated laundry on a dirty Seattle street, and the Chinese diner that had the best eggrolls a few blocks from our apartment. We'd go there when he was having a good night.

I dreamed of the towels I'd bought with his first small paycheck, and the night I used them to clean up my own blood the first time he hit me. The stains never came out, but Joel wouldn't let me throw them out. He said the stains would remind me not to ever cross him. I dreamed of his hands stroking my cheeks and remembered how his fingers curved around my neck. I dreamed of the carnations he usually brought in the next day to say he was sorry and how the blooms wouldn't have even faded before he'd done it again.

But somewhere in the images of the mundane, my dreams turned towards the bizarre. I could see Joel ahead of me on a mountain trail, zigzagging while he ran frightened in the other direction. I chased him, pelting him with questions about Mom, pleading with him to stop. But looking over his shoulder, he screamed, flecks of spit flying from his mouth as he continued to run from me.

It made no sense; it was normally I who was running from him. Confused, I stopped chasing him, and he was soon out of sight.

It was late afternoon in my dream; the sun was struggling against the weight of the clouds, and the forest above me shaded out a good portion of what light there was. I'd chased Joel along a trail that followed the curvature of the mountain. The elevation gain had been steep, and I was breathing hard.

Around me, the wind had picked up and a light, dry snow was blowing. Shivering, I realized I didn't have a coat, and I was barefooted. I rubbed my cold arms and frowned at the blue of my fingertips. Low-hanging clouds trailed across the mountain and, along with the setting of the sun, began to obscure the mountains in front of me.

A movement to my left caught my eye, and turning, I saw my mother standing on a rocky outpoint of the trail. She was leaning far over, her body unbalanced, as she stared at the jagged crags below her.

"Mom!" I shouted, struggling to get to her. I looked around suspiciously, expecting to see Joel, but he was either not here or, at least, I couldn't see him.

"What are you doing?" I asked. I reached for her, trying to tug her away from the edge. But she was persistent and clung to the cliffs. "Mom, look at me!" I demanded. I was relieved when she finally turned towards me.

I studied her face, tracing the lines that crinkled the corners of her mouth. She was still attractive but older than I'd ever seen her in life.

"Mom, answer me!" I shook her gently. "What are you doing?"

A worried look on her face, she pointed towards the forest trail. "What are *you* doing, Tam? You're in too deep. Don't go any further," she pleaded, her voice rising above the wind.

Behind me, the wind rustled and someone called my name. Still holding her by the shoulders, I turned for a moment, expecting to see Joel, but instead I found nothing and no one except the empty trail meandering back down the mountain.

"Tamara, this is wrong," she said. "You will lose far more than you will gain."

*What is she talking about?* I wondered. I tried to listen, to concentrate on what she was saying. I should know what she was referring to, but I couldn't seem to put the thoughts together quickly enough. The voice spoke behind me again. I heard it, but more than that, I felt the reverberations coursing through my bones. My throat constricted, my breath caught.

"I've already lost you, Mom. What more could I lose? He's taken everything," I muttered into the wind.

"No. You still have your soul. Your innocence. Don't let him take it," she pleaded.

I laughed—a sardonic sound. "Joel took those a long time ago."

"I'm not talking about Joel," she responded, lifting her voice louder. But the voice behind me was overpowering, and I had trouble focusing. I looked over my shoulder, searching the forest for whoever was calling to me.

Mom spoke again, but I couldn't concentrate on her words as the voice whispered my name repeatedly. It was hypnotic, seductive, and turning, I dropped my hands from her shoulders and followed the voice back to the path.

It led me back to the trail that cut a singular path down the mountain with no forks to the right or the left. Behind me, it seemed to disappear, leaving me nowhere to go but forward. Reaching a break in the trees, I saw the coastline of Sitka sound spread out below.

It was a naturally protected sound, and the waves lapped gently at the small exposed beach while the larger waves broke on the shores of the many small barrier islands, dotting the entrance to the sound. A handful of rotting logs, their bark stripped away by wind and water, broke up the monotony of the rocky beach.

Having nowhere else to go, as this trail had no branch points, I kept to the path and was soon off the mountain and meandering through the remnants of the forest. The voice continued to woo me forward, and I followed it willingly.

The heights of the mountain gave way to coastal plains, the spruce trees reaching their arms even higher to the heavens as the ground became softer and easier in which to dig their great roots. The dim light of dusk had now waned to complete darkness, and the forest around me became black. I stumbled on the uneven ground, my feet becoming entangled in the underbrush covering the forest floor.

I felt trapped, as if the darkness itself had grasping hands, and I panicked for a few seconds, my hands beating desperately at the cold air before I remembered this could only be a dream.

"I am no dream," the voice whispered back.

"Who are you?" I demanded into the thickening blackness. The presence pushed against me, pressing the air from my lungs and stealing my breath. It seemed alive, a cloying substance capable of trapping me between cold, hard hands.

"My name was forgotten years ago, but yet you know me."

"What do you want?" I screamed into the walls of blackness that contained me.

"Why question what I want? It is you who sought me out. What do you want?" the voice questioned.

Perhaps it was my imagination that infused the voice into the vines of fog that twined their way around my feet, curling between my knees and snaking towards my hips.

"It's true," I breathed into the fog, which crept in thicker than I'd ever seen. Real fear gripped me as the surgeon's words came back to haunt me. The doctor had left to escape this voice.

"It was not for truth that you have sought me out," the voice answered. "And seek me you did, for I have had no human bonds in a century and a half."

"This was a mistake." In my dream, I twisted on one foot, planning to escape the darkness and fog that had congealed around me. My chest felt heavy as if it was being crushed, but I could feel wakefulness just a short distance away. I turned to see it, a lighter spot in a sea of blackness, and began to move in that direction.

"I can give you what you want." The voice spoke again.

"You don't know what I want," I said, but I stopped despite myself, waiting for the response.

"You want what I want. To be free."

"What I want is to be strong. I'm tired of being weak and being the victim. I'm sick of being pushed around. I want him to pay." I struggled to find the air to spit out my words as I slapped at the blackness around me.

The pressure lightened somewhat; it became easier to breathe, and I sucked in large mouthfuls of air.

"I will be your strength and everyone will pay," the voice soothed.

"What's the price?" I questioned, already knowing the answer. Mom had warned me. My soul. My innocence.

I waited for the response, searching the darkness in front of me for some indication of what watched me from within its thickness. But I could see nothing in the black of the night. Not even the outline of my hands when I held them in front of my face. The fog twisted itself farther up my body, curling around my trunk and then passing around my neck. Although it never touched my skin, I could feel its presence as it slithered around me.

"The truly innocent never ask the price, for they are not willing to bargain," the voice answered.

"I am innocent," I started to say, but what was the point? You can't lie to the dead.

Disgusted, I batted away the blackness enveloping me and pushed towards consciousness glowing on the horizon.

I awoke with a slight start, my arms askew as if I'd been in a fight and my neck was sore from where I'd rested awkwardly against the couch. The fire was still burning warmly across the room, but my eyes wouldn't focus and so the flames danced in a golden red haze. A thin line of perspiration clung to my hairline, and despite the heat of the room, I was cold.

The house had taken on the quietness of night when even the appliances whisper their machinations. Only the occasional crack and pop of the fire broke up the stillness. I was alone, and yet I was not. In the background, I could hear a quiet roar.

At first, I thought it was the silence of the house I was listening to, and I ignored it while I got to my feet. I drank the leftover coffee and threw another log onto the fire. I folded the quilt for good measure and put the journal up.

Still the roar persisted, and I clapped my hands over my ears to relieve the pressure that had built in my head to a deafening crush. It only grew louder and I dug my fingers deep into my ears, not caring that my nails dug into the tender flesh. It was like my head was being held between two giant seashells.

I tried the radio, but I could find no tune that would dampen the sound. I couldn't concentrate on reading, and there was nothing on TV. The channels had gone off for the night, the high-pitched bleep and the rainbow display of colors signaling that I should turn the contraption off.

Instead, I muted the blaring sound and stared at the rainbow on the screen, letting my eyes cross until it was a blur of colors. The roar continued in my head, and so I gave up trying to drown it out. I found myself listening instead.

At first, it continued on as a single, monotonous sound with no variation, but as the minutes ticked by on the mantle clock, the roar separated out into peaks and valleys which eventually gave way to individual words.

The voice was muffled, and I strained now to hear what an hour ago I'd tried to tune out. The syllables sounded foreign and yet familiar. Like the Russian I'd spoken in the dream. As the hour wore on, I began to recognize a pattern in the roaring voice, repeated syllables, but the words wouldn't materialize. I couldn't make them out.

Frustrated, I strained harder to decipher the words but still nothing. When I thought I'd go insane with the effort, I tried to hear only the roar again, but I'd lost the ability. Now I could hear nothing but the repeated words. I couldn't ignore them; still I couldn't decipher the hidden message.

Was this what the surgeon had been describing? He said he'd heard the vampire's voice in tormented screams at night and in whispers during the day. What I was hearing was certainly more than a whisper, but not quite a scream. Either the blood had weakened with time or I hadn't drunk enough to hear his shrieks.

Two hours had passed with the constant stream of the vampire's consciousness before I fully recognized what I'd done to myself. If you play with fire the saying goes, you'll get burned. Well, my consciousness was singed now, and the smoke of my encounter was still stinging my vision.

Determined to do the right thing for once, I grabbed the bottle of blood from off the mantle where I'd set it earlier. The cork, worn on the outer edges, crumbled a little more in my fingers, and instinctively I loosened the pressure of my grip.

The doctor had warned that he didn't know what would rise from the fluid if it were spilled, but I didn't care so long as it wasn't in my body. Proximity was my problem, and I didn't want it anywhere near me.

I opened the back door and stepped to the edge of the deck. The day's thick snow spread out across the yard. It looked like a scene from Currier and Ives with the undisturbed snow glistening in the hint of moonlight playing hide and seek with the clouds.

Behind the lawn, the mountains rose up in the background, hard walls of stone, their tips softened by rounded layers of snow. The spruce trees, glazed in ice, ringed the foothills and spread their branches out to hold hands, encircling the yard in a magical ring.

It was a beautiful night. The rain and snow had disappeared for a while and even the wind had quieted down. For once this month, the night was silent yet my mind reverberated with the mumblings of a man buried for two hundred years.

Angered by the contrast, I flung the bottle as far as I could, my voice erupting in a howl with the effort. I didn't watch where it went. I didn't care. I didn't want to know.

It was just past three a.m., and despite having slept for only an hour, I was afraid to close my eyes again. The feel of the vampire's presence and the sound of his voice in the dream were too fresh. His rumblings in my head made me anxious. It was like someone was behind me whispering, but when I turned to look over my shoulder, no one was there. I picked at my clothes and ran nervous fingers through my hair.

*What the hell have I done?* I questioned over and over.

My body begged for sleep. My mind prayed for rest, and that is where I found my only solace. While my mouth moved in prayer, his mumblings died away. I took advantage of the situation and poured another shot of whiskey. It landed with a heavy, hot thud in my belly, where it sunk even lower and wedged itself deep in my pelvis. Bands of warmth spread their way out until my limbs felt warm and heavy. My mind slowed but didn't stop, and I downed another shot. My stomach burned clean through to my back but my brain gradually began to numb.

My mouth was still moving in prayer when sleep finally took me.

I was vaguely aware of being fitful the rest of the night. A strong male voice whispered to me, intertwining into my dreams. He spoke of eternal strength and youth. He tempted me with promises of revenge for anyone who'd hurt me. He spoke of power, and I wasn't afraid anymore.

In my dreams, the moon rose, a tiny sliver, in the clearest of nights. I chased falling stars across the night sky, careening from one mountaintop to another, laughing at the humans below me who struggled to see only a fraction of what I looked at.

How weak they were and how strong I was.

I dreamed of Joel and of blood. It dripped down his arms, hot and wet, and I lapped it up, shredding the skin from his body with my teeth, and it was only the rising of the sun that chased me from his carcass.

# Chapter 7

Realization came slowly, I was disoriented at first. Then piece by piece, small sensations began to make sense. The velvety material under my cheek was my bedspread, the rhythmic creek and moan was the mantra of the aged ceiling fan. I flexed my feet and muscles ached in protest from the assault of my dreams.

The sun had reached the windowsill of my room and cast golden rays across my bed. Forcibly, I shut my eyes until I grew accustomed to its brightness and could stand to open them again.

I stumbled into the kitchen to escape the light, but the sun chased me. I didn't mind so much once I'd found the coffee. Laying thankful hands on the coffeepot, the sounds of percolation reassured me that within a half-hour, I'd be feeling much better. The whiskey sat on the desk where I'd left it last night. I eyed it warily but I was grateful it had been here. I'd slept, at least a little.

The vampire was not with me now. I searched the insides of my mind, listening for the awful roar from last night, and could find no trace of him. I whispered his name aloud, focused and got nothing. It was as if he'd simply ceased to be. I was thankful for the reprieve, appreciative that he couldn't reach me in the daylight.

Two cups of coffee and a warm shower later, my mom's truck and I were twisting down the road. The sun was well into the morning sky by now, but on this side of the mountains, it was hard to tell. Mists still shrouded the small domed peaks that rose from the icy waters of Sitka Sound and reached long gray arms out across the expanse of water. Some of the gray misty fingertips reached the mainland and some didn't.

The town of Sitka lay ahead, the harbor showing the most activity this morning as a few diehard men and women readied their boats for the day. In the winter, Sitka's population decreased by nearly two thirds, and no cruise boats bobbed on their anchors. Not quite the ghost town like the other villages of southeast Alaska, enough hardy locals gathered in the restaurants around the square to keep them open year round.

I considered pulling in for another cup of coffee but decided against it. I was simply not in the mood to be stared at this morning. Word gets around in a small town, and I had no doubt that my history had been discussed and dissected until the rumors were far worse than the reality had been. Not that the reality hadn't been bad enough, but still, speculation never makes a reputation any better.

Instead, I aimed the nose of the truck towards the police station. I'd skipped a visit yesterday and was now determined to get back to annoying the cops until Mom's case was reopened. I was going to get justice for my mother the legal way, I had decided after last night's run in with the vampire.

Pulling in a big breath of air for courage, I opened the door with an authority that I did not feel and walked up to the receptionist. Usually she behaved like a stone wall I had to bust through every time I came and the look on her face told me today wasn't going to be any different. With a land-line phone in one hand and a cell phone in the other, I was a distraction she clearly didn't want around. The glow of the social media page cast a frightening shade of pallor on her skin as I stopped in front of her desk.

"I'd like to speak to the detective please," I said as resolutely as I knew how.

Not bothering to hide her irritation, she pointed towards a short row of chairs before punching a button on the desk phone. “She’s here…” Her voice undulated like the little girl’s in *Poltergeist*. Laughing momentarily at something from the other end of the phone, she tried to smooth the smile off her face but didn’t quite make it. “He’ll see you in a sec,” she said, none too politely.

I rolled my eyes, and thankfully, she went back to her cell phone. No doubt I’d just made a bunch of her online friends hit the ‘like’ buttons in a resounding applause of hilarity.

A round clock ticked the seconds off loudly as I searched for a tolerable position in a typically uncomfortable waiting room chair. After twenty minutes and twenty-three seconds of listening as my life was marked off, I found myself squeezing the bridge of my nose. The coffeepot tempted me from the corner, but I found it empty, the last few drops sizzling on the glass bottom. I started to make more, but the receptionist *tsked* me from her desk.

“Ma’am. The coffee’s for the police officers. Please take a seat. Detective Scott is working on something very important, but he said he’d take a break in a few minutes to talk to you—again.”

“You’re coff…” I started to point out that it was beginning to burn, but she cut me off again, pointing to the chairs. Like a scolded child, I resumed my waiting.

Nearly an hour of my life marched away to the rhythm of that blasted clock as I waited. Mentally, I prepared for another hour when the door to the detective’s office swung open, revealing a small, neat office on the other side. The detective, a former classmate of mine, motioned me in, his cell phone held to his ear by his shoulder. I took the offered seat as he finished up his conversation.

Kendrick Scott was as handsome as ever. And just as arrogant. He’d been that way as long as I could remember. Some people would say it was for good reason. Track star, football star, basketball star… I could go on, but what’d be the point?

Naturally, Kendrick could have gone anywhere and done anything with his classically all-American looks. Tall, fair-haired with a smile that could light up a room from the doorway, he was as handsome as he was successful. But what made him the town hero is that all though he could have gone anywhere and done anything, Kendrick had stayed right here in Sitka to protect and serve the town that had loved him from the beginning.

I guess I could see his charm. If I looked real hard.

"Tamara, how are you?" he asked, clicking his phone shut as I perched precariously on the lip of one of his office chairs. He smiled broadly at me, and if I didn't know him better, I would have at least considered that the grin was genuine. Wow, he was good.

"Well, I'm okay, I guess. I'm sure you know why I'm here. I wanted to check on Mom's case again."

He sighed, leaning forward heavily on his elbows. "Tamara, you know I closed the case. I've told you every time you've stopped by that I found nothing out of the ordinary."

"I know, Kendrick, but I read the report again the day before yesterday, and I keep thinking about that set of extra footprints one of the officers mentioned in his report. I hadn't seen that particular officer's report before, and I've seen several reports with Mom's footprints mentioned, but the other set they found near the point of her fall was new information to me. I just wanted to see what you thought about those since we hadn't specifically talked about them."

I watched him carefully as he shook his head ever so slightly. I might not have noticed the movement if I hadn't been so hyper vigilant. He was thinking of the best way to placate me. He'd never once entertained the idea that there could have been foul play.

Rubbing his short hair backwards, he leaned back, crossing his arms behind his head. "I really didn't think much about those footprints at all. This is Alaska. People fly in from every part of the globe to hike in these mountains. There are thousands of footprints up there. Do you want me to trace them all?" He smiled to lighten the harshness of his words. It didn't help.

"Mom was a good hiker. I just can't see her falling. She knew the terrain and she was so careful..."

He waved me down before I could really get started. "Your mom was getting older. You hadn't seen her in years, Tam," he said, calling me by my junior-high nickname.

A few tears welled up in my eyes quicker than I could recover, and even as I looked away, I knew he'd seen them.

He took a deep breath, raising his hands in the air and pressing them towards me as if he could force my sadness back into my chest. "Look, I'm not trying to pull a guilt card or anything, but, Tam, she really was starting to age. She didn't get around like she did when you left. I'm sure she was looking for herbs or something, you know, like that and got a little too close to the edge."

"I understand that she was getting older, Kendrick, but the footsteps were right behind hers. My ex-husband is a violent man. Couldn't you at least consider the possibility that there might've been foul play?"

He waved me off again, indicating that he was tired of the conversation. His patience got thinner each time I stopped in. "We did. Of course we did. We looked at it from every angle," he answered. "You're going to have to get past this, Tamara. Let it go."

He tugged at one of his nails, polishing it on his jeans before he picked up his cell phone, obviously bored and hoping I'd take the hint to leave.

"The footprints were right behind hers!" I was angry and the words ripped from my throat.

Silence hung in the air, and I considered that he might tell me to get out. I could tell he was considering the same thing.

Calmer, I began again. "The report said that there were skid marks before she ever got to the point of fall. They wrote it off that she was trying to catch herself. The footprints behind hers had a wider stance. I think the skid marks mean she was being pushed, and the wider stance was because that person was pushing her."

"That's a good theory, and I guess you think we weren't smart enough to think about that. But we did. There were no witnesses, and her body was there for a couple of days. Lots of hikers probably walked right past her and didn't even know she was down there. There's probably a picture out there somewhere of some hiker smiling from the place of her fall. You know, they're waving 'hi' to someone back home while her body is right below them. Her footprints obviously matched the shoes she had on her feet. But the other footprints matched back to shoeprints from the most common discount store in the country. Meaning everyone's got some. I've got nothing to go on, even if I did believe it." Holding up one finger in the air, he continued, "Which I don't."

"You could check Joel's shoes?" I ventured.

"No probable cause. No judge in their right mind would give us a search warrant. Tam…" He paused, his lips still pursed together, for what seemed like an eternity, while he decided whether or not to finish what he had started to say. "Besides, his ferry ticket proves he didn't arrive until two days ago."

Sensing something bad was coming by the look on his face, I stiffened. "What?"

Drawing in a deep breath, he looked at me firmly in the eyes. "About Joel, he dropped in a couple of days ago. Said he was moving here because he'd fallen in love, not just with you, but with Sitka and wanted to come back. He hopes he can fix things with you someday so he just wanted to drop in and make sure I knew he was here. He came in on the ferry two days back, and as it turns out, he's already got a job on the mountain clearing logs. He starts tomorrow and he said…"

Squirming before he ever got the words out, I cut him off. "And you don't see anything odd about that? He always said he'd kill me and anyone I loved if I left, Kendrick! Now he's here to try to 'win me back.' Yeah, right! Don't you see a pattern in all of this?"

"I see a man who came here voluntarily to say he was afraid there might be trouble. I see a man who wanted to let me know he had a history with you. Tam, lots of people say things when they're angry. I bet you've said some pretty incriminating crap yourself in the past. I know you two go way back, but he's got no criminal record. A few domestic dispute calls, where I might add, you insisted to the cops that you were fine, but that's it. I've done my homework on him. So unless you can tell me something that I don't already know, this case will remain closed."

"What I see is a first-class manipulator and a cop too damn stupid to notice. And why the hell didn't you mention to me before now that you knew Joel was here? You would think you could've shown me the common courtesy of letting me know that the man I've been running from for eight months was here. As it was, I found out when he called me last night and scared the hell out of me." My chair slid backwards as I flew up to my feet.

"Hey, Tam..."

His voice held that subtle hint of sarcasm mingled with righteous indignation. You can't learn to talk that way; you have to be born with the ability. I hesitated, my purse still oscillating on my shoulder from where I'd turned away from him.

"I'll be watching Joel. And I'll be watching you too," he said to my backside. "Just so you know."

I hated the way he said my nickname. I'd hated it ten years ago, and I hated it now.

"Well, I guess you can watch me die, Kendrick, because that's what's going to happen as long as dumbasses like you are the ones protecting me. And by the way, don't call me 'Tam.' We're not friends."

Without looking back, I pulled his door shut, smiled my best "I'm not flustered" smile to his secretary. "You might want to get that coffeepot off. It's still burning, you know," I said as I walked past the sizzling machine.

I bolted once I was out of the building, my legs pumping furiously as I rushed from the downtown and up the side streets. I'd made this same run a thousand times as a kid. I didn't have to think at all, my mind tracing the well-known course. My lungs were on fire and my muscles trembling by the time I reached the old Russian cemetery that sat just a few blocks from downtown.

It was on oasis, a magical place almost, sitting a stone's throw from civilization and yet so isolated as to feel remote. I'd never failed to walk in the gate and not feel as though I had crossed into some other world or another time.

The cemetery crested the pinnacle of a hill, and inside the gates, the land rose and fell with numerous smaller valleys and summits. Intertwining trails of green moss wound their way through tombstones whose age could only be guessed so worn were the inscriptions. The graveyard fencing was twisted topsy-turvy from the tumultuous tremblings of the ground and barely managed to stay upright. Stone angels guarded the grounds silently, their faces eroded with time and rain. I passed several as I entered, smiling at each one in turn. I'd named most of them at one point and I remembered them almost as fondly as my childhood friends.

Above me, the Sitka spruce trees rose a hundred feet into the air, their limbs stretching out to eclipse the light that sifted downwards. The deep green of forest ferns sheltered my feet as I walked, working in concert with the moss to subdue my footsteps. I followed a trail that twisted its way around both new graves and old until I came to my father's.

Burial sites don't hold up well in Alaska; the ground heaves and twists, pushing upwards unevenly, making it difficult to tell the old from the new. The stones crack and fall apart, creating their own kind of artwork as the jade moss and vinery overtake the broken pieces. That was part of the cemetery's magic. Here the past and present intertwined together so that my dad's grave blended into the mystery of the landscape, appearing neither old nor new. Instead, Dad seemed to change with time, to breathe through the earth that encased him, pushing it up in waves all throughout the cemetery.

It had been a comfort as a child as though he were with me still. I paused to whisper a hello to him. I didn't stay long, pressing my fingers to my lips and placing them to his weathered stone. We'd made peace years ago.

My grandmother's plot rested over the next rise, right next to my mother's. In the ten years I'd been gone, the northern slope of grand-mom's grave had risen nearly four inches above the southern slope. Moss was encroaching on her headstone, and the Orthodox cross at the head of her grave was leaning dangerously, as most around the cemetery were. I knew Mom's would be looking the same soon. She wouldn't mind; she'd appreciate the beauty of blending into the surroundings.

I settled down onto the small bench I'd placed here from my meager funds when I'd returned home. It'd been my first purchase. Resting in the quietness of the cemetery with no one watching, I let the fear that had threatened to control me at the police station reach the rest of my body. While my heart palpitated, my hands trembled, and although I cried slightly, I bit my lip. This place of rest was too beautiful to disturb with my tears.

I'd like to say that I'd become fearless in the days since my amazing escape into the Seattle night, but that would be a complete lie. Joel scared the living crap out of me. I couldn't be angry with the police really. Joel could lie to the devil himself. Combine tall, dark and handsome with charm, add an overwhelming dollop of badness, and you got Joel.

I was dissecting Kendrick's words when a voice disturbed my reverie. Looking up as my name was called, I saw Peter coming towards me. He climbed a small hill, quickly, and then crisscrossed another trail to reach my mom's resting spot, walking through the rotting foliage of summer rather than sticking to the trail.

"Tam, I thought I saw you racing up the street. Is everything okay?"

"Yeah, I'm okay," I lied, wiping an errant tear from my cheek. Graciously, he looked away to give me some privacy. "Just some... um... unfinished business with the police about Mom. And some groceries. Thought I'd kill two birds with one stone, and then I ended up here." I smiled, pretending nothing was wrong.

"I assume it wasn't the produce that sent you careening up here. Something go wrong with the police?"

I shrugged. "Our great classmate, the cop, is a serious screw-up," I muttered.

"Come on, Tam. That's not fair," Peter admonished gently.

I nodded, knowing he was right, but I refused to take back the words.

"So you really do think Lena was murdered. You were serious about Joel last night,," he stated quietly.

I sighed, my eyes closing to squeeze out a few more tears before I responded. "I know most everyone thinks I'm insane." I looked down at the ground. It was embarrassing being the town crazy. I'm not sure how my grandmother dealt with it all those years.

"I don't think you're crazy, but I think you've got a lot on your plate. You've been through a lot with your mom's passing and the bad relationship," he replied.

"Joel killed her, Peter. I know he did."

"But the police don't agree." It was a more of a statement than a question.

"Obviously not. But I know him, and I've looked at the evidence. And to make matters worse, Kendrick told me Joel stopped in a couple of days ago, and the police haven't done a damn thing. He's here! Isn't that some kind of evidence itself? I just don't get why they don't see it." I didn't tell Peter about mine and Joel's conversation the night before. I didn't tell him Joel warned me to stay away from him.

"People see what they want to see."

I bristled at his words.

"I didn't mean that you were seeing it wrong, Tamara. Although you might be, but the police might be looking at it wrong too. People often see what they're used to seeing or what's easiest to see. Or some combination thereof. Don't take it personally."

"Easier said than done." I smiled to take the edge off my words. My tears had dried, and I rubbed my irritated, fatigued eyes.

"Are you getting enough sleep? You look exhausted," he said.

"Strange you should ask." I laughed nervously remembering my dreams and the promises of the vampire.

"So... you're not getting enough sleep. Nightmares? About your mom?"

"Vampires, actually."

Peter looked at me as if I'd just sprouted horns.

"Vampires?" he questioned.

"You know anything about them?" I asked as I laughed despite my circumstances. "Bet that doesn't help my crazy reputation."

"Well, no. It doesn't, Tam. Don't mention vampires to anyone other than me, okay?" He said teasingly.

"Starting to believe some of the rumors of my insanity, huh?" I asked.

"If you're looking to surprise me, just remember, it's really hard to shock a man of the cloth. It kind of comes with the job description and I'm not the same boy you remember from a decade ago."

"Well then, what can you tell me?" I deadpanned.

"About vampires?"

I nodded at him to continue.

"Oh, you're serious!" His eyebrows were nearly at his hairline. I couldn't help but laugh at his expression.

"I'm reading an old journal I found at Mom's house. It's an old ghost story or vampire story or something like that, I guess."

"I'm surprised at that. Your mom *really* did *not* like the occult."

"I don't think she knew the journal existed. It was hidden at the very bottom of an old trunk. So anyways, what can you tell me?"

"Maybe you should be more specific. I think we all know the Hollywood mumbo-jumbo."

I nodded at him, laughing at the ridiculous of our conversation. "Okay. Here goes. First of all, are you a believer?"

"In vampires? Really, are you seriously asking me that? If I say yes, you'll think I'm insane. If I say no, I'm guessing you won't say another word. So I plead the fifth. But I bet I've heard every legend that you have, and then a few you probably haven't."

I moved over, waiting for him to take a seat beside me, anxious to hear his answer. "Of course you don't believe. That would be ridiculous." I studied his silent expression intently. "You don't, right?"

He laughed lightly. "I'm getting the feeling you want me to believe." His leather gloves creaked as he rubbed his knees lightly. "Tam, I entertain the possibility that we don't fully understand everything of the past, and I believe that where there is smoke, there is usually fire—even if only a few coals."

"Meaning?" I asked, encouraging him to expound.

"Meaning that where there are so many legends, how can there not be some inkling of the truth? I also think they are likely a thing of the past, despite what Hollywood says, if they ever did in fact exist."

"Okay, Father, supposing they were 'out there,' how were they created? And more importantly, can they be killed?" I scooped my fingers in the air like quotations for emphasis.

He raised his eyebrows at me. "You're calling me 'Father' now? After last night?"

I smiled, raising my eyebrows back at him, and he continued.

"Technically, that's two questions, and there are lots of answers. Remember, vampire legends originate the world over. I took some classes that dealt with Russian and Slavic mysticism in the past, and so I know those legends best. According to my studies, vampirism was the penalty for suicide or dying in opposition of the Church. There were, of course, a few other bizarre beliefs like falling from wagons and dogs jumping over a corpse, but the most widely held origins concerned the suicides and heretics. Legend also states that they cannot die. You can hold them in the grave, but the only way to kill them is to bring them back into the fold of the Church so that the natural process of death can occur."

"So they could live forever rotting in the ground?"

"No. That's the crux. They can't die, and they can't decay. They are forced to exist, to be aware sun up to sun down, paralyzed with the coming of the day and fighting to escape at night. They become weak, but never weak enough to die. It's an eternal punishment. They are truly immortal. A stake won't kill them, and neither will decapitation. It will contain them," he lifted a finger up for emphasis as he shook his head, "but it won't kill them. Remember, the Bible says there is only one death on this earth and then the judgment."

"That's truly the meaning of hell on Earth," I whispered, more to myself than anyone.

"Why are you so interested in this? It's got to be more than some old journal that has got you so riveted." He turned to face me on the bench.

"Promise you won't go straight to the authorities about my sanity?" I asked, looking at him suspiciously.

"Cross my heart," he replied, tracing the outline of an X on his chest.

I raised my eyebrows even higher, searching his face for the truth.

"Um... you do realize that I'm an actual minister, right?"

I laughed out loud now. "Yes, Father. But you're a man and my track record with men is not so hot."

"Have a little faith and let me redeem my gender." Peter smiled. It was pleasant and refreshing just like dinner the night before.

Taking a leap of faith, I continued with the story. "This is where it really gets weird. I've been going through and organizing some of Mom and Grand-mom's old stuff. Squirreled away in some musty old boxes, I found this journal belonging to a Russian surgeon and a bottle labeled 'vampire blood.' I even found the doc's name in the family Bible. I read the journal, and the surgeon talks about a specific vampire in his writings." Now I truly felt crazy.

"Are you serious?" he asked just as his cell phone began to jingle in his pocket.

I nodded as he put the phone to his ear and listened for a few moments.

Covering the mouthpiece, he whispered, "Sick parishioner. Can I stop in sometime? I'd love to see the journal. And I'd love to see you again."

"Sure," I whispered back at him, knowing I could not let that happen.

"You really are okay up here?" Peter asked, his hand still covering the mouthpiece.

Nodding a yes, I smiled and motioned him away with my hands. He looked back at me once as he walked away, and I pointed towards the front entrance to the cemetery.

Alone, I relaxed into the scenery. I suppose most people find graveyards disconcerting, but this place had the exact opposite effect on me. Some of my most serene moments had been spent here, leaned against the back of a fallen headstone. The dead who slumbered nearby had never objected to me, and I'd certainly never objected to them. Overall, it was a friendly relationship.

This hallowed ground had been the resting place of my people for as long as had been recorded in the family Bible, and it was as natural to be here as my childhood home. In fact, the cemetery had been my first stop after arriving back in Sitka. It seemed fitting. Mom had been laid to rest in this dark ground before I made it home, and I couldn't go home without seeing her first.

When my father had passed at a young age, I'd stopped in every day after school to visit him. I whispered to him about boys, the ones I liked and the ones I didn't, and fights with Mom. And occasionally, I did nothing but describe the weather, a beautiful fish I'd spotted, or a particularly impressive whale spout. It didn't matter really what I talked about, the talking had made me feel better.

Death had claimed Dad early, heart attacks weaving their way through the paternal side of his family tree, and it was therapeutic to tell him about things we'd shared in our short time together.

But there were other happy memories here as well. My first kiss, a chaste peck with Peter, had been concealed here in the lush greenery. Our lips had barely touched. The cemetery had been a perfect place for an egg hunt one Easter morning, and the place to prove your bravery on windy, wet October nights. I smiled, remembering my friends and I as we set huddled together, shivering at every creak of the tree limbs and moan of the wind.

I could have stayed here reliving memories for hours, but I was running out of daylight. It's easy to do when you only have seven or eight hours to start with, and I'd squandered too much time between here and the police station.

I spent the last remaining half-hour of light tidying up the grave sites. Using my hands, I swept away the leaves that had gathered across the soft mounds of dirt. I removed all the dead flowers. I regretted it immediately; Mom's grave looked so barren, and I wished I'd thought to bring some fresh ones to replace the old. Whispering my goodbyes, I promised to visit again soon. I'd bring her favorite lilies when I did.

Before I left town, I bought a few odds and ends groceries, nodding to a couple of old classmates I met in the grocery aisles along the way.

The sun was setting as I loaded two small bags of produce and milk into the cab of the truck, and by the time I pulled onto the highway from the grocery parking lot, not a ribbon of pink could be seen staining the horizon.

# Chapter 8

As the sun set, the roar of the vampire's consciousness rose in my mind like the moon that trailed behind on my drive home. At first, it had only been a niggling in the back of my head, but it grew in intensity until I could again hear syllables, although I still couldn't yet make out the specific words. The voice waxed and waned and was at times so deafening that it forced my hands off the steering wheel to squeeze my temples in efforts to suppress the sounds.

The respite of Peter's comforting presence was soon forgotten as the white noise compounded the anxiety I was feeling about Joel. He was out here somewhere, and he was already manipulating the police. It's one thing to have suspicions but another thing altogether to have them confirmed. What games did he have planned for me?

I pushed the white noise to the back of my mind as best I could and focused on driving. I passed one last car as I drove across the Indian River Bridge, and then I was alone on the highway. The road stretched out like a gray ribbon through a sea of blackness. The mountains to my left and the ocean to my right were virtual voids and despite the moonlight, the ribbon of highway was dark.

It felt lonely and I was scared—scared of Joel and the rush of the vampire's voice in my mind. I'd only been forced to listen to it for a half-hour this evening, and already I was about to pull my hair out. Nervous to the hilt, my eyes were in constant movement between the road in front of me and my rearview mirror, but the highway remained dark and empty as I neared my home.

I've never had a psychic hit, but as soon as I turned off the main road onto Mom's driveway, I felt like the air changed around the car. Maybe it was the vampire's blood pushing through my veins that lent me his sixth sense. Maybe I was just on edge and expecting the worst but something seemed off, though I couldn't put my finger on what.

The drive was narrow, hidden in a curve and nearly obscured by trees. I surveyed every inch of it as I drove the length, expecting to see Joel at every turn. But as I passed the hulking form of each ancient tree, I found nothing but quiet empty shadows. I was so intent on what was in front of me that I'd reached my parking spot before I realized someone had pulled in behind me. The car must have been concealed on one of the side roads that I had passed, waiting for me to drive by.

Now there was nowhere to go. I was blocked in. My yard wasn't big enough to turn around in, and there wasn't a second entrance to the property and my house blocked my going forward. I studied the car in my rearview mirror. The lights, both interior and exterior, were off, and I could just trace the outline of someone in the driver's seat. The tip of a smoke flamed to life in the darkness of the car as the occupant inhaled deeply, and then it waned to only a dull glow. Too fat to be a cigarette, I recognized it immediately. King Edward cigars, Joel's favorite, light up the night like no other.

I watched the glow of the cigar arc out the passenger window and fade into the landscape before I realized that the outline of the driver was gone, and I had no idea where. Pressing hard on the brakes because I was too chicken to put it into park, I sat in the truck, idling, unsure of what to do. Tingles of alarm quivered down my back; I held onto the steering wheel, forcing my trembling hands to grip it firmly. My knuckles stood out white on the dark leather of the wheel, and I stared at them for inspiration.

My head roared, my heart thumped, and I thought I was going to be sick. Begging my brain to concentrate, I searched the darkness that surrounded me, but there was nothing to see, nothing that gave me any indication where Joel was hiding.

The floodlight for the yard had been burned out when I moved into Mom's house. I'd been meaning to have it replaced, but money was tight so it had remained on my to-do list. *I should have bought less coffee,* I chided myself. *And fixed the damn light.*

Thick mists had rolled in from the sound, providing many hiding places even in the small confined area in front of my house. I strained my eyes and searched every crevice of the yard, mentally forming a picture of the different places he could be hiding. In my rearview mirror that I checked repeatedly, his car mocked me.

Except the vehicle blocking my exit, everything looked just as I'd left it. The back part of the house was lit by the lights I had intentionally left on in case I got home later than expected. The porch was illuminated but dimly so; the lights were meant only to provide enough background light so you wouldn't fall going up or down the stairs without destroying the natural ambiance of the view of the sound. I guess I'd forgotten to turn those off when I got up this morning.

The glow from the bedroom light illuminated enough of the living room through the picture window that I could make out the curtains fluttering with the ceiling fan breeze. I couldn't see any movement inside the living room or the part of the kitchen I could make out.

About twenty feet to my left, the forest leaned in on the yard, its border densely dark against the lighter shades of the yard. The trees to my right formed the rest of the cocoon, and I searched the borders desperately for any signs of Joel, but the yard and its perimeter remained silent—menacing actually because I knew my property concealed him.

Feeling the sudden need to look in the bed of my truck, I turned my head slowly, my gut tightening up as I did so. Behind me and to my right, I caught the blur of a movement. My mind shouted a warning, and I barely managed to hit the electric lock as a gloved hand curled under the door handle.

"Dammit!" The curse erupted from him even as he pounded a fist, once, hard into the window. The truck shook with the impact, and I flinched as his fist flew towards me. A short-lived scream ripped from my throat before my mouth clamped shut.

Like a guppy in a fishbowl, I watched as Joel circled my truck. Again, I wished for a cell phone but then remembered I was in Alaska. Cell phone coverage was sketchy at best and nearly non-existent where I sat, trapped.

Joel's long strides carried him quickly around the truck, and trying to watch him made my head swim a little. Adrik's roaring in my head didn't help and increased my dizziness exponentially. For a moment, Joel stopped at the driver's window, arms crossed in front of him. He was fairly tall, so I had to lean in towards the window a little to see his face. He was examining my truck the way a wolf studies the frame of chicken coop.

Catching me looking at him, he leaned down to smile a leering grin at me before turning to walk behind my truck. I dreaded the dizziness but turned my head over my left shoulder as far as my neck would allow to watch him stride behind the bed of my truck. Swiveling my head the other direction, I strained over my right shoulder to find him but couldn't locate him in the darkness.

I screamed again as his hands reverberated against the window to my left. He'd doubled back, catching me off guard.

"You can't sit in this damn truck forever, Tam! Got to come out some time," Joel shouted, his mouth so close to the glass that fog formed, obscuring his face. Originally from Alabama, a heavy southern drawl clung to his speech. "Nah. You'll have to take a piss soon. Never could go long without taking a piss. I can already see you starting to squirm, sugar." He jeered at me through the truck window.

I ignored his words even as I realized I had to pee. Mentally, I cursed the twenty ounces of soda I'd downed at the grocery store. I couldn't sit in the truck all night, and even if I could, what good would it do? It wasn't like morning light was going to bring the cavalry.

"Don't you wish you could do this?" he said as he leaned back slightly. He made a big show of undoing his fly before letting a stream loose on the door of my truck. You could always count on him to be classy.

It was perhaps my only opportunity, and my mind seized on it immediately. Shoving the door open with all my strength, the sharp metal edge caught him square in the groin, sending him to his knees. He sucked in air in a loud whoop as he doubled over at the waist cursing out loud.

I wasted no time slipping out of the truck and sprinting across the yard. Begging the front door lock to open, I was shocked when the key slipped in on the second try. I didn't bother to close it behind me or look over my shoulder. It was a waste of time; Joel would just bust it down if he wanted in.

My hands were shaking as I punched 9-1-1 into the phone that hung on the kitchen wall. It was ancient; the yellow color had faded to more of an off-white with time.

The operator's voice was calm and collected when she answered. "9-1-1. State the nature of your emergency." Her sterile voice was probably supposed to make me feel better. It didn't help.

"Help me! Please. Oh God! My ex-husband's going to kill me! Send the police!" My voice sounded shrill even to me. I screamed my address at her, hoping to God their system was equipped with some kind of GPS.

"Calm down, ma'am. I've got it. You're on the board and help is on the way. Where is your ex-husband now? Is he with you?" she questioned, her fingers efficiently striking a keyboard in the background.

"He's right behind me," I whispered into the phone just as the line went dead.

Joel stood behind me, one hand holding the cord in his gloved hand, the phone jack empty in the wall. Damn those old wall phones. The receiver was still in my hands when he pulled it almost gently from my grip, setting it back on the base.

"I'm gonna let what happened out in the yard slide—for tonight that is. But you know you're gonna have to pay for that little stunt, Tam. You can't hit a man in the balls and expect to get away with it."

I almost nodded my head as he spun me around to face him, like I used to do when he threatened me. I caught myself just in time, but how easy it would have been to slip back into my old role of the victim and in those few seconds, I forced myself to remember all the good in my life that had come from leaving him. I pictured my apartment and the decorations I'd made with supplies bought with my own money from the job that I'd gotten. And I thought of Mom and what she'd said that night when her spirit came to me. He might kill me, but he would *not* own me again. I took a steadying breath to help my resolve.

It didn't hurt that I knew the police were on their way. Joel was no idiot, and he'd heard me give them my address. I'd be safe tonight, and even for the next few nights. Joel was good with the police. When he came for me, it'd be when no one was expecting it. He'd be the thief in the night with the airtight alibi, and I'd be the wrong person at the wrong time kind of accident.

"Where you been anyhow? Thought for sure you'd make it back for your mommy's funeral. What took you so long, girl?"

Next to me, he leaned against the counter, his long legs stretched out in front of him. I could feel his eyes on me, studying my face. I strained to keep my expression passive—like he didn't scare me, like I didn't give a shit that he was here. At least that's what I wanted him to think.

"Don't worry, baby. I sent the old broad some lilies. Orange ones were always her favorite, right?"

"How long have you been here?" My voice was surprisingly calm. Guess that psychology class had helped a little after all.

"Oh, I came a few days after I got the divorce papers in the mail. Friend of mine brought me up here in his boat. I stayed with him out on Indian River. That wasn't very nice, babe, leaving me like that. And that lawyer of yours. She was a real bitch. Got uppity with me just 'cause I wanted to talk to you face to face."

"She knows you talk with your hands," I whispered. "And I didn't want to talk to you ever again."

"But you wanted to talk to your momma, didn't you?" he smiled. "Maybe you should have talked to me first."

He twisted a lock of my hair around his finger, inching me sideways until I was forced to stand directly in front of him if I wanted to stand at all, my head pulled back as far as my spine would allow as he twisted his fingers close up to my scalp.

With my hair as leverage, he held my face still as he ran one smooth finger over my lower lip. I couldn't control the shaking that overtook my frame but I forced myself to meet his eyes, to at least pretend I wasn't afraid of him. It was disturbing after so long to see him again because looking at Joel was like staring a contradiction in the face. How could anything that looked that good be so bad? He was heroine in a pretty box. With a bow on top.

"The police are coming, Joel. Surely you don't plan on being here when they make it," I whispered through trembling lips.

He smiled, leaning into press his warm mouth to my cool forehead covered with the sweat of fear. "I always win, Tam. You just need to come on home," he whispered into my ear before releasing me. "Don't end up like your momma."

Expecting him to leave since the police were no doubt on the way, I was confused when he walked to the sink, filling up a large plastic tumbler with water.

"Sleep tight, babe," he said, raising the glass to his lips and taking a long draw of the water.

I followed a few steps behind him to the door. He left it open as he stepped out into the cold night. I was still confused until I saw him splash the water up onto the door of my truck, washing the urine and all proof that he'd been here away. Smart bastard. Although I doubted the police here would have gone to the effort of testing my truck for his DNA.

He was well past gone before the headlights of the police cruiser illuminated my drive. I was standing in the front door, leaning on the frame for support while they parked. Joel could have killed me several times over before they ever got there.

A long-legged policeman stepped from the car; the lights still on, the engine running. He didn't plan to be here long from the looks of it.

"We got a domestic dispute call, ma'am. What's the problem?" he asked, walking towards my door. One arm swung loosely beside him, the other rested on the stock of his handgun. Another officer warily stepped off to the right. His weapon wasn't drawn, but his gun hand itched so bad his fingers twitched.

I could see the bias in the eyes of the first cop; rumors of me must have fully circulated the department. I should have expected that, as it was a small force.

"My ex-husband was here. But he left when I called 911," I answered.

"Officer Delaney, ma'am." He tipped his wide-brimmed hat as he climbed the steps, taking them two at a time. "Can I come in?"

I nodded yes, moving backwards from the door to let the officer pass. As he crossed the threshold, a sudden wave of dizziness washed across me. My senses swirled around me as the deafening crush of white noise erupted in my brain; bile rose in my throat. Instinctively, I cupped my ears, but the roaring continued unchanged. The voice had quieted while Joel was here but the roar had now returned with a vengeance.

"You okay?" Officer Delaney was asking. I struggled to hear him over the crush in my head.

"I'm all right. Just a headache," I lied and swung the door shut behind him.

One hand still on his gun, he looked cautiously around the living room. "Nothing looks out of place," he remarked, walking on into the kitchen.

The other officer was taking cautious steps towards my small back yard. "I'm going to look around the rest of the yard," he said matter-of-factly to his partner.

Sinking down on the couch in the living room, I waited until the first officer finished surveying the two bedrooms and bathroom of my snug house. His partner had finished with the backyard and was standing beside the porch, busy talking on his radio.

"Like I said, he left when I called 911," I said through clenched teeth, my fingers digging into my temples.

"Just like that? You called the police and he left? Didn't lay a hand on you? Didn't touch a thing?"

"He touched me all right, he just didn't leave any marks. Oh, I almost forgot the veiled threats about killing me. And he all but confessed to killing my mother. Before that, he urinated on my truck and kept me trapped in my vehicle for a while until I managed to hit him with the door and get inside."

"So you hit him first? Without him laying a hand on you?" He pulled out a notebook and started to write.

"He's not here to press charges, Officer. Thanks for coming. You guys have a real good night, okay?" There was no point wasting any more time so I walked to the door, holding it open to give him the message.

"By the way, ma'am, what was he driving?" the officer asked. He waited for my answer with the pen and notebook in his hand.

I exhaled in disgust. "I don't know. I was thinking about surviving! Not cars."

Maybe I'd have noticed if Adrik's roar hadn't been humming away in my head.

"Uh-huh. What was he wearing? What's his name again?" the policeman asked, a touch of sarcasm in his voice.

I must be the worst witness ever. "His name is Joel. Joel Parker." In exasperation, I sighed. "I think he had on flannel. It rubbed across my skin, but I don't remember the color. Detective Scott told me today that Joel was back in town," I added.

"So this was the first time you'd seen him?"

"Since I came back into town, yes."

"What a coincidence." He smirked. "I'll let Detective Scott know about this call in the morning. You do know filing a false police report is a criminal act, right?" he questioned.

"What the hell does that mean?" I shot back.

"Ma'am, I'm just saying it's a little strange. You find out Mr. Parker is back in town today, and then you report he's here tonight. Nothing's been tossed around in the house, and there's not a hair out of place on you. Are you sure your ex was even here? The detective mentioned you might pull something like this," he said, scowling at me as he walked out through the door.

"Here's an idea, Officer. Maybe my ex is smarter than that smart-ass of a detective. So you go right ahead and let the 'Detective' know in the morning," I said, making quotations in the air. "If I'm dead by then, I'd ask you to let him know that too, but I'm betting if I were, you guys would probably never figure it out. Take care," I added as I slammed the door in his surprised face.

A few moments later, the police cruiser disappeared down my drive. Inside the dimly lit interior of the car, I could just make out the outlines of the officers. The front passenger window was rolled down, and a long arm held out a cigarette. Watching them from the window next to the fireplace, I let the curtains slide back into place. I locked the doors more as a precaution than anything else. Joel wouldn't be back tonight.

Doubtless the police would take some routine surveillance trips down to my house during the evening. They would hate for me to turn up missing on their shift. It wouldn't look good after they'd reportedly found nothing a few hours earlier.

It was the safest I'd felt in days, but it was an illusion. I had merely pushed off the inevitable. The day of reckoning with Joel was coming. I'd failed miserably in convincing the authorities that Joel was guilty. Once again, I'd let Mom down.

I was down to my last option.

# Chapter 9

I was digging through the snow before the glare of the cruiser's lights had cleared my driveway. Intoxication and terror had fueled my aim off the back deck the night before when I'd flung the bottle with as much strength as I could conjure. So it was with only the vaguest idea of where the bottle had landed that I began searching.

My fingers were numb with cold and my pants soaked through with melted snow as I clamored across the frozen ground on icy knees. The white noise of the vampire in my mind had become deafening again. A couple of times without meaning to, I stopped in my searching to claw desperately at my ears even though the movements were wasted. It didn't help.

Instinctively, I'd move away from the sound when it became crushing, and I soon realized that if I moved to the right, the roaring would lessen. If I moved to the left, it got louder, to the point of pain, although the words were still inaudible and I realized he was speaking to me in the only way he could, steering me to his blood.

I was in tears from both the pain in my head and fear when I finally felt something hard and round under my right knee. I stretched my hand down through the snow and grasped the rounded contour of the bottle, whispering a thanks to the blanket of snow that had protected the bottle's fall. As I worked to pull it to the surface, I lost my balance and reflexively shifted my knee, snapping the neck of the vial off in my hand.

A dark stain formed in the snow, and I watched in horror as the stain spread quickly across the surface. The snow absorbed the fluid like a sponge, and I felt sick to my stomach. I needed it too much to have wasted the blood like this.

I held the remnant of the bottle up to the moonlight. Only about a fourth of the previous contents hadn't spilt out, and I set it aside for later. I wasn't certain that the remaining blood would be enough, so I scooped the red snow up in my hands and ate it out of my palms, licking my skin where it melted and ran down my forearms.

I felt the vampire's satisfaction as the blood touched my lips and his contentment when it hit my belly and stayed safely down. It was the first peace I'd had this evening. For a few moments, he was quiet and my mind was thankfully silent.

Above me, the stars studded the night sky in a glorious display. They seemed brighter than when I'd first come outside. It's usually so cloudy in Sitka that you can't make them out, but for the moment, the sky was cloudless, and despite my circumstances, I crossed my legs and leaned back, studying the view. My hands were so benumbed with cold that I didn't even notice the icy temperatures as I stretched them out behind me for support and let my head fall farther back to trace the Milky Way's ribbon through space. What would it be like to study these patterns in the stars for centuries?

I didn't have more than a few moments to ponder my own question before my mind was buzzing again with the vampire's unrest. He wanted more of me. My head roared with desires that I couldn't completely make out or fully understand. Except one command which was loud and clear.

*"Drink."*

It echoed repeatedly in my mind until I imagined I could make out the word emblazoned in the stars. It reverberated in the wind, and even the ground underneath me spoke those same syllables. I could feel the earth's utterances in the pads of my fingers even as the pit of my belly burned with hunger for more.

The remnant of the vial rested beside me in the snow and I didn't hesitate as I lifted it to my lips and drank the rest of the liquid. I was committed to exploring this final option because I was trapped even if no one else realized it. How could anyone judge me for the lengths I was willing to go?

But I knew as I sat there listening to the voice of the vampire in my consciousness that I would be judged for my actions. Mom would be so ashamed if she knew what I'd done. She wouldn't understand that I was doing this for her too—that I needed peace for her. And for all that Joel had done to me.

*"And God shall wipe away all tears from their eyes; and there shall be no more death, neither sorrow, nor crying, neither shall there be any more pain: for the former things are passed away."* The scripture came unbidden to my mind, one of Mom's favorites. I guess that was the one beautiful part of her being in Heaven; I would never disappoint her again and she would never know of the unholy things I had done in her memory.

But Peter would judge me if he ever found out, and he'd be disappointed by what he'd see only as impulsivity. He wouldn't understand that I needed to be free of Joel, and that I couldn't face a lifetime of running from him. Peter would think the risks were too great, and that I'd only changed who I was running from.

But I had a plan and no part of it involved letting Peter down. What could go wrong?

I tossed the empty, broken glass towards the woodpile, hearing it explode into thousands of pieces, before I stumbled back to the house, shocked at what my life had become.

It wasn't immediate but within a quarter-hour, I begin to feel blurred, as if the outlines of my body and my mind were smudged and not as distinct as they had been. What were my thoughts and what were not my thoughts were difficult to distinguish.

I was in my own house; the house I'd grown up in, and the interior hadn't changed much in the decade I'd been gone. Yet some of the furnishings looked unfamiliar, as if I was looking at them for the first time.

The light switch on the wall was exactly where it should be. I knew it had been there for years, but I couldn't quite remember what it was supposed to do. I flipped it up and down twice, knowing that I should know and looking strangely at the light flickering over my head. How odd it seemed.

*You need to go to bed*, I told myself.

I walked to the living room door and checked the lock again, fairly certain that the idea was mine, but before I'd turned to go back the bedroom, I decided I would go for a hike.

*There's somewhere I need to go. It's important.*

I was unlocking the doors before I realized it made no sense to hike at ten in the evening.

*What is wrong with me?*

The surgeon's journal lay on the mantle. I picked it up, turning it over in my hands. It looked different I thought at first before I decided that it simply looked older. I remembered seeing it lying on a small cluttered table littered with soiled bandages. I could see the doctor hunched over, scribbling furiously on the pages. I touched his familiar handwriting. I recalled being unable to read it because I was illiterate.

And then I remembered I was bilingual and had read the entire journal cover to cover.

Two lives intermingled in my veins—two sets of memories to piece together and sort through.

Adrik was here. I'd invited him in, and now he was with me. I could feel him, and yet I couldn't quite find him. But he was near, a presence lingering at the edge of my consciousness. He was the constellation that you couldn't see when you looked directly at it, but if you looked away, you could see the haze of stars hovering at the edge of your vision. He encroached on my awareness, and I was feeling more smudged and less distinct with every passing second as his blood seeped into my system.

Fear set in, and I tried to push it back, but I didn't have the strength. I was too tired. Maybe if I'd been more rested and less mentally frazzled, I might have stood a chance. As it was, I gave up and went to my bedroom before I lost all control and ended up on the floor.

My muscles went lax, and I didn't try to stop them as I melted onto the bed. My vision tunneled, the ceiling above me growing more distant by the second until the tiny hollow circle that remained disappeared.

I'm not sure how long I was asleep before the dream began or if I was dreaming at all. The experience was more trancelike. I knew my world existed, and yet I couldn't interact with it. I couldn't feel the ceiling fan blowing above me or see the light from the lamp on my nightstand, and I didn't have the power to stop the vision that formed around me.

I found myself standing in a clearing about fifty feet in diameter ringed by towering spruce trees. They appeared as old, robed men standing guard, their outstretched limbs cloaked in undulating layers of lichens; the tips of their branches pointing like fingers of skeleton hands at me, trapped in the center of the clearing. Nests of snow broke up the dark green of the forest floor while springy moss cocooned my feet. The ground was flat like the coastal plains that stretch along the ocean, and in the distance, I could hear the light lap of the ocean licking at a shoreline.

The moon hung heavy overhead in a near cloudless night. The moonlight glinted on the pockets of snow and the dampness that perpetually glazed everything in the path of the mists floating in from the nearby ocean.

I was not alone. I could feel him behind me, and his presence overwhelmed the forest. Nothing moved. No animal called out to its mate. Not a single birdcall broke the silence. The forest was paralyzed, and I barely breathed myself, my diaphragm frozen with fear.

I didn't acknowledge him at first, except to turn ever so slowly in his direction, my eyes firmly planted on the ground in front of me. I couldn't force myself to look up. I couldn't force my shaking muscles to stay still.

I was still trembling when cold skin brushed my cheek, the caress of a finger that traced a line from my eye to the corner of my mouth and continued down until it rested under my chin. He tilted my head with the barest pressure of his finger until I could not escape his gaze any longer and then I could not look away. I could not force my paralyzed muscles to move.

"You know my name?" he questioned.

My mouth was dry; my tongue felt like sandpaper, and I swallowed, looking for extra moisture, but I could find none. His name cracked across my vocal cords as I tried to speak.

At my efforts, he smiled. But it was a frosty expression—frigid actually.

"And you know what I am?"

I nodded once, the smallest of movements.

"And still you pursued this relationship?"

"I need your help, Adrik," I said finally finding enough air to form a whisper.

"How very refreshing to hear my name uttered by a human tongue after so long. And such a beautiful human at that."

His voice was low, his Russian dialect older and more guttural than I was used to. I struggled to translate, relying on the mental images that floated across the bond from him to me to help understand his words. I swallowed hard as he began to circle my body, his finger tracing a cold outline around my shoulders before spinning me around and trapping my head in his hands. His thumbs traced the thin skin of my eyelids before stroking my cheekbones. His cool fingers traced my trembling lips. There was nowhere to look except at him as he studied me.

He was easily the most beautiful man I'd ever seen, and although I wanted to close my eyes against such scrutiny, it was impossible to look away from such perfection. He might have appeared an angel except his eyes could not have been any less clear or any warmer than glacial ice. His thick black hair was neither short nor long, and a few errant locks arched across his forehead, daring me to push them aside. Spikes of black lashes accentuated the coolness of his stare.

A thin beard ran from his sideburns and traced the thin outline of his jaw before highlighting the contours of his mouth. His tall frame was hard, lean underneath the thin cotton clothing he wore in the dream. His feet were bare as were his arms, and the coldness of the dream didn't seem to affect him as it did me. I shivered with the chill, and even more where his hands touched me.

And touch me he did. Dropping his hands from my head, his hands snaked out to stroke my arms and shoulders, one hand brushing against the underside of a breast. I sucked in my breath harshly, taking a step backwards at the intimacy of his touch. I barely registered the movement of his arm as he forced me to tolerate his hands. I tried to convince myself that it wasn't real. This was all just a dream.

The corners of his lips lifted in a small smile. "What did you think was going to happen when you strengthened the blood bond? Did you think our encounter would be all one-sided? That I would seek nothing in return?"

"The surgeon didn't mention your ability to touch him in the journal," I answered.

"I had no great desire to touch the surgeon," he whispered, his hand sidling down my hip. "I desire a great deal to touch you, however."

His desires drifted through the bond we shared. It made my lower belly ache even while my skin tingled with fear.

"I need your help," I whispered again, forcing myself to concentrate.

"So your innocence is no longer in question, and you are willing to bargain after all. I am glad. I find innocence quite a bore." He continued to stroke my body while he spoke, and no amount of reminding myself that this was a dream helped.

"What will it take to get you to help me?" I asked, struggling to maintain eye contact. Looking at him must be the way a mouse felt looking into the eyes of the eagle that held it.

"A payment of blood, of course," he answered.

"Whose?" I questioned.

"So quick to give up any pretense of humanity," he said. His beautiful lips turned up a little more in a wicked smile. "If only it were that easy, Tamara. But I have a large wooden stake coated in iron through my heart, so although you want this Joel you are thinking of to pay the price for you, I do not see how you can force him to remove the stake embedded in my body. I believe you are going to have to pay the blood price yourself. But I give you my word, once you free me, I will sup on his bones."

"I don't understand," I answered, staring at him in confusion.

"What is there that is difficult to comprehend, Tamara? You have sought me out. Did you not understand the consequences?"

"I knew I would have to bring you up. I just didn't understand that I would have to die for it!"

"I have lain in the ground for two centuries paralyzed by this stake through my heart. It must be removed for me to rise, and whoever does this deed will die a gruesome death. I will have very little control because I am burning with hunger."

I stared at him dumbly while his words sunk into my overwhelmed mind. Finally, I realized the gravity of my mistake.

"No!" I shouted, lashing out with my hands at his face and chest. "I don't deserve to die! Joel does, and I deserve to *see* him dead, and my mother deserves to be avenged. I have paid enough!" I hissed. "Joel has hurt me in ways that you can't possibly understand."

"Ways that I cannot possibly understand? Woman, do you realize whom you speak to? You speak to a man who gave up his soul for revenge, and you shy from simple death? You have paid nothing in comparison." His expression was even icier as his fingers cut harshly into my arms.

"I let you in my head, didn't I? I'll spend the rest of my natural life with you in my dreams. Surely that has to be worth something," I said.

"Nightmares? Did you honestly think that would be the only cost of revenge? Did you believe that you could simply unearth me, and I would be at your service?"

I dropped my eyes, but not before he noticed the guilt in my expression. A poker face had never been my strong suit. His eyes widened with realization before narrowing in a frightening look.

In the next second, fire burned a painful path through my head. I grasped the sides of my skull and screamed as he ripped through my thoughts, ferreting out the secret ones I'd tucked away. The plan I'd hidden was displayed for him to see.

"You miserable bitch," he hissed, backhanding me to the ground.

With no time to catch myself or put up a struggle of any kind, I landed hard on my back, the air knocked out of my body with the sudden meeting of the ground. I watched as my breath hovered above me, a gray wet cloud that I couldn't retrieve.

Adrik was on me before I could draw a breath back into my empty lungs. With one hand, he dug strong fingers into my throat. He tangled the other hand deep into my hair and forced my neck back so it was even harder to find air. I gasped in his hands, struggling to breathe.

*Can he kill me in my dreams?* I wondered. *Was that possible?*

Logic surfaced for the briefest of moments, reminding me that I was not really in his hands in this cold forest. His fingers were not truly curved around my neck. In reality, I was lying on my bed in my warm house.

"If I convince your mind that you cannot breathe, rest assured, you will not breathe," Adrik whispered into my ear.

"It's mind over matter," I mouthed back at him.

Enough air had seeped into my lungs that my diaphragm had relaxed slightly and the pain between my shoulder blades was beginning to subside.

"When I get through with you, Tamara, you will not have enough mind left to worry about," he said, pushing my head backwards into the ground with his index finger. "So your plan was to unearth me and point me toward the blood of your enemy, and in my great gratitude, I would kill your enemy. And then you would stake me in my day sleep? You thought you could locate my resting place, easily enough, through the blood bond. What a cunning little bitch you are."

Having nothing to say, I stared at him coldly.

"You should be warned, it is unlikely I would have let you live knowing where I rest. It is a vampire's greatest secret."

"Then turn me into a vampire, and I'll kill him myself."

"I want no children, Tamara. I will never mark another."

"If you have no control, what's to keep you from marking me when I pull that stake out?" I questioned.

"It requires no more control or effort to rip the heart from your chest than it does to sink my fangs into your vessels."

"Then I'll pull the stake out during the day while you're weak. Then you can kill Joel. It's simple."

"And how do you propose to find me during the day when the sun has dominion and I am incapable of leading you to me?"

Studying his face, the realization of what he was saying and the truth about what I'd gotten myself into slowly worked across my mind like the punch line of some bad joke I'd been too slow to get.

"It is quite simple, Tamara. I make you one offer. Give me your life, and I will give you the revenge you seek. By my honor, Joel will pay for his sins," he answered calmly.

The space between us was very small, made even smaller by the anger that radiated from each of us. The moon hung behind him as he remained leaned across my body stretched out on the forest floor. I could have heard a pin drop on the ground beside me in such stillness.

"It's that simple, huh? Was it that simple for you, Adrik? I don't really understand, honestly. You were accused of rape, not murder. None of your loved ones died at the hands of this woman. How does that compare to the hell I've lived? Joel killed my mother, and he will kill me too."

"I was a slave, beaten like an animal!" his voice roared. Snow rained down from the trees with the echo. The ground shuddered underneath me. I clamped my hands across my ears, but he jerked them down, pinning me to the ground again.

"I lost my god," he continued. "I was excommunicated from the church which was the only thing I cared about. Is it not worse than death when you must give up eternity as well? I would have gladly given my life or selfishly that of my family's if I could have saved my soul. Death pales in comparison."

With each word he shook me until, finally, his anger became too much, and he could find nothing else to say. I watched the rise and fall of his chest as he struggled to control himself before shifting my gaze to his face. Never have I felt such an intense gaze as the one that held me now. The strength of his arms was weak compared to this paralyzing hold of his eyes. I could do nothing but watch as he tongued the tips of his fangs for the span of a heartbeat before lowering his mouth to my neck.

My skin parted beneath his lips and blood rose to meet him. He exhaled longingly against my neck and, wanting more, he pushed his fangs deeper, my vein splitting beneath their hard points. His assault lasted for only a few heartbeats, and then he was gone.

I sat up, my hand catching the blood at my neck, and searched the darkness for him, but I couldn't make him out among the shadows.

A few feet away, a log lay half buried in the snow. I crawled to it and pulled myself up until I was sitting, more or less, while I struggled to catch my breath. The temperature of the dream was dangerously cold, my clothes were soaked through and I was shaking from a combination of temperature and fear. My fingernails were a light blue, and through my clothes, I could feel the roughness of the tree bark I leaned against.

*How can a dream feel this real*? I wondered.

"I remember this night with clarity. I lived it once, many years ago, of course," Adrik answered, reading my thoughts as he solidified from the darkness. "This is where I was interred for the final time on a night just like this one," he said. He tapped the stump with one foot.

"Why here? It just looks like another part of the forest to me," I answered between breaths. Curling my feet through the snow, I dug my toes into the earth, recoiling as the dirt pushed itself beneath my toenails and between the digits of my feet. I could hardly imagine being buried alive in this cold, wet ground beneath my feet.

"It is as terrible as you imagine and much, much worse," he whispered as he studied the pieces of sky visible through the clouds. His expression had turned from cold to pained with that one sentence.

The misery of the experience worked its way into his voice, his emotions coursed through our blood bond, and even though I hadn't experienced what he had, I could feel the terror and fear of what he'd suffered—apparently was still suffering. If the mud on my toes made my skin crawl, I could scarcely conceive what it would be like to be covered with the muck from head to toe.

What would I be like if I'd been buried for two centuries? I might not be able to put together a coherent thought or carry on even the most basic conversation. The surgeon had apparently come closing to losing his mind in a very short time just by hearing Adrik's thoughts, let alone actually living them. And yet next to me, this vampire, Adrik, set calmly and able to put intelligible words together.

"Do not put too much credence into my sanity. It fails me completely most every day when the sun is highest in the sky, when I am so weak that I cannot even flex the fingers of my hands, when I cannot lick my parched lips. That is when my mind turns to foolish babble and I curse every human I have ever known. I curse the dead who sleep peacefully unto the Second Coming and the woman who bore me upon this earth."

"So you're here," I asked, gesturing to the landscape around us. "You're buried wherever this place is?"

Nodding his head yes, he turned towards me once more. "I am buried only a few feet right below where I stand now. It is where I was first cursed. Where I first took human life."

"You're talking about the child. The native child that you accidentally killed." I studied his face, seeing traces of something other than rage in his eyes. They were softer, warmer, if only by a shade.

It was impossible to not notice him as he sank down onto

the log next to me, to not recognize the perfection of his features. The blue ice of his eyes or the way his eyebrows made perfect dark arches above them. I couldn't help but study the strength of his jaw, the perfection found in the curve of his lips any more than I couldn't help but want to brush back the errant locks of hair that tried to hide the budding emotion of his eyes.

"Few emotions are left to me at this stage. I do not pretend to care much for humanity, but I think in becoming a vampire, the strongest of your emotions are what carries over to the next life. They are what define you. For me, it was the experience of Irena and that of the child, of course. It has been over two hundred years, and still the boy's face tortures me."

"Guilt and rage," I mouthed, more to myself than him. "I know them well."

"A potent combination, would you not agree?" he responded.

"Do you still hate Irena?" I asked.

"On that point, I have never wavered. The solidarity of my emotions regarding Irena has softened the blow of lying buried in the dirt these two hundred years. It is also a help that I can hear her screams reverberating through the earth. Unlike me, she was buried on hallowed ground. Her father sought to save her, but he only made her condition more miserable instead. The very ground itself makes her writhe as it works to thrust her unnatural body from its hallowed midst."

"I bet her screams mix nicely with yours," I said, instantly regretting the words before they'd even cleared my tongue. I have no idea what possessed me to say it except that this was at least in part still a dream. My internal filter wasn't fully engaged.

His cold gaze washed across me, returning to lock on my eyes. "Women are the coldest creatures of all."

"I didn't mean it so harshly," I answered.

"'Out of the abundance of the heart, the mouth speaks,'" he responded, quoting the Bible.

"Not this time," I answered. "I feel for you. I really do, and I wish I could help you. Without dying or unleashing you on the entire island, that is. But you can't make me come. You tried earlier this evening. It was you that made me think I needed to take a hike. But I resisted. You don't have the power over me like you did the surgeon."

"No, you still possess free will. I am too weak to force you to me, but I can give you the revenge you so desperately want."

"If I let you kill me, that is," I said angrily.

"The price of revenge is always steep, Tamara."

"It's too steep, Adrik. I can't help you. I won't help you. Desperation pushed me to believe the impossible, to drink your blood in the hopes I could save myself and avenge my mom. But I am not so desperate that I'm willing to die or free you on the innocent people of this town."

"Not yet, Tamara, but time is, as always, on my side. We have many nights together ahead of us."

I could feel the power of his persuasion wash across my senses. Physically, I could feel the tug of the invisible cord binding the two of us together. It was strong but not overwhelming—at least not yet. Still it made me want to go to him, made my heart ache with the desire to help. He smiled at my response to him, his tongue playing across the tips of his fangs, and while my skin should have crawled, it didn't. Instead, his hunger had an effect on me. It burned in my stomach, stoking the anger and rage that I felt towards Joel until I ached, low in my belly, with desires I hadn't felt in years.

"Lust and revenge are merely extremes of the same emotion," Adrik said to my unspoken thoughts.

I swallowed hard, unable to look away from the wicked beauty of his lips. Through the blood bond, I felt his thoughts morph towards the other end of the spectrum, towards lust. I closed my eyes as I felt the brush of his lips across mine and then the light pressure of his mouth, followed by the sweet sting of his fangs at the base of my throat. His hands held my face captive while he traced the contours of my neck with his cool lips. His hands cupped my breasts through my T-shirt before dropping to knead my hips.

"It's just a dream," I whispered in his ear.

"Yes, very true, but how much better to lust a woman of real flesh and blood than those I have conjured in my mind all these years. I never had a woman, you know, but I will have you every night. Mark my words, Tamara, there will come an evening when you lose yourself in passion and come to me, and I will have your blood and your life."

"A virgin accused of rape," I whispered, dropping my head back to allow him better access to my throat. His lust was affecting me. "What about the night you made Irena? The surgeon said her body was in terrible shape. I just assumed..." I began but didn't finish.

Adrik pulled slowly away from me, his eyes cold and glacial again.

"That I raped her."

I nodded, a slight movement, as I drew back from him. If I'd been cold before, now I was frozen by his icy stare.

"I wanted to for what she had done to me. I yearned to abuse her in ways she could understand and appreciate. I craved to hear her screams when I thrust into her. But in the end, I found I could not."

"You didn't want to lose all of your humanity," I said.

A wistful smile touched his lips. "Humanity played no role in my decision. I simply did not want to become the thing of which she had accused me. It was the only remnant of my former self that was mine to control, and I did not want to give her that power."

His passion had cooled, and I could feel his thoughts roaming into the past.

"What happened, Adrik? Please tell me so I can understand. I know from reading the surgeon's journal that you, by complete accident, took the life of that native child and that the guilt nearly killed you. And then you were accused of rape. But how that led to excommunication and suicide, I just don't get."

"It is a convoluted and twisted tale," he said.

"It appears we have all night," I answered sardonically.

He laughed softly. "No, we have every night."

# Chapter 10

Patiently, I waited while he seemed to collect his thoughts, to find the words that would describe what so obviously still affected him. Time had done nothing to dull his memories. In fact, they were sharper, each one an individual barb that he'd cut himself on so many times that I could almost see what his skin would look like if the analogy were real. A tangled mesh of lacerations.

Through the bond, I could see images forming in his mind's eye that played like some ancient silent movie. I watched it play out, fascinated by pictures of a time and of a people who now only remained in the blackness of his thoughts.

"It all starts with the child. His death was the crux around which my story revolves.

"I was a young man when I came to Sitka. My mother had born me into serfdom on a rural estate in Russia belonging to a prominent landowner always looking for new opportunities to make money. The economy was hard, and his cash on hand was at an all-time low, so I was his capital investment in the Russian American Trading Company. As such, I was to be sent to Sitka aboard the next ship making its way to Alaska. My labor would be his currency.

"No merchant ships were planned to travel to Alaska at that time, so my master secured passage aboard the Neva, a warship of the Imperial Russian Navy, where I would be the personal serf to one of the bishops until we arrived in Sitka in addition to providing general labor aboard the boat. The Neva had been dispatched by the Tsar to circumvent the world to prove Russia's superiority at sea. It was a godforsaken trip that seemed at the time to last an eternity.

"Ships are a constant work in progress where no job is ever entirely completed. The chamber pots are always in need of emptying, and every bit of that great boat that touches wind or sea must be constantly scoured so that the timbers underneath your feet do not waste away.

"On the voyage, I had made friends with a peasant named Ivan Korovin. He was poor, but he was free, and in the social structure of the day, our friendship was uncommon. Despite the great gulf of our birthright, we became near inseparable. In reality, his chores were not far removed from my own, and the vast amount of our time was spent together. Without his company, I might have died on the trip over.

"You see, serfs were not a precious resource, and Russia was full of them, so no one was greatly interested in wasting provisions on not only a serf but a sick one at that. My ever-present retching on the ocean crossing did nothing to increase my strength. I believe I survived mainly from sheer prayer and Ivan's compassion. He gave me portions of his rations nearly every day, and I owed him my life.

"Despite our arriving in the midst of a standoff between Alexander Baranov, the then governor of Alaska, and the Tlingit Indian tribe, it was a relief when we finally reached the coast of Alaska and traced it around to the outpost of New Archangel.

"A contingency of Russian Imperial soldiers, members of an opposing native tribe called the Aleutians, Ivan and myself were dispatched to take the fort from the Tlingit. Theirs was a fierce culture, and when faced with losing their most prized fishing grounds to the Baranov, the Tlingit proved willing and capable fighters.

"A small distance from their village, the Tlingit tribe had constructed quite a foreboding palisade. It was built from green spruce trees so that our cannon fire could not breach the walls. The Baranov tried mind you. He tried with all his might to blast the Tlingit out, and when he failed, he decided to starve them out.

"After many long days of constant cannon attack and lack of provisions, the Tlingit sent word of their surrender, and the Baranov felt confident his plan had succeeded. Their notice of surrender was followed by a litany of chants that we assumed to be part of their ceremonies associated with losing a battle.

"A few of the soldiers were entranced by the chanting, such guttural sounds put to a lilting tune. But to me, it had an eerie sound that lifted the hair on the back of my neck. The tune took me back to Russia, reminding me of the tales of my mother's people, the Slavs. We were a people that believed in spirits and demons as much as we believed in the living. I crossed my chest as the music drifted across the ground that lay between us and the fort because I knew that inside those four walls, something frightening and dreadful awaited me.

"Ivan, my companion and not one for superstition, was more concerned of the weather and complained bitterly of the conditions in which we found ourselves. They were abysmal. We slept on the ground when we slept at all. Our skin was constantly moist, as our clothes were poorly suited for the wetness of our environment and we were all soon covered with chaff and rot.

"The chanting droned on for five days, and by this time, anyone who had found any enjoyment in the sounds was now long since tired of it, and nothing remained to take our mind from the rain and fog that continually poured in from the sea. The officers in our group had the good fortune to warm their bones with swigs of whiskey they passed to one another. For the rest of us, there was nothing except the empty promises that the stand-off would soon be over.

"Ivan had just asked again for the fifth time, 'What the hell do you think they are singing about?' when the pounding of drums joined the Tlingit's voices. The slow and steady chant that my heart had been keeping time with began to get louder until it was frenzied and rushed. The beating drums filled my temples. My head ached and my stomach twisted in knots.

"I did not think it could get any louder, sound any more primitive, when suddenly the drums and the chanting ended. It was just after midnight, and an anguished cry, the likes of which I had never heard ripped from the throats of the Tlingit. And then a perfect calm overtook the forest, not a sound stirred upon the air.

"We all watched the fort with trepidation, expecting that so great of a cry could only be followed by some deed of extreme importance. The officers whispered amongst themselves. Ivan shook his head at me. 'What the hell,' he mouthed into the darkness, little puffs of fog forming in front of his face.

"If the Aleutians fighting by our sides understood the chants of their fellow natives, they gave no indication. They looked at one another just as questioningly as we did our fellow Russians. No one knew what to do with the silence. Was this the sign of surrender? A few of the men expected the doors to swing open to reveal a messenger with a welcome on his lips and dusting ourselves off, we rose from the ground. Word, sent by the Baranov, traveled through the troop, 'Stand ready. We take possession now.'

"But the gates did not open, and if the days before had seemed long, the four days that followed that death cry were like nothing we had experienced.

"Stuck in the mist and the rain, tempers flared as we waited for the arrival of more troops. After what seemed like an eternity, the re-enforcements were in place and the decision was resolutely made to take the fort.

"The fog rose from the ocean and followed us as we advanced on the palisade, as if it knew that there were sins within those walls that would need to be covered. Weapons drawn, my fellow soldiers and I approached cautiously and hesitantly. The stake walls of the palisade were intimidating but not nearly so much as the absolute stillness that hovered over the fort.

"As we forced open the palisade doors, I could not calm the foreboding growing in the pit of my stomach. Something was desperately wrong. No voices cried out to meet us, and the odor of death reached me. I gagged on bile before I could swallow it back down.

"The walls of the palisade gave way to reveal a scene that I will never forget if I am to be a millennium upon this earth. Scattered on the ground were the bodies of children. The victims of this war, their small faces contorted in pain and betrayal. Some, partially consumed by the wild animals of the area, lay on the ground while others were left in the makeshift homes, but all were days dead; decay becoming evident despite the cold. Everything rots so much quicker in Alaska, especially the dead.

"Not a man among our group had dry eyes. We were each one appalled by the sight, and every one stood silent, unable to find any words to describe the horror inside the fort. Around me, soldiers forgot to hold their muskets up any longer. The guns dropped uselessly to their sides, metal clinking against coat buttons. The flags of Russia and the trading company fluttered uselessly in the wind behind us.

"Bile rose again in my throat, and this time I was unable to stop the rush of stomach fluids out my nose and mouth. It splattered onto the partially frozen ground beneath me, the only sound in a sea of quiet. I was not alone as I made the symbol of the cross on my chest, whispering prayers up to Heaven for the slain children.

"None of the soldiers or even the officers seemed to know quite what to do next as each one stared silently around; a few began to mill about, turning the bodies over to see if any lived while a few more blessed the ground with their stomach juices. The enemy had gone, leaving only the corpses of dead children and animals behind. Shock had left the Russian army defenseless. If there had been any Tlingit warriors lying in wait inside the palisade walls, their victory would have been an easy one.

"After what seemed like an eternity, the commanding officer wiped the confused expression from his face and waved his hand forward, his movements subdued as if he did not want to disturb the dead lying at our feet.

"Fanning out, we all walked deeper into the abandoned fort, stepping over the sad bodies as we went. Silence hung heavy over the abandoned fort. No birds sang, no squirrels laughed as even nature recognized the slaughter that had taken place inside these walls.

"A keening song whispered to me on the wind the farther I walked into the fort. I turned towards the sound and listened. It was the mourning song of a child barely audible over the crunch of soldiers' boots.

"I found it hard to focus so I closed my eyes, letting every other sound blend into the background. I wound my way through the fort, the song of mourning becoming closer with my every step. It was a native song, and I strained my ears for more sounds that proved someone had survived.

"A breeze blew by me abruptly, reeking of sweat and urine. I jerked my eyes open, startled as the form of a small boy dashed across the threshold of a structure and ran towards the back of the fort. Weakened by injuries and lack of food, the young child did not make it more than a few strides before he stumbled to the ground. Blood stained his leather tunic and crusted the tip of one braid.

"Digging his fingernails into the dirt, the child clawed his way up from the ground, tumbling forward again but managing to stay upright until his worn pants caught on a jagged tree root, bringing him to his knees again. Tears stained his dirty face as he jerked desperately on his pants leg, but the material would not divide in his hands. He cried harder as I approached him.

"I pulled a knife from my waistband as I leaned forward to slice away the imprisoning material. I did not consider how this might look to the child and, frightened by the sight of the knife, the boy lunged forwardly suddenly. His small hands hit me square in the chest, but he was so weakened by the starvation of the last few days that I barely noticed the futile force of his blows.

"It was only as I watched the abject fear on the child's face convert to pain that I became aware of his blood dripping onto the exposed skin between my glove and coat sleeve. I looked down in surprise, the moment hanging in the balance as I realized the boy was impaled on the sharp point of my knife.

"The child mouthed a word that I could not understand before both air and blood erupted across his young vocal cords and spewed out his mouth, spattering my face and clothes in a frothy spasm of death. So much in shock, I stood unmoving, my arm extended out as the child dangled on my knife, not allowing him to sink down on the ground. I could not look away, and I watched as death overtook the child's face, his pupils black and glossy at first but fading to dull.

"It was Ivan who forcibly pushed my arm down and allowed the child to slip to the ground. Only the light thud of the child's body collapsing on the wet soil broke my concentration enough that I spared a glance at Ivan's hand on my arm. I sunk to my knees beside the child and lifted his small frame into my arms.

"Thick black hair lay across the child's face; I brushed it aside with as gentle a touch as possible, unable to look away from what I had done. He was just a boy; manhood had not even begun to trace lines upon his face. His skin was still smooth, his jaw line soft. Now dead, his body began to cool in my arms; his dark skin began to waxen and pale.

"Ivan was watching me with sympathetic eyes but also with pity. He knew what this would do to me. My only solace in being dispatched to this godforsaken land had been my hope that I could minister to the natives. To bring them into the fold of the Church, and now just such a child lay dead by my hand. 'It was an accident, Adrik. A tragedy to be certain, but just an accident,' Ivan was telling me, but I couldn't listen. I wouldn't listen.

"Tears brimmed in my eyes, and in spite of the soldiers gathering around me, they slipped out, running down my cheeks to mingle with the child's blood. For a few short moments, I was no longer part of the world. Time stood still.

"I dared look at no one. I could not face the guilty accusations written on the faces of the soldiers that had gathered around. They were watching me closely. What happens to a serf that kills a child? I knew they were thinking the same question. I did not know the answer; I did not care. A quick death would have been preferable to what was to come.

"The soldiers soon gave me privacy and looked away when I was unable to stop the tears. They bowed their heads when I began to pray and beg the Father for forgiveness. But one pair of eyes remained focused on me. I could feel them boring into the back of my skull. The rage was palpable and the air changed.

"An inner voice whispered for me to look up, to find the source of the rage, to explain the tragic nature of the mistake and to plead for forgiveness. A guilty conscious kept me from doing so, I suppose. Instead, I prayed for a dead child that no longer needed my supplications.

"I was never punished for my actions that day; the Baranov himself sought me out, his voice soft and calm as he said I was not to blame for the tragedy. No record was made of the child's death as it was hardly the kind of report you could send back to the Tsar.

"I often wondered if the lack of punishment added to my guilt. Perhaps if the Baranov had ordered a stripe or two on my back, I would have been able to put it behind me. I needed to feel some pain at what I had done, to bleed for my crime.

"Instead, I became an outcast, more so than I already was as a serf. Soldiers talked behind my back. Conversation would die as I entered the mess hall; the men would draw straws to determine who must take guard duty with me. The Aleutian natives eyed me warily.

"Ivan was the only man who stood by me, who remained loyal with no judgment. It was Ivan who had distracted the guard as I picked up the child's body, carrying it away to be buried that night. It seemed a cruel hoax, after having been murdered, to simply burn the child's body like the rest that were cremated that evening.

"And it was Ivan who held my hand when the nightmares began a few nights later."

I barely noticed when his voice stopped, so engrossed was I in the story that played out through the bond in such clarity that I could see perfectly the child that had died in his arms. I could feel the knife and how it slipped through the child's skin and the warmth of his blood on my forearm. I scratched at my own skin to get rid of the sensation.

What I couldn't brush away was the guilt that vibrated across the bond. Two centuries had come and gone, and this man, considered a monster, was still grieving over the death of a child. They say time heals all wounds, but Adrik was proof that time is not that powerful. His wounds were open and oozing.

He began to speak again, pictures reforming in his mind, as he continued his story.

"From the night of the child's death forward, I relived the experience in my dreams. The nightmares were persistent and inescapable. I could find not a comfortable night of sleep, and soon I was haggard. It was rumored that I was cursed among the citizens of the fort. My countrymen avoided me; the natives considered me possessed.

"I sought out the help of the surgeon, who thought me very near to mad. He treated me with one concoction after another. None of which were able to help me keep my eyes closed. The nightly tortures became so bad that I took to relieving other men of their evening guard duty. I could not sleep after such a nightmare; I was too terrified to close my eyes.

"On one particular evening, the dreams had been so violent that I had woken up gasping for air and beating my arms against the straw bed underneath me. My clothes were drenched despite the cold. The dream had woken me earlier than usual, leaving me with most of the night hours to face, awake and shaking in my bed. Out of sheer desperation, I went looking to relieve my friend Ivan from his night patrol.

"The weather had been particularly nasty that day with squalls coming in from the ocean nearly back to back. A blow-down wind late in the evening had sent ancient rooted trees crashing down the mountains. Afraid for their lives, the hunters scurried in from the mountains and bays with no pelts for their struggles and the fishermen returned with empty boats if they returned at all.

"A gloom had settled over the fort the rest of the day that carried over into the evening. The men settled into their quarters, and the Aleutians hid in their camps that sat alongside our palisade walls. Ivan was only too happy to give up his night duty on such an evening. Normally, he would have argued with me, knowing how desperately I needed to sleep. But as I said, the weather was obscene so I soon found myself walking the perimeter of the fort.

"Night duty brought fears of its own that had nothing to do with the weather. Remember, I was a serf of Slavic descent, raised on the stories of every kind of demon imaginable, and walking those trails was more than a little terrifying. Add in the surprise attacks of the Tlingit, who occasionally stole in from the mountains to seek revenge, and the occasional bear attacks, and you can understand why night duty could be quite dangerous. Perhaps that is the reason I sought it out so much; perhaps I had a secret craving for death.

"The fort was unnervingly dark that night; the fogs rolling in from the ocean so heavy that the lamps of the fort appeared little more than faraway twinkling candles. Rain, mixed with snow, fell continuously. Not so hard that I could not see to walk but enough that it was an impossibility to stay dry. Despite my parka, the rain found inroads into my underclothes and my boots. My gloves could not keep the tips of my fingers warm, and my lips were so cold they ached. Still I patrolled.

"I had just rounded the corner and began my ascent to the farther limits of the fort where the visitors' cabins sat when I saw Irena. Despite the weather and the lateness of the hour, she waited for me on her porch. I stopped, planning to turn and retrace my steps, but she beckoned me forward, saying that her fire had gone out and it needed to be restarted.

"I could hardly disobey an order from her, especially for something as necessary as a fire, given the weather. Her father was the Duke of Kozlow. She was nobility, and orders from her were to be obeyed as from the Tsar himself. Behind her, I could make out, through the windows, the figure of her native maid working in the kitchen. I was relieved; she had a chaperone.

"As a human, I was said to be handsome, beautiful actually. Many women had wanted me over the years, a few men as well. And as a serf, there was very little I could do about it. Beautiful serf children were often abused throughout their lives, and I had been lucky to be spared that by my masters.

"Irena had pursued me for weeks. The gossip around the mess hall in the evenings said she was a prolific lover. Any other man would have given their right eye to be close to her, but I wanted nothing more than to be as far from her as possible. I had avoided her at every turn, kindling her anger against me each time I refused her advances.

"Please understand that Irena was beautiful, and I was not immune to her charms. But my aspirations were not of the flesh; I wanted to be a part of the clergy. I had for months been beseeching the fathers to secure my serfdom from my owner as a donation to the Church.

"Irena was dressed that evening in the thinnest of chemises despite the ugliness of the weather. It was difficult for me to even walk past her into the home. The mists had collected on her skin, and through the moistened gown, I could make out the heaviness of her breasts, the darkness of their upturned tips. Her stomach was flat with youth, her pelvis tilted forward as she leaned against the columns of the porch, making the hollow between her thighs stand out all the more.

"I was a man, and she obviously wanted me, and I could feel myself rising in response. I had never been with a woman, and it crossed my mind to give in to her, to feel myself sinking into the softness of her body. How much easier it would be to not have to fight her. But I resisted, knowing I was struggling for a greater prize.

"I did my best to ignore her as I built the fire back, and soon the heat was radiating such that the air had lost its sting and the glow of the flames illuminated the room. I turned to go, whispering my wishes for her good evening without raising my head or meeting her eyes.

"I noticed then that her maid was gone. The house was small; I could see into every room, and the maid was nowhere. I realized the danger of my situation at that point, but it was too late. Irena was determined to have me and now we were alone.

"She was still wearing her rain-slicked chemise, but she discarded it now, the material dropping to her feet with the heaviness of the rain. She stood between me and the door. It was impossible to reach it without brushing against her skin.

"Looking back on that night, I should have run. I should have fled as fast as I could and given what small amount of money I had to a native with a canoe. If I could have gotten to the mainland, I might have stood a chance on my own. But I was a serf, and the thought of escaping had never occurred to me. I was raised to obey my master on this earth as in Heaven.

"Instead, I stood mute, my eyes cast down, not knowing what to do, but realizing the danger I was in. The seriousness of my situation danced in the air around me. My ears buzzed with fear.

"I felt her hands on my body, first on my arms and then my chest, and next her lips brushed mine. The intimacy of her touch startled me. It was not right for a woman of her station to be touching me. The consequences would be severe for no one except myself. I asked her to stop, pleaded with her in the name of the Church to let me alone.

"But she was the master and I was the slave; I stood paralyzed by fear as she slipped my heavy parka off and tossed it aside.

"'Do not deny me,' she warned. 'I will tell my father you forced me. I can only imagine what he would do to a man in your position who dared to defile his first-born daughter.'

"I had no defense against her. I was terrified. It would do no good to tell my story as I could hardly accuse the duchess of rape. I stood still as a ghost as she removed my shirt.

"I was trembling yet I was hard with desire. How could I not be? Would any man have been any different? She led me to her room at the back of the cottage and, like a lamb to the slaughter, I followed her.

"I do not recall every detail as fearful as I was, but I remember her long nails slicing into my back and my skin raising in angry whelps. She did the same to my neck. With practiced hands, she pulled my virgin cock from my pants, stroking it until I thought I would explode. This was all wrong, and though my body was betraying me in all ways, my mind screamed at me to leave, to protect myself, but it was too late.

"'Kiss me,' she whispered into my ear, and I did, my mouth lowering onto hers. Her lips were hot and demanding; I could feel them swell underneath my own. Her legs wrapped around my waist, her hands kneading and pressing on my buttocks. Beaded blood from her scratches ran down my back and onto the sheets, and I could feel the heat of her at my groin.

"My mind was still begging me to leave, run, anything but stay here in this room. But as so many men are, my spirit was willing but my flesh was very weak. But I was weak with fear as much as from lust. I lifted to push into her heat and..."

Adrik stopped then, the visions in his mind closing down. I gasped slightly as the movie in my head came to a stop as well.

He sat quietly beside me for a moment, saying nothing. His expression was full of self-loathing and hate. Finally finding the resolve, he continued. "Her father and six officers burst through the door. I, the beguiled slave, had been lured into a compromised position. The maid had slipped out the door for the purpose of fetching the duke. The blood dripping down my back and the scratch marks were the supposed proof of the rape.

"You see, Irena was an accomplished whore, but there was another skill she excelled in as well. She was a consummate liar. She began to cry as soon as she saw her father, begging him to save her from me. The maid later confirmed to the Baranov that Irena's menses had stopped. It was only this evening that the maid had realized what was happening as Irena had been too terrified to mention to anyone what I had supposedly been doing to her nightly.

"Now you might ask, why would not some man who knew the truth of Irena come forward? Had I not said she was a whore? But I ask you, why would anyone save a slave?

"The duke was livid. He could not see reason. Not a handprint could be seen on Irena; not a scratch marred her skin. She certainly did not look abused, but no one would have been able to rationalize with him even if anyone had been willing to try.

"Without consulting the Baranov, I was dragged out of the cabin to where a tall pole, used to dress out large game, was sunk into the ground. Blood and scraps of fat littered the ground at its base. It took four men to do it, but my arms were stretched high around the pole and secured with leather so tight that blood oozed from my wrists. I was to be whipped with the great knout.

"Do you know what it is?" Adrik asked me. His eyes had gone colder, harder.

I shook my head 'no'.

"The great knout, as it was called, was essentially a whip, the favored method of punishment in Russia. The handle was the size of one of my arms from which hung a wooden strap the length of my forearm. This ended in a metal ring to which were attached straps hung with knots of leather or wire hooks. The leather was soaked in milk and dried in the sun to make it hard.

"Fifty blows and above were considered a death penalty. Punishment by the knout was so exceedingly brutal that hardened criminals often lost consciousness just watching the sentence carried out on fellow criminals.

"I was never a vain man, but facing that knout, I pleaded with God that I not embarrass myself. That I remain on my feet, that I not beg for mercy, and that I not piss myself, and knowing that I would likely do all three before death claimed me.

"The ropes suspending my arms were pulled tighter such that my feet were lifted off the ground and I could just barely touch the balls of my feet to the earth. I was naked, my buttocks and privates exposed to the entirety of the camp, and I was utterly humiliated. The wind caressed my back, and chills raced the length of my spine. I shook with the anticipation of what was to come.

"Behind me, the men and women of the fort gathered. The duke had wanted a crowd and had sent a soldier to rouse the fort so there would be plenty of witnesses to my humiliation. To my left, Ivan stood, his face immobile until the knout was brought forward and tested by the Duke for strength. He took a step forward then, his face contorting with rage.

"I shook my head at Ivan, reminding him with my eyes to hold his tongue and do nothing stupid. There was no reason we both should die tonight. Besides, he had family to consider back in Russia, and the duke had a long reach of influence. Ivan's family could be tortured with merely a word from the duke.

"At first, I was certain I would die. The duke was a large man, quite capable of collapsing my spine with the whip. As much as I dreaded the pain of dying by the knout, I had no fear of death. I looked forward to it. It would be glorious, for as soon as my eyes closed to the darkness of this earth, they would open in Glory with the light of Heaven to illuminate me forever. There would be no more pain, no more nightmares, and I would never be a slave again.

"I bowed my head so that I could not see the crowd that had gathered around to watch the torture I must endure. Most of these were free men; they had never suffered at the hands of nobles nor faced the knout. They had not starved and withstood the knout for stealing food to feed their family. For them, this was a spectacle only—a sport.

"I closed my eyes and focused on what I would see in Glory instead of the heavy footsteps of the duke behind me.

"'Let this be a lesson to any man, free or otherwise, who thinks that he can lay hands on a woman above his rank,' the duke's voice rang out to the small crowd that had gathered around me.

"There was complete silence except the duke's exhalation as he threw his weight into the first blow. The air sang as the strap flew from his hands and my skin gave way beneath the leather as he sliced an inch wide strip from my neck to my buttocks.

"My body contorted, every muscle contracting along the length of my spine until I felt like a marionette whose strings were held by multiple people all moving in different directions. My blood spurted on the wind, the hot fluid spattering on my arms and face. I danced on my tiptoes, remaining on my feet out of sheer willpower.

"After the first blow, the duke asked for my confession. He promised to stop if I would declare his daughter guiltless. I inwardly resolved to remain truthful and prayed for a quick death. I prayed for forgiveness of my former sins and the strength to endure.

"By the tenth blow, my legs went out from under me, my bladder gave way, and I had lost so much blood that I could barely hold my head up. Still I would not confess to this crime I did not commit. One of the soldiers ran a log between my legs and tied my feet on either side to support me for further punishment; they cinched my arms up higher so the ropes might hold me steady.

"The blows resumed and kept coming methodically. I cannot even begin to explain the pain. My body was afire; the smell of my blood was thick in my nostrils. My back was a twisted mass of pulverized flesh, and my skin lay in strips at my feet, carved off my body like meat.

"I clenched my jaws so hard that I broke two teeth. One I managed to spit out; the other I swallowed in a paroxysm of pain. My shoulders dislocated from the muscle spasms as did one hip. When the crowd had counted out the sixteenth lash to fall across my back, I was certain I would not remain alive to endure another.

"At that point, I was in and out of consciousness. I would return to myself long enough to catch bits and pieces of Ivan's prayers on my behalf. The sound of some animal crying reached the haze of my mind. Sometime later, I recognized the cries as mine.

"The crowd urged me to confess. Even Ivan begged me at this point, but I refused. I was proud, for I had fought the good fight. I had kept the faith. Or so I thought. True hell awaited me, and if I had known that, I would have cursed the duke and spurred him to whip me harder and faster until my blood lay cast on the ground like a crimson cloak behind me. How I have begged that time could have been turned back on itself and I could have died that night, but it was not to be.

"My last conscious thought was to search the crowd for Ivan, for our eyes to meet and for him to know I had not been defeated. But it was not Ivan's eyes that met mine. It was the cold glare of Irena's maid. Her rage was palpable and familiar. It was the same rage I had felt the night the native child had died in my arms."

Adrik paused here, and I sat quietly beside him. The log underneath us was cold, and although I was still only dreaming, I couldn't help but shiver at both the wintery landscape and at the brutality he had experienced.

Light snowflakes had begun to drift down from heavy gray clouds that stood out in the dark sky. I pulled my knees to my chin, balancing carefully on the rough bark beneath me, but grateful for the warmth of my own skin. Oblivious to the weather he was creating around us, Adrik stared silently ahead.

If I could have thought of any words of comfort, I would have said them, but I had nothing but questions.

"Why didn't the duke whip you until you were dead? Why stop?"

"There were two reasons, I think, looking back on it," Adrik resumed. "The foremost being that he wanted my confession so that there could be no reproach of Irena. Being with child, she could not marry into the royal family, but with my confession, she, at least, would not be a harlot. Her family would have borne great shame if she had simply been a woman of loose standards.

"Secondly, Russian executions were unusually brutal. If the convicted became unable to bear the sentence, he would be cared for meticulously, and all efforts made to save him so that the sentence could be finished. So the duke hoped to save me so that he could whip me again. That was the way of things."

I nodded at his answers, and he continued with his story.

"The shivering of my bones is what woke me a few hours later; my teeth were clattering together from fever, and I awoke to find myself slung across a thin, miserable cot in a cell within the blockhouse used to house the occasional prisoner.

"My back had been dressed with plaster-coated rags in an attempt to staunch the bleeding and control infection, but it was clear the surgeon's efforts were failing. My skin was hot and damp to the touch, and blood soaked through the plaster such that it leaked onto the dirt floor. The sheets were sullied from a combination of blood and sweat.

"Fifty lashes and above was nearly always fatal. I had suffered forty I was told, and although I might have survived back in Russia, my chances were not good here in Alaska. The fort was lacking in bandages, nursemaids or even a clean, dry room in which to house me. I was grateful, for I so badly wanted to die.

"Against odds, however, I managed to survive the night, and I awoke the next morning while the surgeon changed the plastered rags on my back. The strips had dried into my wounds, pulling out dead tissue when the strips were yanked from my lacerations. The treatment was harrowing, and luckily I was in and out of consciousness while the surgeon worked on me. He slipped me whiskey to drink, to help cut the pain, but my bowels were so constricted, I could not keep it down.

"I awoke once more that afternoon at the insistence of a native woman who helped me drink a few sips of broth. She would not make eye contact with me as I begged to speak to one of the fathers. I know now that the lack of a father's visit should have been my first signal that things were not right, but I suppose I was too delirious to realize the oddness of the situation.

"I was allowed no visitors in those first two days, save the surgeon and the native who changed my bandages. Loneliness set in such that I began to look forward to the torture of clean bandages. At least I was able to see a human face.

"Each day was the same. The surgeon came in the morning, followed by a few sips of broth when my screams had died enough that I could swallow. The broth came again just before sunset, after which I spent a cold and miserable night with only myself and my thoughts to keep me company.

"And I thought a lot. Of my parents back at home, my brothers and sisters who remained in serfdom. I thought of Ivan often and, surprisingly, very little of the woman who had done this to me. I was dying after all; it was obvious to everyone, and I had no room in my heart for hatred and anger.

"My body convulsed with fever. My urine was little more than blood. My bowels had turned to water, and despite the surgeon's skilled hands, fresh blood still oozed from my wounds. I had survived the beating to die slowly by infection and blood loss.

"But I was concerned only for making my goodbyes. I missed Ivan. There were many things I needed to tell him. I wanted to pray with a father and hear my favorite scriptures once more.

"It was late in the afternoon; I had finished my broth and snow was falling thickly outside. I watched it through the one small window on the far wall of the blockhouse and only enough light filtered in that I could trace the largest cracks in the wooden walls with my eyes. Expecting a long and lonely night, I was surprised when the door to the blockhouse swung open.

"The wide form of the archimandrite, the highest ranking church official of the fort, teetered on the threshold. He hesitated for a moment as his eyes adjusted to the darkness before committing to the first step through the doorway. He lifted the hem of his garment in both hands, screwing his mouth up, as he looked distastefully around the room. I did not know the man personally, but I knew of him, and he was not renowned for visiting the poor and afflicted. How he came to Alaska remains a mystery to me.

"From my cot in the corner of the cell, I watched him as his eyes searched the darkness for me and chills lifted gooseflesh on my arms. Not so much from the cold air but from the visitor himself. Something was wrong. Very wrong if the highest-ranking father at the fort was here to see me.

"Finally locating me in the darkness, he settled himself down in a chair positioned in front of my cell. I could have reached out and touched the rich fabric of his cloak if I had dared. Instead, I tugged the cotton blanket I had been given higher on my shoulders and struggled to sit up in deference to his position.

"The archimandrite, Father Solinov, folded his soft white hands gently in his lap and watched me momentarily before he began to speak. The full weight of his authority had settled across the room so that even the dust motes no longer danced in the thin ribbon of light bending through the window. I was terrified.

"'Child, I have come to check on your well-being,' he said. His voice was thin and reedy like his arms and legs. He was too soft and too cultured for a father in this wild frontier.

"'I cannot lie, Father. Neither body nor soul is well. Have you come to pray with me and give me comfort in my last hours?' I asked hopefully. My voice was barely audible even in the hushed silence of the room.

"'And I cannot lie, child. I am not here for your comfort. I come for your confession. Give voice to your sins for as the scriptures say 'by the mouth, confession is made unto salvation.' You are not long for this world. Death waits either from the knout or from the sickness that rages in your body. God's justice will not be denied. Confess so that He may forgive you. So that the young Irena can have justice and that your conscious may be clean as you cross the veil.'

"'Father,' I said, 'if confession were possible, it would be given. But how does one confess what one has not done? How does one admit to a crime that one has not committed? Is that not a lie and yet another sin? And then how does one ask forgiveness for the second sin without making bad the prior confession?'

"Exhaustion was taking its toll on my mental and physical strength, and I dropped my head in my hands, fighting a wave of dizziness that threatened to make the world go dark. It had happened several times in the last few hours, but each time, I had been unmercifully brought back to consciousness by the pain in my back.

"'Son, there is a witness. The native woman who serves Irena bears witness to your vile rape of the future Duchess. Why would she lie against you? What logic is there in this charade that you continue?' His face lifted in a convincing smile.

"I stared back at him, unconvinced. During my imprisonment, I had considered this from nearly angle, and I knew the Archimandrite would gain from my confessing to this sin. The stripes on my back had washed part of my innocence away. I had begun to see the world and the players in it in a less loving light. If the Archimandrite could obtain an admission of guilt, the duke would no doubt be in his gratitude. He might even be brought home to Russia; at the very least, his standing for the next highest ranking in the Church would be enhanced.

"The surgeon had been urging me to confess for days, arguing that the sentence would be lighter, and there was a chance I might live through the rest of the knouting. I had spent many hours comparing the few choices I had, and I knew there was only one correct path, to simply hold to the truth.

"The matter was very straightforward to me. How could a man admit to such a heinous crime as rape simply to save his life? Admitting to such evil was surely evil in its own right. Could God forgive me the sin of lying done simply to save myself? Was it not possible that what had occurred and what was still to occur was merely a tribulation that I must endure even if it cost me what most men held so dear? My life was not so valuable to me. A better place waited.

"I suppose the father could see the resolve in my face when I answered him. 'What appears a charade to you, Father, is simply my burden to bear. I will not admit to such a deed despite these women who bear false witness against me. Innocence is mine and will remain so in death.'

"The passion of my words could be heard in the small confines of the quarters, despite my weakness, and I raised my eyes briefly from their place of deference to the archimandrite to look him in the eye for one moment. There was no mercy in the face that stared back at me. Not a hint of kindness or understanding.

"'No, my child,' the archimandrite said, 'you will not die an innocent man. You will die a condemned one. For since you cannot find the conviction to atone for your sins and are determined to persist in your disobedience, I have no recourse but to excommunicate you from the Church which you claimed many times in the past to hold in the highest esteem. I feel our trust in you these past months has been misplaced. We have welcomed you with open arms. We have loved you as a brother. We have prayed for you, and yet you have revealed your true nature—a lion in a den of innocents. Until you have recognized your crimes and confessed, you cannot enter the church or take sacraments. You will die soon, and it will be a final parting as they lay your bones on unhallowed ground. For there on that dismal ground, your remains will never rot, and in that unnatural state, you will lie until the Judgment Day, unreconciled to God. May He tug at the strings of your heart and bring you to your senses before death carries you beyond His mercy forever.'

"Hearing the words as the man spoke them, I, at first, did not react. It was surprising to hear them pour forth from the mouth of the archimandrite so easily, as if it bothered him not at all to speak them. He cast my soul aside like one casts out the garbage, without a second thought. I could see in his expression that he enjoyed stripping away the one thing that mattered to me. Surely I had misunderstood him.

"I cast a questioning look in the direction of the man. 'Father, did you just...'

"'Yes, child. I did.' Twisting the corners of his mouth down, the father feigned sadness but laced in his voice was a coldness that gripped an icy hand around my heart.

"A great void opened in the pit of my belly and, the pain forgotten in my back, I lunged to my feet. I gripped one of the cold metal bars of my prison in one hand and forced my face as far as it would go between two others. With my other arm, I reached desperately towards the archimandrite. He took a step back as I did so, watching me surreptitiously for a moment before turning to leave.

"'Father. Father! Please, I beg of you. Do not do this. The Church is all I have.' My hands twisted towards the priest in midair as if mentally willing the man to be touched by my destitution.

"'Yes? Is there something you wish to say?' He smiled eagerly at me, waiting for words that would never come.

"'Father. Oh, God, please, Father. I beg you. I cannot confess something I have not done. It would just be another sin. It would be wrong. You are condemning me. Please, have mercy on me.'

"'I turn deaf ears to your lies. When you are ready to confess, call for me and I will come. Remember, you have so little time left.'

"His words died on the wind as he turned and stepped out into the fading light of a winter day but not before I caught a small smile of satisfaction on the face of the man who should have been there to bring me comfort.

"With the loss of my soul came the loss of muscle control, and I slid down the bars to land on the dirt floor of my cell. I watched the door that the father left through battle with a wind gust. Fluttering for a matter of moments, the heavy door finally ceased its struggle and banged closed with a finality that matched the words of the priest, leaving me truly alone without even my religion to comfort me.

"In all of my years, I had never experienced such devastation. It raced across my every fiber, and I cried aloud, hard sobs wracking my body as I pleaded to the heavens. I grasped the bars in front of me, shoving violently against their uneven surfaces. As I did so, my wounds split asunder, blood soaking through the bandages so rapidly that my trousers could not contain it. But still I continued to push and pull against the bars, my loud cries no doubt heard by the passersby outside. But no one would come to the aid of an excommunicated rapist.

"It was the first time in my existence that my mind had been unfettered by the Church. Hate was a foreign emotion to me, but I embraced it as it began to breed in the wounded remnants of my soul. Devastation morphed into rage, and an idea began to take hold as I sought out a method of revenge on the woman who had orchestrated my downfall. No doubt, she knew of what had been done to me and still she had not retracted her lies.

"Glancing down at the floor as rivulets of blood coursed down my back, I noticed a small pool of it at my feet. I let go of the bars and slid down the cold walls of the blockhouse as I studied the red fluid. My shaking hand paused in midair, my fingers curling into the palm of my hand before I found the resolve to draw one finger through the bloody puddle.

"How badly I craved Irena's blood. I wanted to see it on my fingertips and dip my hands into it. I wanted her cursed eternally as I had been. And yet I could not reach her for she was far removed from me.

"I studied my blood closely, watching as it began to congeal on my fingertip. It had a pungent odor, and I gagged thinking of how it had dripped from the deep wounds of my back. Then I thought the unimaginable. I was already excommunicated. Why not go the next mile?

"Suicide would ensure that I rose from my grave in such a form that I could pass my curse on to Irena. She would suffer as I did; I would make sure of it. My mind was no longer held in check by thoughts of purity, and so I made my plans.

"The ceiling rose above me, forming a peak in the center of the cell. Thick logs made up the supports, two of which ran the length of my cellblock. The blockhouse had been constructed out of strong Sitka spruce in the shape of an octagon. Only the one small window served to provide any light. No one outside would notice my activities. If they did, they would likely be too late to stop my plans.

"My hands were accustomed to hard work, and the blanket from my bed came apart easily in them. My anger bred strength for my arms and legs, and a few moments later, I had a serviceable noose.

"I used the bed turned on its end for a scaffold to stand upon as I tied the noose to the supporting beams. I held onto it while I rested and considered my plans. Did I really want to do this? I thought of my options one last time.

"Confession was not a possibility. I had not raped Irena, and confession of the crime would bring no resolution to my soul, for I could only be re-instated to the Church if my heart was truly repentant.

"My excommunication was complete, and despite how I felt about the priest, I believed the man had the power to do it. He was the archimandrite after all. Had he not been vested with the right?

"I was terrified, but my terror was not as deep as the hatred and rage brewing in me. Never had I allowed such violent emotions to take hold of my heart, and I could only interpret this as proof that I truly was cut off from everything good and pure.

"As I hovered at the edge of my human life, I did not question that I deserved my fate, for I most certainly did. Tonight, I would finally pay for my sins. The native child would be avenged. Perhaps the archimandrite in his priestly heart had recognized me for what I was. He simply had discerned the wrong sin.

"I could forgive him but there was no room in my heart for Irena. She had to pay for her sins as well. Interested only in securing Irena's fate, I pushed all hopes of reconciliation from my mind and focused on the noose, using both hands to cinch the knot tightly around my neck.

"I trembled with my exertions and the bed frame shook underneath my feet. My heart beat wildly in my chest. My breaths came quick and shallow, and although I would be beyond death in mere moments, I felt more alive than I ever had.

"Looking death in the eyes gave me sudden clarity of vision. I realized for the first time how young I was and how many regrets I had now that I had no remaining years to live. In my too-short life, I had never even considered looking for love nor had I bothered to make many friends. Other than my mother, there would be no woman to mourn me. My existence would end with me, without children to prolong my life with their remembrances of me, no grandchildren with whom to boast grand tales of my youth.

"And for the first time, I could feel the inkling of caring about such things now that it was too late. But even as I craved these things, my heart hardened when I thought of all I had lost.

"I lifted my arms out to my sides, inhaling my last lungful of air, and leaped with all my remaining strength, bringing my feet down on the shaky surface on which I stood.

"The bed frame splintered under my weight, and with nothing to stop my fall, my body whiplashed against the strongly braided rope that hung me. My body gyrated wildly in the air. I grasped at the rope out of sheer instinct, but as I had expected and relied on, my upper body strength was not enough to pull the weight of my body up and allow me to suck in a breath. Even if I could have, it would have been futile, as my strength would eventually wear out, and I would strangle once more.

"I clawed desperately at the rope but soon lost the ability to hold my arms above my head and both limbs, not quite in unison, dropped heavily to my sides. I sucked hopelessly for air, my belly caving in with the effort. Long after my vision tunneled, I could still feel myself spinning on the axis of the rope that held me.

"My body listed for what felt like an eternity. My human death did not come from a broken neck. Instead, I strangled on the noose, so I had time to focus on the women who had put me in this predicament, lest I forget in death what in the last moments of my life had become so important."

# Chapter 11

Adrik's voice died away and the memories of his past stopped playing in my head. I felt him slightly disconnect from me. The bond was still there, but he'd closed his mind for a moment. I suppose like humans, some memories are too important not to share but too painful when you finally do. He needed a moment of privacy, and I let him have it. A few minutes passed before he lifted his head and looked at me.

"I'm so sorry for what happened to you. I had no idea," I said.

"Irena paid for her sins. She and I are even now and I need no one's pity."

"I don't pity you, Adrik, but I am sorry for all that you lost. Still, I don't understand how committing suicide allowed you to curse Irena," I said.

"I was already excommunicated, so my chances of rising as a vampire were good. If I committed suicide, it was almost a certainty I would rise a vampire, and then I could curse her with my fate by marking her. Revenge was my main concern, so I did everything in my power to ensure my transformation.

"It was Ivan who cut me down that next morning and buried me. And it was because of him that my plans worked. He did not know it, of course. I had asked the native woman who served my meals the morning of my last day alive to carry a simple message to Ivan saying I fully expected to be dead by morning so serious were my wounds. My only request of him, even before I was excommunicated, was that he bury me in an unknown location and allow no one to desecrate my body. The people of the fort would have been anxious to see me staked in my casket since they considered me cursed after the incident with the native child. In those times, any oddness associated with a person could result in a stake through their corpse and the thought terrified me.

"Ivan honored my request, despite my suicide, and retrieved my body the morning following my death. He buried it in the one spot that not a soldier from the fort was brave enough to enter, the ground where the children had been killed in the Battle for Sitka. It was long considered cursed, and no man—white or native—would approach it. Ivan was my one true friend. He must have been terrified, knowing the old legends that I would rise and come to him. Still, he proved as loyal in death as he had been in life."

"What was it like?" I questioned. "Rising?"

Adrik took a deep, unneeded breath, holding it inside for what felt like several minutes but was surely much shorter. "The experience is difficult to explain to one who has never died and the act did not happen immediately as I had expected. Rather, it was a process that unfolded over days. My consciousness returned first, but it faded in and out as a human fades in and out of sleep before fully waking for the day.

"The semblance to my human existence ended there, for nothing else seemed even remotely related to the condition in which I had previously lived. No part of me felt human. My chest seemed a void for not a thing stirred within the cavity. My heart was silent, and my lungs were nothing more than dead space. Even my skin had a smoothness that could not have belonged to a man. My every mortal ache and pain was gone and the hideous burn of my lacerated back was only a memory.

"My body was alive with a thousand new sensations. The pads of my fingertips danced across the wood of my coffin and I could feel each splinter. I stroked the coarse wool of my garments and could count every fiber. My body was muscled and whole underneath my hands. My member sprung to life in my hand as I stroked its length. I felt strong. Immortal. Death had not touched me.

"But not everything was as glorious as my immortal body. While my sensations were strong and new so also were the hungers that burned in the pit of my bowels.

"Naturally, I wanted blood, and the mere thought of the substance would constrict my throat and cause my bones to ache. The smell of my friend Ivan hung heavy in the air of my coffin, and each time I inhaled of its sweetness, I would gnash my teeth and scream in hunger. My throat burned the same as a man on a deserted island surrounded by an ocean of water that he could not drink. My mind conjured images of waterfalls running with blood and rain that turned red upon my skin.

"But I had other cravings, some expected and some not. I, who had been so deathly afraid of the terrors of the night, now longed to be a part of that darkness. The night called to me, and I ached to be free of my prison. The muscles of my legs begged to stretch and join the other predators that roamed the woods. I missed the magic of the moonlight and the whip of the wind on my skin.

"My mind was free as well and every thought that had been shut off to me before was opened up. And thus, I craved all the vices I had denied myself through the years. I longed to hurt the men I had prayed for only days before. I wanted to know the feel of a wanton woman's hands. I wanted to experience drunkenness. I feared nothing, except that final Judgment Day, and since I had sinned the worst sin that could be sinned, what fear had I in a few more?

"And each one of my sinful urges centered on Irena. How I desired her! The thought of her bones crushing in my hands and her blood running down my throat made me dizzy with anticipation. I wanted to see fear bloom in her eyes when she realized my plans for her.

"All the self-control I had once possessed was tossed aside. My patience was destroyed, and I lusted for blood and revenge with such fervor that I would beat my hands and head against the coffin lid in my angst to escape.

"And nothing held me in the grave except the earth itself. I lay in unhallowed ground in a simple wooden box. My body was whole and intact. My arms unbound, and no Crucifixes ground through my body. No rocks in my mouth to still my bite. No bed of garlic to burn the skin from my bones. I had been buried without a single sacrament of protection.

"Fools! All of them. Even Ivan who had buried me in this pristine condition. To bury the condemned man without any protection from the unholy nature they had forced upon me. It was as if they believed in good but not in evil.

"But I could find no way out of my grave, and I was weak from lack of sustenance. I clawed the underside of my coffin lid until my nails broke off into the wood. That tomb and the dirt heaped upon it would have been no match for my strength if I had tasted even a swallow of blood.

"In desperation and boredom, I turned to gnawing at my arms and hands. I cleaved the tissue from my bones, and when I had chewed through all the flesh I could reach and could find no more blood, I gnawed my exposed skeleton until shards of bone lodged in my teeth. And when not an unmarked spot could be found on my arm bones, I cried. Pitiful guffaws that could have been heard from atop the grave if any other creature had been close enough to hear. When I could no longer find the energy to cry, I would return to my bones and gnaw some more.

"In the daylight hours, I simply listened to the sounds of the world above me while I lay paralyzed by the sun. Without my crying, the wildlife would venture back to the forest around my gravesite but never close enough that they would step on the grave. When my body was re-animated during the night, the animals would scatter, for they recognized my state clearer than any human. Animals do not question what their senses tell them is real.

"The beginning of the thirteenth night of my imprisonment found me noisily sucking on one scarred arm bone. Divots marked its surface where my teeth had gnashed the bone in my desperation. Not a shred of tissue remained from my mid upper arms down to my fingertips, and the bones of my hands clinked against one another as I moved.

"I was half-listening to the night sounds above me while I worked on my gory task. The stillness, brought on by my presence, weighed heavily on the world above. Not a living animal could be found stirring near my grave, and it was only the uneven patter of rain drops tapping the earth of my gravesite that provided any noise at all.

"Against the backdrop of the rain, a new sound began to take form. It was a soft thudding that became slowly more insistent as it approached until I could recognize the pattern of a man walking. A shiver of excitement rolled up my spine, my muscles contracting so strongly that they lifted my body from the coffin floor before dropping me back down again.

"I froze in place, my teeth clenched upon my own bone. I struggled to relax and turned my face from my arm to study the sounds above me. I was as silent as the proverbial grave, and I dared not even blink for fear that the sound would reach the passerby above me. It was illogical, of course, but the knowledge did not quell the fear.

"The footsteps were the first human sounds I had heard in my new life. I was certain they belonged to a man, a native male to be exact, for the steps traced a confident path through the dark forest overhead. The white men of the fort could not move so calmly through the woods. Their gait is offset by the constant looking over their shoulder. They are not at home in the wild.

"I lay tensed in my coffin, unmoving and unblinking, as the footfalls approached my grave and then hesitated before finally coming to a stop. Above me, the man shifted his position in reference to the newly dug grave; his knees creaked as he bent to examine the fresh dirt. The rub of his leather-skin parka reached my ears along with the light tinkle of oyster shells sewn on for decoration.

"Though I could not actually smell him, my mind imagined his fragrance, and I went mad with hunger. My hands clawed desperately at the coffin lid; my nails scratched deep grooves down its wooden length. I bucked against the wood of the coffin, but it would not budge with the weight of the earth that pressed it down. I fought my enshrinement with skinless fists.

"The grind of the human's joints as he stood to go reached my ears, and I began to cry once more as the only human who had ventured close now began to move away. Howls of pain tore from my throat. I roared my disgust so violently that my own ears ached with the noise.

"The man hesitated then at the keening sounds coming from underground, and I heard his heart palpitate and pick up as he listened to the inhuman sounds coming from the grave. His breathing became harsh, and he lurched forward, gaining momentum, to sprint for safety.

"Frenzied by the reverberations of the human's heart, I went completely insane inside the coffin. I twisted violently, screaming and growling more like a wild animal than a man, and in pure instinct, I reached out with my mind, imagining the feel of the dirt under my feet and the scent of his blood in the air.

"As I did so, my bones collapsed from within and my skin melted away, and I felt the hard confines of the casket in its final attempt to contain me before I melted through the layers of wet dirt and leaves. From a thick mist, I materialized atop my grave.

"It was my first view of the world as a vampire, but I did not take time to appreciate it. I was too focused on the hunger burning in the pit of my belly. The scent of the man permeated the forest, and it was so strong and fresh that I could nearly see it winding through the trees like a red ribbon. I followed it without a second thought.

"I caught the human just as he entered the mountain pass that would lead him back to his people. No doubt, he had thought himself safe, and that whatever beast he had heard from under the ground was long since put behind him. Perhaps he even questioned whether he had heard anything at all.

"His breath was coming in loud wheezes and, unable to run any longer, he sucked in deep mouthfuls of the cold night air as he slowed to a walk. The beadwork on his tunic danced with the effort of his breathing. The smell of his sweat mingled with the warm smell of blood, and his muscles shook with fatigue; the clamshells decorating his hair tinkled nervously around his head.

"Confident of his escape, he was focused on reaching the mountain pass and did not see me until I was close enough to clamp one hand around his throat. I lifted him up so that only the tips of his moccasins could reach the earth and his feet danced underneath him as he searched for traction in the dirt.

"He brought his hands up and fastened them on the bones of my forearm, his eyes widening in surprise and terror at my lack of skin. Although I could see the sickened expression cross his features each time his nails scraped my exposed bones, he still clawed desperately at my arm, trying to break my grip.

"When he realized my grasp was a death hold from which he could not escape, he stopped struggling and looked me full in the face. 'Are you the Kushtaka?' he asked me in between the gasps of his lungs.

"I had learned enough Tlingit and Aleutian as a human working among the clergy that I could understand the basics of their speech and a few of their customs. The Kushtaka was the river otter man, a shape-shifting creature that captured men in the woods or in the sea. The unhappy victim was then drowned and taken back to the underwater home of the river otter and turned into another Kushtaka. The victim would never be reincarnated back into the clan of his people and would never walk in paradise. Instead, he would haunt the forest and the coastline for an eternity, searching for his own victims.

"'No,' I shook my head at him. 'I am not Kushtaka.'

"By this time, the human had dropped his hands from my arms and hung limply in my grasp. I was watching the blood drain from his cheeks when I saw a fleeting hope cross his face. A moment later, I felt the tip of his knife cut through the skin of my belly as he tried in vain to disembowel the dead.

"My blood ran cold down my legs and dripped onto my naked feet, staining the snow underfoot, and I released him as I stared at the ground underneath us. The native took a step back, repulsed at the red fluid that had sprayed across his own belly and now dripped from him to the ground as well.

"He looked at me with a new terror now as he recognized that my blood was not warm. It did not steam upon the wind, and I did not drop to my knees as one whose belly has been ripped asunder.

"'I am not the Kushtaka,' I repeated again. 'I am vampire.' The word had no meaning to him and he only stared at me dumbly for the span of a breath before his body braced to sprint.

"I caught him in my arms before he could get more than a step, and I forced his head back so I could look at him and he surrendered his gaze willingly.

"There were many things I wanted to tell him, and I found that as our eyes locked, I could reach his mind without the need of speech. I showed him what I was and I promised him a quick death and swore that I would deliver his body to his people so it could be burned in their way. I would not keep him from paradise.

"I could have pressed my will upon him and made him mindless as I took his life. But that is not the way to deliver death to a warrior. He did not want to die, but he was not afraid. This man deserved the dignity to face his end like a man, to look it full in the face and make his peace.

"I gave him these moments before I turned his knife upon himself. His hand remained on the carved, bone handle as I placed the beveled tip over his fluttering heart. Basking for one more moment in the glow of its pounding, I plunged the stake between the native's ribs, skewering the organ on its point. His heart spasmed once but did not beat again as his mouth opened, his last breath of air flowing out and into the wind.

"It took only a few moments for the blood flowing forward in his body to stop in its journey, but with my hunger raging, I marked those seconds each as an eternity. Finally, his eyes became hollow and the muscles of his hands quit their twitching.

"As he collapsed, I lowered him to the forest floor. His dead eyes watched me as I sunk my fangs into his elbow. The artery was still hot, and I drank until I could expel not another drop, and for the first time since my rebirth, the raging fire in the pit of my stomach was dampened, if not quenched.

"As I rose from him, I felt new—more alive than I had when life had truly been mine. I inhaled a deep breath and extended my arms over my head, the flesh already regenerating as I did so. I stretched upwards as high as I could before twisting my torso to either side. Strength rippled through my muscles as I flexed my arms and legs. The cool air tickled the skin of my scalp as it ruffled through my thick hair and waved lacy fingers across my exposed skin.

"I felt whole now, and looking down, I took note of my nakedness. Smooth skin, gleaming even in the moonless night, rippled across the thick muscles of my chest. My abdomen was finely notched as it tapered to a tight ligament that stretched between my hip and groin before flaring out slightly across the taut muscles of my thighs and buttocks. My phallus thrust forward proudly, each inch hard and firm from my recent feed. I stroked it once, anticipating its use another night.

"I flexed the muscles of my arms feeling the strength. I sucked in the air, tasting the forest in the back of my throat. Throwing out my chest, I let out a blood-curdling roar, listening as it reverberated off the mountains. I had run without breath and my heart lay as still in my chest as if I were truly dead indeed.

"Without a fearful thought, I scaled the cliffs that led to the mountaintop with only the tips of my fingers and my toes. I climbed so quickly my skin barely grazed the granite walls. Without the need to remain jointed, I could stretch ridiculous distances, and with my newfound strength, I could hold on to the cliff with one hand and swing far to the right or the left.

"I had reached the tree line of the mountain above which nothing grew. Ice hung in sheets and bits of it dug sharply into my skin. The air was thin, but I had no cares—no worries. I was as icy as the landscape around me, but I had no fear of this frozen wasteland. It was my empire, and I was a vampire, cold and glorious. All the chains of my previously constrained life had fallen away, and I did not care that no part of me appeared human any longer.

"Lying in the shadow of the mountain below, I could make out the body of the man I had killed. I felt no guilt, but I had no argument with the human. The native had simply served as the bait to draw me from the grave. He had unleashed the powers that I did not know I possessed.

"I had promised him a quick death, which I had delivered. I had also promised to deliver his body to his people so that it could be burned. I lifted my head to the wind and sucked in a lungful of air, tasting the flavors that flower across my palate. Once you smell blood, you will never forget the fragrance, and it was easy to recognize the small band of humans that lay ahead of me in the dark. Probably a hunting party that wanted something different than the usual seafood fare of their diet and had come looking for black-tailed deer.

"Or perhaps they preferred the taste of settling old scores with the Russians. The human I had killed had been traveling in the general direction of the fort before he stumbled onto my gravesite. Perhaps he had been bent on vengeance.

"Not that I was concerned. I had no care for the humans at the fort, although I did not wish them any particular harm. That part of my previous life was gone, and my humanity seemed a faraway notion, a quaint idea that had once weighed heavily on my mind. I was beyond that. Their schemes and affairs had no bearing on me now. Except Ivan of course, who had been my friend, my one true ally despite my vanishing humanity, and for Irena, who owed me a debt of human blood.

"Finding the small encampment of humans posed no difficulty, as the stench of the human excrement surrounding the camp acted as a beacon for any predators—including me. Stretched across the front of the small camp were two smoking racks which proved a couple of their hunts had been successful.

Only partially smoked, the meat meant that the natives had no plans to move their camp immediately. Three brush lean-to's stood a few feet to the south of the meat racks. Each one was small, approximately six feet long and three feet tall and the open ends of the structures were covered by the thin wool blankets that the trading company was so fond of handing out as gifts.

"There were three men and one woman asleep in the shanties. None woke to my presence as I positioned the native's body beside the small fire that gently burned, releasing smoke to preserve the meat. I deposited the corpse, shying away from the fire as I did so as even the dim flames evoked a deep fear in my core.

"I backed a respectable distance away and crouched low to the ground as a human stirred inside the tent. The young female turned restlessly in her sleep, her breath sliding out in a long sigh. As she twisted, her pulse naturally increased for a few seconds before falling as she succumbed to deeper sleep.

"I could not leave once I had listened to the utterances of her heart. I pressed myself against the damp ground, bits of leaves and moss digging into my skin as I listened to the woman. Desire finally overcame the logic that I had taken enough blood for one night. I was merely greedy as I crept to the brush shelter and gently swept back the skin curtain just far enough to allow my form. In one step, I crouched over her sleeping body.

"Black hair in a tumble around her head, the native woman lay with her lower body turned towards the sleeping man beside her, her upper body turned slightly away from him. Both hands rested on her abdomen, flattening the material of her dress to her body, her breasts tugging on the material with each breath.

"Lust coursed its way through me like lava filling my blood vessels, and the air on my naked skin felt even cooler in contrast to the hot air rolling off of hers. I leaned ever nearer to her. Her dark skin clashed with my paleness as I traced the smooth skin of her neck with one icy finger.

"A slight flutter of dark lashes was her only reaction to the vampire that knelt beside her. Feeling a power rise up in me, I pressed my will upon her, forcing her further into sleep as I trailed cool fingers down to massage a limp nipple. I applied more pressure, twisting it gently in my fingers. A stiff peak formed in my hand and her legs parted slightly beneath the blankets.

"As her pulse rose, my desire grew rapidly until my erection lay thick along my leg. I would take this woman tonight; there was no reason not to give in to my wants. The dawn was hours away yet; time remained on my side, and I could spirit her into the darkness and no human would be the wiser until morning. I would be safely in the ground before they awoke.

"I slipped my arms underneath her sleeping form as I whispered deep sleep into her subconscious and lifted her to me. She was very beautiful, or perhaps it was simply that she was the first woman I had beheld with my new eyes. Her dark hair lay draped across my arms. Her lips were red with youth, and her body corded with muscles from hard work. How different from the soft and lazy Irena.

"Irena. Just the thought of her name cooled the need for the woman in my arms. The grip of revenge was stronger than my physical need and I decided to savor my ardor, the peak of my wanting for Irena. In her unwilling arms, I would slake my all-consuming lust.

"I took one last look at the sleeping woman and found her inadequate for what I really wanted. I would find no satisfaction in her body, and so I placed her back in her sleeping blankets, untouched and unmolested.

"The native men I killed and consumed before heaping their bodies into a great fire that would usher them to their afterlife. The woman I left alive. No doubt she would return to her people with stories of a murderous Kushtaka that had spared her life. I had given her a gift actually, for she would be considered blessed and be regarded as a powerful shaman.

"Turning from the camp, I lifted the last tendrils of my

control from the woman's mind and slipped into the darkness. Dawn was coming, and I could feel the paralyzing power of the sun. The very thought of it created in me a longing for the dirt I had been created in. I could no more have ignored the call of that ancient tradition than the cry for blood."

# Chapter 12

The gruesome images rolled to a stop as Adrik stopped thinking of the past for a moment, and I was glad. Seeing those innocent men die was painful to watch, and worse yet was the flutter I felt in my abdomen while he talked. It reminded me of watching one of my cousins pull the wings off butterflies as I kid. I was mortified and yet I couldn't look away.

"Why are you judging me?" he asked, sifting through my thoughts. "It is simply my way. Besides, I see the same blackness in you. I know the things you wish to do to Joel."

"I'm not judging you, but those native men were innocent. They had done nothing to you. Joel, on the other hand, is an asshole and deserves everything I want to do to him."

"Ahh, I see. You think there are degrees of murder. Perfectly legitimate to kill for the sake of revenge, but hunger, now that is another thing entirely."

He was mocking me, his eyes narrowed with sarcasm.

"Not that I care, Tamara. I can hardly stand in judgment over you for wanting revenge. I certainly sought it out and I would do it all over again."

"Then what are you saying?" I asked hatefully.

"Recognize your actions for what they are before you do them. The consequences will be much easier to accept if you do not think yourself falsely accused."

"Like you, Adrik?"

"No. Nothing like me. Just advice from a man that could not

take his own counsel."

"Tell the rest of the story please," I urged, wanting to put an end to our tense conversation. "But first can you tell me why you had to return to the grave. Why couldn't you go somewhere else?"

"I cannot explain the tenets of vampirism, only tell you what they are. From the time of our rising, we cannot leave our gravesite for six months. We are bound to return to it at daybreak. It is a calling that we feel in our bones, and even if we try to ignore the call, we cannot. Our body will, of its own volition, return there. Perhaps it is nature's way of providing protection for our friends and family since our whereabouts will be known for that time period. Just like the crowing of the cock, I think. He crows not to tell the vampire when to go to ground but instead to tell the humans when it is safe to open their doors.

"But there was no protection for Irena when I came for her the evening following my rising. Daylight was a long-lived hell, but as the final rays of the disappearing sun lost their clutch on the landscape, my muscles awakened. I was renewed. Fresh blood coursed through me, and I licked my lips. The taste of the men I had killed the night before lingered still and I savored it.

"Certain the world above me stood in darkness, I closed my eyes and let myself fall apart. I passed through the layers of my grave and stood, whole, above my crypt.

"I flexed my muscles, not out of any need but simply because it felt good. I took in a deep breath, and my chest expanded as the air passed across my vocal cords, spilling down in lungs that no longer needed air. The sweetness of newly fallen snow danced across my tongue, a sharp contrast to the earthy rot of the grave.

"In the breeze, my skin cooled, and looking down, I took note of my nakedness. Pale, I would appear the alien, the outsider. Clothes were a necessity, and at first, I thought to dig to the depth to my coffin and retrieve the burial clothes.

"It had been two weeks since I had awoken, and each night I had dug a fingernail through the wood of my coffin lid to mark the time. The outline of the grave had begun to fade as leaves, stained dark with rain, blew across the turned earth of the crypt. I did not wish to draw attention to the gravesite by disturbing it, and so, unclothed, I walked towards the fort with thoughts of blood on my mind.

"My movements were silent, and in only minutes, I stood on the outskirts of the fort. Approaching from the northern end to avoid the sea, I melted to the ground where the tree line met the cleared land of the fort.

"Becoming part of the landscape, I lay in the shadows as the smells of the fort washed across me. I could see the garrison atop the Round Hill, the most secured portion of the encampment. A soldier stood lookout in the blockhouse, smoke from his cigar hanging neatly around his head, making his fur hat look like a round, gray blob. He gazed out at the ocean and paid no attention to the ground at his feet.

"From the middle of the fort, cattle stamped their feet nervously. A sheep bleated, its fearful noise unnoticed by the sentry standing atop the Round Hill. The soldier in the garrison had pulled out another cigar, and another young corporal had climbed up to join him. They talked quietly of fur prices and the rising cost of fresh meat.

"To my left, the cabin Irena shared with her father stood alone. The surrounding buildings were not currently in use, and only the light from Irena's lamps broke up the darkness. I could hear her laughter mixing with the deeper voice of a man. She had a caller, and I was not surprised at the smell of lust leaching out from the interior of the cabin. The beat of their hearts was thick and full as they recovered from their activities. Another human, a woman, walked softly around the front room of the cabin, her steps quiet but sure.

"The sound of those three hearts was almost more than I could bear, especially that of Irena's. Their very vibrations shimmered the air around me. My body pulsed with each beat. Pulling me forward, like strings on a marionette, I rose from the ground to my full height and soundlessly I walked towards the cabin where she lay.

"I studied the entrance to the small cabin before I drew too close. On the small porch, a wet, muddy rug covered the lowest step; the roof had been freshly swept of spruce needles. Lamplight flickered in the thick glass of the south-facing window; a curtain wavered in the slight breeze that found entrance through a crack.

"Inside the cabin, the human male prepared to leave. He slid his legs into his trousers, donning a well-worn shirt. It rustled against the hairs on his chest. Outside, I licked my lips, my tongue running across sharp fangs, and backed away from the porch.

"I waited as the man's heavy footsteps thudded from the bedroom and passed through the living space, out the door and into the yard. Reaching the bottom step, the human pulled a cigar from his coat pocket. The match he struck on the sole of his boot illuminated his face as he lit his smoke.

"He crushed the match underneath a heavy boot and inhaled deeply of the cigar. The smoke he blew out hung about his head briefly then twisted away on the breeze. He adjusted his crotch with his other hand and softly laughed out loud as an amusing thought crossed his mind. He kicked a small rock around with the toe of his boot as he studied the ground in front of him.

"He had lifted his hand to his mouth to take another draw before he realized his fingers were empty and the cigar gone. 'What the h...' he began, spinning quickly around on his heels to study the darkness around him.

"His words died into my hand as I clamped one across his mouth. As a man, I would have been stronger than him. As a vampire, he was putty in my grasp, and I pushed his head back so that our eyes met. I studied the human as I inhaled deeply on his smoke. The warmth of the tobacco felt good as it spread through my lungs.

"Blood pumped harshly from his heart and fear colored the lustful scent that clung to him. He sweated in my hands; he shook, and it colored his cheeks. He began to fight, and I crushed him against the hardness of my body. 'Sshh,' I whispered, blowing smoke into his ear.

"But I did not want him to fight. I wanted to look at him, to see the way his pupil crushed his iris when it dilated. I wanted to watch the fluttering of his eyelashes and study their deep yellow color as they swept across his green eyes. I wanted to listen to his heart and feel the fine hairs of his arms lift against my skin.

"The night before I had killed the native man quickly and efficiently. I had been too hungry to enjoy myself. Tonight was different, and I was mesmerized by this human I held in my arms. It was illogical since only a handful of days ago I had been a human, but still I could not help but marvel at the beauty of such a delicate creature and how utterly alive he was.

"He was studying me as well, and I could see that he recognized me. He knew who I had been, and he knew what I was. And I had known him. I cannot say we had been friends, but we certainly had not been enemies. It was no matter; I had every intention of killing him.

"But first I had questions. 'Whose footsteps do I hear in the house besides Irena's?' I asked. Lifting my hand from the man's mouth, I wrapped long fingers round the human's throat, keeping his body close to me lest he cried out.

"'The... the maid,' the words whispered from his clenched vocal cords.

"'The same maid that testified against me?' I questioned him. He nodded his 'yes'.

"'Irena's father is drinking with the Baranov?' I asked. Again another yes.

"He started to beg then, and I shushed him with my thumb on his lips. How soft his skin was under my hand. I stroked the fullness of his bottom lip with my thumb before replacing it with my lips. A good night kiss, so to speak, as I sucked the air from his body, crushing him against me and squeezing the remainders from the bottoms of his lungs.

"His ribs cracked under my hands, and I could taste his fear in my mouth. I wanted his blood, but I could not risk making a child and so I let him strangle.

"He ceased to struggle after only seconds, and when his heart had made its final sound, I pushed his neck back and drank until blood dripped from the corners of my mouth and wet the ground under my feet. His body discarded in the ocean, I returned to Irena's home with only minutes lost.

"The house, although poorly lit, stood out in the darkness, its far corner only a stone's throw from the forest. Behind the curtains, I could see the shadow of a human roaming the room. It did not belong to Irena, as it moved with too little fanfare.

"I knocked at the window and was happy to see the shocked expression of the maid who had accused me of rape as she opened the door. Her face flushed despite her dark skin; her breath caught in her throat. Quickly, her hands formed the symbol of the cross against her chest and nausea rolled through me. But I was not deterred.

"'Let. Me. In.' I hissed the words through the semi darkness of the porch into her face. Hatred rolled across my body as I stared at my accuser. I lifted one foot to cross the threshold, but it caught in some ancient tradition, held eerily in midair. The woman laughed at me.

"'Do you plan to hide behind these walls forever?' I asked her. I promised her death with my undead eyes and smiled with my inhuman lips.

"'If that is what it takes then the answer is yes,' she answered.

"'And what of your children? You, who will not live forever. Who will protect them from me?' I asked.

"She spit at me now words of intense hatred and anger. 'You have already cursed my child. Why do you think I have done these things to you? Why did you think I sided with this she-devil?'

"Looking at her in a new light, I stepped back slightly from the door, my hands falling limply to my sides. 'He was yours. The native boy I killed was your son.'

"She studied me with eyes as cold and dead as mine. The air

changed around me, a cool chill wrapped around my form. I had felt these emotions before, the day the child had died in my arms.

"'You buried him in the ground. You damned his soul, and now he can never enter paradise because you put him in the dirt,' her voice broke. She stared into the distance. 'I cursed you that day.'

"'I meant to honor him. I did not want to see his body burned in a mass grave,' I argued. 'I buried him so that he might have peace.'

"'You cursed him,' she hissed at me. 'We are Aleutian. We are not of your kind. Our ways are not your ways. We do not put our dead in the ground to rot. You interfered with what you did not understand, and now my son is a slave to death for eternity. He can never walk in paradise. And so, I cursed you.'

"'I have cursed myself,' I answered.

"She eyed me defiantly, unafraid momentarily of what stood before her.

"'You do not give me enough credit. You believe in your own power but not of mine. My power traveled here with the sun when it first spread its light upon the earth. The Tlingit tell a story of your kind. They met ones such as you before my people. You see, many years ago when the earth was young and fresh and still covered in sheets of ice, a monster followed the trail of winter's path to a village full of mighty warriors. But the warriors were safe and warm in their homes, their baskets full of dried fish and venison for the winter. The monster could not reach them, and it paced the mountains gnashing its teeth. Finally the snows melted and spring arrived and the warriors went out to find fresh meat and fish. The monster was hungry, and many warriors did not return home. Women disappeared from the village. Their empty bodies were found scattered in the forest. The remaining warriors stalked and killed the beast; its heart burned upon the fire. But the monster was strong and did not want to die. It wanted to drink the blood of humans forever, and so its heart, when thrown on the fire, burst into uncounted mosquitoes which flew away. And so the beast lives on and cannot die, for who can slay all the mosquitoes? Now, you are the mosquito. You will never die, and you will drink human blood forever. You cursed my son, and I have cursed you. We are even.'

"In the background, I could hear Irena. I could smell the scented bathwater clinging to her skin. She smelled of lust and roses. I gripped the doorframe and the wood crumbled in my hands. I chaffed under the restriction. I wanted her so very badly.

"'Yes, we are even,' I said. 'I cursed your son, and you cursed me. But now you must protect yourself. What do you offer for your own life?'

"She eyed me suspiciously for a moment before taking a deep breath of resolution. I knew she had no love of Irena. She was her servant after all. I had been a servant as well, and I had not loved my masters. 'Come in,' she said and stood back from the doorway.

"I stepped through the now powerless threshold and caught the servant's chin in my hand. 'Tell me truthfully, did Irena act of her own free will or was she merely your puppet?' I questioned.

"'She is her own person. She was in a bad way with a child growing in her belly, and to be married into the royal family,' the maid answered, 'she needed a scapegoat, and I suggested you. After all, your many rejections stung her pride. My people are powerful—our shamans strong. Over the years, I have poisoned your sleep, and the night that you were accused, I drew you from your sleep and brought you to us. But she was as guilty as I. Without her accusing words, mine would have meant nothing. Your life was meaningless to her.'

"'The child,' I whispered more to myself than to the maid. 'I had forgotten.'

"'The child is dead; Irena's womb was poisoned by her father,' the maid answered.

"'To whom did the baby belong?' I asked.

"The maid only shrugged her shoulders. 'Does it matter?' she asked.

"She was right. It did not matter at all. I pulled her face close to mine so that she might see the levity in my eyes. 'Leave this place and speak of me to no one. Do not return. I do not care how you accomplish it, but if I ever see you after this night, I will feel no obligation to spare your life again.'

"She held my gaze evenly, considering my commands and deciding she could live with them, she nodded once, and I let her pull from my grasp.

"'Woman,' I caught her arm as an afterthought as she stepped past me, goose bumps standing up beneath my fingertips. 'My intentions were truly to honor your son. His body lies three strides west of the eastern trail fork. Perhaps he can still find peace.'

"Her hardened expression melted somewhat, but she did not look at me as she spoke. 'Perhaps there will be peace for you both,' she said and walked away without looking back. I waited as she disappeared into the darkness before I turned to reap the only peace I knew I would ever find.

"Unaware of my presence, Irena continued to bathe in the back room. The tinkling of water dripping from a lifted limb drifted through the thin walls of the house and into the living space where I stood. She hummed to herself as she leaned back into the tub, a satisfied moan on her lips.

"With footsteps as light as the air itself, I entered her bedroom, coming to stand silently behind her as she soaked in the water. Mist rose from the heat of the bath. A clock chimed the top of the hour from within the living room, its sound causing her to startle. A dollop of water splashed over the side of the tub, pooling on the hardwood floors below.

"She felt my presence behind her, and she whirled in the bath only to find the space behind her empty. She called for the maid, 'Anna! Get in here! You should not leave me alone.'

"Angry, she leaned back into the bathtub, but her skin crawled, and she could not get comfortable. Getting no response, she shouted again, 'Anna! Now! I want to get out!'

Again she waited.

"Exasperated, she kicked at the water with her toes, splashing it onto the floor. "Well, you are just going to end up cleaning a mess if you do not make haste *now*!' Irena waited a moment, then thrust her foot sharply down into the tub again, showering the wall in front of her with warm water. It ran down the wallpaper that only the rich could afford, collecting on the baseboards.

"'Anna?' Irena's voice now held somewhat of a question, but hearing my soft footsteps behind her, she stood up, her backside to me. Expecting Anna with her robe, she pushed both arms out behind her as I slipped the robe onto her arms and across her shoulders. I reached round in front of her and brought the edges together, nuzzling her neck.

"'I thought you left...' she giggled, placing her hands on my arms. Her fingers traced across my cold skin, but it took her a couple of breaths before her mind caught onto what the pads of her fingers were telling her. Her breath hitched and her heart paused in her chest.

"My skin was wet with rain. Bits of dirt and leaves still stained me from the grave, and she lifted muddy hands from my arms, holding them up at strange angles as if they did not belong to her.

"My physical and emotional needs were one and the same, and I pressed them both against her. My body was naked, and so was my mind as I allowed the rage to pour from me to her. My consciousness caressed her mind while my hands roamed her body. My need for revenge pressed hard against her backside. I let my mind race unfettered through hers, ripping away whatever pretenses she used with everyone who thought they understood her. No one knew her the way I did in those moments.

"Irena was a petted, petulant woman whose every craving had been instantaneously granted. She lacked any real emotion or true feelings for anyone with the exception of her father. I am not sure if love is what she truly felt for him, but she did at the very least respect him. She appreciated his head for business and his logic. It was a trite and small emotion, just beginning to bud with age, but it was there.

"But although I searched every crevice of her conscious and unconscious thought, I could find not one shed of remorse for what she had done to me. I was nothing to her except what the chaff was to the grain. Necessary to provide a service but worth nothing once the service was complete.

"That is not to say she did not feel contrite, for she felt very sorry indeed but only because she had to face the unhappy consequences of her actions. Her contrition was not that of the woman who realizes her sin and falls humbly on her knees to beg for a forgiveness that she knows she does not deserve.

"'Your lover is dead and your maid is gone. Your father will no doubt drink late into the night, so I have all evening to enjoy you.' I spoke the words, although she could see my thoughts as I forced them into her mind. I spoke only because I enjoyed the way my voice made her shake all the more. I wanted to reach all her senses.

"I lifted her from the bathtub, my cold hands leaving a trail of dirt across her skin. Touching her reminded me of the silk curtains that hung in my master's house. As a child, I had stroked those curtains once and my mother had whipped me out of fear of our master's response. Irena was the smoothest, softest person I have ever touched.

"The robe I had placed on her fell apart as I swung her up in my arms. Her skin was alabaster white, unmarred and unmarked. Her breasts heaved from fear in the lamplight, the darkness of her nipples disappearing into the shadows along with the deep triangle where her legs met her body. Drops of rose-scented water slipped onto my feet as I carried her to the bed.

"I pushed the robe farther from her body and lowered myself onto her. After the cold of the grave, she was like a hot fire on a winter night. My skin tingled next to hers; my fingertips burned with her warmth. She tried to shrink from me and from the unnatural feel of my skin on hers, but I would not let her.

Instead, I pulled her closer so that every part of her body touched mine.

"'Is this not what you wanted?' I teased. 'Why do you pull away from me? Is my skin too cold? Is it too wet? Does the dirt from my skin stain the purity of yours?'

"She was too frightened to speak and could only stare at me dumbly. I could read from her mind that she had never paid for any of her actions before and she was clearly stunned that she would be held accountable now. Her mind was grasping for anyone else to blame.

"'Let me be clear, Irena, that it was by your sins that I was judged and condemned. By your sins, everything important to me was stripped away. Not your father's, although he will pay for his part in my suffering, and not your maid's. Your actions were solely your own.'

"Still, she had nothing to say. No words by which to console me, and I certainly had none for her. What I wanted was to hurt her in every way imaginable. I wanted to strip away her dignity, her beauty, her pride and arrogance. I wanted to touch her everywhere and in every way that was horrifying. I wanted to defile her.

"In her conscious thought, I recreated the man that I had been a mere fourteen days before when my hands had been as warm as my eyes. My human lips caressed hers while our legs intertwined in the throes of passion. In this vision, I came to her as the beautiful servant that she had desired.

"I caressed her body with my mouth; my hands roamed her breasts, and she arched her back to push them farther into my hands. I nipped at their fullness, my fangs sliding easily through her skin, but she never noticed as deep under my control as she was. Her body and mind were both throbbing with need, and she opened herself up to me, begging for me to enter.

"Then I pulled those happy, comfortable images from her mind and let her reality shine through. The hands that plagued her were cold and dirty. Her breasts were pressed against the filth of my body, and there was not enough warmth in my eyes to inspire anything but utter despair. I was poised to enter her, and she could feel the warmth of her own wetness.

"'You wanted me, Irena and you have been wanting me for the last half-hour, and now I am going to give you what you have asked for.'

"She begged me then, offering me things that are of no value to the undead. Money, possessions. Position. Things which had been of no value to me before my transformation and which certainly meant nothing to me now.

"I laughed at her offers and positioned myself to take from her what I had already paid for with the whip. With my every thrust, I would peel the skin from her back with my nails, and finally I would crack her body asunder with the force of my desire.

"But in the end, I found I could not do it. I could not be the rapist that she had claimed I was. I would not give her that power over me. She would not dictate what I was or had ever been.

"No doubt, I still caused her plenty of pain. I marked her more times than I can remember. Her skin came off her back in long thin strips that made her beg for mercy. The joints of her limbs bent easily in my hands while her bones crumpled with my lightest touch. Multiple puncture wounds covered her body, graze marks leading from one set of fang marks to another. Blood streaked her white skin, and what I could not capture with my tongue stained the sheets and the walls.

"I left her haphazardly on the bed. She was quite a mess, and I disguised nothing. Her eyes gazed unseeing at the ceiling above her. Her mouth was pulled back in a grimace, her teeth shiny and white against the blue of her lips. Her thick blonde hair, clotted with blood, lay out in waves against the red-stained bed sheets.

"Her heart still beat, straining to circulate what small amount of her life blood remained. Just enough to keep her alive until morning when her father would find her. Just enough that she remained semi-conscious of her surroundings. Her only movements were to try to wet her lips and blink her eyes. I smiled in approval; she would be quite a vision for her father.

"The night was still young by the time I had finished with Irena, and still no one had come for me. It seemed the maid had been true to her promise. I had pulled from Irena's mind that her father would not return for several hours, so I had time to consider what I would do when my actions were discovered.

"It was only a matter of time, of course. The condition and nature of my death would have the occupants of the fort on high alert, so when news of Irena's attack made its way around the fort, I would be the first and only suspect.

"Ivan would come himself. He was a man of honor. He always had been, and he would no doubt blame himself for agreeing to bury me with no precautions, as I had asked of him.

"I was under no delusions as to the outcome of my future. I could not run or hide, for you must remember, as I said earlier, that a vampire cannot leave his first tomb for six months. We are bound for that time to the homeland of our vampire birth and to our grave. Ivan had buried me, and so he would find me.

"What would I do when my only friend came for me? Would I kill him and feast upon his blood? Would I curse him as I was cursed? I swore to myself that I would not. I would rather feel the fire of the stake at his hand than taste his blood upon my lips. If I must be staked, let it be his hand that thrust the blow.

"The duke lingered long at his card game with the Baranov that night. I helped myself to a change of his clothes while I waited. I then settled onto a chair beside Irena's bed while I carved a stake out of a stick of firewood.

"Irena stirred as I did so, opening her eyes and looking wildly around the room. Her gaze finally settled on me. She struggled to sit up but could not find the strength and dropped her head back down into the fullness of the blankets. Sluggishly, she licked her lips and swallowed, hoping for speech. Her hands trembled from the combination of fear, pain, and exhaustion.

"'What will happen to me now?' she whispered through her bruised lips.

"'Now you have only to die, and my plans will be fulfilled,' I answered.

"'What will happen... when I die?' Her body shuddered with the thought.

"I leaned over her now so that she might see the full truth in my eyes. 'You will awake, buried under the ground in a tomb from which you cannot escape. The priests will ensure that you are buried correctly with crossed arms and crucifixes. Perhaps they will decapitate you so that you spend eternity with your head buried between your knees and facing Hell. And you will scream inwardly, you will curse the day you were born, but no one will hear you. I should know, Irena. Because of you, I have been there.'

"'I will not be the only one,' she sneered at me. 'This time, you will not escape the grave.'

"'It is the price I willingly pay to ensure your suffering. And that of your father's.'

"Her eyes widened as she remembered the duke. 'My father, please.' Irena's voice quavered and broke in a sob. Her tear ducts spasmed with the effort, but she had no fluids to spare on tears. 'Please don't hurt him,' she pleaded.

"'Why should he be spared?' I asked.

"'Father loves me. He did not know of my lies.'

"'Perhaps he did not care,' I answered as I continued my work on the stake.

"She continued to shake her head no. The blood that had dried in her hair cracked and splintered with her movements. 'No. He knew nothing. He is innocent.'

"'What exactly did he not know, Irena? That you were a whore and a liar? Or did he not know that he took the one thing from me that mattered? I must say I am surprised that you are wasting breath upon him. I did not think you cared for anyone that much.'

"'Please,' she begged again.

"'Have no worries. It is only you that I desire to spend eternity with. I have no designs on your father's eternal soul. Only his happiness.'

"'He did those things to you out of love for me.' Her voice

sputtered and nearly gave out as she coughed up some specks of fresh blood. I had deeply lacerated her neck. She exhaled and blood plumed from her lips in tiny red bubbles.

"'He will always love you, Irena. That is why it will hurt so much.'

"I tired of talking to her now and whispering an incantation that she could not ignore; I pressed my will forcefully through her mind and pushed her dying body back into sleep."

"The duke did not see my disjointed figure sitting in the corner when he returned in the wee hours of the morning. Vodka mingled with his breath and sweat lined his armpits from the walk home. He was cursing silently to himself about the Baranov and the indecent amount of money he had lost to the man over cards when he walked into Irena's bedroom to check on her.

"The lamp still burned in the corner of the room, and in its light, Irena's blood glimmered dully. The duke let out a garbled cry when he saw his daughter spread out on the bed. He took a step backwards from the shock and swung around to look behind him. Turning quickly back around, he produced a weapon from his pocket, an intricately carved revolver, and swung it from one corner of the room to the next. I had touched his mind so that he did not see me watching him from my corner.

"With hesitant steps, he approached Irena's bed, mumbling crooning noises that only parents can make for their children. He thought her dead, but like any human, he hoped that by not knowing for sure, it would make it not true.

"He patted her leg gently once he reached the bed as he whispered her name again, and getting no response, he stretched out a tentative trembling hand and pushed her neck to the side. His fingers traced the puncture wounds of my fangs in her neck and then followed the track marks to her shoulders and down to her wrists. The bones of her hand crackled under his fingers as he turned it over. Pulling his hand away, he stared numbly at the blood on his fingertips.

"Irena had stirred at the pain in her hand. Blood bubbled on her pale lips as she tried to point out my presence to her father. But he was too occupied with the thoughts that I was pressing into his subconscious to understand her.

"'*She is no longer your daughter. She has risen vampire. You must protect yourself. You must protect the reputation of your family. Put her down.*' My words fanned through his mind, bringing to remembrance childhood fears and years of legend and lore.

"'Child, I am so... so sorry for what has befallen you,' he whispered, tears mixing with his saliva while he spoke. His voice broke; his back bowed with despair. His right hand curved around the stake I had left upon the bed. He did not question its presence.

"'Father, I am still your little girl.' She struggled for each word. 'Please listen. Feel my heart beating. Feel.' She groped for his hand, placing it on her chest. 'I am alive, Father. There is still time. You can save me.'

"Under his hand, her heart beat out an unnatural rhythm. But he did not recognize it. The image of the demon I had created in his mind was too strong. Tears streamed down the wrinkles of his face like water through mountainside gullies. He had aged, it seemed, literally in front of my eyes.

"'Irena, forgive me for bringing you to this accursed place. I am so sorry. How will your mother ever forgive me? She warned me time and again this was no place for a lady. I would not listen. I can never forgive myself.'

"'Father. Listen to me. I am still alive. There is time. Remember the legends. Bring me the vampire's heart, and I will be free of the curse.' She desperately tried to bring his mind around while I mocked her efforts from the corner.

"'He cannot hear you, Irena. He hears what I want him to hear. He sees you as I have told him to see you, a vile demon who must be put down,' I said to worsen her despair.

"'Yes, child, you will be free. I will save you,' the duke

whispered into her ear as he pulled her close, placing a father's kiss on her cheek. 'Do not fear, child. You will be buried with all the rights of the Church. They will not put your body on unhallowed ground.'

"'Father. No. I have been marked. I need his heart.'

"But the duke heard nothing else she said, and with one last kiss to her forehead, he drove the stake through the fluttering heart that beat beneath his hand.

"I smiled as his daughter's heart sputtered underneath the tips of his fingers, struggling to squeeze out another ounce of blood before finally giving way to utter stillness. She stared up at the one man who had truly loved her as he watched death steal across her features.

"Tears of pain trickled from the corners of her eyes. Her mouth moved, her eyebrows lifted slightly, and leaning down, he placed his ear to her mouth, but the words died on her lips. Even I did not know what she had hoped to say. He wiped one last errant tear from her cheek with a bloodstained finger as her eyes turned dull.

"Pulling my hold from his mind, I peeled away the image of Irena that I had created for him, erasing all vestiges of myself in his subconscious. I let him see that she had been human still when he drove the stake through her heart. I brought to life in his mind the beautiful first-born child he had held in his arms, the precocious daughter with blond curls that hung to her waist, the daring young woman he had presented to society. I let him relive their first father-daughter waltz, watch again as she took her first step, first horseback lesson, stutter her first words, and then I let him hold her in his arms one more time.

"'*What have you done?*' I whispered to his subconscious as my final parting gift, leaving him alone to answer the question.

# Chapter 13

"Irena's body was found, alongside her still sobbing father, shortly before nightfall that evening. The fang marks on her body left no doubt as to what fate she had suffered. The duke, inconsolable, had stood vigil beside the body all day. The Baranov had found him, leaned against the bed, muttering about murdering his daughter. He could not be comforted and finally was loaded onto a ship bound for Russia and shipped away. His last request was that Irena be interred on holy ground, and he paid the archimandrite handsomely for the privilege.

"The daylight had been lost by the time the search party entered the forest to hunt me down. Ivan, when confronted by my handiwork, had agreed to lead the way to my grave. I had been waiting all day, my mind a haze of anxiety and dread that they would come while I was yet incapacitated.

"It was with great relief when the lingering sun dropped behind the horizon, and I was finally released from my paralysis. I had dissolved into a vapor of consciousness, passing through the solids of wood and earth before coming together atop my grave.

"It was to be my last night free, and with that knowledge, I inhaled deeply, replacing the stale air of the tomb with the freshness of the forest. The Aurora Borealis danced atop of me; as a human I would have missed its glory as it was too faint for mortal eyes, but tonight as a vampire, I watched the ribbons of color as they snaked through space. The breeze was stiff, and the salt of ocean spray danced in the air and burned my eyes.

"The forest had been alive above me while I had yet been in my tomb, but now as I stood above it, the sounds of the forest died around me. A few hundred feet away, a bear made the sudden decision to abandon a recent kill. An otter slipped into Indian Creek within the forest to my right while an owl rustled the air above me as it took off from a nearby tree. It did not like my presence it seemed. Smart bird.

"On the wind, I smelled Ivan and the men that followed him. Fear dripped from their armpits and escaped onto the wind from their mouths as they breathed it from their core. Their hearts tapped out a staccato I could palpate in the air, and although it had only been a day since I had fed, my mouth watered and my appetite swelled. Mine was a hunger that could not be satiated; a desire that could not be laid to rest even though I was the one now being hunted.

"The hunting party was close; I could hear them stumbling through the underbrush. The high-pitched rub of parkas on tree limbs, the rattle of one man's lungs, and a whispered prayer for safe return by another proved the group grew close.

"I considered, for a short moment, escaping into the blackness of the forest or feasting on their blood. But for what purpose? I had promised myself that I would never harm Ivan. He and I had been closer in life even than brothers, and my thirst for blood would not see me separated from him. Escape was not possible since I was compelled to return to my gravesite come morning; if the deed was not performed tonight, Ivan would return at dawn. I was doomed either way and I preferred to meet the stake upright and on my feet.

"I was considering the immortality of the stars when I heard the group of humans step out of the forest and into the clearing where I stood waiting. My skin tingled from their nearness, the fine hairs on my arms lifting like the mantle on a dog. My mouth watered, but still I gazed at the heavens, memorizing the patterns of lights. I knew I would not see them again for a very long time—possibly never.

"There were seven of them—six white men and one native. The smell of their clothes and diet would have given their race away even if I could not have seen their skin. Fear permeated the air around each of them, but the native had a calmness that none of the white men could approach. He had no fear of death, only of the pain that came with it, and his bravery flavored his scent.

"Garlic and salt also mingled with their fear. They had carried the substances with them, and it overran their coat pockets and satchels. One human carried a torch, the fire wavering in the wind with the tremble of his hand. All of them, even the native, carried a cross, and despite the distance between me and them, its power caused my eyes to burn. I closed my eyelids to the sight.

"'Adrik,' Ivan spoke aloud. 'We have come to put you to rest.'

"'What makes you think I will let you, brother?' I asked out of curiosity. Did he love me still as I loved him?

"'It is because we were as brothers that I know you will submit to me,' Ivan answered.

"To the rest of the men, I asked, 'And the rest of you, should you not have waited until daylight to come? Here in the darkness, you are weak and strength belongs to the undead.' I murmured into the cool wintry air, my voice equally icy. I would not hunt Ivan, but the others were fair game. I owed them no loyalty.

"Surprise and recognition crept across their expressions as the reality of what they were facing, what they had come here to do, became real to them, and suddenly the idea did not seem as noble as it had when they started out.

"'What was the strategy? Did you think the vampire would simply surrender to your stake?' I questioned the group.

"'We could not wait till morning just to see who would die tonight,' Ivan spoke.

"Fright oozed from their skin, stronger now, and carried towards me on the wind; I swirled the taste of their pheromones on my tongue. Their fear was intoxicating and having energy of its own, I drank it in, unable to quell its power over me.

"Ivan, standing center, was flanked by the others. He trembled slightly in my presence, and his face was contorted with a disgust that not even the empathy in his eyes could overcome. The men that spread outward from him, an odd assortment of hunters and soldiers, beheld me with nothing but contempt. These were hardened men, tough, accustomed to working in the worst conditions, facing the most violent of predators, but now they were unsure of themselves, having never faced the likes of the monster that stood in front of them.

"One of the men stepped slightly forward of the others now. He was more boisterous and verbally threatened me. The others of the group eyed him warily and warned him to stay back. I remembered this man. His name was Alexei and we had worked together on repairing the palisade at the fort many times. He was known for his temper and his tenacity. He was not known for restraint.

"Tonight, his breath reeked of alcohol, and I could smell the odd mixture of untempered courage and stupidity in his sweat. He seemed an odd choice for such a dangerous expedition, and I could see by the nervous glances of his fellow hunters that they agreed with me. I studied him until Ivan's voice broke my attention.

"'Irena is dead, Adrik. You have what you wanted. Let us get this over with tonight,' Ivan said, his voice steady enough to the human ear. To me, it wavered, his fear apparent.

"'The victory was sweet,' I acknowledged. Running my tongue over my fangs, I smiled at the men. They swallowed hard with disgust at my double meaning and I laughed aloud at their pious disgust. 'How innocent you all pretend to be! How many of you had not wanted to taste her? And some of you had, and yet, here I stand, dead by your sins! Even yours, Ivan, my best friend! You tasted her too. Was it your child that once lived in her belly? So I chose to taste her after all. What was the harm in that? Did I not deserve the pleasure?' My questions met only the cold silence of their judgment.

"'The priest judged you guilty. It is proof enough for me,' Alexei snarled as he lunged forward, pulling a sharpened tree branch from out of his parka.

"I sidestepped him with barely a registered thought, and he rushed past me without realizing I had ever moved. The jab of his stake met nothing but empty air.

"His face crumpled with fear as he realized he had missed. Before he could react, I twisted his large frame round so that his back was to my chest. I pulled the crudely made stake from his hand and turned the weapon back on him. His heart beat wildly in his chest as I pushed the wooden tip through the first layers of his skin. 'The priest judged poorly,' I said as his hot blood flowed down my hand, and unwilling to deny myself, I brought my fingers up and licked the sumptuous fluid from my skin. Anxious for more, I pushed his body forward with my other hand, feeling his body shake on the stake as I impaled him. I lost myself for a few moments in his taste when his heart had ceased.

"Dropping his body to the ground as an afterthought, I glanced back at the other men, who had fanned out behind me. They had made no move to save the man as I killed him, and so distracted was I by his blood, I had not noticed their movements or their trickery.

"'Was he the bait?' I asked Ivan.

"'Not intentionally. But we were each willing to sacrifice ourselves to save the people we love,' Ivan answered.

"'I would never hurt you, Ivan. Nor any of your kin. You need not have made a sacrifice of any of these men.'

"'I know you would never have intentionally hurt me, Adrik. But you have chosen evil over good, and so it will color your every action. You cannot choose which part of you it will affect.'

"They had encircled me, crosses of various shapes and sizes held up into the air in my direction. Some were made of simple wood, others ornately carved of oak, and others cast in metals but all wrapped in power. I was entrapped by the strength and no matter which direction I tried to go, I could find no way to breach the power of their circle.

"Spinning round, my eyes searched desperately for a weakness, but the humans, stretching arms out to one another now, held to the cross of the other so that the circle of men was unbreakable. Their bond magnified the power of the cross, and my eyes burned. My skin crawled, and I could go neither forwards or backwards. I thought to go straight upwards and made an attempt to jump and catch hold of the branches that reached over my head, but in the weakness brought on by the crucifixes, I was unable to rise more than a leg's length above the ground.

"Ivan pleaded, urging me to submit to the stake, and although I had no desire to hurt Ivan, it was proving more difficult than I had imagined it could ever be to give up my reign on this life. Far easier it had been to hang myself and snuff out my human life that I should have held precious than it was to submit to the power of the stake.

"'Adrik,' Ivan's voice, calm and gentle, spoke from behind me. 'Please, brother. Do not make this harder than it needs to be. Let me help you retain some shred of decency. Do you not think enough blood has been spilled here?'

"Turning around at his question, I found Ivan had joined me within the confines of the circle. Two other men had joined hands behind his back and let him in, thereby keeping the integrity of the perimeter. In one hand, he held a crucifix, and in the other, a stake, sharpened to an ugly point that he leveled at me.

"'Do you recognize where we are, Adrik?' he asked, indicating the forest around us with the stake squeezed tightly in his hand. 'It is more than the unhallowed ground where your body was laid, brother,' he murmured.

"At first, I did not understand where Ivan's questions were leading. I studied the ground underneath my feet. It appeared nothing special. The earth was cool beneath my bare feet. In the distance, I could hear the slap of waves lapping at a shoreline behind us. To my right, the river that helped to create the peninsula we stood on flowed towards the sound where it would intermingle with the salt water of the ocean.

"And then with sudden clarity, I realized the irony. The ground beneath my feet was a clearing because only a few short years ago, it had been a fort, the same fort where I had killed the native child. I searched the ground, half-expecting to see the blood of the child still staining the ground. It was a human memory, and I had nearly forgotten its intensity until Ivan's words had brought it to remembrance.

"I turned my hands over, remembering the color of the child's blood on my skin. How warm it had been but how quickly it had cooled in the breeze. 'The child's blood is still on my hands,' I whispered. And I felt the shame, the guilt, all over again.

"'There is much blood on your hands, Adrik. I wish that it was only that of the child for those stains were not really there, only imagined. But surely Irena's blood and the innocent men you have killed will stain your hands for lifetimes to come.'

"'I care only for that of the child,' I spoke back, staring at my hands, at the imagined stains.

"Ivan's thrust was strong, his aim good. So entranced by my guilt, I had taken no notice of the whisper of wind that moved towards me as he struck. The stake entered my chest and seared my heart as it passed through the dead organ.

"I watched my cold blood run down my chest and drip onto the same ground that had soaked up the blood of my first kill. How inhuman it looked, not even warm enough that it would disperse on the remnants of ice that laced the forest floor. A red monstrous stain that proved my guilt and my inhuman nature.

"More stakes followed, but I scarcely noticed. Instead, I memorized the contours of my best friend's face until sapped, my great strength gone, I fell to the ground. I lay haphazardly with my limbs askew. Ivan leaned over me. I felt the touch of his warm hands as he brushed the locks of hair out of my eyes. His tears fell salty onto my lips as he whispered promises made years ago between two peasant men, cramped together in the dirty underbelly of a Russian ship. He would send word to my mother of my death and my love for her. His first-born child would carry my name. He would pray for me every day. And he would never forget me.

"Ivan's warm hands were the last kind touch of humanity that I felt before two soldiers hoisted my body. Ivan's fingers slid across the tips of mine as the soldiers began the march to the fort. It was the last I saw of him for many, many years.

"That night proved more painful that anything I could have ever comprehended. Dying as a human paled in comparison to the suffering I experienced that evening.

"Terrified, the humans had lit the interior of the surgeon's quarters with such large sums of candles and lanterns that the illumination burned my eyes. The flames of the candles danced menacingly next to the table my body rested on, and my skin crawled with the heat and the fear they would burn me first and then bury me seared in the ground.

"Perhaps the flames would have been easier, after all, than the torture they meted out. In being vampire, it was if I deserved no dignity for first they stripped me naked, studying me as if I was nothing more than an experiment gone wrong and not the man that I had once been. And worse still, at my feet stood the archimandrite, the man who had allowed my soul to be cast from Heaven. How I hated that he saw me in my weakness.

"My punishment was made worse as next the surgeon grasped the many stakes that pierced my heart and examined the blood that oozed from the entrance wounds. He rubbed every inch of my body with garlic oil. My skin flamed in response. Although silent to the men who stood over me, my shrieks drowned out every other thought in my mind. The garlic soaked into my skin, which broke and bled underneath the oil, allowing it to penetrate even more. No part of me was untouched by the flames of the oil, and to make the humiliation worse, he packed my every orifice with the whole herb. Blood ran from my eyes and across my cheeks.

"But the surgeon had more punishments planned. He slashed my elbow and drained me of blood, bringing my hunger raging to the surface. I thought I saw a moment of pity as his gaze traveled the length of my pain-wracked body. I snarled at him, hissing with pain. I did not want his pity.

"The only respite was the sight of Irena's body laid out upon a cot in the corner of the room. She was quite dead, but I could see through my tortures that her body had been treated with the same contempt as mine. To the humans in the room, she was nothing but an empty corpse, but she was anything but the shell they assumed her to be. Deep within, I could feel the stirrings of her restless, undead spirit beginning to form. The transformation was still early, but already her rage was smoldering. If this fort ever disturbed our undead graves after tonight, they would be lucky, I thought, if it was me they awoke and not her.

"Finally I was dressed in some cast-off wool garments and carried back to my grave. It was a long journey in the hands of the four shaking humans chosen to convey me. Their every misstep shook the stakes in my chest, and if I my frozen tongue would have worked, I would have begged for mercy.

"By the time we arrived to my previous burial site, the coffin was half-full of water from the rain that had moved in during the evening. It covered my face as the soldiers dropped me down into the watery hell. For besides fire, nothing creates such fear to the vampire as water.

"It sloshed up and over my face. It drained down my throat and filled my lungs. Paralyzed by the power of the stake and the garlic, I could not even close my mouth against its cold, dirty stream.

"The men did not even have the graciousness to close my eyes. I could do nothing but watch through the ripples of the water that covered my head as a hunter leaned in over the casket. Slicing one more metal stake through my heart, he hammered its beveled tip into the wooden bottom of the crypt.

"Above me, stars twinkled amongst the clouds that moved

to the east. The rain had ended and a thick fog had rolled in from the coast. It weaved itself in tattered strands along the forest floor, intertwining amongst the legs of the human that bore witness to my suffering.

"In a last bit of cruelty, a heavy metal cross was dropped onto my chest. It burned, settling deeper as it seared into my chest.

"Above me, the humans laughed as the cross burned my skin. They leaned in over my coffin and boasted of the hell that awaited me after a long watery grave. Eventually growing tired of the sport, they sealed me in the coffin, nailing thick metal studs into the lid.

"Immortality does not always have a nice ring to it. Especially when facing an eternity of torment. I was young as a vampire and had only ever been young, even as a human. Perhaps if I had been more mature in one of my lives or had spent a decade or two at ground of my own choice, the pain would have been more bearable. Perhaps I could have looked ahead and saw that nothing on this earth would last forever.

"But as it was, I could not see beyond the day or the week, let alone the months and years that lay ahead. I lived only in the now. I could not see that time washes away all pain, all wounds and destroys everything that is not eternal, and that these shackles binding me so tightly would in some future dissolve in what must be the boundless abyss of time.

"As strong as the iron used to construct the cross on my chest, as vigorous as the herb that weakened my body, and as virile as the wood penetrating my heart, I was stronger and more eternal than even the elements themselves.

"Burn the vampire into ash and can we not yet come forth? Even ash is still solid in your hands. Water cannot drown us, earth can only bury us for so long, and wind can only blow us so far. What cannot decompose cannot be destroyed. Unnatural in life, we remain unnatural in death. Unchanging, unmoving, we remain frozen between two worlds—between life and death.

"If I had been coherent when thrown into my watery coffin, perhaps I would have laughed at their shortsightedness.

Instead, the water I cursed has been my friend over the years. It washed away the garlic oil from my skin. The herb in my body lasted the longest, but it too eventually eroded.

"Alaska is a land alive. So very alive that the ground shudders with arduous growing pains. Over the years, my grave shifted with the movement, and one particular upheaval forced my bound arms apart. How good it felt to be relieved from the cross created by my own limbs.

"The wood of my coffin lasted longer than I expected, but it, along with some of the stakes, finally gave way to wet and rot, reverting back into the soil from which it had sprang. With each element removed, I gained more mobility. I could not rise, but when darkness reigned, I could at least flex my fingers or blink my eyes.

"The iron cross was the last sacrament to keep me pinned beneath the earth. It had seared into my skin so deeply that it rested upon my heart, and I could not escape it. I gnashed my teeth and cried out to the world above me but no living thing answered me.

"For fifty years, I laid there. Fifty years of sorrow and suffering had dragged on in an endless hell when one morning I heard the approach of footsteps. Unlike the steps of those who only passed through the forest, these footfalls hesitated, backing up and then taking a few steps to the right or to the left, before finally settling on a path that brought them directly overhead my grave.

"These were not the sounds of a young man on a hunting venture but instead the hesitant steps of an old man. I heard the creak of his bones as he lowered himself next to my burial spot.

"It was midmorning, and the power of the sun was on the earth, so my paralysis was deep or my fingers would have been digging into the earth with the unbearable pain caused by the human's closeness. Above me, the man's heartbeat was erratic, and his ancient lungs wheezed with his exertions. I did not care that he was old or near death. I cared only for the hum of the blood passing through his stiff old arteries.

"The human did nothing more than sit there for a quarter of an hour before his wheezing finally came to a stop. It was then that he began to speak to me in a voice that had aged with time but whose tenderness I would have recognized anywhere. Even now, the thought of that tender tenor brings me some measure of comfort.

"Ivan talked for hours that day. How glorious it was to escape the confines of the grave, if only in his words and stories, and see the world through Ivan's eyes.

"How he had changed over the years. And the fort as well. No longer a peasant, Ivan was now a man of some position. Serfdom, it seemed, had ended in Russia, and I would have been freed if I had lived. He had proved himself reliable over the years and had picked up a trade. My friend had become a respectable miller, and in doing so had gained a wife and children.

"But his home was nearly empty now and death knocked at my friend's door. Three sons had stayed in Alaska, although only one had remained in New Archangel. One daughter had married the fort surgeon and remained in New Archangel. His last child died within a month of birth; the boy had been christened and buried in the small cemetery atop the hill. His wooden marker had since given up the ghost to the elements, but still Ivan visited there at least once a week. This lost child had brought him immeasurable pain, for he had taken his mother with him.

"In the decades since my staking, the fort had changed as well. Gone was the shabby village and replacing it was an honest town of trade and a busy harbor. The Church at last was firmly established; the natives well assimilated, for the most part, into the religion of the Russians.

"Even the name had changed. Many people now thought of New Archangel as 'Sitka.' The deep superstitions of the Russians were slowly being replaced as men of learning now resided in New Archangel. There were even visions of a college. Even the Church had lost many of the old Slavic beliefs that had been so prevalent when the fort had been established.

"Long since forgotten was the vampire who had been staked and buried in a distant corner of the forest. Such a legend, such a monster had no place in this modern, civilized Sitka. Whatever rumors had been told of me, whatever fear I had instilled in the men who had put me to ground had died with them. Ivan had outlived them all and I lived on, it appeared, only in the mind of my best friend.

"Ivan's health was poor, his breathing raspy. He had to stop often to catch the breath that rattled loosely in his lungs. How I envied him, for he was not long for this world. His body's suffering would end soon, and that is what brought him, gasping for air and leaning on a cane for support, to my grave that early summer morning.

"He sat beside me that day, describing in detail the things I had never experienced in my short life. He described the joys of marriage and the feel of his children when he held them in his arms for the first time. He described the emotions of watching his family grow and in being able to provide for them.

"And he talked of the archimandrite and how he had died an old man in his bed not even a decade past. Ivan had approached him once many years back, begging him to rescind my excommunication. He had looked at Ivan as though my friend had become unhinged, a light smile lifting the corners of his mouth.

"'My child, I do not believe in such superstition. Forget such nonsense. Turn instead to the firm instruction of the Church,' the archimandrite had said, forming the cross upon his chest.

"It was the last time Ivan had mentioned me to anyone. Never had he spoke of me to his children or his wife except in nightmares that he explained away as only ghostly tales told him in his childhood. He had suffered the knowledge of my fate in silence, having no wish to burden his family with such stories.

"Of Irena's father, Ivan recounted how he had died at sea for no apparent reason; the man had simply wasted away. The crew aboard the vessel, knowing he had staked his own daughter, weighted his body after his death and cast him overboard, fearing he was vexed and might reappear in the morning.

"Of Irena, Ivan said nothing. Perhaps he was afraid the very mention of her name might bring me out of the ground despite the cross under which I struggled. Perhaps being a father had changed his mind of her over the years. Likely he could not bear the image of her, a woman, suffering the same fate as me.

"Finally he spoke of my crimes against my own humanity and the potential I had thrown away for revenge. 'Was revenge worth what I had given up?' he asked time and again.

"I was thankful then to be stilled by the sun. I was glad that my lips failed me, for Ivan would not have understood my answer if I had been forced to give one.

"It was late summer, and so the days were longer. Not long before sunset, I heard him begin to dig at the ground surrounding my grave. I guess if you bury a vampire, you don't forget where you have put him, for his hands went right to the spot. Ivan scratched furiously at the dirt, but as with all things, his muscles were not what they had been when we had been young. His heart palpitated all the more with his struggles and his breath came in short gasping wheezes, but still he continued until I saw sunlight for the first time in five decades.

"Ivan sat down beside me then, recapturing his lost breath. The sweat of his labors flavored the air, and I could smell a sickness in his lung that was revolting even to me despite my great hunger.

"The sunlight, gratefully, had ebbed by now, and my muscles began to move. My hands flexed at my sides, and I bared fangs at him, straining the muscles of my neck as I struggled to reach him. Howling with hunger, I threw my head back in hopes of the momentum to dislodge the cross that lay seared to my chest. Luckily for Ivan, something that powerful cannot be moved, and he remained safe. I had no control at this point. It had long since been robbed of me by the hunger.

"Shaking his head sadly, Ivan shushed me, whispering calm words mixed with soothing sounds, as you would a mad man. I cried for blood, begging him to give me but a taste.

"'I am sorry, Adrik. My time on this earth grows short, and one fear plagues me, leaving me unable to die with any semblance of peace. Since the night I forced a stake through my best friend's heart, I have considered your plight.'

"'I wake each morning considering your suffering. I think to bring your comfort. I am nearly able to convince myself that you were never truly the animal you were accused of being. But then I muster myself out of bed and, walking about the village, I see the children, the innocents and reason whispers to me that you must never rise. Know that I will love you as my brother for an eternity and forgive me the actions I must repeat. The cross still holds you but I have come to re-enforce your bindings.'

"For several moments, he studied my face. His expression was blanched with sadness, and then hardening with determination, he reached a shaking hand inside a bag strapped at his waist and removed a stake of iron. The metal gleamed despite the darkness, and I shivered at the thought of its purpose, dreading the pain that it was certain to bring.

"'Brother,' I struggled to utter a coherent word between hisses of hunger. 'A concession, Ivan. Please,' I pleaded.

"'What, Adrik? Anything, save your release, and I vow to make every effort to see it done,' Ivan promised.

"'Do what you must here and then see that you secure Irena as you do me. Do not let her escape her punishment.'

"He stared at me first with shock and then with anger that gave way to disgust.

"'A half a century of sorrow and still you think only of vengeance.' Ivan raised the stake, his arms shaking with exertion while he spoke. 'I see now how deserving you are of this fate. You have become no different than the woman who did this to you. Perhaps the passing of yet another century will find you more remorseful.'

"'Please, Ivan. You gave your word,' I hissed through the hunger.

"Nodding his head in agreement, he brought his arms high

above his head, and with the full effort of his failing strength, he pushed a new stake, forged from iron by his own hand, through my heart. Producing a rock from his waist sack, he pounded the stake into place until it had passed through my body and was buried to the hilt in my chest. The tip passed deeply into the dirt and held me completely immobile once more.

"The pain was exquisite; I had forgotten its sharpness. How insensate I had become with the lack of stimulation. Fire erupted from inside my chest and radiated out to every fiber of my body.

"My last sight was Ivan's hand as he closed my eyes. His tears for my sins mingled with the dirt as he filled in my grave. I cried for different reasons. It was not for sadness but for want of blood.

"Ivan never made good on his promise to secure Irena. He choked on his own blood in a paroxysm of coughing not one hundred yards from my grave but I did not mourn for Ivan, instead I grieved for myself. His was my last connection to humanity and he had entered Paradise.

"After his passing, I existed only in the cold, wet blackness of the earth. If the fifty years I had spent in the ground before Ivan visited my tomb had been wretched, there are no words to describe the next century and a half.

"One would think that the years would begin to fold in upon themselves. Instead, the marking of time became my obsession, and I have marked its passing second by second.

"Until you, Tamara. You are the first bright spot in two centuries of endless nights."

# Chapter 14

The clouds had slowly fallen apart in the black sky, and as they did so, the moon slid out. At first only a sliver that lit the edges of the furrowed clouds was revealed but finally a solid silver disk that illuminated the earth with such force that it could have passed for early morning slipped from the cloud cover.

That great ball of light was the focus of my vision when Adrik pulled away, leaving me alone with my thoughts for the first time that night. I stared at it through the window from my bed, at first confused but finally with the comprehension that I was no longer one with Adrik.

The bond was still there. I could sense it, invisible and yet tethering, but Adrik was closed off to me. I could feel nothing from him. No more a part of the buried vampire, I was just me, the girl who had lost too much. The one with her own grudge.

Beside my bed, the clock ticked off the seconds slowly into the quiet of the room, seeming louder than I'd remembered. Maybe I'd just become much more aware of time. After all, I felt as though I'd spent a century with Adrik, enshrined in the ground. It may have been a dream, but it seemed as real as the last twenty-eight years of my real life.

One thing is for certain. I'd never felt more alone than I did at this moment. Adrik was gone. I searched my thoughts for him, vainly bringing up the most terrible of his memories to evoke a response but could find him nowhere.

Screaming his name in my head, he didn't answer, and I was angry. It seemed unfair and cruel that after I'd lived his torments that he should desert me like this. I wanted to tell him of mine. Didn't I deserve that courtesy? I was alone in my head, and I didn't like the sensation. After so intimate a bond with Adrik, such aloneness felt unnatural.

Even my skin, when I held my arm up to the moonlight, looked pathetically mortal. Humanity clung to my body; my eyesight was normal, my hearing weak. And even as everything in this room was familiar and everything about my body felt whole, it also felt surreal, as if I were out of place and not really a part of this home at all.

To my left, cotton curtains waved lightly in the breeze of the ceiling fan. Beneath me, the sheets felt too smooth, too comfortable. I squeezed my quilt between my fingers. I was warm, and my belly grumbled for food and not blood.

It was darker in the living room; the windows in the adjoining kitchen faced west, and I didn't bother to turn the lights on as I had sought out the gloom. My head ached and numbly I chewed a pop tart to quell the growls of my stomach.

Feeling disjointed, I swallowed the odd-tasting food, washing it down with a partially full glass of water that I must have left sitting on the table from a forgotten day. Yesterday. It felt lifetimes away.

I left the warmth of the house, choosing the chill of the back deck over the comfort of the house. Trained by fear for Joel, I scanned the most distant reaches of the yard but saw nothing that looked out of the ordinary. Tonight, there were few places to hide with the moon so bright that not even the shadows were dark.

I slipped into a large deckchair and sucked in the pungent smell of the spruce trees mingling with the earthy scent of the forest. A light breeze rippled the limbs of the evergreens, the long strings of lichens trailing in the wind. To the north, the howl of a dog split the quiet night, but it was distant, and I was unconcerned that it meant anything was amiss.

The world was alive with activity around me. A large male

bald eagle landed near the top of a tall cedar. It was nearing sunrise, and the bird prepared to begin its daily hunt. To my right, a bat careened wildly at the edge of the yard. But I knew better, it knew its way around even more than the eagle.

Everything moved too fast after the quietness of the grave. Only the mountains, with their ancient majesty, felt right. Unchanging and unmoved, they stood as a backdrop to the ever dying and renewing world around them. I felt more connected to Adrik watching them, and lulled by their steadfastness, I drifted towards sleep.

Somewhere between sleep and awake, I sighed with relief and not without a little contentment when I felt the caress of Adrik's presence in my mind. It made me feel safe and comfortable. How illogical since Adrik was bloodthirsty and condemned.

But he had been my confidant. He knew my darkest secrets. He did not judge me for wanting Joel dead, and he understood the desire for revenge all too well.

"Yes, you are safe with me," Adrik's voice whispered into my sleep-dulled subconscious. But I knew better.

"No. You're a killer but..." I started to say but paused as I realized I was unwilling to put the rest of my thought into words.

"And so are you," he finished for me. "You have wished him dead many, many times. It is the same thing, Tamara. And exactly why you are so safe with me. I could spill your blood in the blink of an eye, but I could never judge you, never condemn you for what you crave to do to him. Is that not the greatest comfort of all, to be free of the reproach and disapproval of everyone?"

I felt some of the tension drain away. How refreshing to not have to pretend that I had any humanity left where Joel was concerned. Adrik would never stand in judgment of me.

"Joel deserves death and so much more," I responded.

"Of course he does," his voice was seductive and sweet as he spoke of murder. "Release me, and I will rip him limb from limb.

I give you my word."

I believed him. Why shouldn't I? Adrik was a killer, but I had seen his soul and he was no liar.

"And who else would die?" I asked. "How much more blood would it take to fill you?"

"Does it matter?" he countered.

"Of course it matters." Disgust filled my mouth with a bitter taste. "I only want to kill Joel. I don't want to hurt anyone else."

"Then you are not ready." He paused for not even the breadth of a second. "But you will be. You are so close."

"What about you?" I asked, changing the subject. "Is there any good thing that can be done for you? I mean real help?"

"Re-communication to the Church is my only option, and the archimandrite who performed the act is long dead."

His despondency and the finality of what awaited him rang through the bond like a death knell.

"Surely any priest could reverse the excommunication and bring you back to the Church."

"I am afraid it is more complicated than that. The lineage of the archimandrite is the most important, and it is only that lineage that can help me. But it would not matter, Tamara, if the man stood before me today. I have no remorse for my wrongs. I would do them again."

"Do you think of her?" I asked, speaking of Irena.

"Only every other thought," he answered back.

"I want to help you, Adrik," I murmured, realizing that the inkiness of the night was beginning to fade into a hazy gray. How powerful would the bond be at daylight? There was still so much to say.

"Tamara, I too feel the power of the sun. Despite its presence, the bond will still be strong because of the amount of blood you have consumed. Strong enough that you can feel me but not likely understand my thoughts and words. You must understand that I, at times, have no control over my mumblings. In one sentence, I will beg you to come to me, make promises that I can never keep, and in the next warn you away. You must understand this. I freely accepted the consequences when I cheated death that night. I have no regrets. And no illusions. I am a killer. Never trust my promises of safety. When I was well fed, I had control. I chose my prey, but after this long, I am like the poised snake. My prey will choose me.

"When I first felt you," he continued on, "I thought back to the doctor and the theft of my blood, and I hoped you would drink every vial he had taken. Then I could drag you, forcibly, to my grave, and I would be free. That you were a woman was obvious from your first drink, and I thought to make you culpable for Irena's sins because of your womanhood. But after wandering through the brokenness that lives in you, I know you are as much the victim as I. And now I find, I do not want to hurt you. But make no mistake, I would. I already have."

"You haven't hurt me, Adrik." But it was a lie.

"Haven't I? You are now eternally connected to me. My every thought, my every suffering will be yours to share. I will haunt you night and day. When the sun rises and my body falls slack, my mind will cry all the more, and when the sun sets, I will seek refuge from my own thoughts and will seek you out. I am laid bare to weakness. The Bible says man cannot serve two masters, for he will love the one and hate the other. My master is hunger, and I do not fool myself by thinking otherwise. I will hurt you further if given the chance. Be careful that you do not present the opportunity."

What he said was undeniable. We'd been as one, and he was not just hungry, he *was* hunger. I had felt it myself, understood its power, and I had no intention of unleashing it on my home town.

"Adrik, what did you mean when you said I wasn't ready for revenge but I would be?" I asked.

"Rage burns in you, Tamara. You have your own hungers, and eventually they must be sated."

It was the last intelligible words we exchanged. The earliest rays of the sun erupted over the top of the mountain range in a golden glow that chased any lingering darkness away.

The sky remained clear as the sun climbed the horizon, without the usual thick cloud cover that typically dominated the sky over Sitka. The sunny disposition of the morning left him wordless and weakened, but I could feel him still, battering against the back of my mind.

I knew he suffered, remembering from the dream how the sun, even on cloudless days, caused his bones to ache. I remembered his need to stretch when not even the tips of his fingers would flex.

The taste of the loneliness gagged me as I felt it wash across him. The desperation of being trapped beneath the earth made me shudder as I remembered the feel of the bugs on his skin and his water-filled lungs. I could taste the bitter burn of hunger in the back of his throat and feel the parchment that was his throat.

Distantly and only in the barest of whispers, he spoke, but I couldn't understand him. I struggled with the harried, frenzied voice, but in the end, it was like the constant buzzing of insect wings, and it left me feeling anxious.

It was miserable. Not only the sensations that I experienced through the bond but also knowing Adrik was trapped in such a hellish existence. I wanted to help him. He was, in a bizarre way, a friend and confidant, and part of me loved him so how could I leave him in this state and do nothing? And yet how could I help him?

I've always considered myself weak. The counselors at the shelter had worked to convince me I was stronger than I gave myself credit for. They were wrong. I could not stand the barrage of his thoughts in my mind.

Adrik had said it was comforting to have someone to share his thoughts with, and yet now, while he lay tormented, I decided to desert him. I could not listen to his mind anymore.

I spent the next hour praying, and while my lips whispered words to the Lord, my mind was safe from Adrik. But I can only pray for so long it turns out before I get distracted. My mind would wander, and Adrik's consciousness would vine its way back into my thoughts, and I would find myself awash in utter despair.

I dug through Mom's small collection of jewelry and between the hundreds of handmade bracelets and earrings, I found a small crucifix on a leather cord. I tugged it over my head but found little relief. Adrik's frenzied voice still reverberated in my mind. I needed something stronger to overcome the bond.

The hallowed ground of the cemetery would give me the greatest relief I decided, so I called Peter, asking if he could meet me there again. Perhaps if anyone could think of a way to help Adrik, Peter could.

# Chapter 15

The road into town clung to the coast for most of the drive. Fog had rolled in from the sea and lay in fat heavy patches in the roadway. In the distance, I could see the next system of clouds working its way in. The sun was being inched away by the clouds, and Adrik's voice was getting stronger.

In reality, the drive was short but seemed longer with Adrik's constant barrage of my mind. It was with a great sigh of relief that I stepped across the threshold of the hallowed ground of the cemetery, all traces of the blood bond evaporating as I did. I breathed out the anxiety that had been with me all morning.

I found Peter sitting on the small bench that framed Mom's grave. Deep in thought, his fingertips rested on his temples and his eyes were closed. The brown of his raincoat camouflaged into the brown trunks of the evergreen trees that mingled amongst the gravestones and his feet were buried in the spongy moss that crept across the cemetery floor.

"Only a true friend would meet me in a cemetery two days in a row," I murmured as I set down beside him, hoping I didn't startle him.

He smiled as he turned to look at me. Locks of his blond hair lifted in the breeze and his eyes, a deep green, twinkled as they had as a teenager. It took me back fifteen years when he'd stolen a kiss. I wondered if he remembered that moment.

"Only a true friend would trust me with their secrets in a cemetery," he responded. "But I'm beginning to wonder if you have a love of the morbid."

"I feel a certain peace in this place that's hard to explain. My family's here I suppose," I explained as I leaned forward to remove a wilted flower from amongst a bundle of lilies that rested atop Mom's grave. The bouquet hadn't been here yesterday evening when I drove away. Strange, I thought, that someone would bring flowers so late yesterday or so early today.

"Your family's not here, Tam. They're in a better place."

"Of course I know that, but I still feel connected to them here. Maybe it was all the visits as a family to Dad's grave or the times I escaped here as a kid. I also spent quite a few hours here with you, or have you forgotten?" I gave him a nudge with my shoulder, hoping to jar some memories lose.

He smiled but didn't answer. "So, what's brought us here today?" He gestured to the damp greenery around us.

"First of all, let me reiterate once again that I'm not crazy," I said, eyeing him suspiciously.

"Okay. Let's make the assumption that's true." He was teasing me, but I could read concern in his eyes as he studied me.

"Seriously, Peter. I'm about to shock you."

He held his hands up defensively in front of his chest. "Seriously. I'm ready."

He wasn't, I knew, but I forged ahead regardless.

"You remember that journal I told you about?"

He nodded his head slowly and cautiously, his eyebrows disappearing into the locks of gold that framed his forehead as if he were agreeing to meet the devil himself.

"What I didn't tell you was that in the same trunk, I found a bottle of what looked like blood. The label, which was written in the same handwriting as the journal, said it was 'uppyr krov.'" I paused, letting the Russian translate into his English functioning brain.

"Vampire blood?" He said questioningly. His eyes widened somewhat and I saw him swallow a little harder than normal.

I nodded my head. I couldn't help but smile a little at his reaction. It was so Peter. "Yeah," I said, "vampire blood."

"That old bottle sitting on your mantle the other night. That's what you're talking about," he spoke quietly.

"Yeah, now this is going to sound really strange but I drank some of it," I continued despite his raising eyebrows.

His eyebrows cinched up even higher as he brought his hands down on his knees with a light slap as he took a deep breath. "Naturally! Of course you did. Because that makes *perfect* sense."

I nodded my head yes, my face coloring in response to the look of sheer disbelief that overtook his face. "Peter, it's real," I whispered.

"Real? As in, it really is a bottle of blood that this surgeon collected a couple of centuries back from a suspected vampire or you think it's actually vampire blood?" He turned to fully face me on the small bench.

"It *is* vampire blood, Peter. I know it is because I drank enough that it formed some sort of bond, and I can feel him, the vampire, in my mind. He's visible in my dreams, and it's just exactly like you said. It is exactly like all those legends you told me about. You know, how he can't die, he can't decompose, and he's imprisoned forever in the grave."

Taking a deep breath, Peter took my hand, folding it over in the warmth of his own. "Tam..."

I cut him off. "Peter, I know I sound crazy, but I'm not. This is real," I said harshly.

"Tamara, listen to yourself!"

I jerked my hand away at the condemnation in his voice.

"You said I could talk to you about anything. Well, here I am trying to talk to you, and I don't need any judgmental crap right now. Listen. Please." I kept my gaze firmly leveled on his, hoping he'd see the sanity in my eyes.

Around us, the wind picked up slightly and the heavy drops of rain that had collected earlier on the tree branches showered down while I waited for him to answer. He wiped away a drop that had landed on his eyelashes before squeezing the bridge of his nose for a second. Finally, he looked at me again, his eyes moved back and forth between mine for a long while before he looked away.

"You're right," he nodded. "Sorry. I won't interrupt again. Tell me," he said politely, but I could see the worry in his eyes. It was the same look he used to give me when he'd see Joel and I together—like seeing a fly in a spider web. You know the poor fly is doomed, and when you think about how the spider is going to tear the fly apart piece by piece, you start to reach for it out of pity. But you stop because it'll just come across another spider soon enough. I guess I'm a lot like the fly.

Peter was the salt of the earth; the kind of guy you should listen to when you didn't know which way to go, when the decisions all seemed like muddy, blurry trails that faded off into the trees. He wouldn't lead you astray, but listening to my gut or anyone else for that matter had never been my strong suit.

"You said yourself yesterday that you kept an open mind. Keep one now. I did, and I'm telling you that I've met this vampire. Not in this world," I gestured to the wooded area around us, "but in my dreams, and he's as real as you and me. I understand how hard this must be to buy into, but I need your help. I need your steadiness."

He nodded, his lips pressed firmly together but at least no longer squeezed into a blanched thin line bisecting his expression. "Fine. My mind is open. I'm not saying I believe you—at all. But if any of this is true, how can I help?"

I breathed out a sigh of relief. It had warmed up considerably and only wispy fogs of my breath dissipated on the air rather than the clouds that had hung around my head earlier in the morning.

"Thanks." I hesitated briefly before a rush of words overtook me. "Look, you've always been a good friend, and I've never thanked you enough. I know I hurt you in the past, Peter. The way I left and didn't even say goodbye. And then never writing or calling. It was wrong."

Relief followed immediately; I'd been needing to say that

again, even though I'd already apologized once. Sometimes it felt like I'd spend the rest of my life apologizing.

"You don't owe me another apology, Tam. An explanation maybe, but not an apology. I hope someday to hear your reasons, but right now, I want to focus on this vampire. So 'he's as real as us'... keep going."

"Okay, here goes. This journal was written by a surgeon named Klim Semenov in 1808. He gave an account of a man who was accused of rape and then excommunicated from the Church. The man committed suicide and then rose a vampire before he was staked by his best friend, Ivan. The thing is, when he was staked, this doctor bled him out and kept quite a bit of the blood. I'm not sure what happened to the rest of it, but one bottle remained in the trunk with the journal."

"And being the logical person that you are, you chose to drink it," he stated, exasperation underlining his words.

"Only a couple of swallows the first time, and the dreams were pretty mild, enough to pique my curiosity and scare me a bit but nothing dramatic. The next time I drank a little more, and the dreams became much more vivid. The bond seemed to get stronger the more blood I consumed until the vampire actually had the strength to pull me into this vision where I could read his mind and he mine. His memories were as real to me as my own. Kinda like I'd lived them alongside him. The intensity was incredible. It's really hard to explain, Peter; it was like I'd lived a completely different life. I think it was as close to reincarnation as you can get."

"Okay. Suppose this is true and you aren't simply delusional, what does he want?" Peter asked, acid leaking into his voice despite his placid face. "Or better yet, what do you want? You must have drank it for a reason."

"He's lonely," I breathed out. How ridiculous I sounded even to myself.

"Lonely? That's it? He's lonely like I'm depressed after spending two centuries in this grave and I'd like to have a tea party? Or lonely like, I'm rabidly hungry and as soon as possible, I going to rip your throat out with my teeth and drink your blood?"

"Well," I paused, "probably..." I started.

"Be honest, Tamara. It's the second choice, and you know it. If any of this true, he wants something from you. Don't be a fool to think he's just lonely, and don't make the same mistake you made ten years ago. This man or... vampire... or whatever he claims to be, is dangerous."

Anger crawled up my throat, wrapping hot fingers around my vocal cords. My voice came out in a tight squeak. "This is not about Joel."

"Isn't it?" he questioned harshly, scanning my face with his eyes. "Isn't this exactly like you and Joel? He was dangerous. He wanted to own you, and you couldn't see the truth that everyone else could see even though it was right in front of your face."

"I'm not blind, Peter. I know what I've gotten into this time. You're right about me wanting something as well," I answered.

His eyes went wide with surprise and then faded to disbelief. "God help me. I can't believe I'm hearing this. And I can't believe I'm saying this either, but if this vampire is real, then my guess is that you both want something very bad from one another. He wants to be freed, and you want some very bloody revenge."

"And what if I did? What would be so wrong with that? Joel killed my mother."

"You don't know that!" he stated back forcefully.

Starting to stand, I reached for the coat that I'd peeled off and laid across my knees. "Forget it. I should have known; you're just like everyone else."

On his feet before I could get to mine, Peter pressed his hands onto my shoulders and I flinched. This is where Joel would have hit me. I waited, still and quiet out of habit. Realizing his mistake, my friend pulled his palms away, calmly, lifting them to where I could see them.

"Sorry, Tam. I didn't mean to get upset. I just don't want to lose you to any kind of madness again. Not now. When I'm so close to having you back."

The bench below me was still warm when I sat back down. "Joel killed her, Peter. I know it as sure as I'm sitting here."

Lowering his tall frame down beside me once again, he took one of my hands in his. "Let's say that's a definite. Will killing Joel change that? Will staining your hands with his blood erase the past? It will only end up destroying you too. Let it go, Tam."

"Joel will kill me. Can't you see that?" I pleaded with him for understanding. "I'm as good as dead if I don't do something drastic. I need an edge he can't expect."

"You want an edge? Then leave here. Sell that house and get off of this island. It's a big world, Tam, and you can get so lost in it that he can't find you. I'm selfish, and I would love to keep you here. But I'd rather you be safe. I would rather you be happy. Just like ten years ago."

"You just said you didn't want to lose me again, and now you want me to leave?" I questioned, confused.

"Knowing your safe, alive, and happy. That's not losing you, Tam. That's finding you all over again."

I shook my head, my arms crossed stubbornly across my chest. "No. No! I cannot leave here. It's not just about me. Mom deserves justice. Joel needs to pay. Besides, I can't run for the rest of my life. And that's what I'd be doing, Peter. Running. And I'm done with that."

"And by 'pay', you mean what exactly? Would you be satisfied if he was charged with your mom's death? Would it take a conviction? The death penalty? You could spend your entire life waiting for any of these to happen, so what line has to be crossed for you to be happy, Tam? Would it be enough if I said I believed you? I believe that Joel killed your mother. He's a dangerous psychopath, and he is guilty! Is that enough?"

"No, Peter. I want him to..." I stopped, not wanting to give him the satisfaction.

"Suffer. You can say it, Tam. You want him to suffer. That's called revenge, not justice."

He waited for me to admit it, but I refused. Instead, I forced my eyes away from his, watching a fat white bird that had settled onto a tree limb a few feet away. It pecked at the remnants of a few red berries clinging to the wet wood.

"Revenge always comes back to haunt you. When you curse your enemies, the spell finds its way back to you through someone you love. Revenge is a net that never fails to be broader than you give it credit for, and if you cast it out, you need to be prepared for what you catch."

I couldn't help but smile, even if the expression was a little cold and uncomfortable. "Yeah. Adrik said I wasn't ready for revenge." I didn't add that he'd also said I would be soon.

"Who's Adrik?" Peter asked. "That's a name you don't hear very often. Who is he?" He looked puzzled.

"Well, you wouldn't know him. He's been buried under the ground for over two hundred years."

"The vampire? His name is Adrik?"

"'What? You thought he didn't have a name?" I laughed.

"I've heard that name somewhere. I just can't put my finger on where. Maybe from Dad?" He questioned out loud.

I shrugged my shoulders at him. "I'd never heard it before. I looked it up in an old book of Russian names that Mom owned. It's a really old Russian name."

"It'll come to me. Keep going. Why'd he say you weren't ready?" he asked, his skeptical expression softening slightly.

I sighed heavily, knowing I sounded like a complete fool. "Forget it. I realize with each sentence how absolutely nuts I sound."

"We're way past worrying about that small point," Peter reminded me. "Spit it out."

I shrugged. "Fine. Adrik offered to kill Joel if I let him out of his tomb. And I said no because I didn't want to die, of course, but I also didn't want anyone besides Joel to die. So he said I wasn't ready for revenge if I was worried about collateral damage."

"I didn't know vampires had so much intuition," Peter said. He had such a peculiar expression that I wished again for a cell phone. It would have been a perfect camera-phone moment.

"There's a lot you wouldn't guess about him. I spent a century with him, Peter. At least that's how it felt. He's certainly a killer but not cruel. And he's not a liar. He reminds me often that he chose this life. But you can't imagine how horrible it is. I can still taste the dirt between his teeth, feel the gritty water on his face. And that's nothing compared to the emptiness of time." I shivered remembering what I'd experienced. "I started down this path to help myself, but now I want to help him too. He doesn't deserve this. I know what he did because I lived it with him in my dreams and despite the people he's killed, he doesn't deserve this special form of hell."

I turned to Peter when he didn't respond. His eyes were squinted as if he was looking backwards into time or searching through old memories in his past.

"Peter?" I rubbed his arm to bring him back to me. He looked up, startled, and drew in a deep breath.

"Sorry. I was remembering something Dad told me a long time ago. Listen, Tam. You don't owe this Adrik anything. Look at me," he spoke firmly, giving my hand a tight squeeze. "You said he committed suicide after he was excommunicated. He's beyond your help. He's beyond anybody's help. Leave it alone. The only person who could help him is some ancient dead bishop likely buried layers down somewhere below our feet," he said, pointing to the ground beneath us. "Put this entire experience behind you and forget him."

"I can't. How can I? I'm no different than him. I won't lie to you; I wish Joel was dead. I'd kill him myself if I thought I could get away with it, and maybe even if I couldn't. So how can I just walk away from this man or vampire or whatever he is and leave him suffering alone when I'm no different than he is?"

"You walk away because that's the right path for you. He's beyond your help," Peter said, grasping my hands again. "You're still salvageable. Flesh and blood, hands clean of any wrongdoing. You're different from him because unlike this Adrik, you haven't justified to yourself the collateral damage that your revenge would cost. He clearly did. Innocent people died because he justified his actions. When you reach the point that you justify the suffering of innocent people so you can serve up your own revenge or when you tell yourself that you'll be careful and no one else will get hurt, you're no different than Joel. Or this Adrik. Walk away from all of this and don't look back!"

My hair misted drops of condensed mist as I shook my head. "A part of me loves him, Peter. It's like I spent a century with him. I can't forget. I can't walk away." I spared him the details of being tied to Adrik for the rest of my life through the blood.

"You love him." Peter laughed, bitterness seeping into the sound as he scrubbed his hands across his forehead like he was rubbing away a headache. "Why do you always love what's so very bad for you? Do you want to be the victim? Is this some weird variation of the Stockholm syndrome?"

My initial reaction was to be angry, but it was a well-deserved blow. How could Peter know that Adrik understood me more than him? Understood that I was tired of being the victim.

Peter was quiet for a several minutes, and I gave him space for his thoughts, not saying anything else for the moment. A fine grainy snow had begun to fall from the skies, making little twangy sounds as it hit the rain jacket lying across my lap. I slipped it on, glad for the down lining against my body. Above the canopy of trees, the clouds piled upon each other, obscuring the sun.

"Have you ever heard the poem of the girl who fell in love with death?" Peter murmured.

I shook my head no.

"'Here lies the girl who fell for death. He stole her heart and took her breath. He kissed her as he took her life. She should have watched out for that scythe.'"

"Where'd you hear that?" I asked. "It's actually kind of... beautiful."

"Read it on a tombstone in Ireland a few years back. The poem may be lovely but death is not, Tam."

"I wasn't planning on dying, Peter. I just wanted to borrow a little strength or find an unexpected edge. I'm not going to do anything stupid. I'm not going to make anyone else suffer."

"You already have," Peter murmured and rubbed his hands across his face. I could barely make out his words so I didn't comment.

What little of the afternoon light remained was fading fast. Thin fingers of fog were beginning to poke through the ground cover and settle in the little valleys of the cemetery like heavy hands. The temperature had dropped again, and our breath leached away on the light breeze.

"I would do anything to protect you, Tam. From Joel. From vampires. But I can't save you from yourself." He brought my hands up, his lips grazing the backs of my hands, before setting them back down into my lap. "Don't do anything rash. Please just walk away from all of this."

He waited for a response, the snow drifting down around us to land lightly on our jackets. Dusk had nearly overtaken the island, bringing with its darkness a quieting of the winds. The flakes now swirled in the easy breeze rather than pelting us as it had earlier.

He stood, punching a few keys into his cell phone, and I knew he had to go. No doubt his parishioners needed him more than me. I wanted to reassure him before he left that I wasn't as foolish as he thought. Tell him I'd listen to him for once; I'd walk away from all of this craziness. That I'd leave with him now, book a flight at the airport and get the hell out of here.

But the tether of the trap I'd set for myself held me firmly to the bench. Beyond the confines of the hallowed ground waited the stream of Adrik's consciousness, and the knowledge that I'd never be free of him weighed heavily on my mind. What would it be like to face his cries for mercy on a daily basis until I took my final breath? Would insanity eventually deliver me to him just so I wouldn't have to listen? How long could I last when I hadn't even been able to make it through this morning?

Peter waited patiently, giving me plenty of time to make the right decision; I avoided his gaze. Instead, I studied the new bundle of lilies on Mom's grave. Orange lilies, they were my favorite, and it struck me then how odd it was for anyone who knew Mom to have placed them on her grave. Her favorite color was pink. It had been the one girlie thing about her. One end of a pale yellow card lifted on the breeze, and I pulled it out of the paperclip holding it to the ribbon.

I scanned it quickly, expecting a distant relative or one of her church friends. I'd send them a thank-you note for thinking of Mom. "Some things are worth falling for," the note read in a too-neat print.

The hair on my neck stood up while a tingling began in the center of my chest, expanding outward and trailing down my arms and legs. My skin went cold and flashed to hot. Sweat beaded under my arms and between my legs. Nausea cramped my bowels and gripped my throat.

Joel had often left me speechless, and this time was no exception. Six little words that would prove nothing. To anybody except me. But they were meant for me, weren't they?

"Tam, did you hear me?" Peter asked, breaking the silence that had overtaken me.

Plastering a fake smile on my face, I smiled at Peter, knowing what I had to do.

"Peter, I didn't realize how much I missed this place until I came back. How much I missed you. How much I *will* miss you." I paused, letting my words sink in. "I'm going to take your advice and catch the next flight out to Seattle tonight. I didn't look back the first time I left, but this time, I won't be able to stop looking back."

Part of what I said was true. I would miss him. I would miss Sitka, but not because I was leaving. I just didn't plan on being a part of it for much longer. In the moments it took to read the card on the flowers, my mind had been made up. I was very ready, just like Adrik said I would be.

But I needed to know that Peter wouldn't worry about me and that he wouldn't try to save me. That he'd be safe. He was the one person who still meant anything to me.

"Part of me is jealous, Tam. You know how badly I wanted to

leave here. How I wanted to change the predestined course of my life," Peter answered.

And I did know. It was the exact reason I'd avoided him like the plague when we were teens. I'd craved freedom from the predictable. "You still have time," I urged. "Take your own advice. Start a new life somewhere else and find that adventure you always talked about when we were teens." I wanted him to be safe and how much simpler it would be if he left this island.

He smiled but shook his head no. "I guess I've truly became my old man. I've learned to appreciate the predestined plan, and this is where I'm meant to be. Just like my father and his father before him. All the way back to when Sitka was first settled."

*That's a long, long time to be stuck here*, I thought to myself, and no sooner than I did, I saw my friend with new clarity. "You can trace your pastoral lineage back to the founding days of the city." I spoke my thoughts aloud.

Nodding, he answered, "Yeah. Imagine trying to break that mold."

I smiled at my good fortune, knowing I could ensure his safety now. Standing, I took one of his large hands in mine, tracing the curves of his lined palms. "I came back to find some peace about Mom, but I found you instead. I'm glad you were here with her when I wasn't, and I can't ever thank you enough for that. If I could make a wish, it would be to have the last ten years back. I wouldn't let you go again, Peter. I made some really big mistakes, but letting you go had to be the biggest one of all."

I studied his face in the waning light, attempting to burn the image into my mind. This is the way I wanted to remember Peter. Youthful. Strong. The green of his eyes. He started to bring my hands to his lips but instead, I lifted my arms to his face and pulled his mouth to mine. I kissed him with all the passion that he deserved for the last decade and for all the years that we'd never get to spend together. He returned my embrace, pulling me in close to his body with powerful arms.

For those brief moments, I didn't think of Joel or Mom. Or

what could have been or what would never be. I didn't think of the cold ground or the tombstones around us. I just let Peter hold me for the last time.

"You need to go," he said matter-of-factly as he pulled away. "There should be a few seats left on the nine o'clock circuit flight."

"I know. You go on. I'm going to say goodbye to Mom and Dad one last time." I motioned to their graves, tears brewing. I looked away quickly so I could hide my emotions. They were too strong, and I feared he'd see through my façade.

"Call me when you get to Seattle. I'm not letting you get away so easily this time. It should have been me instead of Joel," Peter said, his voice strained. He squeezed my hand, kissed me lightly on the lips and turned to walk towards his car.

"I won't call for a while. I'm not going to take the chance that Peter will use you, somehow, to get to me. Like he did with Mom. We'll find each other again when this thing with Joel is all blown over."

"I'll be watching for you then," he said. "That's a promise, Tam." He turned away quickly, I suspect, so I could not see the tears that I knew were in his eyes.

"Peter, one more thing," I called after him.

He stopped, turning only slightly towards me. His face was still averted and his hands were pushed deeply into his pockets. "Anything," he answered.

"Don't check on the house. Don't go anywhere near it. If Joel catches you out there, it will put him into a rage. He knew how I felt about you so please don't put yourself in jeopardy."

He nodded, and I turned so I didn't have to see him leave. Moments later, the whine of his car engine cut through the silence of the cemetery, and I was alone.

Even though the cemetery was only a short distance from the center of town, it was absolutely quiet. Light from the bordering houses barely penetrated the darkness. The graveyard was set into a depression at the top of a small hill, and I was visible to no one here in the darkness.

Violently, I jerked the arrangement of lilies from atop Mom's grave, throwing them as far as I could into the brush that bordered the path. Tears that I'd hidden from Peter streamed down my face. The emotions I'd kept in check exploded out, shrieks ripping from my throat, and I buried my face in my hands so there was no chance anyone would hear me.

I shook roughly from head to toe with so much more than just anger until my muscles ached and I sunk down beside Mom's grave, the wetness of the ground sinking into the knees of my jeans. Curling into the fetal position, I cried until my eyes went dry and my lungs simply refused to spare any additional breath for sobbing.

I lay there in the dark and wet for a few moments longer until I forced myself to my knees again. My terror tried to keep me on the ground, but my rage drew me to my feet. With raw vocal cords, I whispered my goodbyes to my parents. In a few short hours, I'd never set foot on hallowed ground again.

From the time my feet struck the ground outside the cemetery, I felt the barrage of Adrik's mind. Every vestige of daylight had vanished, leaving me open and exposed. Though he was weak compared to the former strength of when he was first made, the onslaught of his consciousness was still like a battering ram. I felt him start to sift through my thoughts like sand in a child's hand.

His cool humor radiated across the bond. "It seems you are ready now," he whispered across my thoughts.

"He needs to die," I said aloud to no one in particular.

Adrik said not another word as I drove to my house. I grabbed a few clothes and put them in a suitcase so it appeared I'd packed. I wrote a note for Peter, fully expecting him to ignore my warnings, reminding him of the danger of Joel and left it on the table.

In my mind, Adrik only laughed.

# Chapter 16

The Sitka airport sits on a small island just to the west of town. I crossed the small bridge and parked my car in the center of the parking lot, leaving it so that Peter would see it and believe I'd left for Seattle.

The local airline flies in circuits around southeast Alaska. The last flight of the night would be leaving shortly, and I bought a ticket to further convince Peter that I'd left. The ticket took all of my cash, but it didn't matter. What I was about to do didn't require money. Then I left the airport in search of Joel.

The walk was long; rain pelted down from heavy, low-lying clouds, but I had all night. Besides, he would be easy to find. He'd always loved his beer.

He was leaning against an ancient jukebox when I pushed open the door to a hole-in-the-wall bar on a side street just off of downtown. The interior was dark, meant to convince you that some degree of anonymity existed in this small town. Smoke hung around his head as he leaned in towards a girl, sucking on his cigar in a vulgar display. He held a beer bottle loosely in his left hand. With his right, he was stroking the inside of her bare arm.

Joel turned in my direction, no doubt feeling the heat of my gaze, as I walked towards him. The girl at his side reached out for his arm to pull him back towards her, but he shook her off, walking a few feet towards me.

"I got your message in the flowers," I whispered, leaning

forward to speak softly in his ear. I tolerated his arms as he intertwined them around my waist.

"You need to come home," he whispered intimately as he placed warm lips to the skin of my cheek. "You're real selfish, you know."

"How's that?" I asked.

"You keep on putting other people in danger. Like that priest friend of yours," he spoke into my ear again. He'd pulled us onto the small dance floor. We swayed slowly to the music. His large hands slipped under my jacket, stroking my back. I forced myself to accept his touch.

"Time's running out for you, babe," he whispered.

I smiled. "No, it's just beginning. Be careful of the priest, Joel. I've been to the police about you every day. They will notice if something happens to him. I'm going to disappear for a while, but don't give up on me. I'll be back. You better stick around. Cross your t's and dot your i's. You wouldn't want to give anyone the wrong idea by running off, okay?"

I pulled away, and he didn't try to stop me. He wouldn't make a scene in the middle of a crowded bar. He really didn't like witnesses. I watched him closely until I'd backed out the door, and then I ran as quickly as I could down the fog-entrenched street. I wouldn't be around to find out, but I'd bet good money he'd be looking for me just as soon he could walk out of the bar unnoticed.

I ran the nearly two miles to Totem Pole Park, which had been formed years back from the land where the Battle of Sitka had been fought. A walking trail had been cut through the forest marked by copies of original totem poles. The last totem of the trail marked the location of the Tlingit Indian fort where the Tlingit had held off the Russians in 1804. The land was still cleared here in remembrance of that fateful day, and Adrik was buried somewhere in that clearing. The park headquarters were closed this time of night, but it was a simple thing to jog around the corner and disappear into the forest that edged the street.

The darkness of the night was heavy, blanketing the woods so thickly it was almost impossible to make out my hand in front of my face. Scattered ribbons of fog wound through the trees and drifted across the ground. It gave the park a haunted feeling and broke up the blackness around me.

The wheels of an occasional car gritted against the highway that followed the contours of the park, and the headlights would flash through the trees behind me, creating a myriad of strange figures from the gnarled and broken tree limbs. I caught my breath a hundred times thinking the outstretched arms of a felled tree belonged to Joel. It was a relief when I'd finally stumbled far enough off of the road that the lights could no longer penetrate the denseness of the forest.

My breathing was ragged by this time, and I leaned against a damp tree for support. I was hot from running, and steam lifted from my skin when I slipped off my jacket and tied it around my waist. Around me, the forest was unnaturally quiet. Not even a bird broke the silence.

Adrik had been relatively quiet over the last hour, but now I could feel him grow restless as he sensed my presence in the woods. Closing my eyes, I emptied my mind of everything except the tug of the bond and let it carry me forward into the dark.

Moss-covered tree limbs pulled at my clothing and dug into my face. My shoes twisted in mud that sucked at my feet, and I fell to my knees a few times, but I didn't dare open my eyes. I could sense Adrik more without my eyesight interfering with the tether of our bond.

Without vision, the bond became nearly palpable with every step I took closer to him, and I followed it into woods. His every thought was of me. The beat of my heart played in my own ears as he focused on the rhythm. His mouth watered and I could taste his saliva. I felt him dig his fingernails into the palms of his hands. I heard the sound of my footfalls through the bond. His fangs cut into his tongue, and I tasted his blood in my mouth.

The bond was a band of energy. With each step in the right

direction, it shivered in anticipation. With every misstep, I could feel the tension gather as it jerked me back onto the right path. It became so powerful as Adrik focused his every thought on drawing me to him that I simply had to point my foot in a given direction and instantly I'd know whether it led me to him or away.

The last of my footfalls brought me directly over his grave. He whispered to me that I had arrived. That he waited.

On hands and knees, I knelt down and began to tear wildly at the ground. No one was around to tell me I was defiling a state park; it was only the two of us, and I dug my fingernails into the wet ground with as much force as I could.

His grave was on the edge of the clearing, and in the center stood the final totem pole. The evening was so dark that the great pole cast no shadow whatsoever onto the empty ground around it. Only the drifting fog draping itself around the pole illuminated its ghostly form in the darkness; the eagle at the top of the totem glared at my actions.

I turned my back on its knowing stare and dug my fingers even farther into the dirt, throwing clods of earth into the air behind me. Despite the few rocks that I came across, my nails gave way as I clawed through ancient and rotted root systems.

Needing more purchase in the wet earth, I grabbed a nearby tree limb and snapped it in half across my knees. With every muscle fiber in my body, I used the limb to gouge deeply into the packed forest floor.

I pulled at the years of caked dirt and roots until my every muscle burned with the fire of exhaustion. And then I would see Joel's face in my mind and know it was the last image my mother had seen. Hatred and rage ran hotter than my exhaustion, and I pushed past it, digging until a sharp metal tip bit into my skin. I jerked my hand back, gritting my teeth against the pain as blood welled to the surface and dropped like hot wax onto my legs.

I sat back and studied the metal for a second before striking the metal tip protruding from the ground with my tree branch. Adrik spasmed in pain; I could feel the agony across the bond, and I knew I'd found the mark.

Using the metal tip as a guide, I dug through the muck until my fingers scraped across the clammy feel of wet skin. The sensation startled me and I jerked my hands back but for only a brief second before I sucked my breath in for resolve and began to unearth his body from the stake upwards. I focused only on his chest and head, careful to keep his arms and hands buried.

Weakened by time, the iron stake and cross could not keep the muscles of his chest and neck from contracting, and ever so carefully, I began to clear his head and neck. I started high, smoothing the mud and debris from his hair, the locks of which had grown long, curling through the mud.

He jerked angrily with the slowness of my movements, anxious to be free of his centuries-old prison. His body convulsed upwards, lifting his head farther from the mud that encased him. With each movement, jet-black strands broke from their muddy molds and snaked across my skin. I struggled not to jerk backwards at the slimy feeling. I couldn't afford to let his hands get a hold of me before I accomplished my plan. I doubted he had the strength to move too much against the stake, but I wasn't about to take the chance.

I'd be guaranteed nothing but death if he could sink his fingers into my wrists or my heart. It would be a simple matter to kill me and then drink my blood as it poured from my veins, and I'd get nothing in return.

When I had cleared away the muck and could make out his features, I grasped the stake firmly in my left hand and twisted it violently forward and side to side in his chest. Underneath me, I could feel his neck contract in a silent scream, his lungs too full from years of dirt to be able to make sound. Twisting it harder, I urged him to lie still, promising him no further pain if he did what I said.

Steadily, he relaxed underneath me, but I kept one hand on the stake while with the other, I resumed freeing his head and neck from the clutches of his tomb. Using my thumb as a scoop, I scraped grainy layers of mud from his eyelids, and I pried his dirt-caked lids apart so he could physically see me for the first time.

While I could barely see him in the dark, having to rely more on touch than anything else, I knew that he could see me with absolute clarity. Reflected in my mind was my own image. My face was dripping with muddy drops of perspiration, and my hair hung down in sodden locks that framed my face. My lips were curled back over my gritted teeth.

He bared his fangs at me, and I ground the stake harshly into his chest to show him who had the upper hand. Through the blood bond, I sensed the intensity of the pain, but I dared not to ease even the slightest pressure on the stake. I needed this small upper hand.

Sucking in his breath harshly, I watched his nostrils flare with my scent. He remained buried from the mid-chest down, and I sat atop him. Between our bodies, I guessed there was about twelve inches of dirt through which I could barely feel the heaving of his chest as he tried to suck my scent deeper into his lungs.

He couldn't rise against the metal stake Ivan had replaced through his heart to pin him to the ground. But still he could flex his arms and legs enough that I could feel them twitching through the dirt between us and he could lift his head slightly. When I twisted the stake, his body went motionless except the hiss of air through his clenched teeth.

"Are you able to listen? Try to concentrate," I calmly whispered to him. His mind was an angry, hungry red haze. I was getting images from him but not much in the way of coherent thought given the proximity to my blood that continued to drip onto my jeans.

"We can help each other, Adrik. I know how to release you not only from this grave but from this life altogether. I really can help you."

Through the barrage of thoughts I was getting, I made out an occasional sentence that made sense, and I let up on the stake a little, allowing him to think more clearly. He lifted his head slightly and began to cough decades of dirt out of his lungs.

"There is no help," he said through the bond.

"There is. I promise."

He didn't need me to tell him my plan; he could read it clearly in my thoughts.

"What about the collateral damage?" he asked, small amounts of air beginning to pass across rusty vocal cords. His Russian was guttural and harsh, but with the help of the bond, I understood him.

I felt my answer float through my mind. I left it there, unwilling to push the words out of my mind. *"I don't care anymore."*

Whatever remorse I felt had melted away earlier when I read the note left on Mom's grave. Peter had said I wasn't the kind of person who rationalized away the victims, to justify the suffering of others to satisfy my own self.

He was wrong, of course.

I'd justified doing exactly that ten years ago for nothing more than a man when I'd abandoned my family and friends. I saw myself clearly even if Peter didn't. But this time would be different. This time, I'd protect Peter. The whole island might die, but Peter would be safe.

His safety would not be an issue. Because Peter was the key to helping Adrik. How had I missed the connection for so long? Peter was the direct descendant of the archimandrite, the same one who'd excommunicated Adrik. No doubt, the bloodline went back a great many years, but it was the same one. Peter could release Adrik from this life by re-communicating him and Adrik wouldn't lay a hand on him, knowing that Peter was his only way out of this hell.

"What makes you think he will release me? He is of the archimandrite's blood, after all." Adrik's voice was barely audible, and I strained to hear him.

"You don't know him the way I do. He's kind. Peter would never want anyone to suffer," I answered, tracing away the dirt from one eyebrow.

"I find that hard to believe having known his ancestor." His voice was a rasp over clenched teeth.

The flavor of something sinister and violent wafted across the bond from his mind. It was different from his usual hunger but the sensation was fleeting, and I couldn't make it out. He focused on my smell, and his hunger pulsed so greedily that it drowned his other thoughts. He wanted to distract me, I knew. And it worked. I had my own revenge to plan.

"You have to believe me, Adrik. Peter's good—sincere. He will help you."

"The way he helped you?" He asked snidely.

"You can't help someone who doesn't want help. But he tried," I answered, thinking back to Peter's advice. A sane person would have taken it. "What I want is to see Joel dead." I spoke again. "I wanted that more than I wanted Peter."

That same sinister feeling floated across the bond, and I could taste it on my tongue. It was sweet at first, spreading out until it coated the insides of my mouth, and I swallowed in response and nearly gagged as the sweetness became so thick that I could barely breathe past it. I choked and started to ask him about his dark thoughts, but before I could, the sensation was gone and he was speaking again.

"Then the last vision that crosses Joel's dying eyes will be your beautiful face, Tamara. And as you lap up the blood that pools around his body, remember that nothing tastes quite as sweet as revenge."

My sight had finally adjusted to the inky darkness, and I could just make out the glittering of his eyes in the blackness. Sitting up to gain more traction, I grasped first the cross, pulling it from beneath the earth. His skin sizzled where it touched him as I jerked it away from the burnt tissue it was adhered against. Then, I clenched the stake more firmly as I lowered my bleeding right hand closer to his waiting fangs. He gritted his teeth, hissing violently as I shoved the stake side to side to gain control of his body.

The timing had to be perfect. The tip of the stake had to come out just as he lifted his lips to strike. A little too fast and the stake would be out, releasing him before he'd bitten me. At that point, I'd merely be dead. I needed his mark on my skin before I died if I was to rise.

Deciding a little insurance was best, I tasted my own blood with my tongue, and he went crazy beneath me. With bared fangs, he flexed his neck upwards, straining to get to me.

He was past reason, and I couldn't find a coherent thought anywhere in his consciousness. I took a deep breath and jerked the stake as hard as I could, feeling it slide out of the ground beneath him, through his body, and out into the air over my head.

The force of my pull would have thrown me backwards if his hands hadn't erupted through the ground to catch my back. So frenzied by my blood, he'd buried his fangs deeply into my wrist just as the stake had cleared him.

His body followed next, coming up out of the ground like the trunk of a tall tree as he rolled from the ground onto me, pinning me with his weight. His body was cold and wet; my t-shirt rubbing against his naked skin was no protection against the iciness of his body. I shivered beneath him out of both terror and exposure. My fate was sealed, my wrist bore his mark, but that didn't mean that I'd die well.

I'd chosen this but I couldn't stop the few warm tears that slipped out of my eyes from the pain and the fear, mingling with the mist before finally cooling on my cheeks.

He drew heavily on my wrist until I felt the tips of my fingers start to tingle and then finally go numb. A moment later, he angrily pulled his fangs out and plunged them into another artery. Only seconds had passed before I sluggishly realized that the second artery had collapsed beneath his hungry lips.

Lying beneath him, my head was spinning, and my vision starting to tunnel as he lifted his head from my arm. He studied me for a moment before he touched my chin with a finger, rolling my head to the side to look at him. Through the blood bond, I was vaguely aware that he was calmer, the hunger that had filled his head still present but through its red haze rational thoughts began to surface.

"Where is your home?" he asked, speaking both internally and aloud.

I was past speech, past forming collective sentences or complete thoughts, but his mention of home brought images of my childhood to mind.

I saw Mom standing on our porch, waving to me as I ran to the school bus, my grandmother cleaning fish in the backyard. Images of Peter driving me home in his dad's restored convertible mustang, my arms waving wildly back and forth in the wind as he took the curves a tad too fast.

Long-forgotten images of my dad surfaced to ripple across my slowing mind. He and I riding bikes to and from town, groceries stacked up in the little baskets above our tires. Dad smiling at me as we swung on the front porch, the warmth of his cradling arms while we watched the silver moon rising from the ocean.

With a map of the island and of my house in his mind now, Adrik brought my body back closer to his, penetrating the skin of my neck as he sliced his fangs into a hardier vessel. More tears slipped out of my eyes from the pressure of his bite and trickled down my face, leaving warm little trails across my cold skin.

The stake that I'd pulled from his chest rolled out of my palm, landing with a dull thud by my head, which seemed buried in sand. I was numb from the waist down except my feet which ached with a chill that had settled into the bones. It hurt to even breathe.

Death hovered around me, and I wished for the warm, yellow comforting light that those near death described, but it never came. I suppose that beautiful feeling is reserved for those not cheating the grave.

"I'm so cold," I felt my lips move, whispering to nothing and no one in particular.

"Soon, Joel's blood will warm you. It will flow through you like a fine wine." Adrik's words sounded like molasses dripping from a bottle somewhere in the distance. His wet lips brushed mine. They were warm against my cold skin, and I sighed when he pulled away from me—warm with my blood.

I'd never felt so much pain and even in my darkest days with Joel, I had never felt so much cold or so empty. Pain traced the length of my numbed limbs and I hardly realized it when Adrik jerked me from the ground. He was standing now, dirt and mud still dripping from his body. I swung easily in his arms as he began walking.

I remember nothing of the trip to my home. I recall only watching the porch-swing from a distance shudder in the wind as Adrik laid me on the ground in the forest bordering my yard and the sounds of him digging deep into the earth.

I drifted amidst an inky blackness until I felt myself being shoved into a wet, earthen hole Adrik had dug. I began to fight him, preferring to die in the warmth of my bed rather than this sodden grave. "It is safer this way and it is a necessity. You must lie in native ground for the passing of six months' time," he spoke. I fought him anyways because I was too far past reasoning to truly understand.

The tomb tunneled into the ground at an angle so that I could only make out a sliver of silver sky as Adrik pushed me through the entryway and into the cavern he had created. The root systems of the plants overhead trailed across the skin of my face, tangling in my eyelashes and tickling my lips. I tasted dirt on my tongue and felt the grit between my teeth as I was buried alive.

Panic started to overtake me even more, and with the little strength that remained, I clawed at the earthen roof over my hand. At least I think I did, perhaps it was only wishful thinking that I could still move my fingers. Adrik grasped my hands in his, jerking them down as he whispered to my sodden brain.

"Focus on the one for whom you accepted the vampire mark. See his face, remember his scent. Relive his hands upon your neck, his breath on your face. Think of the loved one he took from you and see her broken body. Make his countenance your last image, and it will bring you across death quicker. You are marked now. It matters not how you die or where. I will not leave you."

I quit fighting him and did as he said, and despite the pain and the cold, I could feel the heat again of my rage as it traced my numbed limbs. I pictured Joel's face inches from mine; I let his shouts fill my ears. I relived his every slap and felt again his doubled-up fists.

I let the terror of his rampages regain a foothold in my mind, remembered how I'd shaken with fear. Felt my face flush with shame when Joel slapped me the first time in our little apartment.

He'd laughed at me, my skin swollen with the imprint of his hand, that night as he'd shoved me down into the bed. And that's the way I pictured him in my mind now. Cold green eyes above high cheekbones that arched over a cruel mouth that could speak words that would make the devil blush and with the same tongue talk the pants off nearly any woman he wanted.

It was the face my mother had looked up at as she fell to her death, and I focused on every detail and recommitted to memory his every feature and line. Hate kindled deep in my chest and I let my mind run with the possibilities for his future sufferings.

My thinking was so tunneled that I no longer felt Adrik browsing the contents of my thoughts. I didn't see it coming when he snapped my neck. My last breath flowed out of my body; I felt it blow across my lips even as he slipped his fangs into the underside of my upper arm.

# Chapter 17

It took thirteen long and agonizing days for my body to catch up with my mind, and by the time I could first begin to stretch my muscles, I was burning with a hunger so intense that fire would have paled in comparison if it had been licking at my skin.

On the final evening of my confinement, I'd pushed up through my shallow grave into the fresh air of night with blood on my mind, specifically Joel's blood.

Joel's smell lingered in the yard around my home; I suppose he'd made a few visits to check out the rumors of my leaving, and the perfume of his blood drove me to distraction. The scent swirled through the remains of my lungs and coated the insides of my mouth. I licked my lips at the thoughts of what I'd do to him.

Adrik had urged patience, warning of the need for greater control before I took revenge. Angry, I lunged at him when he dared to contain my dark desires. I hissed menacingly in warning that he should leave me to my own plans and bared my fangs. He raised his eyebrows at my threats and returned a hiss so loud that it hurt my ears, but I was too headstrong and heady with my own strength that I dismissed his.

I twisted gracefully through the air, landing within inches of where he had been, but he was gone before my feet had even settled into the soil. Behind me, he reappeared with his fangs at my neck, and I realized how easily he could have severed my head if he'd wanted to.

"I know how you crave to taste him. And you will but take the time to enjoy it. Revel in the blood of another this night. Surely there is someone else worthy of our particular brand of pain? Your first kill will be difficult to control." He spoke the words into my ear. The blood bond hadn't survived the transition, and I was alone in my mind.

It was an easy choice. I had no second thoughts as I slipped through the forest towards a modern residential district just off the main highway. The unhelpful Detective Scott lived in a moderate home at the end of a cul-de-sac. The streets were dead, all of the neighboring homes darkened by the late hour, as I walked barefooted up to his front door. My knock echoed loudly in his entryway.

Behind the door, I heard the rustlings of bedcovers being thrown back. Adrik had melted into the shadows of the porch, and I stood alone. I knocked again, hearing the man inside slide something off a counter. I assumed it was his gun, and I smiled at its uselessness.

"Who is it?" Kendrick called from behind the door, and I put my face directly in front of his peephole.

"It's Tamara, Lena's daughter. Can we talk?" I spoke hesitantly, wanting to sound weak.

He sighed heavily and muttered something about stupid women. "It's three fricking a.m. It can wait until morning, Tam. Go home." He turned away from the door.

"Please. I need to get something off my chest. I really need to see you," I pleaded, letting some of my desperate hunger bleed into my voice.

Behind the door, his heart beat confidently, and I shook a little in anticipation. He sighed, a curse word hanging in his throat. I heard his hand run through his hair. I remembered his arrogance, and my mouth watered.

I could smell Kendrick everywhere. On the doorframe where he passed by on his way to work each morning. From a chair at the distant end of the porch where his scent mixed with coffee. That's where he began his days; behind me, I could hear the ocean driving away at the shore. No doubt, he had a lovely view of the coast. A shame he wouldn't see it again.

His smell was consuming, and suddenly I wanted in this house badly. Grasping the doorknob, I twisted it. Naturally, it was locked, and I shook it violently in my hands. It seemed little to stand between me and what I now wanted so badly. I raised my hand to force the door open, but from the corner of my eye, I saw Adrik and he shook his head at me. Kendrick had to invite me in. It was part of the magic that protected humans. My fangs were descended, cutting into my tongue in my anger, and I tasted blood oozing into my mouth. Reluctantly, I pulled my hand from the doorknob and waited for the human, my former classmate, to open the door.

"I hope to God this is important," he muttered as he slid the bolt lock out of place and opened the door.

"Thanks, Kendrick," I said, my head down a little so he couldn't see my face too well in the shadows of his blinding front porch light.

One large hand rested on the doorframe, his gun held casually in the other, he was only a little nervous, and it barely tinged his flavor. He should have known something wasn't right by the way I'd shaken his doorknob, but he'd been lulled into a false sense of security over the years. Taking a quick survey of the yard and completely ignoring me, the real danger, he motioned with his hand to come in. But I needed to hear the words.

"Can I come in?" I asked.

"For the love of all that's holy, Tam. Why do you think I'm holding the damn door? Get your ass in here," he spit out. "Just take your shoes off."

It's an Alaskan custom that you don't wear shoes into someone's house. It's very rude.

"I'm not an imbecile," I said as I stepped across the threshold, angry that he thought I had no manners. "I didn't wear any."

For once, the detective had nothing to say to me as his eyes dropped to stare dumbly at my naked feet. His puzzled look slowly morphed into confusion as his gaze traveled up the rest of me.

My skin was pale, ashen with hunger. The tattered remnants of my clothes were heavy with mud and leaves. Twisted dreadlocks of hair hung around my shoulders and dripped large dirty raindrops onto the perfection of his floor.

He brought his gun up, the holster dropping with a clap onto the tile at his feet. The leather case was soon followed by the weapon itself. His hand remained lifted in the air; his brain not quite up to speed that I had knocked the gun from his grip. He started to speak, but I slipped one hand hard around his neck, cutting off his air before he could tell me to leave.

He went limp in my hand, his eyes rolling backward into his head as he lost consciousness, and I lowered him to the floor, not bothering to get any farther into his house. I was simply too hungry. The artery in his wrist split easily under my nail and I bent my head to taste the red stream. The flavor was so powerful it made me dizzy.

Regaining consciousness as I loosened my grip on his throat, he began to fight, and I smiled as I flung one leg across him, pinning him easily underneath me. One weak scream escaped his lips before I clamped a dirty, bloody hand over his mouth.

Maybe it was the taste of his own blood that stained my skin that caused him to fight harder or the sudden realization that death was sitting on his chest. His eyes went wide, and he thrashed violently for a few moments before he became too weak from the blood he was losing all over the tile floor.

"Why?" Kendrick kept mouthing against the palm of my hand.

I leaned down so he could get a good look at my face and hear my words over the terror that was overshadowing his mind. "You're a detective, Kendrick, but apparently not a very good one. You're asking the wrong question. Right now you should be asking *how*. *How* is this happening? *How* is Tamara holding me down so easily? *How* did she get fangs? That's what you should be questioning. Not why! The why is simple. You didn't pay enough attention to my mom's case and I had to go to extreme measures. If you had asked more questions when my mom was killed, you wouldn't have to ask questions now." With my every word, I tapped his forehead for emphasis until his head was ricocheting from my touch.

I think I saw a light bulb go off in his eyes just before I brought his arm up, the artery still pumping, to my mouth and let his heart pump his life into my mouth while he watched.

Exsanguination is not an unpleasant way to go. It can be rather slow, depending on the artery of course, but not particularly painful. It seems you just drift slowly away as your vital organs get less and less blood. Your vision tunnels, and you lose sight of what's killing you.

Kendrick Scott, former classmate and bad detective, struggled weakly for a while longer until that peaceful, 'I'm dying', calm came over him. His pupils dilated slowly until they fixed and the dullness of death took the shine from his eyes.

Dead now and no longer in danger of turning him vampire, I sunk my fangs into his neck, retrieving every drop that I could find. I did the same at every juncture of his limbs where the arteries ran close to the surface of the skin. And when it was over, I backed slowly away from the body, only mildly shocked at what I was now capable of doing.

Adrik had been right to find a stand in for Joel for my first kill. I'd been so hungry that my lust would have gotten out of control with Joel, and I would have killed him too quickly, as I did this man. I didn't hate Kendrick; I didn't like him, but I didn't hate him, and so his death didn't excite me the way Joel's would have. Still, I'd killed him so quickly. His blood had pumped out in rhythmic gushes from too large an incision and an immediate need to fill my hunger.

"I want more," I said to Adrik as I returned to the porch, leaving Kendrick's body lying on the floor of his entryway.

He shook his head, a decisive no. "Slit his throat and anywhere else you marked him," Adrik said. "We cannot let our presence be known."

"No one's going to think of me when they see him," I laughed, drunk on the power of taking his life.

"Your beloved Peter might," he hissed back at me.

He was right. I could see that despite the haze of invincibility that clouded my mind, so I did as I was told.

With Kendrick's body taken care of, Adrik took my hand and pulled me into the woods that nestled the cul-de-sac in a cloak of darkness. I scowled, dreading to return to the dank tomb Adrik had created for us. It was a necessary evil, our protection at least until I could travel. Six months, and I'd be free of Sitka. For now, we would sleep beneath the earth.

But the night was far from over. It was barely past two a.m., and the sun didn't rise till nearly eight. I'd forgotten for the moment the coming of the dawn and the power of the sun. The knowledge that I'd lay paralyzed in the ground again in a few short hours was eclipsed by the fresh blood that filled me.

I wanted to careen through the woods, chase the wind that teased my skin. Scents of the previous day's hikers rushed around me, and I wanted to track them down in my state of euphoria. Adrik held me back, whispering caution. A small island is no place for a vampire so we'd have to be careful. Bodies stack up quickly in such a place.

For a moment, I considered defying him and giving in to the feeling of freedom that came with my nearly indestructible body, but the memory of Peter held me to Adrik's side. He'd certainly think of me if too many people were found dead in so small a time frame. Adrik needed less blood than I, and he'd already killed once, a young hiker still out in the woods at the wrong time, since I had released him from the grave.

We traveled the rest of the way through near silent woods, the quiet broken up only by the occasional crack of a stick underneath our feet and the call of a few birds.

The rain had passed for the moment as we climbed the steps to my house. Entering through the back door, we were careful to wipe our feet on the dirt-crusted rug outside. Peter, despite his promise, had come to check on the house several times. It was important that he not know I was still here so I certainly couldn't leave my footprints all over the house. But how nice it was to be here, in my own home, and to not have to ask permission to enter.

I could smell Peter; his fresh scent marking the doorways and the kitchen counter. Adrik noticed too, his nostrils flaring as he picked up the scent.

"He has been here again. He is becoming a nuisance," Adrik derided me from the kitchen. "We will have to deal with him soon."

Twice now, Adrik had risen from our daylight confinement to find that Peter had been to my house. Tonight, Peter's scent burned a path of longing through my veins that made my head spin and my dead heart ache. I traced his path through the house, caressing the wooden doorframe he'd leaned against and buried my face in the jacket he'd forgotten on the coat tree in the corner of the living room.

Tonight, Peter's scent lingered heavily around a small hallway table that held the family Bible. Although I couldn't touch the holy book, I held my hand above the pages, wondering what he'd found so interesting here. There was nothing unusual about the Bible except that it was old. My family had used it to record our lineage for generations. When Peter and I were children, Mom had read from it to us in Russian.

Beside the Bible, a few relics that Mom had kept lay around the family heirloom, a wooden cross hand-carved by a native man who lived in town and some beautiful beads from an ancestor's long since dilapidated wedding gown. Certainly nothing special and nothing that should pique Peter's interest.

I turned my attention back to the Bible again. Tonight, it was open to the pages listing my family tree, and I read the familiar names that had never meant anything to me despite Mom's best efforts. The first few names on either side were ancient Russian names whose birth dates and death dates were presumptions only. Dad's side of the family had originated with Yegor Semenov, the same surname as the owner of the journal and blood and I whispered a quiet thank you to him for saving his family's possessions.

Mom's family had originated in Russia as well. Her first ancestor to be buried in Alaska was named Ivan Korovin. It was this line that had intermarried with the Tlingit many generations back.

From the concentration of his scent, Peter had spent considerable time studying my family tree. His scent had imbedded in everything around the table. A pencil lay beside the Bible as if he'd been taking notes, and a nearby notepad was laced with the perfume of his skin. I'd picked the paper up, planning to take it to the grave with me that night. Lost in thought, I didn't notice Adrik watching me. He was leaning against the doorframe when I turned around, still holding the pad of paper with Peter's scent to my face.

"What was he doing here?" Adrik asked. "What interests him so in that Bible?"

"I don't know," I said, shrugging my shoulders. "He's a preacher. All Bibles interest him I guess.

Adrik raised his eyebrows skeptically at me. "I think his interest lies more in you, Tamara."

"Maybe. But he's lost to me now. I chose this life over him, and I have no regrets."

"He does not think you are lost to him, or he would not keep coming here. You cannot leave here for six months, which makes us very vulnerable. If he continues to be so inquisitive, Peter will become a problem that we must deal with."

"Peter is my friend. He's done nothing wrong. Besides, he can help you," I said across the darkness of the room. "He's the same to me as Ivan was to you. We cannot hurt him."

"You are the only help I want," he said, leveling his gaze at me.

Adrik was wet—we both were—from our hike home through the woods. Beads of water clung to the dark lashes rimming his blue eyes, like lush ferns lining the blue of a mountain spring. They brimmed with hunger. It was our first night together after I'd risen. He'd lain with me each evening, patiently awaiting my waking.

"You are thirsty. I was selfish with the blood tonight," I said. "I see the hunger in your eyes. I should have offered some to you."

"I have had the blood of another since I first laid you in the earth," he murmured, his eyes growing hungrier. "But the remembrance of your blood lingers still on my tongue. And the feel of your skin."

Thirst and desire flared in me again, but this time from deep in my groin. It flared up and outwards until I felt it tingle down into my thighs and up into my chest. Blood danced on my tongue as well. Peter's scent skipped across the air between us, an aphrodisiac even to me, who loved him so dearly.

The kitchen was no place to indulge the thirsts that teased us both now. The living room seemed a more appropriate place. Logs from one of my last human chores lay stacked neatly in the corner next to the fireplace, and soon a roaring fire blazed, warming the blanket-covered floor for the two of us whose skin was cool to the touch.

I was filthy. It seemed Adrik had figured out the concept of running water and had helped himself to a few old clothes of my father's. At least, I thought I recognized them. No invitation was needed to my house as it was not owned by the living.

I still carried the dirt of the grave and more than a little of the detective's blood, and so I pulled him with me to the shower. He may have understood how to turn the sink on for a quick sponge bath, but his eyes went wide with the warm water streaming from the showerhead. It was a glorious feeling to step under that hot flow and let it wash away the layers of filth that clung to my skin.

The shower was small, but after I was certain that every speck of blood and dirt had washed down the drain, I pulled Adrik into the enclosed space with me. He hissed sharply as the hot water slapped his back the first time and tried to sidestep from the unusual sensation.

Laying my hands on the smooth muscles of his chest, I forced him back into the water, feeling with my fingers the warmth working through him until it spread up through the pads of my fingers splayed across his chest.

He watched, at first apprehensively, as I lathered my hands up with the soap and spread it across the firm muscles of his chest. My fingers worked his skin and muscles harshly and layers of grime from two centuries fell in sheets to the bottom of the shower, leaving pale smooth skin in its wake.

Lifting upward on my toes, I washed his shoulder-length hair, the water running through it to cross his forehead and fall heavily across the fullness of his red lips. Becoming accustomed to the sensation of the water, he tilted his head back farther, letting the stream hit him full in the face. His fangs were bared, his lips parted. I watched as water streamed across his mouth and followed the contours from his angled jaw to his smooth chest. It hung in the hair of his belly and trickled farther south, and I hurried to finish washing him.

The blankets were hot to the touch as we settled down in front of the fire, the colors of the flames rippling across our wet skin. We seemed the perfect combination tonight. He was full of lust for body and blood. My willingness to give him both was evident on my face as he reached a hand towards my naked breasts.

Splaying one large hand across first one and then the other, he sucked in unneeded breaths as his fingertips met my fire-warmed skin. My nipples puckered as he fingers traced their shape. Leaning backwards on my arms, I tipped them into his now eager hands, and he lost his tentative touch, kneading my breasts harshly.

Droplets of water from our previous shower dripped from his head onto my belly as he leaned his head across my chest to take a nipple into his mouth. He bit first one and then the other. Lifting his head, he caught sight of the water drops trickling down my belly. A flick of his tongue caught them before they reached my belly button. His eyes slid to the dark triangle where my thighs met my body.

Still leaning back, I spread my knees somewhat as he rubbed

first one finger and then two into my closely clipped hair. He pushed my knees a little farther apart with his hands as he reached his fingers down to trace the valleys that he couldn't see.

His fingers slid into me, and I moaned slightly as he began to move them in and out, his thumb massaging me outwardly. With his other hand, he lifted my body up, and in between strokes of his fingers, he slid the length of his cock into me. I hissed lightly in response as my every nerve ending lit up from my pelvis to my core.

In the light of the fire, his muscles strained with his desire as he thrust into me. I wrapped my legs around him, forcing him deeper with each flex of my feet. His lust was building with his every stroke, as was mine, and I could feel the vibrations of his orgasm building deep within him.

Sitting back on his heels, he pulled me to straddle across him and with two more strokes, I took the virginity of this supposed rapist as he came forcefully into me. He buried his fangs deeply into the juncture of my neck and shoulder and drank until the contractions in my pelvis had stopped. I would have to feed again soon so strong was our moment.

There are some memories that are eternal, I think, remaining as bright and vivid in your mind as the day they were experienced. Like the first time I kissed Peter. His lips were soft and his hands warm as they cupped my face. I was human then, sensations not quite as strong, but that quick touch of his lips will warm me forever. In the same way, the taste of my initial kill and the feel of Adrik's arms encircling my waist on my first risen night will never fade.

# Chapter 18

The Roman philosopher Seneca once said that revenge is an inhuman word. He was later sentenced to death by suicide by the dictator Nero. How ironic that he chose death by exsanguination and slit his wrists before stepping into a hot water spring where he bled his life's blood out. The quote had made little sense to me when I had first began to study philosophy but now I saw it with new clarity. Revenge had, after all, stripped me of any shred of compassion I had left for Joel. If a trace of connection to him had existed in me, it had poured out the same as Seneca's blood the night I committed myself to this path.

Certainly, I didn't feel very human as I looked down from the waving spruce trees at the squat travel trailer clinging to the edge of the mountain. It was crowded onto a littered irregular lot with a tiny rectangular storage shed and an old rusted out jeep. I doubted it was more than twenty feet long and eight feet wide and it sat humped against the wind and surrounded by a variety of tools needed to debride the trees from the side of a mountain. Joel's car, I recognized it from the night he had trapped me in my yard, set a few feet away.

Like a cat, I hid precariously but effortlessly along the length of a tree limb, unaffected by the ice coating the bark. Neither did I look human suspended here above the ground, my straight, black hair waving in the cold wind that shook small clods of snow off limbs and dumped them onto the ground beneath my perch.

Several lots had been cleared out on this side of the mountain but so far none of them were occupied except the one below me. Joel was working up here; most likely in exchange for free room and board while he cleared the trees to make room for a level house pad. Sitka was growing and eventually these lots would sell and homes would be built, even if they were only tourist or summer housing. And when they were completed, riff-raff like Joel would have to move on.

But tonight, it was just him and me alone on this mountain, the face of which grinned headlong into the wind. Adrik had left an hour ago as I had stretched out on the tree limb about fifty feet up the eastern face of a large bodied Spruce tree and I remained exactly as he had left me, blending into the dark tangle of limbs.

Below, Joel sat protected in the metal shell, exhaust fumes boiling from a stack in the roof of the mobile home. His lights glared on the freshly fallen snow, and I could make out every word of the TV show he watched above the whistle of the wind. He had disappeared into the house shortly after Adrik and I arrived, reappearing only to throw the browned filter from a cigar out into the yard marring the perfection of the snow. His littering only made me hate him more, if that were possible.

His scent had filled my nose and despite my hatred of him, I could not help but appreciate the beauty of his flavors. Testosterone, which Joel had in spades, has such a pleasant aroma and I inhaled of him deeply and let him flow down into my lungs and wash across my every sense. Even now, the flavor still lingered in the air. My mouth watered, filling with the sweet anticipation of what Joel would taste like.

I had watched him nightly now since I first rose, well over a week ago. Frankly, I had surprised myself that I had managed to keep him alive so long. My last living thought had been of his death and as my mind began to wake from crossing over death, the same thought had consumed me.

Tonight would be perfect timing. I was thirsty but not out of control and I had spent the last week remembering all the reasons I hated Joel. His every slap, his cold words, my mother's death. I dredged up each bad memory, reliving them again and again while the sun held me captive in the ground.

No matter how bad the memories hurt, I focused on the way his hands had felt wrapped around my neck the first time I had made him really angry. I forced myself to remember the touch of his hands on my back each time he pushed me over the footboard of the bed and the humiliation of seeing myself in the mirror when I was so helpless.

My transformation to vampire had left me immortal and strong but it could not suppress the buddings of fear that built up in the pit of my belly while I re-lived the worst of my human moments nor did it keep my heart from aching as I imagined how my beautiful mother had felt freefalling to the earth. But the transformation did bring me ripping my way through the earth in a glorious rage on my first night as vampire and the sun would never protect Joel again.

The snow had stopped; the clouds curling away to reveal a brightly starred sky as I swung my legs over the side of the tree limb I was draped across and dropped to the ground. Out of habit, I bent my knees with the impact, landing quietly in the snow. I was barefooted and my tracks were small in the white blanket covering the ground.

The mountain was quiet tonight with the exception of the noise from the inane reality show Joel was watching. The wind had died down since I arrived and a bird that had been calling from deep within the forest had slipped so far away I could no longer hear it. The smoke from Joel's cigar oozed out from around the windows, the smell intermingling with gas fumes from the exhaust. The scent of boiling coffee joined in the fray.

I walked quietly to the door of the trailer, still not quite certain of what I was going to do to him but as I raised my hand to knock, I decided I just didn't have it in me to be civil and hope for an invitation. Instead, I placed my hands under the frame of the trailer and felt around until the strong metal braces that supported the floor cut into my hand.

The trailer was relatively small and it took very little effort to flip the metal box onto its side. From within, I heard the surprised shriek of a man caught unawares as the furniture flew topsy-turvy around him. The smell of slightly charred skin mixed with the smell of coffee wafted through the air. The lights to the camper flickered once before the electricity gave up its connection and everything went black and the fumes became stronger as the gas from the broken pipe feeding the mobile home leeched into the air.

Inside, I could hear Joel shuffling as he struggled to pull himself upright. His shrieks had turned to cool curses as he realized he had survived and I waited, less than patiently, as he located the now oddly positioned door and climbed out. I laughed a little at the doomed man who poked his head out of the camper like a worm from the dirt and peered nervously around in the dark.

No doubt Joel thought he had been hit by a blow down from the mountain. Wind events like that did happen and it was not unheard of to lose a vehicle or a mobile home to one. Cursing the weather that he had always hated, Joel slowly climbed out of the trailer before patting himself down and sighing with relief when his hands came away without any blood. It was only then that he noticed the burns on his right arm where the coffee had hit him and he cursed again as he pulled his sleeve down to protect the injured skin.

He surveyed the damage walking two steps to his right and then another three steps to the left, his hands rubbing backwards from his cheeks to his neck while he gathered his wits. From a distance, I watched, amused at his discomfort. "Well shit," he finally expounded into the darkness before kicking the bottom of the trailer that now faced the air rather than the ground.

For a moment, Joel resumed cursing the weather and Alaska before he pulled his cell phone out and then kicked the ground with his boot when he realized the cell phone service didn't reach this far up the mountain. "Dammit," he cursed again as he slammed the phone shut. Still shook up, he turned towards his car and then remembered the keys were in the trailer. He was having one of those nights and I smiled knowing it was going to get worse.

I could tell by the look on his face he was considering crawling back into the trailer but the smell of propane was strong and finding the keys in the swirled contents of the trailer would be like looking for a needle in a haystack. One more curse word slipped out of his mouth before he turned dejectedly towards town. I guess he was going to walk back but I saved him the effort and stepped out of the tree line from where I was watching him.

He saw me standing starkly against the backdrop of the forest that shrouded the small yard and he jerked back, stumbling, but managed to keep his balance at the last moment. I understood why he was spooked. I had not looked for my reflection in the mirrors of my house, too scared I would not see one, but I could see the unnatural paleness of my skin and how it gleamed in the partial moonlight almost like marble. I could feel the strength of my muscles and see my hair snaking across my near naked shoulders for since I felt no cold, I had worn the less restrictive clothes of summer.

A specter in the woods, I stood perfectly still while he blinked hard, once, to check his eyes but when he opened them I was gone and I watched him from the heights of the trees while he whirled around searching the darkness for where I might have went.

The rise and fall of his chest picked up even more than when he had climbed from the trailer and I could smell the fear oozing from his armpits. He mouthed my mother's name once as he tried in vain to pierce the darkness with his human eyes and just seeing those syllables on his lips brought my rage to new heights. How dare he utter her name!

But then I realized that to him from this distance I might look like her ghost. Mom and I were both of medium build with streaming black hair that fell to our waists. She had been a hair shorter than me but not by much. I had her eyes and her lips and now I had the pale skin of death. It was her specter that tormented him and I wished I had thought of the idea myself as he began to run wildly for the road. I cut him off at his driveway as I materialized from the thin air to stand in front of him.

"I want to talk to you, Joel," I said in Russian knowing that it would trigger unwanted memories. Mom had never deigned to speak English to him. He bolted backwards, his mouth slack-jawed and his eyes wide, before he finally turned his back to me and dashed without thinking into the blackness of the forest.

I let him run wildly into the woods as it was exactly where I wanted him to go before I took to the trees, skimming their great tangle of limbs in pursuit, while he careened out of control on the forest floor beneath me. He attempted to stick to the trail and he did for the most part except when I flew slowly enough from one tree to another that I appeared like a ghost at random moments and then he would crash to the ground.

Two times he fell so hard, his feet entangling in a tree root, that I thought he would not get up but fear propelled him on and his fingers dug into the wet ground for purchase before he managed to claw his way to standing and continue his wild run into the night.

The trail led him round the side of the mountain for a couple of miles before joining with another trail that led towards town. Joel stopped here at the fork in the trail as he did not have the breath to go another foot farther and he searched the darkness for the specter that chased him. Unable to find me, he did not fight the fatigue this time when his legs went out from under him. I watched from the tree tops as he lay on his belly, his head turned to the side with his eyes closed. His chest heaved for air and I could hear the pound of his heart against the ground under his chest.

When he opened his eyes again, I was on my knees beside him in the snow. He started at my presence and pushed backwards looking for footing but the slick of his shoes gave way in the snow and he dropped back down onto his back again.

"Lena," he whispered unbelieving into the dark as he stared up at my face.

I leaned in closer so he could see my features more clearly. "You know she's dead. You killed her."

His eyes widened for a moment before he blew his breath out harshly into my face. He smelled of coffee, cigarette smoke, and fear. Pissed off when he realized it was just me, he slapped the ground in anger with his right hand before raising it to wipe the sweat from his forehead. "Tam, you fricking scared the shit out of me."

I smiled at his stupidity. How quickly he had forgotten what had pursued him from the trailer and he'd brushed my mention of Mom's death aside as if I hadn't spoken at all.

"Why aren't you scared now?" I asked, innocently.

"I thought I saw something. Like a ghost or something. But I guess it was just you."

"Like my mom's ghost, Joel? And seeing me instead made you feel better. But why?"

Still struggling to catch his breath, Joel screwed his face up at me in confusion. "What the fuck are you talking about? You must have lost your damned mind chasing me through this godforsaken wasteland. It's forty below and you're sitting here babbling asking why I'm not scared anymore. Why on God's green earth would I be scared of a little piece of crap like you?"

"Because you should be. You know, Mom would have had far more mercy on you than me," I responded not really listening to his words. I was speaking more for my benefit than his.

"Your Momma got what was coming to her, Tam," Joel whispered leaning in close to me as if we weren't alone and the forest was full of ears. "All she had to do was tell me where you were and I would have walked away. But no, she had to play the martyr."

"It's sort of funny, Joel, that you believe in ghosts but don't consider the possibility that I've changed," I said continuing my part in our tangential conversation.

"Changed? You? You were the most predictable piece of this

entire game, Tam. All you had to do was disappear when you left me. Drop your mom a one liner and skedaddle and I would have never found you. But you were too selfish. You had to make your peace with her instead of leaving her in peace."

"The only peace I've had since I met you was the day I left. Then you stole it when you took my mom but tonight I'm going to get it back. So I want you to run Joel. You really need to run and hope to God that the smell of the fear in your blood makes me so crazy that I won't be able to remember everything you've done and I end up killing you far more quickly than I want. Or else it's going to be a very long, miserable night for you."

I pulled him roughly to his feet before he realized I had grabbed his arm. His skin was warm against mine and under my thumb I could feel the swell of his still racing pulse. I swallowed hard, forcing the rage back down. Letting my head drop back slightly, I pushed my fangs forward from my gums as I parted my lips just enough that Joel could glimpse their tips.

"I want you to feel something," I said pulling his head to my chest. He struggled against my hand on his neck and nearly lost his balance, his arms splaying out to his sides like a man on a tightrope, but I held him upright, his ear against my skin.

"Feel," I demanded again and his body went still except for the working of his lungs and his eyes twitching back and forth as his brain tried to rationalize what was happening. "What do you hear? Do you feel anything?"

Nothing moved around us. The forest was silent, the wild animals having recognized the presence of a stronger predator, and the only sound that littered the night air was the whisper of the wind and the full rich hum of Joel's heart paired with his irregular breathing. He listened in earnest this time and I caught his sharp intake of air when he realized my chest was dead quiet. Not a breath stirred. Not a single heartbeat.

He began to back slowly away from me, his hands slithering up and pushing against my belly as he struggled to break my hold. I let him go, laughing wildly at the look on his face. Joel was staring fixedly at me, half believing but arguing with logic that this couldn't be happening. He looked like he belonged in that famous painting of the man on the bridge screaming with the sky on fire behind him, his silent mouth formed into a desperate 'O' and his hands drawn up alongside his face.

"Run, Joel," I whispered and pointed into the mountains and for once in his miserable life he didn't argue but instead took one last look at me and sprinted away and into the darkness of the forest.

My every instinct said to pursue him. The sight of him running from me and the taste of his fear drifting through the air stirred something that was almost uncontrollable. The thrill of pursuit, I suppose, which has brought every predator to bear since the beginning of life as we know it. It's the reason you don't turn your back on a growling dog or run from a horse in an open pasture. Seeing the backside of someone as they turn tail will bring out the beast in the best of us.

But while my gut screamed to bring him down immediately, my logical mind urged me to wait. To let him get some distance ahead. To let his fear rise and grow until he could hardly reason. So instead of pursuing him, I climbed the mountain that loomed behind me while I waited.

The climb was quick and soon ended in a jutted shelf where I stretched out and surveyed the town of Sitka below me. The city spread out as a cluster of dim lights along the shore. One side open to the sea and the other three hemmed in by mountain peaks that thrust sharply towards Heaven.

In the distance, the now dormant volcano, Mount Edgecumbe, stood shrouded in mists as she leapt from the ocean floor and the full moon hung dull beside the mountain crest, too obscured by expectant gray clouds to be of much use.

In the valley, a church spire stood tall and straight. As a human, I could barely have made it out from this distance but as a vampire, I could see the shape and strength of the metal as it mingled with the mists. The steeple belonged to Peter's church, the same church Mom had attended, and seeing it made me think of my friend.

I missed Peter. I missed his friendship and I missed the

opportunity of what we could have become and I couldn't keep from wondering if he missed me too? I pictured him as I expected him to be. Leaned back in his Dad's high backed rocking chair with his feet stretched out towards the fire. A steaming cup of coffee mixed with a little Bailey's to his right and a Bible spread out in his hands with his notes for tomorrow's service between two chapters, reading while the rain tapped a comforting staccato on the roof of his family home.

That's how I wanted to remember him, safe and warm in his home doing the things he had been born to do, and I wanted him to remember me the way I had been meant to be. Before Joel scarred me forever. Before I sold my soul for revenge.

Luckily Peter would never see me as I was now, I thought to myself, as I stood and dropped off the side of the mountain cliff fifty feet to the ground below and turned in the direction that Joel had fled. Luckily, Peter would never see me as I would look tonight with Joel's blood spread like banners across my skin. Secure in the knowledge that Peter was safe and putting him out of my mind, I started in the direction that Joel had went.

I found him with no trouble; it was too easy actually. There wasn't any sport in it at all. Not that I expected it to be. It's hard to outrun and out maneuver a vampire in the darkest hours of the night. He was huddled under a large log that had been felled several years ago by the looks of the weathered bark. He was shaking, his fear billowing out like clouds of smoke from a damp fire into the cold clean air. A beacon that was impossible to miss.

He never heard me coming and so I caught him unawares as I jerked him feet first out from under the log. His screams were hoarse as if he'd been crying and his hands clawed desperately for anything to clutch but could finding nothing. Flipping him over on to his back, I pushed him down into the snow with one bare foot as he raked my legs with his broken fingernails.

"Tam," he mouthed through gritted teeth once he quit screaming. "Please."

"I liked it better when you were screaming," I said as I grabbed the hair of his head and began to drag him further up the mountain. "I remember screaming quite a bit when the shoe was on the other foot."

"What happened to you!" he shrieked, his body bouncing harshly on broken rocks and jutting tree limbs as I drug him behind me.

"You happened to me," I answered calmly, turning around to stare at his stricken face. "You turned me into this."

"Into what? This isn't possible. Into what?" he kept repeating.

"That will be the best part, Joel, because you when you come to yourself, you won't even know what hit you. They say ignorance is bliss but in this case, I don't think that's true."

"When I come to? So you're not going to kill me?" he asked desperately.

I rolled my eyes. "Don't be so literal. Bad choice of words. Of course, I'm going to kill you but I'm going to do so much worse and the best part is that the worst part will never end. It'll just keep going and going and going."

I drug him the rest of the way up the mountain while he alternated between crying and begging for mercy. It wasn't until I stopped at the edge of a sharp mountain crag that his voice died away. For the first time, I think he realized where we were. I pulled him upright to a standing position and leaned him far out over the rocky outcropping so that he could see the valley below. He was shaking so hard he lost bladder control and his urine poured out his pants leg, staining the snow at his feet.

"You don't have to do this, Tam," Joel pleaded as he eyed the valley below, unable to look away. "Please. I'm sorry for everything I did to you. Sorry about Lena. I didn't want to kill her."

I jerked him upright so that his face was inches from my bared fangs. I hissed in his face, "Don't speak her name. Don't you dare ever speak her name and I don't want to hear any more of your lies. I want to hear you beg. I want to hear my name gurgling in the blood pooling in your throat."

"You'll never get the satisfaction out of me," he sneered, pretending bravery just moments after begging for his life. I guess he had realized this wasn't going to end well, no matter what he said.

I smirked at his bravado. "I promise I will," I said and then I lost myself while I slipped the skin from his body in long streamers, tasting his blood as I went. His bones turned to sawdust in my hands and his nerve endings flamed in my fingers. His organs dissolved with my touch. And I was true to my word. His cries for mercy were harrowing. Even to me.

But the night was simply too short to make up for all of the evil he had done and some people should suffer for an eternity. So when at last, his exhausted heart could find little else to pump out, I slipped my fangs deep into his neck and cursed him with the kiss of immortality. With one final act of revenge, I leaned his still conscious body over the edge of the cliff where Mom's last moments of life had been spent watching him as she fell to her death.

"I want my face to be the last thing you see while you fall. Like yours was for her," I said as I flipped him over so that he was facing me. Nothing touched his back except the caress of the wind coming from the canyon below.

He was angry now and resigned, I guess, to dying. His previous shock at his nearing death was gone. Now there was only hatred. "I should have killed you the night I caught you at preacher boy's house. I've had a hundred opportunities but I was trying to give you another chance to come home."

"You only wanted another chance to control me, Joel. But those days are over."

He laughed at me then, blood flying from his mouth into the wind. "I'm still controlling you, Tam. Just look at what you did to get back at me. Nothing's changed. I always said we would be together forever. Turns out, I was..." His last words converted to a scream as I thrust him off into eternity.

I just couldn't listen to him say he was right.

I buried him in the woods close to where he had been staying but not before I wrapped him in tow chains from his truck and staked those chains to the ground. I shoved a crowbar through his heart and deep into the ground underneath him and then I passed every other tool I could find in his truck through his chest and belly until his body looked like a pincushion. Through his eyes, I drove two long tree branches. I put rocks in his mouth so that his parched throat would have no rest when he awoke. With two more metal tools, I dropped them into place so that they formed the Cross upon his chest, happy that his skin would be afire for the life of the metal.

I filled in the grave, satisfied that his suffering would be eternal.

Joel's body was cooling in the ground, and I danced through the forest, drunk on his blood and strength. The forest was alive around me, and I'd never been more alert to all of its wonders than now in the glow of my most savored kill.

The lush ferns caressed my bare feet as I raced from one side of the island to the other, stopping only when my feet dipped into the icy waters of the Pacific Ocean. I scaled first one mountain and then another, passing through the ring of near frozen clouds encircling the great peaks to bow before the great white moon that turned my skin a more unnatural shade of white.

How beautiful and glorious to be standing on that mountain with the blood of my enemy on my hands. Below, I could see nothing but billowing clouds stretching on for as far as my eyes could see. Above, the Milky Way twisted across the sky in a brilliant glow of whites and blues, competition for the stark white of the moon.

It was only when my skin began to crystallize in the frozen air of the mountain that I decided to leave. The blood high was waning, and I now wanted to lie in the arms of my lover in my own bed before the sun drove us to the paralyzed condition we hated. So I pirouetted one last time on the mountain peak, whispering my goodbyes to the moon and dove back down the side of the mountain, using the giant crags as stepping stones.

# Chapter 19

Joel's blood was still frozen in a thin layer across my skin when I took my first step out of the dense perimeter of forest bordering my house. I was jittery with excitement to share Joel's suffering with Adrik but before my first footfall struck the yard, I knew something was terribly wrong. I froze in place and drank deeply of the night wind. Blood laced the air too strongly, a perfect mixture of testosterone and iron intertwined with terror. I recognized the scent. My mouth watered, and at the same time, my belly cramped low in my pelvis.

The evening was nearly silent except for the gasp of an injured man. The sound reached out from my home through the darkness to bring me to my knees. I recognized it immediately and I had no choice but to lock my legs and cling to a nearby tree for support. The thought of facing what I knew was happening behind the walls of my mom's house made me want to turn and bolt into the woods, but I could hardly leave Peter to face Adrik alone. The first step towards the porch was hard, and the second was even worse and by the time I reached the porch, I was shaking with fear.

The door to the living room stood ajar and from where I stood on the porch, I could see Peter slipping in a small pool of his own blood, his left foot sliding out from under him. His nails skittered across the hardwoods as he struggled to pull himself up. A large gash ran the length of his right arm, and warm bright blood dripped from his index finger onto the floor. The ancient wood soaked it up like nectar.

Peter had managed to reach his feet and he spared only the shortest of glances on me as I stepped across the threshold. His eyes flicked nervously away from me and towards the corner at something I couldn't see but I was too riveted by the arc of red that leached in a near constant stream from his arm to the floor to pay much attention to what he was looking at.

I wanted to reach for him, to staunch the wounds on his arm but I dared not touch him. Instead, I forced myself to turn away and confront his attacker.

"What have you done?" I screeched at Adrik, who was standing in front of the fireplace, his back against the stone hearth. His tightly squeezed fists were the only indication that he had any emotion at all. Otherwise, Adrik appeared calm and collected.

"Only what I had to although I plan on doing far more. Your precious Peter came to stake us." He gestured towards the corner that Peter continued to glance at nervously.

I took a few more steps into the room so I could see where Adrik was pointing. An iron cross had been knocked across the room. One end had penetrated the paneling on the far wall; the other end had created a perfect C shape scar in the dark oak floors where it had spun in a circle after a glancing blow off of Adrik's broad forearm. The scent of his charred skin from where he'd made contact with the cross permeated the room. The smell touched a deep-seated and ancient fear inside of me, and I shivered, averting my eyes from the power of the cross.

"He must be more fool than foe to seek out our kind after dark," Adrik said as he pushed forward from the hearth to advance towards Peter. "Or perhaps he wishes to join us."

"He can *help* you!" I answered, catching him by the arm as he started to walk past me towards Peter. Adrik jerked his arm away from my hand and continued to advance on my friend. I shoved him back harder this time, nearly knocking him off balance.

"Adrik, he can help you. Didn't you hear me? Why hurt him

when he could be the answer to your prayers?"

"I have no desire to waste my time on prayer."

"That's not true, Adrik. This life brings you no true happiness. We both know that. Why would you want to hurt the one man who can bring you peace?" I questioned.

Adrik's gaze touched mine briefly, but he ignored my last comment completely and pushed past me again.

"He came to stake us! Had it been left to Peter, you and I would have spent the next century writhing in the dirt."

"He wouldn't do that to me," I argued, keeping myself between him and Peter.

"The way his ancestor did not trade his religion for favor and political gain? Peter would have slid that stake through your heart to the hilt without a second thought, Tamara."

"He wouldn't have hurt me." I couldn't look Adrik in the eye as I protested. I could feel Peter's breathing pick up behind me. His heart sped up as I lied for him.

"You are a fool if you truly believe that," Adrik answered.

"He's my friend," I said simply.

"His nature will not allow him to be your friend. He is your judge and your jury."

Behind me, I felt the air stir as Peter bent over slightly, trying to use his shirt as a tourniquet to slow the flow of blood from his arm. He'd bled a great deal, and I knew Adrik was thirsty to taste him. Joel's blood still coated my throat, and I was grateful for it quieted the hunger for a moment.

"Tamara, you have to end this," Peter whispered to my back. He was speaking English, and I could sense the irritation in Adrik at not knowing what was being said. "You know I'm right," he continued.

I kept my eyes on Adrik but spoke in Russian. "I asked you to not come here, Peter. Why didn't you listen to me? Why didn't you trust me?"

"Trust you! When you were under the influence of him? I didn't believe you at first when you told me about the blood and the journal. But when you said Adrik's name that day in the cemetery, it triggered something in my memory. Something that Dad had read me from his great grand-father's journals. Stories that I thought were never any more than fairy tales. I'd given them no credence at all. But I'd never been able to forget his name. Do you have any idea what you've done, Tam?"

"I know exactly what I've done! And I would do it again but you've not answered the question, Peter. What have you done! And why did you come?"

I felt the unwanted answer swell in the space between us and become a separating wall. Peter was on one side and I on the other. I should have known the answer, of course. It was obvious now that the question had been asked, and I desperately hoped Peter wouldn't have the courage to tear the wall down. That he would just leave the answer unspoken. But of course, Peter had never been a coward like me.

"To save you, Tam. You are your own worst enemy. And to save all of us from you. Myself included," Peter answered.

I turned to Peter as I was forced to recognize the truth. The words were out, and I could no longer ignore them. He had torn the wall down and now I had to face him. He'd come to stake me, just as Adrik had said.

Behind me, Adrik laughed a low and deadly sound. "She now begins to see the light," he commented.

"You came to sentence me to the grave, Peter, even though I would never have hurt you. I swore to myself that I would keep you safe, and I would have if you had just trusted me! How could you have done this? Would it have been so easy to put me down like that?"

"If I'd come for no other reason than to drive that stake through your heart, it would have already been done. I'd have come in the daylight when you were defenseless. But I didn't, Tam. I came to save my friend before so many bodies stack up that she can't remember who she even is. Ten years ago, I should have marched down to that dock and dragged you off of that ferry. I should have gone to Seattle and found you when you didn't answer my emails. But I didn't, and I've lived with those regrets every day. It's a little too late to make up for the last decade, I realize, and I'll have to deal with that for the rest of my life. I can't save your life now, but I *can* save your soul."

"I don't need saving. I haven't done anything wrong!" I hissed at him. "I was the victim."

"But you didn't have to be the victim, Tam. Not this time! You had the strength to walk away from Joel all those months ago in Seattle. All you had to do was walk away from this too."

"Joel killed my mother, Peter. He would have killed me in the end. She and I deserved justice. Can't you see that? Couldn't anyone see that? Why am I the bad guy in all of this? The only thing I'm guilty of is figuring out a way to beat Joel at his own game. I wanted justice, and I got it!"

Peter shook his head at me, his breath blowing out in a harsh stream of air as he jabbed a finger in my direction. "No! Justice would have been proving Joel guilty. A steadfast determination to see that he legally got what was coming to him. Justice would have been giving your mom what she wanted, which was to see *you* happy. Not condemned to eternal separation from her," Peter answered.

He took a deep breath and paused. "What would your mom say, Tam? Have you thought about that at all? It would make her sick to know what you've done. She would hate this. She died protecting you, and now her death was in vain."

I was angry now. Angry that he dared bring up Mom and then make it worse by saying her death meant nothing. Without a preconceived thought, my right hand arced gracefully and effortlessly wrapped around Peter's neck as I brought him to his knees in front of me. He forgot about his bleeding arm as he reached up to pry uselessly at my fingers. I could feel the scratch of his fingernails against the skin of my hand and forearm. His carotid ricocheted erratically against my thumb. In the palm of my hand, Peter coughed out what little air he had left in his lungs.

"Kill him, Tamara. Let us drink the blood of our common enemy together," Adrik said from behind me.

I stared hard at Peter for another moment. My rage felt like a mass of swarming yellow jackets in the pit of my belly. My fangs descended sharply against my tongue, and my left hand flexed dangerously at my side. Instinct whispered to slit his neck, and I barely recognized the snarls of anger that came from my throat.

Apparently neither did Peter as he watched me with the strangest look I'd ever seen cross his face. There was the expected fear of course, and that was painful enough, but it was mixed with pity. I knew the look. I'd seen it all too often over the last few weeks. It had just never come from him. He'd always been the one to give me far more credit than I had ever really deserved.

It hurt to see Peter stare at me in such a way. My fangs lost their edge, and the growls died in my throat. I'd sworn to protect him, and here I was threatening him. The anger went out of me like a deflated balloon, and I loosened my grip on his neck. The knowledge of what I had to do crystallized in my mind.

Peter sucked in air gratefully, the fight leaving his body as he relaxed into my hand. His fingers loosened from my own although he still gripped my arm for support.

I pulled him gently to his feet and continued to hold him in my grasp while he regained his balance. His legs were unsteady and his gaze told me he was a little dizzy from the lack of oxygen. I could hear his heart working hard to keep up. He nodded at me that he was okay that tried to pull away from my grip.

But I refused to let go. Instead, I placed my hands on either side of his face. I ached to touch him one last time. I ran a finger across his lips and the strong line of his jaw.

"Peter, you have to leave. Take my family Bible and keep it next to your heart. Adrik cannot touch you as long as the Word of God touches your skin and he cannot control your mind. Take Mom's crucifixes and go straight to the church, stay there, no matter what Adrik threatens. I'll keep him from following you and in the morning, when the sun has risen, leave this island and leave no trail by which he can find you. Take the advice you gave me only two weeks ago."

I let go of him and backed away so he could see my words were in earnest.

"Adrik," I spoke over my shoulder. "You have to leave too. You are no longer tied to this ground. The six-month period of confinement has been over for you for ages so you can rest anywhere, and on any ground."

I spoke Russian. Peter was more fluent than I was in the old language. He'd been raised on it the same as I. They could both understand me, and so they would each know what I was saying. I would sacrifice myself for the both of them. Adrik could leave and would be safe from Peter, who would be protected from Adrik.

"And what of you, Tamara?" Adrik spoke from behind me. "He will come for you at first light and he will put you to ground for good. He cannot be trusted."

Peter was watching me just as I watched him and I knew that Adrik was correct. Because Peter was good. He was honorable and he would always do the right thing. No matter the personal pain that it caused him.

"I know, Adrik. Believe me, I know. But Peter is the Ivan of my story and I have to keep him safe," I answered.

I heard only the rustle of wind to my right as Adrik sailed through the air. My eyes were still locked with Peter's as his mouth began to open in a scream that never had the chance to fully form as his breath was knocked from his body. Peter's lips pulled back, and I could see his gritted teeth as blood erupted from him in that same instant and sprayed in a wide arc as Adrik's nails tore geysers in his chest.

The spray hit my mouth, and the taste spread out in the purest of sensations across my tongue. Behind me, it spattered against the back wall of the living room and sizzled in the remains of the fire Adrik had built when we'd risen earlier this evening.

It was like my feet were in quicksand, and my head in a fog. By the time I reacted, Peter was a dying man with blood pooling around where he'd fallen. I reached to shove Adrik away from my fallen friend, but my hands clutched only emptiness. I looked to the far side of the room and found him facing me defiantly.

I made first to bend towards Peter, and then indecision struck, and I changed course mid-movement, charging towards Adrik, but I pulled up short before I reached him. What was I going to do? We couldn't kill one another, and locking into a violent battle with him would do Peter no good at all.

"How could you do this to me?" I hissed as I turned back towards Peter.

"You are not thinking clearly, Tamara. You think you understand the pain of being committed to a century under the earth, but you cannot possible comprehend," Adrik answered. "This human is not worth that price."

"He was worth everything," I whispered as I gathered Peter up in my arms. He moaned slightly as I did so and resisted my grasp, struggling to get a handhold on the rug underneath him but he was weak, and his grip broke with no effort on my part.

His breaths were coming in ragged bursts through his clenched teeth and between the gashes on his chest, I could see his collapsed lung attempting to work as he struggled for air. The lacerations were shallow on the far right side of his ribcage but became deeper as they moved to the left side of his body, and just before the sternum, they were deep enough to have reached the lung. The wounds continued across his left chest before becoming shallow again and fading to mere graze marks. His legs lay at an odd angle to his body and twitched uncontrollably. With my left hand, I could feel the bones of his severed spine crackle in my hand.

His neck had been heavily damaged as well. One large neck vein had been reduced to threads of tissue only and blood flowed from it at a fatal rate. He would have already been dead if it had been an artery. Instead, this blood was the dark oxygen-starved fluid that seeps from veins.

Lowering my lips to his forehead, I kissed his clammy skin gently. Perspiration was beading in his hairline. His cheeks only minutes before hot with anger were now blanched with pain and fear. In front of my eyes, his lips paled and deepened to a blue.

"Peter... Peter..." I couldn't quit saying his name, but I could say no more. It would have been demeaning to apologize for what he'd warned me would happen. I, who'd listened none at all, could hardly whisper a contrite apology now into the ear of a dying man. Even if I could have, it wouldn't have mattered. Peter was ignoring me completely; my empty words falling on deaf ears. His attention was focused entirely on Adrik.

"Tell me, Adrik. Is this how you repay Ivan's kindness to you?" Peter asked. Blood bubbled out, mixed with foamy air, from the wound on his chest. He didn't have long, and he'd stopped struggling to escape as he recognized the seriousness of his situation.

Adrik looked both confused and angry. "What could you know of Ivan?"

"I know you swore an eternal oath to him that you would never harm him or any of his children," Peter choked out between breaths. "How does it feel to know you broke that sacred oath?"

"I honored the oath to my friend," Adrik said between clenched teeth. "How dare you question my loyalty. Remember it was I who was speaking truth while your ancestor was turning out lies! You are either very brave or very stupid. I never visited revenge on the archimandrite. Maybe I should get it now, priest."

"Someone should question your loyalty, Adrik, because you're too arrogant to do it yourself. You swore you would never hurt Ivan or any of his kin but you marked Tamara, and so you marked Ivan's bloodline. And now she is sentenced to the same hell you chose for an eternity."

Adrik's eyes narrowed and he hissed dangerously towards Peter as he raised one arm to deliver what would no doubt be a death blow. "You lie. Just like your ancestor," Adrik spoke.

"Are you so certain, Adrik? Years ago, my father told me your sad tale and how you pledged allegiance to one man, the very man who staked you. The only man who you not harm. That man's name is written in Tamara's family Bible. Ivan sired her mother's bloodline, and so he sired Tamara. How arrogant to think Tamara had no connection to him just because she did not carry his name."

I watched as Adrik's expression changed from suspicious to anger and then his lips curled back with pure self-loathing. He looked at me with new eyes and then dropped the threatening arm he held up towards Peter to his side. Walking haltingly to my family Bible that still set on the bureau in the hall, his fingers hovered inches from the page as he traced the names down.

But Adrik had been a serf. He'd never learned to read, and so I leaned Peter gently against the couch at his urging and went to Adrik, holding him, as I confirmed his worst fears by reading the names that he pointed to. I read Ivan Korovin's name in a hushed whisper, barely get the syllables out as I knew the pain it would cause him.

I pulled Adrik back to the living room, away from the condemnation on that page, whispering to him that he hadn't known, and neither had I. It wasn't his fault, I promised him. But he didn't listen to me. Blood-filled tears ran down his cheeks.

"You did this to her, Adrik. This is your fault." Peter struggled with the words as his breath would only come in short spurts.

"No. He didn't know!" I shrieked at Peter. And immediately felt guilty as more of his blood leached onto the floor with his exertions.

"It is exactly like we talked about, Tam. When you reach the point that you justify the suffering of innocent people so you can serve up your own revenge or when you tell yourself that you'll be careful and no one else will get caught up in your plot, you always end up hurting those you love. Adrik hurt Ivan, the one person that loved him. And the one person Adrik loved."

The speech took the last of his energy and he dropped his head back against the couch. He gulped in large mouthfuls of air as his eyes rolled backwards. His chest heaved with the effort, and the muscles of his fingers twitched from lack of blood. His legs were rolled outwards with no muscle tone to keep them upright.

Adrik shook my arms from off his shoulders, not wanting my comfort, and sank down to the floor. I suppose he thought I knew somehow, about Ivan, and let him mark me despite his promises. But I was innocent in this one thing. I had no idea Ivan was a part of my family tree. "I didn't know, Adrik. I swear."

"I am even more damned than I knew," Adrik responded as much to the room as to me. His eyes weren't focused, and I knew his thoughts were somewhere in the past. I waited what seemed like an eternity for him to gather himself. Finally, his eyes cleared somewhat, and he looked at me unhappily. "If Peter means to you what Ivan meant to me, then go to him. Forget that he meant to stake us for he certainly had good reasons. You have little time left to say your goodbyes, and we both know he cannot be saved from death any more than we can be saved from hell."

I looked back at Peter resting against the couch. I had been angry at him for coming here tonight. I had been angry that he'd planned to drive a stake through my chest. But I was angrier still that he'd heaped guilt on Adrik, who was more fragile than he understood. But Adrik was right that I loved Peter, at least as deeply as I was capable.

Despite my anger, I gathered Peter back into my arms and caressed his cheek, wiping away the tears of pain that trickled from his eyes. Peter was minutes away from dying. His wounds could not be repaired, his spinal cord was severed, and most of his blood had run out in a river on the floor. Adrik came and knelt beside us, dejected but looking for absolution. I hurt for them both.

"Tam, please lift me up. I can still help him," Peter whispered to me.

I did as he asked and supported his head and body in my arms. He stretched out one hand towards Adrik, grimacing when his hand touched the coolness of Adrik's arm, but he kept it there. Adrik barely responded at all, except to part his lips slightly at the bloody hand on his skin.

"Adrik. Confess your sins. You were mistreated, I realize that. But you chose the wrong path." Peter's voice wavered, but he persisted.

"They excommunicated me. By the sins of another, I was judged and sentenced," Adrik hissed. "It was not my sins."

"It WAS your sin that condemned you. *You* should have trusted God. But instead *you* made your own path, and now the children of Ivan's children have paid the price. Tamara has paid for *your* sins."

Peter spit out the words forcibly with the final adrenaline rush that accompanies death and then collapsed against me as his hand dropped from Adrik's arm. His face paled suddenly as his heart palpitated and skipped a couple of beats. His body jerked as the pain of a heart attack ripped through his chest. The sound of the dying organ filled the room, and I gathered him even closer in my arms.

"Peter, I am so sor..." I began to whisper, but I couldn't get the words out. My voice died in my throat. I buried my face against his chest.

"Confess, both of you while there is still time, and we will open our eyes in Glory together," Peter pleaded with me with both his eyes and words. His right hand found mine, his fingernails digging into the palm of my hand. "Please, Tam. Time is precious. At least to me," he added. "I want to be with you forever. I always have."

Adrik turned towards me but I avoided his eyes. I didn't want to hear his words. I didn't want to acknowledge what I knew was coming. I dropped my head down but gently he lifted my chin so that I had to meet his gaze. And then I was trapped by the power of his eyes. The eyes of a man broken, a man who has been forced to acknowledge his crimes. The eyes of my maker.

"Tamara, forgive me for bringing you into this life and for abandoning you in it now. I could live with all the other sins I have committed, but the knowledge that I have betrayed the one person who meant anything to me is too much. I do not know if God will welcome me, but I have to try."

Adrik waited for a moment, but I was too dazed to speak. Peter would be dead soon. Adrik was speaking of contrition, and I realized I soon would be alone. I could find no words.

Adrik pulled me against him. He caressed the back of my head, and I leaned into him for strength before I trailed my lips up to his forehead and kissed him gently. "I forgive you for whatever you think you did to me, but my sins are my own. We were both ignorant of my ties to Ivan, who will be so happy to see you when you open your eyes in Heaven."

"Come with me. Accept the forgiveness that is offered and follow me into the afterlife."

I nodded at him and smiled as I placed his hand in Peter's. "Find your peace, Adrik. I'll find mine too."

Peter's fingers were colder even than mine, but he managed to curl them around Adrik's. "Confess, Adrik. Say the words. Quickly!"

"Forgive me, Father, for I have sinned," Adrik said and just listening to the words made me somewhat nauseous.

The change in Adrik was instantaneous, and I watched as the purest peace washed across his face. It was the first true smile I'd ever seen cross his features. His expression relaxed, and his eyes for a moment became even brighter. In his happiness, I saw his true beauty. Not just that of his face which was as heavenly as his body, but I could see the true man that he had been. The goodness that his vampire nature had tried to strip away but could never completely remove.

"Follow me, Tamara," he said in a voice I didn't recognize. It was as if his body had become hollow, and he was speaking from a void.

I smiled at him again, and as I did so, his body caved in upon itself. Dissolving into millions of grains of dirt, his remains scattered and skittered across the floor, filling in the cracks of the floorboards and landing briefly on the blood spatters before being absorbed into the clotting fluid on the floor. It rose up in a great cloud of dust and overtook the room and the smell of dirt and decay filled my lungs. Adrik had finally died the natural death he had avoided for two centuries. Heaven had welcomed him. I'd had no doubts that it would.

In my arms, Peter stiffened again as his heart fired off another rapid succession of beats. His face twisted in pain again, and he clutched my hand more tightly.

"He's at peace, Tam. Come with us, and we'll be together for an eternity."

I stroked his hair. I touched his cheek. His body shook with the chills of a dying man. I held him closer, tears rolling from my eyes and dropping red blotches onto his chest.

"Confess, Tam," he urged me again. His voice was dying away, barely a squeak over the wheeze of his lungs and he forced the words out by sheer will power.

"He deserved it. Joel deserved to die," I whispered angrily.

"What about Kendall Scott? Or the hiker that was found in the woods or the other two people who disappeared off the island in the last two weeks? By whose sins did they die?"

I had no answers.

"And now me, Tam. I'm dying even though you swore to protect me. Was your revenge worth it? Do you feel any remorse?"

"Of course I do. I love you," I shrieked at him but I couldn't meet his eyes. I hated what I'd done to him. I'd meant to protect him, and here he lay in my arms struggling to breathe his last.

"Then prove it," he mouthed, the words barely whispering across his lips.

"Father, forgive..." I began.

"Confess Ta..." he started but couldn't finish. His heart sped up again momentarily and then settled into a slow march towards death. His eyelids started to close, but from sheer will power, he forced them open. His gaze held mine. "Please," he mouthed but even I couldn't hear him. No air moved across his vocal cords. He simply didn't have the strength to whisper even another word.

"Father, forgive me," I began again.

The corners of Peter's mouth lifted into a smile as he waited for my final words. He nodded at me slightly for encouragement and he closed his eyes. His expression was calm. Trusting. He deserved so much more than I had ever been capable of giving him.

"Father, forgive me. For I am about to sin. Again," I whispered into his ear as I bent my head to his.

# Epilogue

The philosopher Confucius once said that if you plan to embark on revenge, you should dig two graves. One for your victim, and the second for yourself.

I'd laid Joel in the first grave, and in my own grave, I placed the cold body of my childhood friend and the last person on earth who'd had any faith in me.

I had sworn that I would protect him, keep him safe and in my arrogance, I honestly thought that I could. Instead, I'd taken everything from the man I'd sworn to protect. At least the things that were important to him. His God. His identity. No doubt Peter would think it the cruelest trick of all. The priest turned vampire. The Father with no god.

Both his blood and his spirit stained my hands because there would be no repentance to save his soul. He couldn't ask forgiveness for my sins. I was the one who needed redemption and I felt no contrition at all, only remorse over the consequences and not the actions that caused them.

Already, I could feel the beginnings of Peter's reawakening as he crossed through death. A restlessness was brewing. A rage that I could nearly taste was burgeoning somewhere deep in the remains of his dead heart.

Would he understand when his body caught up to his mind? Would he forgive me or would he chase me across the earth seeking his own revenge? Would he understand that I couldn't live without him and yet I couldn't die with him?

No matter the outcome, I could not leave Peter even if I wanted. The two of us were tied to this same grave for the next six months and we would either meet the sun each morning wrapped up in the arms of passion or in the throes of bitter rage. Eternal enemies or immortal lovers.

For now, while I still could, I pulled him into my arms as the sun began its ascent into the sky, and with the last movement of my lips, I told him I loved him.

# About the Author

DL Atha was born and resides in Arkansas. She is a practicing internal medicine and wound care physician. She happily lives with her three children and husband on a farm where she enjoys reading, writing, farming, and raising flowers and herbs. Some of her favorite things are horses, chocolate, flowers, and books, while her least favorites are anything that occurs before nine a.m.

www.ingramcontent.com/pod-product-compliance
Lightning Source LLC
Chambersburg PA
CBHW070317260626
47160CB00003B/865

* 9 7 8 0 9 7 9 3 3 5 6 5 5 *